T0165262

A Dubious Mission

A Colton Banyon Mystery

Gerald J. Kubicki

iUniverse, Inc.
New York Bloomington

A Dubious Mission
A Colton Banyon Mystery

iUniverse books may be ordered through booksellers or by contacting:

iUniverse
1663 Liberty Drive
Bloomington, IN 47403
www.iuniverse.com
1-800-Authors (1-800-288-4677)

ISBN: 978-1-4502-2976-0 (pbk)
ISBN: 978-1-4502-2978-4 (cloth)
ISBN: 978-1-4502-2977-7 (ebk)

Printed in the United States of America

Library of Congress Control Number: 2010907556

iUniverse rev. date: 7/9/2010

Yesterday is History
Tomorrow is a Mystery
Now is the Present
Accept the gift.

—Hindu poem

Prologue

June 14, 1936
Thar Desert, Punjab
Northern India

The Great Abu hung from the tightrope. He was known as one of the best tomb hunters in northern India. Abu was twelve years of age and knew that he would have to give up his financially rewarding life soon—that is, if it didn't kill him first. He was starting to grow and would soon be too big to scurry around in the dark holes that he frequented. On a hot afternoon, he had been playing near the bazaar in his local town when suddenly four huge men grabbed him. The men were different from the local constables, much larger and all had yellow hair. They were all dressed in black uniforms that Abu had never seen before.

The one with the scar on his face inquired of Abu, "Are you Abu, the hunter?" He spoke in English, a language that Abu understood, but the accent was not British.

"I am the Great Abu."

"Good," replied the man in a sinister voice as he approached Abu. Suddenly a burlap sack was thrown over Abu's head.

Sometime later Abu realized that he was no longer near the bazaar. He found himself in the middle of a desert. He had never been to this place before. How would he be treated? Most of his employers had been respectful while he recovered a bracelet that had fallen down a well or gathered antique objects in old ruins. The employers treated him well and respected him because he was unafraid of the underground creatures and spirits. It was said that he could cast a spell on the things in the holes and paralyze them while he went about his work. His grandfather, the local fakir, had taught the magic of his trade to him. As Abu rubbed his eyes and sat up, he realized that these men knew nothing about respect. They had tied his hands to a pole.

Abu now stood in the blazing sun. The dust blowing in his face prevented him from focusing on the tall man standing in front of him. He stood with the bright sun to his back. Abu's head hurt. He ached from hunger. He wished he could reach his pockets, where a small stash of dried fruit would provide a source of nourishment. "Why have you captured me when I was willing to work for you?" he asked the tall man.

"My name is Herr Schmidt," announced the man. "I have a job for your unique skills. You have been brought to this secret location to find something. We'll pay you well for your services."

The mention of money quickly changed Abu's attitude. "I'll do your job," Abu eagerly agreed.

"Of course you will," the man replied with a sinister tone that was lost on the young boy.

It was just after noon when the men started to lower Abu into the dig. This hole was the worst he had ever seen. While it was freshly dug, the walls of the hole seemed ready to collapse at any moment. The hole was dug in loose sand held in place by heavy wood and was about three meters wide. Abu knew that it was a long passage because of the huge mountains of sand around the site.

Thick rope scratched the soft skin under Abu's arms. They had equipped him with a light torch, which lit up the way without fire. Abu had never seen one before; fire was his mode of illumination.

Fire in holes helped keep the spirits and others at bay. The men had told him that all that was required of him was to follow the x markings and find a piece of rock with writing on it. He was warned that he must not read the writing on the rock, which they described as a "tablet." It was, in fact, a useless warning since Abu could neither read nor write. Nor could he understand the importance of a rock.

When Abu hit the ground, he found himself standing on cool sand. He untied the rope and wrapped it around his hand so he could pull it; then he looked around. He was surrounded by rock passages that resembled building walls. Abu had seen many structures like these before and knew that he was now standing in an old village that had been buried underground eons ago. Several of these villages were scattered throughout all of northern India. Abu had visited some to investigate their treasures. This town was buried deep, maybe fifteen meters deep, and Abu could tell that the passageway had only recently been cleared. He noticed piles of sand everywhere and smelled the scent of recent fire torches. *Where are the workers?* he wondered.

About twenty meters along the narrow two-meter-high pathway, he came upon a small courtyard with several open doorways. He noticed the small x on the door directly in front of him. As he prepared to enter, his senses came alive. First he noticed the smell. It was the thick smell of death. Something bad had happened in the room. Then there was the noise that wasn't a noise, but rather a smooth vibration that caused the hairs on the back of his neck to rise. *Naja naja is in there.* Abu could deal with the king cobra; he had met him many times before. He knew from experience to move slowly, to maintain eye contact, and to use his secret weapon. After all, he was considered a special hunter. Abu brought the wooden whistle that hung from his neck up to his lips and began to play the hypnotic music that his grandfather had taught him. The light airy music was played with one hand on the flute and one hand on the light. Cautiously he moved forward.

Shining the light through the door, he beheld small wooden tables spread around a medium-size room. To the left was a long, high table. *A tavern.* As he turned to his right, the light fell on a large hump on the floor. The hump turned out to be three bodies, all with yellow hair. As he played the light over the bodies, Abu observed that the men had died horrific deaths. Their mouths were distorted in a permanent scream, their muscles all contorted. He recognized that the men had recently died from snakebites from naja naja. They had died less than two days ago. Usually a cobra bite would take three or four hours to kill a man. They should have had enough time to reach the opening, and yet there were three men dead here. *Many naja naja.*

Quickly Abu rotated the light to see if the snakes were nearby. He continued to play the sinuous rhythmic music that always tamed the snakes. But he was feeling the sudden rush of real fear in his throat. So many snakes would be difficult to hypnotize. Then he noticed the tablet. It was about half a meter wide and less than a meter long; it was thin and could easily be carried under his arm. It was standing upright, like a tombstone, with its bottom buried in sand. The dead men, spread out like a fan around the base, had found the tablet and, in the process of picking it up, were attacked by the vipers. They had all died in the rush to get away.

With extra care, he crept closer to the tablet, all the while considering the risk of grabbing the rock and running. He had moved only two steps when his light shone upon the base of the tablet. The base was moving. What he had mistaken for sand was, in fact, hundreds of small snakes writhing on the ground. *Naja naja nest.*

Suddenly Abu knew how the men had died. They had missed seeing the snake nest under the tablet. The mother snake was probably in the middle of the pack. Death would have been quick but painful. There was only one chance of getting the tablet and retreating alive. Abu had just begun to tie a loop with the rope when loud shouts filled the air. Abu turned and bolted out the door before the snakes could strike. He ran down the passageway, quickly reaching the opening high above.

"Stop shouting," he yelled up to Herr Schmidt. "You will excite the naja naja. They have already killed your workers."

"Did you find the tablet?" Herr Schmidt bellowed.

"Yes, but it is very dangerous in there."

"Bring it to me, boy. Bring it now."

"I—" It was as far as Abu got.

"I'm not interested in excuses; get me the tablet," commanded Herr Schmidt. "I'll double your reward." That was all the motivation Abu needed.

"More slack on the rope," Abu yelled. "When I tug on the line twice, pull the rope in slowly, and you'll have your tablet."

As he carefully returned back down the passageway, Abu knotted the end of the rope into a noose. *So much trouble over a piece of rock! Why is this rock so important? This village has been buried under the dirt for so many years that no one even remembers that it was here. What could possibly be written on a rock tablet that men are willing to give up their lives to retrieve it? Maybe I should ask for more reward.*

Back in the tavern, Abu stood very still. He was using his whistle as he kept a sharp lookout for naja naja. After a few minutes, the movements from the snake pile slowed down, allowing Abu to make his move. Two chips were missing around the middle of the tablet. He expertly tossed the rope around the tablet. He then pulled slowly on the rope until it tightened around the tablet and caught hold in the chipped areas. He pulled harder. As the tablet began to fall over, it landed facedown, crushing many snakes. The rest were in a frenzy—biting on the rock, throwing themselves in the air, and spitting venom.

Backing out the door, Abu moved up the passageway, pulling the tablet slowly as he went. A dozen snakes followed, biting at the movement. Most soon began to slither away back to the nest.

Now he tugged twice on the rope and watched as the slack was taken in and the tablet glided across the sand heading for the exit hole. Abu followed, watching out for naja naja all the way.

"You can lift it out now," called Abu. He watched as the tablet disappeared above him. He could hear cheering and sounds of joy above. Herr Schmidt was speaking excitedly in English, then in a language Abu did not understand. "The Aryan race will rise again. Adolf will be so pleased."

"Throw the rope back down for me," yelled Abu from deep in the hole. "Throw the rope back down." But the yellow-haired men seemed to have forgotten that he was in the hole. He no longer heard any sound.

Abu was shocked that they would leave him in the hole. There was also the uncollected reward. His anger rose. "I am putting a curse on your tablet," cried Abu. "May the spirits of honor invade all who possess the tablet and guide its path back to me, in my lifetime," he added. He then pulled some magic dust given to him by his grandfather from his pouch and blew it into the air above. With that finished, Abu proceeded to climb up the sides of the deep hole.

Part One
Conspiracy

Chapter One

Present day

Colton Banyon rubbed the day-old growth on his rugged but still handsome face as he peered out the master bedroom window from the second story of his home in the far suburbs of Chicago. He now lived in a small two-story town house condo in the equally small village of Streamwood, Illinois. He had lived in better places. It was just before dusk on a sweltering day in early August 2009. He reflected on his past precarious life. Life was a cycle, and his had been on a downslide for a few years now.

He noticed a large white van that entered his street and parked at the end of the small cul-de-sac.

It was too hot to go out, and he didn't want to sit at his desk anymore, having already spent the entire day calling people—"networking," as it was called in business. He had checked all his Web sites, executive recruiters, and friends. There had not been even one job for which to apply. Money was now in short supply, and like most fifty-something-year-olds, recreation was sometimes just thinking.

How had he gotten into this mess?

He was contemplating whether to sell the house to pay some bills or possibly going the all-American route and declaring bankruptcy. He'd received several ads from bankruptcy lawyers on the Internet. It depressed him that even they knew he was having financial difficulty.

If he had to, could he start all over again? These are just material things. He had lost possessions before. After all, two divorces can wipe a man clean.

As he continued to ponder his future, he examined the van and noticed that there were not any trade advertisements on it. It had no specific markings of any kind on it.

The sound of the van's doors opening brought Banyon out of his reverie. Four men, with shaved heads and dressed in black outfits, exited the van. They appeared to be carrying small black boxes. The men headed across the street and toward his condo, which was about fifty yards away.

Since it was just before dusk, Banyon strained to see out the window. His senses told him that something was not right.

Banyon trusted his senses, and they were screaming now. These men were not repairmen. He wondered if they were about to rob him. There had been several robberies in the area. Banyon watched as the men seemed to huddle and then turn toward his condo. Their movements were swift, showed planning, and almost gave the impression of a military strike. As he stayed in the shadows, he observed silent hand signals. Two of the men broke away to circle around the house. Quickly Banyon ran to the back of the second floor in time to see one of the men pulling the grate off the basement window well.

Basement windows were the easiest way to enter his house, as neighbors would hear nothing and see nothing. The window was hidden from view in the window well. What Banyon was able to make out was terrifying. A man with a large swastika tattooed on his thick neck was pulling a ski mask over his head.

Banyon bolted from the window. With two men in the front and two in the back, there was no way out. The open plan of his house allowed anyone to see the second floor as soon as they entered the door. They would find him in a matter of seconds. He had to get away now. He didn't even have time to grab his cell phone, which was on a charger in his downstairs office. The lone way out was through the attic. He hoped that it might take them some time to find the door leading to the second-floor laundry room.

As he closed the door leading to the laundry, he heard the basement door opening and footsteps roaming to the front of the house. They would be checking all the closets, bathrooms, and under the bed in his downstairs suite before they went looking upstairs, he hoped.

Stealthily Banyon climbed the stairs to the attic and emerged into a large open area. As he pushed open the attic window, it occurred to him that the window was at least fifteen feet above the short steeply pitched lower roof. He would have to drop down right in front of the large picture window that he had been looking out of only moments ago. Dropping down was not an option for him. Ever since he had fallen off a roof as a child and hurt his knee, Banyon had nursed a fear of heights.

His very survival depended on pushing back his fear. If he could stand on the window ledge, he might be able to climb to the top of the roof. Sweat stung his eyes. The prospect of climbing onto the roof deepened his terror. At fifty-four, he was not used to much physical exertion. Yet he had no other choice. He had to go, now.

Teetering precariously on the edge of the window, he groped for something to grasp. Even though he was six feet tall, he could barely reach over the roof's edge. Finding nothing to use as an anchor, he realized that he would have to hang from the roof edge and slide, hand over hand, down the roof angle. After about three feet, his hands were bloody. He pushed back the pain. Finally reaching the end of the ledge, he encountered a gutter and a two-foot drop to the lower roof. Letting go of the ledge, he hoped to land on his feet. He hit the roof on all fours. To his surprise, he stuck.

He bolted for the cinder block wall that divided his house from the neighboring house, vaulting over it easily. He followed the roofline to the end of the town house. The unit at the end was but one story high. Sliding over the edge, he grabbed the satellite dish antenna that was attached to the wall and dropped to the soft garden. He ran for his life.

When he was a child, his family had lived in the woods. Banyon didn't own a bike back then, so whenever he wanted to get anywhere fast, he ran. Running had become second nature to him.

That was then, however. Now thirty years of smoking had taken its toll. Banyon knew he could not run for long, so he raced for the small stand of trees a block away. Once inside the woods, he stopped to catch his breath. Crouching behind a thick bush allowed him to observe the back of his town house without being seen. It was still light enough to see from his position, and the streetlights had come on as he was running across the road. Temporarily secure, he tried to compose himself. He had to critically analyze his suddenly dangerous situation.

Who were these guys, and why were they robbing him? Was this really a robbery, or was it something else? Suddenly he noticed movement in the late dusk light.

A lone figure was standing on the roof of the town house, scanning the area. The figure left abruptly. Banyon was frozen in position. *If they are robbing my house, why is one of them on my roof?* Colton Banyon had been accused of being paranoid more than once in his life. He was paranoid now. He could think of no one who could be considered an enemy. True, he owed some money, but not to loan sharks. His sardonic New York wit had, on occasion, pissed off a few people—but not on a criminal level. He was virtually an unknown in the small village of Streamwood. *What to do?*

He could run to a neighbor, but this could put the neighbor at risk. He considered trying to get to a business or a public phone to call the local police, but it was about half a mile to the nearest business, a gas station. *Too easy to stake out.* Sometimes the best strategy was to do nothing. The complex where Banyon lived was built around a circle with only one entrance/exit point. Banyon lived near the back of the complex, off one of the many culs-de-sac that branched off the main road. After a ten-minute wait, headlights appeared up the street. The van rounded the corner and drove right by the bushes where Banyon was hiding. The van was a Ford Aerostar. He could see Illinois license plates, starting with the letters *GPG*, but the numbers were too hard to see. *This should give the police something to go on in tracking the men.*

He wondered if any of the men had been left behind in the house while the others went to stake out the gas station. No, that would leave the lone man vulnerable to getting caught. Banyon decided that the most logical thing to do was to return home and call the police. While the men had seemed professional, they had left some loose ends. Banyon figured that they were after his valuables after all and no one would be in his house. He wondered what they had taken.

Cautiously Banyon crossed the road. He was careful to stay within the shadows. In a few minutes, he reached the basement window well and noticed that the window and grate had been replaced. He ran around to the front door and found it locked. Why would burglars lock the door after leaving? And why would they take the time to replace the window well and grate? *What is going on here?* Turning his attention to the garage, Banyon punched in the code on the keypad, and the door obediently went up.

His Lincoln Town Car loomed large in the space. Nothing seemed to have been touched. If anyone were in the house, they would now know that Banyon was in the garage. Banyon knew that the garage door leading into his house was locked, but he also knew that he always left his keys in the ignition of his car when it was in the garage. He went to the driver side and reached in the open window to grab his keys. As he pulled them out of the window, he dropped them.

When he crouched down to retrieve the keys, he noticed a small wire that was attached to the underside of his car. Although he'd never before seen a real tracking device, he'd read about them many times. The small black box with a wire antenna was secured to the rear of the undercarriage of his car. He suddenly recalled that the men had carried small black boxes as they left the van. Many stores offered products for protection, recording, and detection of movement. You could even buy some of those items at the local RadioShack. But tracking devices? Banyon wasn't quite sure where they were sold. Certainly ordinary thugs had no need to put tracking devices on the cars of their victims.

He now knew that he could enter his house and there would be no one there. Although he was suspicious by nature, his paranoid meter was hitting maximum. Banyon the businessman dealt in high-level strategies, and this was clearly one. The hair on his neck bristled as he silently opened the door. *Are there listening devices in the house? What else could be in the small boxes that the men had carried?* If they had bugged his house, the men would know when he was home and could pick him up, kill him, or do to him whatever they had in mind. He had to hurry since the opening of the garage door might have set off some of the bugs.

Nothing was out of place. He needed his wallet, watch, and cell phone. The face that stared back at him from the bathroom mirror needed a washing. His green eyes had turned brown. It was a sure sign that his emotions were raging out of control. He was frightened.

He ran to the office in quest of his cell phone. It seemed untouched. Hurriedly he programmed the house phone to forward all calls to his cell. He wondered if he should attempt to find the bugs but decided to leave that to the police. He had to get out of the house immediately.

Back in the garage, Banyon looked under his car for more bugs. He failed to locate any more. His organized mind was now in overdrive. Next on his agenda would be to find a place to stay. But first he needed to report the break-in to the police. He didn't want to hang around his house, as the men might come back. The police station was only a mile away. But it was a place that he didn't want to go. He had a history with the Streamwood Police Department. *Once a criminal, always a criminal.*

But if he took his car, the men would know that he was on the move. He wondered if he could detach the tracking device and leave it in the garage. But if the men came back while he was at the police station, they would find it, and the evidence would be gone. Suddenly the solution seemed very simple—take the bug off his car and place it on the car of a neighbor. It was night. No one would be going out, and the police could retrieve the device quickly. His neighbor's car was just outside his garage. Carefully he removed the magnetized bug from his car and carried it to his neighbor's. Surely the people who monitored the bug would not notice a ten-foot change in location. He attached it to the bottom of the neighbor's car. Satisfied with his handiwork, he fired up the Lincoln and headed for the station. He took a back road to avoid the gas station—just in case.

He tried to focus. Okay, what did he know for sure? The men were after something. If this was an ordinary robbery, why attach a tracker to his car? Why him—was it something he knew or owned or something he had access to? It made no sense. His life was just business and his extended family. Almost everything he owned was new. The last divorce four years ago left him with his clothes and a few artifacts from his departed parents. Everything else in his house had been bought within the last two years. He did have his father's war medals and coin collection. Were they after his mother's spoon collection? Maybe his old books were the draw. He did have his Russian grandmother's atlas from the 1900s written in Cyrillic. He should have checked to see if anything was missing, but he was scared and in a hurry. He could check later. Suddenly a speed bump alerted Banyon that he was in the parking lot of the Streamwood Police Station.

Chapter Two

Many modern police stations do not have a receptionist. Instead, duty officers with guns man the front desk. This station was smaller than most. The village of Streamwood had less than five thousand people. Banyon had been there about a year ago. It was on September 3, to be exact.

That had been another horrible experience in his life. He had tried to bury the memory. But he remembered it all too well.

Banyon and one of his employees had just finished opening accounts at the Streamwood bank. They intended to transfer the business accounts after Banyon's planned move to Streamwood at the end of the month. He started the car, put on his turn signal, swiveled his head, and was about to pull out into traffic when it happened. *Bang*, something hit his car.

"Look out," his employee cried after the fact.

"What the—," was all he could muster.

"Some kid on a bike hit your car," she said in a panicked voice.

Banyon was out of the car and around to the front in a flash. A preteen boy lay on the ground near the right front fender.

"Are you all right?" Banyon asked.

"Yeah." The boy was checking his bike for signs of damage.

"Where'd you come from?"

"The alley, over there." He pointed to the small alley that was often found between houses in the Chicago area.

"You've got to be more careful," Banyon scolded. Banyon watched him pick up his bike. Other than the seat being turned, there was no damage to the bike. A slight scuff mark was located on the right front fender of his car.

"What's your name? Do you want us to call your mother? Are you all right?" The boy did not answer. Instead, he grabbed his bike and started to leave.

Suddenly two more boys arrived on their bikes.

"Leave my brother alone," a big one yelled. "You run him down. We gonna sue."

Banyon ignored the verbal abuse and tried to give the boy his business card. Finally the boy took it and put it in his pocket before taking off on his bike.

"Have your mother call me," Banyon yelled after the boy.

The other two kept up the abuse, which started to piss off Banyon. "I'm gonna get you, sucka," yelled the antagonist.

"Let's get out of here," his employee pleaded. Banyon got back into the car. He intended to report the accident to the police, but he decided to call his insurance man first.

Banyon was a New Yorker and had spent many years becoming street-smart. He had witnessed unbelievable things and had firsthand knowledge of man's incredible ability to be vicious and vengeful. He remembered having seen a taxi clip a pedestrian on Broadway, and all of a sudden, there were four people lying on the road, all claiming to have been run over. Some people tried to profit from anything, especially someone's misfortune. He also knew that the boys saw that he drove a black Lincoln. He was sure that they had written down his license plate. To the boys, such a car meant money.

He called his insurance agent to report that a nameless kid on a bike had hit his car. The kid was uninjured and had left the scene quickly. The insurance man said that they got these cases all the time and not to worry. Banyon went to the police station and filled out an accident report with the help of Officer Dean. Dean took the paper and said that Banyon had nothing to worry about. Banyon never heard from the mother and soon forgot about the accident.

On August 31, he moved into his new town house—three months later than the builder had promised. He had changed the address on his driver's license and on all the credit cards months earlier. He had forwarded his mail to the Streamwood post office, located in the only shopping center along with the bank and the grocery store, and had stayed with his girlfriend, May, for the interim.

On Monday, September 3, Banyon finally got around to going to the Streamwood post office. The weekend had been a flurry of activity, as his three boys along with May showed up. They all pitched in to install fixtures, build bookcases, hang art, and set up his office. As he left the post office, the door of a rattletrap car was flung open. A skinny black woman got out. Banyon presumed that she was approaching him to ask for directions.

"You ran over my boy. What I gonna do with the hospital bills? You owes me," the women prattled.

Banyon then saw the boy get out of the car, bouncing a rubber ball basketball-style.

"I been lookin' for you," she continued. "Been here every day, lookin' for your Lincoln. The police been lookin' for you too."

Banyon was stunned. She had come to the mall every day for a month looking for him? The card that he had given the boy had his new Streamwood address on it. But she had never called his phone. Why not? He wondered if this was a shakedown or whether she was righteously vengeful.

The boy hadn't appeared to be hurt, but then again, he was no doctor.

"I gave your boy my card. You didn't call," he stammered.

She was now in his face, spewing all kinds of accusations. "My other boys said you was flying down the road and hit him, didn't even stop. The law gonna get you."

Banyon was beginning to panic.

"Look, you have this all wrong. I filled out an accident report. I'm going to call the police as soon I drop these letters in the mailbox." As he left the post office, he encountered an officer with his hands on his hips. He straddled the roadway, facing Banyon with sunglasses on and looking mean.

The woman was standing behind the policeman, pointing over his shoulder. "That's him—that's the man that done hit my boy. He was gonna hit me too, right here in the parking lot."

"Let's go. We're going to the station house," the officer announced. "It's only a half block away. Can you drive there, or do I have to cuff you and take you in?"

"I'll follow you," a shaken Banyon replied.

At the station, he was put into an interrogation room and was told to wait.

He had seen enough *Law and Order* shows to know that there was someone watching through the glass. After ten minutes, Officer Dean came in and said the detective handling the case would be there soon. In the meantime, would Banyon mind if they took fingerprints? Banyon told Officer Dean that he had filled out an accident report. Dean said that he would look for it. Banyon started to say something but bit his tongue. It seemed that every time he opened it, something bad happened. After all, he knew he had nothing to hide, and he had a witness, his employee, to back up his story.

As they were rolling his fingers, Banyon tried to remember if he had ever been fingerprinted. Had the government done it at the army induction center? That would have been thirty years earlier.

The detective entered the room. He introduced himself as Detective Heinz. "Just a couple of questions. We had a hard time finding you. It took awhile to run your plates, and the license bureau gave an address of a vacant lot. We thought that maybe you were a fugitive or something, and of course, we had Mrs. Woods calling my captain every day. You care to explain all of this?"

Banyon had already started to feel better. "Well, I changed all my records before moving into my brand-new house. The house had delays. The last four weeks were spent at my girlfriend's. I moved into the town house on August 31. I had no idea that anyone was looking for me; I wasn't hiding."

"Let's talk about the accident. Were you going east or west on Irving Park when you hit the boy?"

"First of all, I was at the curb of Park Avenue, south of Irving. I was stopped when the boy came out of the alley and hit my car. I didn't hit him."

Detective Heinz took out the accident report that had been filled out by the boy's family and read the report. "They have several unbiased witnesses, including two other people who saw you run down the boy."

"Look," replied Banyon, "those boys are related. One said that he was his brother. They were not there at the time of the accident, and I have an adult witness who was in the car with me. I even filled out an accident report with Officer Dean. Check out my car, and you'll see that he ran into me."

"Let's do that now," Detective Heinz said as he stood up. Passing through the lobby, Banyon noticed Mrs. Woods talking to the desk cop.

"I wants his name, where he live, don't dis me, I's the one caught him." Apparently she felt that there was a bounty on Banyon.

Outside the office, Carl—on a first-name basis now—looked over Banyon's car. There were no scratches on the front and only a smudge on the fender by the right wheel well. "This, of course, means nothing as you have had three months to have your car repaired," the officer commented.

He and a frustrated Banyon returned to the room. "Can you fill out an accident report? We are going to have to check out everything."

"But I filled out a report last year," whined Banyon.

"Yeah? Well, we can't find it."

"Fine," said Banyon. He knew that he had a good driving record. Hadn't had a ticket in over nine years, ever since he had gotten rid of the 911 Porsche. Banyon completed the form and handed it to the detective, who then left the room.

A few minutes later, Detective Heinz came in with two tickets: one for failure to yield right-of-way and one for leaving the scene of an accident. "Your court date is September 16," he said with a grin. "Just make an appearance and plead guilty. There'll be a small fine—you have a good record."

Banyon was incredulous. "You're saying my story is not right, that they are right, and you haven't even checked anything out?"

"Ula has many hospital expenses on record. The captain says that this has been on the books for a month. Ula Woods has driven him crazy, and tickets need to be issued. Take it up with the judge."

Banyon sat in Cook County Court, awaiting his case. He noted that most of the cases involved repeat offenders, and the black female judge was handing out small fines one after another.

Finally his name was called, and he headed to the front. A group at the other end of the court stood up and started to the front as well. It was Mrs. Woods, her son, and the two other boys from the accident, along with some thuglike knuckle dragger. Banyon had not seen the man before, but he seemed to be related to Ula Woods. The judge looked up and asked, "Who is the defendant?" Banyon raised his hand.

Before he could speak, Mrs. Woods said, "He hit my boy, Judge, he hit my lovely, sweet boy." And then she proceeded to cry.

"Sit down and be quiet," the judge said, but it was too late; it already had registered in her brain.

"Mr. Banyon, you are charged with leaving the scene of the accident and failure to yield right-of-way. How do you plead?"

Banyon had talked to his lawyer and longtime friend before coming to the courthouse. The lawyer had advised him to plead guilty and to pay the fines. "The woman wants you guilty so that she can sue your insurance company. People do this every day. If you plead innocent, they will have a trial right there, and you will lose anyway. You would be responsible for the trial costs and maybe a sentence as well." Banyon knew that Mrs. Woods had set up a good strategy and would probably win. The boy now had a neck brace and a limp. He had not been wearing the items earlier. The group also included a man wearing a sharkskin suit that screamed "ambulance chaser." In all, six people comprised the "Woods group"—six to one. *Not good odds.*

But Banyon was innocent, and this was wrong. He had raised his own children to believe that if you were right, you stick by your guns. He opened his mouth to speak and noticed Officer Dean. He had entered the courtroom just as Banyon was about to reply. *Seven to one.*

"Guilty, Your Honor," was all he could say.

"Since you have a clean record, we will give you ninety days' supervision," Her Honor said.

Hey, not bad, thought Banyon.

"And fines totaling six hundred dollars."

Later, after he had paid the fines and was subjected to three hours of waiting for the signed documents, Banyon finally headed for the restroom. As he started to leave the bathroom, the knuckle dragger appeared in the doorway.

"You were very lucky, man," he said in a deep voice. "If you had pleaded innocent, I was going to have to jump you before the trial later today."

"Why?"

"To make sure that you would lose, man."

Banyon was scared, although he tried not to show it. "Right here, in front of the police?"

"Man, it was all set up. The lawyer would walk in and swear that you started it—after all, I am Ula's little brother. You a vengeful guy and wanted to hurt someone. Nobody would believe you," the bear said.

"But I pled guilty," Banyon stated.

"Yeah, now we can sue your insurance company. We get our money."

"What happens now?" asked Banyon.

"I'm going to let you leave."

Banyon headed to the front door of the courthouse, feeling defeated, punished, and lower than a snake in wagon tracks. Officer Dean stood leaning on a wall near the entrance. He grinned at Banyon. *I wonder if he is part of this or just some "I don't give a shit" cop who wanted to get the bad guys without trying to find out the truth.* Banyon knew that if he had another run-in with the Streamwood Police Department, he would not get a fair shake.

A year had passed since then. Banyon walked up to the bulletproof-glassed counter of the police station and stared at Detective Heinz. Detective Heinz recognized him immediately.

Banyon didn't know where to begin but remained stoic. "I want to report a crime."

"Another car accident?" asked Detective Heinz as he reached for the accident report. Banyon winced.

"No, there has been a break-in at my house."

"And when did this alleged break-in occur?" asked the detective.

"About a half hour ago," Banyon replied.

"And what was taken?" inquired the detective.

"Well, that is the problem. As far as I could tell, nothing. But there was a break-in."

Before Banyon could tell him about the bugs, Detective Heinz said, "Listen, I don't have time for pranks. All my officers on duty are currently busy with a large fire that was started over on Barrington Road. I've got no one to send to investigate."

In that split second, Banyon learned two important things: first, Detective Heinz was the boss. All that bullshit last year about the "captain" was baloney. The second was that the fire could have been started on purpose.

"Was the fire an arson job?" Banyon asked.

"What do you know about it?" Heinz asked, suddenly suspicious.

"Nothing," Banyon quickly responded, "but the men that were at my house didn't seem to be worried about the police showing up. Also, even if they didn't take anything, they did leave some electronic devices."

Detective Heinz's grin had disappeared. Just then, the hotline rang, and Heinz grabbed the phone.

"Detective Heinz, Streamwood Police." After a few minutes, he asked, "Are you hurt?" There was another pause. "Okay, ma'am, just stay in the Blockbuster Store until I get there. Ma'am, I don't understand Indian, slow down." He slammed the phone and started to get up.

The alarms were ringing inside Banyon's head. *My neighbor is an Indian woman.*

"What happened?" asked Banyon.

"A woman was assaulted in the Blockbuster parking lot, at gunpoint no less. This is turning out to be a shitty day."

"Did she give a name?" asked Banyon, starting to hyperventilate.

"You have something to do with this?" yelled the detective.

"I think that the Indian woman is my neighbor. It could have been the men looking for me. I put one of the bugs on her car."

"You'd better come with me. You have some explaining to do."

During the short trip along Irving Park Road, Banyon explained why he put the tracking device on his neighbor's car.

Detective Heinz looked at him in disbelief. "What kind of stuff are you into? Why would you put a neighbor at risk?"

"I didn't think that she would be going out. I'm sorry. I just wanted to hide the device in case the men came back—you know, it was evidence."

"What do you do for a living?" the cop asked.

"I'm just a business consultant," said Banyon, shrugging. "I have no idea why they were at my house, no idea why they would put bugs and tracking devices in my house, and no idea what these people want from me."

As they cruised into the Blockbuster parking lot, Banyon recognized his neighbor's Honda. Almost before Detective Heinz had stopped, he was out of the car and looking under the car. The tracking device was gone.

K. P. Patel was standing in the window of the store as Heinz walked toward her. Heinz was six foot two and had a big barrel chest. He was very intimidating and towered over the slight, frail-looking young woman.

"Mrs. Patel?"

"Yes," she acknowledged.

"You called the station?"

"Yes."

"Are you all right?"

"Yes."

The woman was visually shaken. She was dressed in the traditional sari. This one was silk. She had on a small undershirt that did not completely cover her body, revealing a small ring in her navel. Banyon knew her to be a silent gentlewoman of less than thirty, who spent most of her time with her two little children. She never spoke when her husband was around.

Heinz was gearing up to question her when she seemed to muster enough courage and started to speak.

Her accent was slightly British. She explained that she had been returning a video to Blockbuster when a white Ford Aerostar with Illinois plates pulled up next to her. She was talking on the phone at length with her sister when it happened.

"Four men got out and circled my car. The leader had a gun. Imagine that, a gun to steal my video. Anyway, I kept my doors locked, and next thing I knew, they were back in the van and headed west on Irving Park Road." She pulled in a breath, which caused her chest to rise and hinted of curves below all that cloth. She continued, "They tried to appear like the military but were very disorganized. Only two had masks all the way on. Of the other two, one was young, maybe twenty. The other was older, maybe forty, and had the gun, a Steyr M40, same as you are wearing." She pointed to the weapon on the policeman's hip. "I would not be able to recognize them, but I'm sure about the ages. Oh, and they had hard rock music on the radio, you know, lots of drumbeating and screaming. The words seemed foreign to me."

Stunned at the completeness of the report, Detective Heinz and Banyon looked at each other. Banyon asked, "You didn't, by chance, get the plate number?"

"I am sorry," she said. "I only got the last three numbers, and the numbers were two, zed, and two." She had said the three numbers precisely, with slightly parted lips.

"What the hell is 'zed'?" demanded Detective Heinz.

"It's zero," explained Banyon.

"Please, my name's Pramilla," she announced with complete composure. "Why is Mr. Banyon here? He lives next door to me."

"How do you know that the gun was a Steyr M40?" asked Detective Heinz, ignoring her question.

"In India," Mrs. Patel replied, "my father taught me about guns. I've lived with guns all of my life. I know a police gun when I see one."

Banyon looked at her as if seeing her for the first time. There was something very appealing about her. She looked regal. As she stood tall with her back straight, the slight breeze rustled her cream-colored sari. Her long black hair lay straight. It flowed halfway down her back.

"Did you notice anything out of place or different around your neighborhood today?" The inquiry came as the detective looked up from the notepad.

A delicate index finger, with perfectly polished red nails, ventured up to touch the bottom of her chin. "I thought that I heard someone on my roof around dusk, but I wasn't dressed to go out and look." A small smile crossed her face. The smile said she was naked.

"Well, Mrs. Patel, it's like this," Heinz started, "we have your statement, but no evidence that anything happened. I'm not saying that it didn't happen, but we don't have much to go on. I'll type it up, and if we get a break, I'll let you know. I doubt that you will see these guys again."

"I understand. But it would be nice to get the riffraff off of the streets," Mrs. Patel countered.

"Do you want to call your husband, or can you drive yourself home? I'm heading that way and can follow you," he added. "Mr. Banyon can ride with you if you want."

"My husband would not like that." It came out as a typical reply by an Indian woman, as she snuck a peek at Banyon. Banyon was intrigued now and sensed that she was not as controlled by her husband as she appeared.

Detective Heinz was pensive and bounced his pen on the notepad. Then he spoke like a true veteran detective, waiting for the last second to catch the person off guard. Detective Heinz asked, "Before you go, is there anything else you can tell me about the men, anything at all?"

"When they opened the sliding door," she started, "a book fell out. One of the men scooped it up and threw it back in the van."

"Was there anything special about the book?"

She seemed hesitant, almost shy.

"What did you see?" Heinz probed.

"I think it was a religious book," she finally said.

"Why do you say that?"

"There was a religious symbol on the front." Her voice had fallen to a whisper.

"Can you draw it?" Heinz urged, as he flipped to a page in his book and offered it to her.

Slowly she raised her hand. But instead of taking the pad, she slid her fingers smoothly into the top of her undershirt. Banyon was mesmerized. Detective Heinz stood staring as Mrs. Patel rummaged around under her shirt. The hand came out with a pendant. Gracefully she laid it across her chest. "It was this."

Banyon was astonished. The pendant was a swastika.

No one said anything. The most hated symbol of the Western world was on the neck of this gentlewoman. Was there something more mysterious about her? What, in fact, did Banyon know about her? He started to look around to see if there were any white vans around. He saw none. *How is this connected, and what the hell is going on?*

Before either of the men could think of anything to say, Mrs. Patel again spoke. "It's a religious symbol." It was a straightforward statement.

She explained that the swastika was, in fact, the second most holy symbol of the Hindu religion. The word "swastika" came from ancient Sanskrit and was connected to the beloved elephant-headed god referred to as Ganesha. Ganesha is the god of good luck. Hindus routinely put the symbol over doorways and thresholds and at the beginning of account books.

Mrs. Patel went on to say that the pendant was a good luck charm and was not exactly like the Nazi swastika. The edges on the pendant were pointed counterclockwise, while the Nazi swastika was pointed clockwise. The history of the swastika could be traced back over three thousand years and to cultures in Asia and Europe and even to the American Indians.

Banyon knew many things about history. He had studied fascism all his life. He had a degree in history and was an avid reader. He knew that the Nazi movement was still around but sometimes changed its name.

He spoke up. "The swastika was the symbol for the Nazi Party. In the broader sense, it meant hatred of people that were not like Nazis; it is often the symbol for white supremacy. White supremacy meant racism and the need to not just dominate, but actually eliminate, all others that were not pure ethnic white people."

"Come on," Heinz said. "You're telling me that Nazis exist today?"

Banyon replied, "Actually Chicago has always been a hotbed for white supremacy. Movies like *The Blues Brothers* made fun of the movement, but the white supremacy movement is no joke."

Mrs. Patel joined in, "Fascism is everywhere." She nodded her head as approval to Banyon's words.

A list of facts continued to roll through Banyon's mind. "There are over two hundred white supremacy groups in the United States. In Illinois, there are twelve white supremacy groups. Almost all are chapters of the mysterious Altar of the Creator church. The leader, Joe Kroll, the self-appointed 'pope' of the church, has studied law and uses it to his advantage."

"I have read his name on some police reports," admitted Heinz.

Banyon continued to speak. "There is a logical reason why Chicago and surrounding cities continue to have white supremacist organizations. Most people don't realize that the upper Midwest, especially Wisconsin, during World War II housed prisoners of war. At one time, there were more than twenty thousand German prisoners interned in Wisconsin. They were spread out all over the state in thirty-eight different camps. Local newspapers documented that the German prisoners were often seen drinking in neighborhood bars during the war. As you went north from downtown Chicago, the German population kept growing; and Milwaukee, only ninety miles north of the Loop, was already very heavily German. Many Germans settled there in the eighteenth century and made Wisconsin the beer and bratwurst capital of the USA. The prisoners of war mixed in well with the locals, and many prisoners never returned to Germany after the war ended. To this day, they continue to live in the area. Some of the prisoners, according to the Anti-Defamation League, were former Nazis who had somehow changed their identities, but not their attitudes."

"You seem very knowledgeable," Mrs. Patel noted sweetly. Banyon had by now become very impressed with her.

"My father was a military hero during World War II. I have been fascinated by what happened. You know that history repeats itself, right?"

"I have read about white supremacists. They are sometimes called Aryans. What is the difference?" Mrs. Patel asked shyly.

Now up to the task, Banyon responded, "The Nazis discovered information about the Aryan race from ancient writings of other cultures that had come in contact with the Aryans. They were misguided in believing that the swastika was also an Aryan symbol."

"But my understanding is that the Aryans lived in India," questioned Mrs. Patel.

Banyon nodded his head in agreement. "The Aryans were a nomadic tribe that settled in northern Iran and India. They believed themselves to be ethnically pure and superior. Little else is known about this extinct race, and no one has ever found any written history. The Aryans, however, were the model used by the Nazis as the cornerstone to develop the Third Reich."

"Why use them as a model?" the impatient detective asked.

"No one really knows," answered Banyon. "Hitler was a believer in ancient cults. The word 'Aryan' is derived from *ayas*, a Vedic term meaning 'metal' or 'people who used metal,' as in swords and so on. Also, there are many references stating that the Aryan people were involved in 'struggles between light and darkness.' This can be interpreted as good versus evil or perhaps light-skinned versus dark-skinned. We do know that the Nazis spent much time searching the deserts of India for artifacts."

"You sound like a bookworm," the feisty detective remarked.

"Education is not one of my shortcomings," quipped Banyon.

Detective Heinz tried to summarize. "So, was this a religious book or a Nazi book?"

"The symbol I saw was the Nazi symbol," Mrs. Patel replied.

Banyon was searching the placid beauty of her liquid brown eyes. She lowered her face in shame, as if she had disappointed someone who needed her help. This was a more complicated woman than at first appeared, he thought. Although she was reluctant to get involved, Banyon felt that there was something competent, and tough, lurking just below the surface of that creamy skin.

Suddenly there was a noise. "Great," said Detective Heinz as he snatched up his ringing mobile. "Go ahead, Dean."

"Just came on duty, and there is no one here, just a black Lincoln in the parking lot. What's up, Chief?"

"Where've you been, Dean? You were supposed to be on duty two hours ago. I'm up to my ass in coincidences right now; plus there is a big fire over on Barrington Road. You stay at the station and man the phones until I get back," the detective ordered.

"Where are you? Is anyone with you?"

Heinz didn't particularly like Officer Dean and thought that Dean might be after his job. But, Heinz had to admit, the number of arrests that Dean made was well above average. Revenues from tickets and fines had never been higher. There were, however, some serious concerns about Officer Dean.

"Just man the phones. I'll be back in half an hour," Heinz ordered. "And don't call me 'Chief.'"

"Do you want me to run the plates on the Lincoln? Maybe have it taken to the police impound? It would give me something to do." Dean was digging for information, and Heinz knew it.

"Just do what I told you. I'll be there soon," the annoyed Heinz replied.

"Roger, Chief."

Heinz noticed that Banyon was now agitated. He turned to Heinz and said, "Dean was the one who arrested me last year—he knows my car."

"I realize that," admitted Heinz.

Chapter Three

The caravan was headed west on Irving Park. Mrs. Patel was in the lead; Banyon and the detective trailed two car lengths behind. They were heading in the same direction that the van had taken.

"What do you know about Officer Dean?" Banyon inquired.

"That's police business," growled the veteran cop. "Steer clear of it."

Detective Heinz shot him a mean look just as Banyon's cell phone rang.

"Jesse, I'm kind of busy … What?" Surprise registered on Banyon's face. "Is everyone okay?"

"I'll just be a minute," Banyon said to the detective. "It's my sister."

The detective's right eyebrow was raised.

"No, I don't think it has anything to do with the ghosts," Banyon said into the phone. Both of Detective Heinz's eyebrows were raised now.

"Did the police find anything to go on?" Banyon asked.

Eventually Banyon said, "No, everything is great here." More pause.

"Actually, I'm on my way to Las Vegas," Banyon finally said. "I'll be gone about four days, and I'll touch base with you when I return."

Before Detective Heinz could ask a question, Banyon pressed a button on his phone and put his head to the receiver. Banyon had decided to call his three children. The final call was to May.

"May, it's Colt, you all right? Hey, I'm going out of town for four days. Got a pen? Okay, write large and clear." He spelled out the hotel and gave her the number from memory.

"No, it's business. I'll watch my money. Just remember to put the note on the refrigerator. Did you put my name on it? Thanks. Call you when I get back." He was very happy with May, but she had declared that she was "taking a break" some weeks ago. He hardly heard from her and wondered if that meant they were "just friends" now.

Banyon was checking on his children and girlfriend. Banyon was also feeding his family a plausible story for dropping out of sight for a while.

Detective Heinz began to wonder whether Banyon was scared—or was he very calculating? Banyon seemed to react quickly and think fast. Heinz asked, "What happened to your sister?"

Banyon looked straight out the window and hesitated before he answered the detective. "All three of my sisters' houses were broken into, just about the same time that those men were at my house. My sisters all live in the same town. This is too much to be a coincidence. Somebody is after something, and my family is now involved."

Heinz was quick to reply. "So far nothing makes sense. You have this outlandish story, no evidence, and a neighbor that could be in on whatever it is you're trying to pull, and now you're talking about ghosts. Who or what are the ghosts?"

They had been parked in Banyon's driveway for some time. Now Mrs. Patel began to gently tap at the window of the cruiser. Banyon opened the window just as Detective Heinz asked the question.

"Jesse, my sister, said that someone called her earlier in the evening, saying he had information about the ghosts. All she had to do was meet him at our old house on Speonk-Riverhead Road at eight thirty at night. He didn't give a name, but it wouldn't have mattered as Jesse was hooked. She called both of our sisters, who also wanted more information about the ghosts. They all trouped over to the old house—sisters, husbands, and children. But after they waited for two hours, no one showed up. My sisters thought it was just some prank, but when they returned home, they all discovered their houses had been rifled. Not much had been taken—just some old relics, war stuff from my father. The police have no leads. The timing of the burglaries was considered a coincidence. The police predicted that some friend would probably show up with the things taken, and the earth would continue to rotate."

"That doesn't explain the ghosts," Heinz said dryly.

Mrs. Patel was leaning in the window. Banyon caught the scent of her perfume and a slight hint of garlic and other spices. Her eyes reflected genuine concern.

Banyon sighed and began to tell about the ghosts.

"The house I grew up in was haunted. I know that sounds like I'm nuts, but believe me, something was in that house. The house was built before the turn of the century. It was a Cape Cod with an enclosed front and back porch. A German immigrant, Wolfgang Becker, built the house. When the stock market crashed in 1929, Wolfgang's business died a quick death. His wife and son returned to Germany shortly afterward, leaving Wolfgang alone in America.

"He became more despondent when, in 1936, he got a letter saying that the United States government was annexing his land. It was then that he hung himself in a bedroom closet. When we lived in the house, it was my closet." He explained that the Banyons all believed that Wolfgang was the ghost.

"That's fascinating," Detective Heinz observed. "I've always enjoyed a good yarn."

Banyon continued. "My father bought the land at an auction—the going rate was fifteen dollars per acre in 1946. The house had been vacant since 1936.

"My brother, Jim, came along in 1949. A year later, I was born. Then my three sisters spread out over the next thirteen years. Grandparents, uncles, and various other relatives had extended stays at the country house. It was drafty and made noises."

"And when did you first see the ghost?" Mrs. Patel asked.

"I was about ten when I first became aware of the ghost. No one in my family would ever stay overnight in the house by themselves, and nobody went into the cellar alone. The cavernous basement was built from bricks and mortar. It had several connecting rooms that didn't seem to have any purpose. A constant wind blew from somewhere down there. We swore that the wind sounded like moans."

"Why didn't you just move out?" asked Heinz.

"Well, after many years, my family adjusted to the ghosts and went about our business. Many of our friends wanted to stay overnight to see the ghosts. Sometimes the ghosts appeared with an outsider around; sometimes it didn't."

"But you must have been very scared," Mrs. Patel commented, with searching eyes that locked in on Banyon.

Wanting to conclude the discussion, Banyon replied, "As we grew older, each of us left the house as soon as we could. We hoped that the ghosts wouldn't follow. Soon after the last child left home, my parents sold the house. My family members all know that there is such a thing as ghosts. As I've grown older, the ghosts still haunt me, and I still won't sleep facing a wall."

"What happened to the house?" asked the curious detective.

"The house now lays vacant. The last residents used it for an office for their landscaping business but moved abruptly when the owner had a heart attack on the premises. It stands today as an eerie monument along the Speonk-Riverhead Road. My sisters go by the house occasionally. They're on the lookout for lights, moans, or things out of place. We all hoped that we were done with the ghosts. They've already had too much influence on our lives, and now this."

Mrs. Patel looked at Banyon sympathetically. "I too believe in spirits."

"Are ghosts the same thing as religious spirits?" Banyon wondered out loud.

Banyon wanted to continue, but Detective Heinz ended the conversation. He pointed to Mrs. Patel. "You go home." Then to Banyon, "You come with me; I want to see these bugs."

"My home would have been the first place the men headed upon discovering that I had removed the first tracking device. The devices are probably gone," Banyon said as he opened the garage and went in through the kitchen door. The spice rack was lying on its side. Inspecting the upstairs, he found the mirror in his bedroom askew. The clock in the office had been moved. Everything else in the house was how he had left it. Turning to the wall behind his desk, he saw the nail hanger sticking out of the wall, but no frame. His father's war medals were gone.

Deciding that the situation was getting out of hand, Banyon gave the surprised detective the first three letters of the van's license plate. He apologized for not giving the letters to the detective sooner. He told Heinz that he didn't have much trust in the department. Banyon went on to do a complete search of the house. As he moved from room to room, Detective Heinz sat at the dining room table, placing phone calls in between making notations in his book.

Banyon went into the office to check his e-mails. He scrolled through the many spam e-mails and found two from recruiters that were requesting more information on behalf of a client. He saved those and erased the others. As the screen rebooted, one new message appeared. "Call me later. I have something to tell you, Pramilla." A cell phone number appeared at the bottom of the e-mail. They had lived next door to each other for a long time, but Banyon could not recall giving her his e-mail address.

He went back downstairs to face Detective Heinz. Heinz said, "I'm going back to the shop—nothing to find here. If there were men in the house, they wore gloves."

"How do you know that?"

"I'm a detective, remember?" He then added, "Do you see any cleaning bottles anywhere? They took them after they cleaned up any prints."

"Will you give me a ride?" It had occurred to Banyon that he had parked his car at the station house only three hours earlier, yet it seemed like centuries ago. "What should I do? I can't come back here."

"If I were you, I'd find someplace to stay tonight. I've got work to do back at the station. I'll run the plates on the van," Heinz said. On the ride back to the station, neither spoke.

Once at his car, Banyon got in and then out again. He looked under the car but saw nothing. He failed to notice the face in the station house window that was staring at him with unmitigated hate.

Chapter Four

A few minutes later, as Detective Heinz was just adding sugar to his coffee, Officer Dean stormed into the kitchen area. "Chief, can I go now? I need to check up on something."

"Have you checked on the van and plates, as I asked you to do an hour ago?"

"Sure did!"

"And?"

"The van was stolen today at around two p.m. The plates didn't belong to the van but were reported stolen about three hours ago. The report is on your desk."

"Did you include the names and addresses? Did you talk to the victims? You're not going anywhere until you finish the job that I have assigned you." Heinz added more sugar to his coffee as Dean stomped from the kitchen. Heinz heard Dean slamming his fist into his desk. He watched Dean from the window in the kitchen. Dean collected some papers, stomped into Heinz's office, and dropped the papers in the in-box. He turned around and went back to his desk briefly before leaving the office.

Heinz eventually returned to his desk and started his computer. He called up the system and queried Colton Banyon's file. The detective noticed that there was virtually nothing of interest in the file, just the usual statistics. He also noticed that Officer Dean had recently opened the file. He first thought that Dean had looked up the Lincoln, even after he had been told not to. However, the time stamp said that the lookup had been done yesterday. At that point, Heinz spilled his drink and began wiping up coffee from his lap. *Where was Dean?*

Chapter Five

Banyon headed out of town in his car. He reasoned that the men who were after him would have a larger area of search if he put distance between himself and Streamwood. He suddenly felt an urge to talk, and picking up his cell phone, he called the number supplied to him by Pramilla.

A man's deep voice, with a hint of an Indian accent, answered.

"Pramilla, please."

"Who's calling?"

"Colton Banyon, your neighbor."

"I'll get her for you."

"Colt?" She said it in a silky voice. "I knew you'd call." It was a simple reply. *I am too predictable,* he thought.

"I got your message," answered Banyon. "Are you in more trouble?"

"No, but I wanted to tell you something." She sounded excited, the way a woman sounds when wanting to tell how much she saved on a new dress.

"All right, what is on your mind?"

"They're racist," she purred.

"Who's racist?" The concern was evident in his tone.

"The police, they're racist. Believe me, I know, I've seen the results. Two of my friends were beaten and money extorted from them. As soon as I moved in here, a policeman came to my door and warned me that it was a dangerous neighborhood. He said that it was expensive to look after us and asked for money."

"How much did he ask for?" Shakedowns were a common occurrence in many parts of the city, especially in the Asian and Indian communities. After all, this was Metro Chicago.

"Five hundred dollars."

"Did you pay?"

"Of course. We have corruption in India too."

"How many times have you been approached?"

"Just once, but I'm afraid that Officer Dean will come again soon." She said this as if resigned to the inevitable.

"Did you say 'Officer Dean'?"

"Yes."

Banyon wasn't too surprised. He had begun to put the pieces together. The small amount of money figured too. These guys don't want to be noticed, so they take what they can get and run. It sounded as if Officer Dean was involved in some kind of extortion ring. Banyon also wondered about his accident from last year. Dean was probably involved in that too, he decided. After all, the accident report that Banyon had completed had mysteriously disappeared.

"Don't worry," soothed Banyon, "I don't think they will return."

She suddenly asked, "Where are you, Colt?"

He wasn't sure if it was safe to tell her but decided that she was trustworthy; it would be fine. For some strange reason, he wanted to trust her.

"I'm out looking for a place to stay tonight since I don't think it would be wise to go home. At least until Detective Heinz tells me something."

"Why don't you stay here? I have an extra room. Just leave your car somewhere. I'll pick you up."

After he carefully considered the offer for three or four seconds, Banyon replied, "Can you pick me up at the Airport Hilton? I'm going to park my car in the lot. I told several people that I'm going out of town."

"I'll be there in a half-hour."

"Thanks, Pramilla," he said solemnly.

"Oh, one more thing," she interjected. "I want to hire you."

As he stood in front of the stylish Hilton Hotel at O'Hare, Banyon had the sensation of having been there before. Of course, he had been, countless times, waiting for someone to pick him up. However, he was usually waiting for a limo, not some mysterious woman. He'd been flying in and out of O'Hare for over thirty years and had racked up over a million miles on several major airlines. In the last several years, however, he'd hardly been to the airport. He was not afraid of flying, but it was because of the drop-off of his business. After the last few trying years, many businesses tightened their belts and stopped spending. Many companies now had huge concerns about whom they employed. Several large accounting firms and consultants had been implicated in the downfall of several large corporations. The fallout was a drop in business for all consultants, resulting in Banyon's current precarious financial position. He had recovered some in recent years, but his business was hanging by a thread.

His reminiscing was broken by the sound of a horn. A small gray Honda was parked down the driveway. A thin delicate hand snaked out to wave.

As he opened the door of the Honda, he realized that he had not planned on what to say on the drive back to Streamwood. He was, however, aware of the scent that would forever remind him of her as he dropped into the seat, closed the door, and fastened the seat belt.

"Thanks. You don't have to do this, you know."

"I know, but you're my neighbor. Besides, I'm kind of involved since you put that device on my car." She spoke gaily.

Banyon was putting up his guard. Women had an uncanny ability to make him feel guilty—everything was always his fault.

"I am sorry about that. I've dragged you into something that you shouldn't have to deal with."

"Nonsense," she snorted, jerking up her head as she spoke. "I've already had experience with these racists. Maybe you and I can stop them."

Banyon doubted it, but he said nothing. Glancing sideways, he took notice of her appearance. She was now dressed in black spandex shorts and a red tank top. For the first time, he saw her legs. Banyon was truly a leg man. He didn't care about breasts like most men. Pramilla had great legs. He could see that they were long and well tapered, colored by a good tan. She was very light-skinned.

"What did you tell your husband?"

"Well, actually," she said, flipping her delicate hand for emphasis, "I'm not married."

"But ..." It was as far as he got.

"You think that I'd tell that racist Heinz that I was single?" It was spoken with a fire in her voice. "I'll tell them nothing."

"But..." Again, he was quieted by her retort.

"It's my sister, Previne, who you see with Keri. We are similar, Previne and me."

Banyon was mystified for about thirty seconds. A beer commercial was playing in his head. "I love parties that never end ... and twins." They were twins. An erotic thought passed through his mind. His cheeks turned red at the thought.

"Well, that certainly explains a lot," he muttered, mostly to himself.

"I thought it might," she said with a provocative smile.

At least now he wouldn't have to be worried about a knife cutting off some of his private parts in his sleep. "I'm feeling a little more comfortable now. At least I have someplace to stay tonight and can face tomorrow with more energy than I feel right now."

"Colt," Pramilla said, "I remembered something else about the people that tried to take my video."

"What?"

"The young one wore shorts with a logo on them. The logo was '88.' I checked it out on the Internet. Do you know what it means?"

A bell went off in Banyon's head. "Yes, I'm afraid I do. The letter *H* is the eighth letter in the alphabet. 'Eighty-eight' stands for 'Heil Hitler.' Last year a large discount chain had inadvertently been selling merchandise with the '88' logo. A lot of people were very upset, and the product was pulled from the shelves. It was a public relations nightmare. The Altar of the Creator church owned the company that sold the merchandise. You should call Detective Heinz and add it to your statement, but I don't think that it will matter."

Pramilla changed the subject. "Colt, do you really believe that there were ghosts in your house?"

"Everyone in my family is convinced. I know there was something there. In truth, the fact of actually having ghosts in the house had been a key factor in my decision to leave home and go to school as far away from Speonk as I could get. I may even have spent my life traveling and moving to make sure that they never found me again. The ghosts have had a profound effect on my life."

"I want to hire you," she said. "I want to hire you to take me to your old house and look for the ghosts."

Chapter Six

Detective Heinz was having his own epiphany back at the office. Coming out of the bathroom, he was once again accosted by Officer Dean.

"I got Joe to man the phones. He just came in from the fire scene." Dean informed his superior that the huge fire had been put out. "Joe said that the fire was set by some black punks. I want to interrogate them when we find them."

"I didn't know you were in charge," a sarcastic Detective Heinz replied.

"I know how to handle them better than you," Dean replied. "But I'm in a hurry."

"Hurry?" questioned Detective Heinz.

"I've got to go to church tonight after my shift," was all Dean said before leaving.

Heinz had already decided the Dean was a problem. He was overzealous, didn't like authority, and clearly didn't follow orders. Heinz resolved to pull his personnel file. But first Heinz decided to check on the stolen van and plates.

He started to review the reports. The first victim had been a seventy-five-year-old woman, who reported her van stolen that afternoon. He dialed her number to inform her that the police were working on the case. He noted that the listing was for the Streamwood area and the address was familiar.

"Hello," answered a rather shaky voice.

"Mrs. Kleinschmidt, this is Detective Heinz from the Streamwood Police Department. I wanted to talk to you about your stolen van and to assure you that we are searching for it."

"Oh, I am not worried. Michael will find it again."

"Mrs. Kleinschmidt, has your van been stolen before?" he prompted her as he frantically tried to boot up his computer.

"It happened once before. Your officer Michael brought it back right away. He even had it washed. I hope this isn't about the reward that I gave him."

"Reward?"

"Just a small one—I'm on Social Security, you see."

"You said 'Officer Michael.' Is Michael his first name?" A furrow was now burrowed deep into the detective's brow.

"Dean is his last name, of course. I've known him most of his life. He comes from a very good German family. He lives just down the block, next door to Ula Woods, the colored woman with all those boys, with all different last names."

His computer was now telling him that the woman's van had indeed been stolen six months ago. A day following the report, Officer Dean had located the stolen vehicle. There was no record of the van being kept for evidence of a crime.

Heinz quickly wrapped up the call and dialed the number of the person that had reported stolen plates. At the same time, he had been accessing the files on Glen Minor, the second victim. The phone rang only once.

"Mr. Minor, this is Detective Heinz of the Streamwood Police Department. I'm calling about the stolen plates that you reported today."

"I don't want any trouble," was the nervous reply. The voice was high-pitched. Heinz pictured a small fearful man.

"We are looking for your plates. Any idea who stole them?"

"I can't say." Again a very nervous reply.

"Can't or won't?" an irritated Heinz asked.

"Officer Dean always takes care of it—why are you calling me?"

Detective Heinz had finally accessed the victim's file. Mr. Minor reported stolen plates an incredible three times in the past two years. Officer Dean returned all of them in less than two days every time. As before, the plates were never used for evidence in any trial.

"Mr. Minor, I am Officer Dean's supervisor. Has he helped you before? Your license plates appear to have been stolen several times in the last two years."

Minor began to stutter. "I … I … I … do I need a lawyer?"

"Why would you need a lawyer, Mr. Minor?" A small click told Heinz that he was talking into an empty phone line. *How big is this case? Is there a tie between Banyon and Mrs. Patel? Who are the bad guys? What do they want? How is Dean involved? Every time I turn over a stone, Dean's name pops up.*

As he sat at his desk, a shudder went down his spine. He nearly jumped out of his chair when he heard a squawk on his walkie-talkie.

It was Officer Dean. "Send backup to 312 Bartlett Drive. I found the van."

Detective Heinz stewed in the dichotomy. He had been acting captain for three years now—ever since the real captain had died of a heart attack. He'd been a custodian, put off making changes, and avoided waves with management. He had just been babysitting until the village hired a new captain, rather than managing the station. Some had taken advantage, and now this—corruption. He was slowly reaching a decision.

With new resolve, he announced to the empty station house, "That time is over. I'm going to get to the bottom of this mess, find out how deep this thing runs, and clean up this house."

He began working on a plan. He would start with Officer Dean and his arrest docket. He could cross-reference his arrests, tickets, and all the cases where Dean had been involved. Next he would find out the names of Dean's friends, both on the force and in Streamwood. He would then collect information on Dean's mysterious church. Heinz did not know if he could trust anyone in the department. He needed help.

Whenever a small-town police station needed help, it turned to the state police. They had the manpower to help. Streamwood didn't. An hour after Detective Heinz made a call to the Illinois State Police Department, Agent Loni Chen was dispatched to Streamwood.

Chapter Seven

Heinz had arranged to meet Agent Chen at a breakfast restaurant away from the village of Streamwood. The state police commander had promised that Agent Chen was fully qualified to help with the analysis of the crime data, but she had never been a field agent. "She is a little different" was how he put it. Heinz was still organizing his notes when she appeared at his table. "Agent Chen," she said, flashing her badge.

She was Chinese, about five foot two, with long straight black hair that traveled all the way down to below her waist. She had deep brown eyes and a slim figure that was accented by a big gun on her hip. She was dressed in silky black pants that flowed as she walked. A small red jacket covered her white T-shirt. She was definitely a fine-looking woman. Detective Heinz was dressed in his usual jeans and polo shirt covered by the ever-present police windbreaker. He felt severely underdressed.

She was all business. "Green tea," she said to the waitress in perfect English.

"Only on St. Patrick's Day, honey. We just got old-fashioned yellow Lipton tea today," quipped the waitress.

"That will be fine," Chen said softly. Her eyes told Heinz that she often had to deal with women who treated her with a bit of disdain. Apparently Agent Chen didn't do small talk.

She got right to the point. "What information can you provide about your situation?"

"I'm just getting started myself, but it looks like at least one of my officers, Officer Dean, may be shaking people down. Then there is an alleged assault on a woman. This all seems to be tied to a break-in, illegal listening devices, stolen property, arson, and maybe even bad manners." The last part was a joke that was totally wasted on Chen.

"And you want me to do what exactly?"

Feeling a little uncomfortable because of her abrupt approach, Heinz said, "If there is a conspiracy at my station, I want it stopped."

"Conspiracy? Why didn't you just say so?" a now animated voice replied.

"It will take me three days of investigation to determine the facts, and I'll help with the arrests."

"How do you know that it will take three days?" a surprised Heinz asked.

"This is a small town, small department." She was calculating in her head. "Eight hours to view your files, three hours for background on Officer Dean—I already know about his church; we have been tracking them for years. It will take seven hours to interview everyone involved." Her head was tilted now, deep in thought. "I'll want to have access to a cot so that I can get four hours of sleep per night."

"Agent Chen, why the rush?" asked a bewildered Heinz.

Ignoring his question, she continued. "We need to find a reason for me to be at the station, something that will not alert the conspirators. Maybe I could be your girlfriend doing some secretarial work, you know, to catch up. Of course, you'd have to be there too. That will work. The other officers are not in the station all the time, right? You do want to end this conspiracy quickly, don't you?"

"How do you know that I am not married?" a cynical Heinz asked.

"Well," Chen replied, "you don't wear a ring, you dress like someone that hates laundry, and you didn't stand up when I sat. You are untrained."

"Are you real smart?" It was the only thing that Heinz could think of to say.

"Yes," spoken with not a touch of ego.

Heinz was grinning inside. He dared not show anything to this beautiful machine. "My girlfriend, huh? I haven't had a date since moving up here from St. Louis."

"Is the timing acceptable to you?" she asked, sipping on her yellow tea and watching him from over the rim of the cup.

"You'll have to conceal that gun," he responded, wondering where that bulky sidearm could be stored on her hundred-pound frame.

"I've brought others."

"Well, let's get started, girlfriend."

She had come by train from downtown and had grabbed a cab to the IHOP. She carried one small bag, a briefcase, and no purse. During the ten-minute ride to the station house, Agent Chen filled Heinz in on The Altar of the Creator church.

"We've been aware of their activities for some time. They have twelve branches throughout Illinois. They're fascist." Her voice was vehement.

"They've done very little that we can pin on them. We know about the record company, a distribution company, and their leader, Joe Kroll. Kroll is the 'pope' of the church and is smart. The church is a cover. Anyone can start a church and become an ordained minister. There are advertisements on the Internet to start a church for under a hundred dollars. While the state police haven't been able to pin any drug connections on them, we know they're thugs for hire. We're cooperating with the FBI. The FBI has jurisdiction over any interstate crime. The main church in Peoria is a storefront for anyone that wants something, especially illegal, arranged. They're also into extortion, burglaries, and working people over. Some of their members, if not all, have neo-Nazi white supremacist tendencies. Whenever any of them is arrested, they never indict the church but take the rap in silence. Dean is listed as a deacon at the local church in Aurora, about ten miles from here. I wanted this assignment to get more data on the church. Isn't this exciting? Maybe you and I can shut down the church." She was all but bouncing in the car seat. Agent Chen had turned into an overexcited little girl. Detective Heinz kind of liked that.

True to her word, as soon as Agent Chen was shown to a desk at the police station, she went to work investigating Officer Dean. Heinz watched her fingers fly over the keys.

He'd given her a desk in the open space that was in front and visible from his office. Agent Chen was in full afterburner, calling headquarters with information requests—state headquarters had bigger computers—reading Dean's file, and reviewing the arrest history of the Streamwood Police Department, all the while appearing to be doing some routine task. She worked with her head down. Her black hair covered her oval face. Pencil flying over the paper, she took no breaks—no coffee, cigarettes, or bathroom. Within three hours, she appeared at Heinz's door with a report, a pad of paper, and a smile that said "I told you I could do it."

"What have you got?"

"Your officer Dean is quite a character," she said as she slid onto the chair in front of his desk.

"Michael Fredric Dean was born on July 5, 1959, in Wisconsin. His parents were Cora and Manfred Dean, of Black River Falls. Mrs. Dean was from the Norwegian Hanson clan, which has hundreds of family members in the many isolated coulees in the area. For your information, a coulee is a valley surrounded by many hills. People up in northern Wisconsin explain that they live in such and such a coulee. Coulees were a geological anomaly. When the great glacier came down from Canada during the ice age, it somehow didn't cover a portion of the land that ran from Eau Claire south to the border of Illinois. As a result, hundreds of small hills and valleys were left, a stark contrast to the otherwise-flat Midwest."

"I thought coulees were a Chinese thing," quipped Heinz.

This merited him a blank stare. "Manfred Dean's origins were hard to track down. He just appeared in Black River Falls in June 1946. He was about thirty at that time. We could not find anything about him until I discovered that there was a German prisoner of war camp about twenty miles from Black River Falls during the war. Dean's real name was Krauz, and he hailed from Munich. Captured in North Africa in 1942, he was sent to Camp McCoy to wait out the war. He had apparently met his wife during this time, and he returned to Black River Falls shortly after the war. He changed his name to avoid any anti-German backlash. He was a machinist by trade, a tool and die maker. In 1963, he moved his family to Streamwood. Mrs. Dean had relatives there. He worked for International Harvester in Chicago and retired in 1986. The couple died in 1988, when their car drove into the side of a synagogue in Skokie. Manfred had a record for assault, mostly from fights. His coworkers described him as arrogant, precise, with no sense of humor. He viewed anyone not German with tremendous contempt."

"You got all this information in three hours?" Heinz was beginning to admire this woman.

"There is plenty more," Chen replied. "Dean has lived in Streamwood all his life, except for the army years. After barely graduating from Streamwood High School, he enlisted in the army in 1977. Two high school teachers told me that Dean was more interested in football than school. He was known as the Assassin on the field, primarily due to his aggressive tackling and attitude. He was suspected of several cases of vandalism at the school. But someone else always came forward to take the blame."

"What about his army file?"

"The army was not very helpful, as his files are off-limits to civilians, even the FBI. From what I could gather, Dean was an MP—you know, military police—for several years. He left the military three weeks after the death of his parents. The rest of his file is closed to us. This could mean nothing, or it could mean a lot.

"Due to his MP background, he was able to get hired in Streamwood in the fall of 1988. He lists church, golf, racing cars, and bowling as his interests. He has never been married and lists his emergency contact as Judy Kroll, the wife of Joe Kroll."

"Well, Agent Chen, kind of sounds like the profile of a loner. What do you think?"

"Call me Loni, please," she purred. "After all, I am your acting girlfriend."

"Okay, Loni." He liked the way her name rolled out of his mouth. "What should we do now?"

"I think that I need to borrow your car."

"Why?"

"I feel the need to go bowling."

Detective Heinz started to take apart the report. It was a cross-reference of Officer Dean's cases and any name that appeared more than once on a report. Agent Chen had handed him the report as she had entered the office. He marveled, "I didn't know that our system could do this." Heinz observed sixteen names noted twice, with eight noted three times. One name was noted six times—Ula Woods.

Chapter Eight

The old man sat quietly in the living room of his house located on Tanners Neck Lane. His age was indeterminable, but he was very old and had lived a full and remarkable life. His eyes were alert but rheumy. His vision was sometimes cloudy. Yet his inner vision, supported by the voices in his head, was as strong as ever. He knew that he would succeed in his mission. The voices had convinced him with their singsong riddles about the future. "The time will come, you are the one," they would announce.

The sprawling ranch house overlooked Moriches Bay. The old man had tired of the outdoors and now spent his time seated at his desk. He was planning a mission of great importance, not just for him, but also for all humanity. It consumed all of his waking hours. The time to complete the mission had finally come. He just needed a little help, and he knew whom to involve, whether they wanted to be involved or not.

He hadn't driven in the past ten years. Instead he depended on various services to bring him whatever he needed. His one companion was a Polish housekeeper, who came each day and stayed long after the housecleaning dictated. Stella was fifty-five and unmarried, with no prospects. On occasion the old man had small presents sent to his home and gave these to Stella in exchange for brief favors. The need for favors came further and further apart now—after all, he was almost one hundred years old—but it still existed. To him it was a measure of existence. He had no friends and no relatives; he knew only a few people by name. His longtime friend had died a decade earlier. His several contacts and controllers had died of old age. Of course, he was passed on to other contacts, but those new people had never proven to be true believers. The old man had only one remaining obsession, and he intended to complete his mission before he died.

At that very moment, Joe Kroll was ripping one of his members a new asshole.

"How could you screw up this bad? You're a dipshit. Here we are on the verge of a new horizon for the cause, and you screwed it up. In all the years

I've known you, you've been a screwup. The Lord God has given us a miracle, and you screwed up." Kroll was firing on all cylinders, orating to an audience of one.

"Our forefathers' dream in America is just a few days away from starting, and you screw up. I should've let them put you in Leavenworth. You would have made a good wife for some big black horse-hung animal—or maybe a Jew. Maybe I should drop you as a deacon in the church as punishment."

Dean had an uncontrollable temper going all the way back to high school. Kroll, who had known him for over ten years, knew how to push the right buttons. No stranger to violence himself, Kroll could feel the rush of adrenaline that he always got when violence was near. He felt the sweet electricity of tension, the smell of fear. His brain was alerted for any sign of aggression. In his pocket, his fingers had already laced through the brass knuckles that he always carried with him.

Dean was ready for a fight. But Kroll had mentioned the one thing that Dean feared—loss of his position as deacon. All his life Dean struggled to be a leader.

He tried to be conciliatory. "Joe, we know where the guy lives, and we'll find him. He can't stay hidden; I have people looking for him everywhere. I have the resources of the department. Even that idiot Heinz thinks that Banyon is someone with something to hide. I've sent a man over to his girlfriend's house to see if he's there. I'm expecting a call any minute."

Kroll actually liked confrontation; it made his blood boil. Whenever his blood boiled, he always developed a need for sex. Not just any sex, but rough sex. Kroll was now consumed with sexual desire and knew that he would hunt later that evening. Dean had often hunted with him.

Dean was feeling the arousal as well. "Kind of reminds me of Okinawa. You were yelling at me just like that back then."

"Damn straight," shot back Kroll. "I sure as hell will never forget that adventure."

"The army should have never sent us to that cesspool. The crazy Japs were always accusing the American military of raping their girls. Didn't they get it? We won the war and could put as many men on Okinawa as we wanted to."

"Yeah, but you know our yellow-bellied leaders. They always knuckled and paid off the families."

"But we stopped that, at least for a while, didn't we?" Dean reasoned.

"You almost got us hung, as I recall," replied Kroll.

"It wasn't my fault," cried Dean. "When that girl came at me with the knife, I knocked it away and bear-hugged her while you interrogated her brother."

"But the confrontation had gotten you aroused. I saw it in your eyes. Her little legs were tangling, and her skirt was rising. I knew that something was going to happen."

"But, Joe, you were the first one to hit her."

"Well, she wouldn't shut up. But you hit her many times. Then you raped her."

"You did too," exclaimed Dean.

"Michael, you hit her one too many times. She died, for Chrissake."

"But I fixed it, Joe. I killed her brother, made it look like a suicide after he killed her."

"We were lucky. You do realize that, don't you?"

Twenty-five years later, Dean was still reliving the event. The blood rushed through his veins. He was not ashamed of what they had done; he was proud. They had saved a fellow Aryan, showed up the inept military government, exterminated some Asian garbage, and been sexually satisfied, all in one fell swoop. He couldn't wait to have a chance to do it again sometime. A phone rang, breaking the trip down memory lane.

Dean opened his cell phone. "Where is he?" Dean screamed into the phone. He hung up abruptly. "The asshole has gone to Las Vegas, to some convention. Our guy saw a note at Banyon's girlfriend's place. He was posing as a telephone man and saw the note on the refrigerator. Banyon will be back in four days. I told you we would find him."

"You'd better call the old man," a worried Kroll replied.

Dean was the only one to communicate with the old man. He didn't want Kroll to take over and take credit for his work, but he was a little afraid of Pierce. Before making the call, he thought about his history with the old man.

He had first made contact over two years ago. He had been reading the "personal services" ads in a mercenary magazine. The ad read "Need to identify a fingerprint. Can you help?" He had taken the job for five thousand dollars, half up front. Dean could not find the print in the police data banks but knew a female clerk at the FBI in Chicago who liked rough sex. She also came up empty. The owner's prints did not exist, or they were not in any database.

The print appeared in the police database about a year ago. Dean called to notify Pierce but never heard back from him. Suddenly he was summoned to the old man's house. His voice was wheezy but clear.

"Come to see me. I have something for you to do and will pay handsomely for your services. It might lead to the one thing that you have always desired. You may be the one I seek. I will need to know that you fight for the cause.

Bring documentation that you believe." Dean knew that the cause was white supremacy. The old man was one of them. That had been just four days ago.

Dean had arrived at MacArthur Airport at a little after noon. It was a two-and-a-half-hour flight. MacArthur, located in Ronkonkoma, is about halfway between New York City and Montauk Point, the end of Long Island. Long Island could be accessed by any of New York's three main airports, but MacArthur saved hours in commuting time.

Dean rented a car and, after collecting a map, made his way to the Long Island Expressway. Heading east he noted the flat contour of the land. There were also fewer houses lining the highway than he expected. Taking exit number 70, he proceeded to Montauk Highway and passed through the small town of Eastport.

Continuing down the highway, he came upon a sign for Speonk. Finally he reached Westhampton and Tanners Neck Lane. Turning right, he followed the tree-lined road. He could smell the scent of the ocean now. As he came around one more curve, he saw water. It wasn't the ocean. It was a large bay. Coming to a halt at the end of the road, he noticed a brick-walled compound to his right with iron gates and no nameplate. Walking to the gate, he depressed the button on the wall.

"Who is it?"

"Your visitor from Chicago."

"Leave your car where it is and walk up to the house," the voice ordered.

"Fine," Dean said as he scanned the landscape for cameras. He saw none. The house was set back from the road some hundred feet with a circular driveway. The ranch-style house had been built with red brick and covered with a shake roof. The door opened before he got there. A medium-size man stood in the opening. He had stooped shoulders and wore a dark suit. The man appeared to be very old, maybe ninety years old or more. He looked frail with stooped shoulders and seemed to have trouble standing up. There was something in his hand. Drawing closer, Dean recognized a Luger pointing at him.

"Nice gun, German Luger, relic from World War II," Dean said with no trace of fear. He didn't believe that a gun that old could even fire. Dean was an expert on guns, and this one needed work to fire.

"Good of you to notice. I trust no one." He waved the gun in such a way as to encourage Dean to enter.

As he passed by the old man, Dean could feel a chill come from the house. A grandfather clock ticked in the background. All in all, the house reeked of loneliness.

Dean was ordered to raise his hands and to lean against the wall. He was expertly frisked and ordered to turn around. Once again, he was staring into the barrel of the Luger.

"Michael Dean. I'm here at your request. We talked on the phone just yesterday. You do remember?"

"I may be old, but I'm not senile. You are either here because of greed or because of the cause. Which is it?"

"Both. I'm a businessman."

"Good, I have a proposition for you. First we are going for a little ride—you drive." Dean was ordered to walk slowly, two steps ahead of his host.

When the two men reached the car, Dean was instructed to open the trunk. The old man put Dean between himself and the open trunk. Satisfied that no one was there, he ordered Dean to open all the doors. With his gun still trained on Dean, he stood back.

"Get in and drive where I tell you." He took out a piece of paper and handed it to Dean. On the paper were precise directions. A long straight road headed north and stretched for as long as the eye could see. Dean learned from the map that it was the Speonk-Riverhead Road. Six miles along, Dean turned onto a dirt road, which continued slightly uphill. He was told to stop near a crest.

"Out," the old man ordered.

They walked to the crest; it revealed an open meadow. Dean could see for miles. The land was dotted with stunted pine trees. A town was outlined in the distance. A body of water lay to the right. Yellow-white sand was everywhere. The only sound was a slight rustling of a breeze in the barren woods.

The old man gestured toward the water. "That's where Long Island forks."

"That's quite a view," Dean agreed.

The old man smiled. "Beyond is the Sound and Connecticut in the distance. The trees behind us prevent you from seeing the Atlantic Ocean. The ocean is nine miles from this spot."

"That water is a lighter blue. Why?"

"That is Peconic Bay. It's between the two forks of Long Island. It's a sandy-bottom bay. Sometimes the water is as clear as in the Caribbean."

Dean took his word for it.

"That hill in the other direction represents the highest point on eastern Long Island. This hill that we're on is the second highest."

Dean asked, "How high is it?"

"Three hundred sixty-five feet and three inches," replied the man.

Dean asked, "You've measured it?"

"I had it surveyed—I own it."

"Impressive."

"In fact, I own all the land around here and all the land up the road on which you have just driven. It's sacred to me, and there's something hidden in the land that I must have. You can help me find what I search for, or you can die out here—it all depends on how committed you are to the cause. How committed are you, Mr. Dean?" The gun was leveled at Dean's chest. "If you cannot document your commitment to the cause, you will die out here where no one will ever find you."

Dean knew the gun was useless against him. He was too fast, and the gun had not been maintained properly. He could easily overpower the old man, and so he faced the next task scenting opportunity.

Dean took off his coat, dropping it to the ground. He then pulled his turtleneck over his head. Turning around, he showed the man his back. A tattoo covered almost the entire surface. The giant swastika had one other feature, the word "Aryan" underneath, written across his lower back.

"Thank you," the pleased man uttered.

Dean saw tears in the eyes of the weary old man—a man who had been hanging on, waiting for someone to come. Dean was someone to help him complete his mission, someone who believed. He would be the one that Pierce used to finish the job. The gun, now pointed to the ground, soon disappeared in a pocket. The old man stepped forward.

"My current name is Walter Pierce." His right hand extended to shake hands with a confederate. "I am pleased to meet you, Michael Dean, very pleased, indeed."

"The picture you sent me was taken out here, wasn't it?" As soon as Dean had said it, he wanted to take it back.

"I will explain everything in due time, my son." The old man spoke as might a teacher to a student.

Returning to the car, they started back down the road toward Westhampton. Pierce directed Dean to drive to a small restaurant in the downtown area. They were seated immediately in an inconspicuous corner. Both ordered local lobster.

As they ate, Dean commented, "The food and service is good here, surprising for a resort town."

"I own it." A slight grin came this time from Pierce. "We need to stop at the bank before we head back to my house—to get you some cash, if that is acceptable?"

"Just don't tell me that you own it," joked Dean.

"But I do," Pierce said, grinning. "It has three branches."

Paranoia kept Dean sharp and kept him from stepping into many bad situations. Looking around before speaking, Dean said, "You haven't shown me your tattoo. How do I know that you are a true believer?"

"That's because I don't have one. It would not have been prudent to have that kind of identification in my time. But I do have my signed orders, signed by Admiral Canaris. He signed the orders to start this mission; you will finish it."

"My God!" exclaimed Dean. "I know who Canaris was. He was the head of the Abwehr, the military counterintelligence service. Canaris was one of the top Nazis during World War II."

"Actually, I knew them all: Canaris, Himmler, Heydrich, Ribbentrop, and even Hitler. They sent me on this mission, and now I've found you to complete it. You can be the savior that I've sought."

"Are you a sleeper?"

"Hardly," Pierce said, now amused by Dean's excitement. "I was born here, just a few miles from this very spot. My task was to be finished by 1942. Alas, it remains undone."

"You haven't completed your mission after over sixty years. Why can you complete it now?"

"That's the reason you're here—you can complete my mission for me. Come now, we must leave. There are too many ears here. What I need to tell you will take all night."

Back in the car, Dean asked, "I left you a message almost a year ago. Why did you wait until this week to call me back?"

"That's no mystery," said Pierce. "I needed to make certain arrangements and also have you checked out. I'm not sloppy. Now I have a question for you. Is the print on the picture Colton Banyon's?"

"How did you know?" Dean was surprised.

"I suspected," was all that Pierce would admit to. "But it is the name of the person in the picture that I really need. Find Banyon and get the name from him."

They traveled the rest of the way in silence. As they left the car and walked toward the house, Pierce turned to Dean. "Under no circumstances is Colton Banyon to be harmed. I don't care what else you do, but don't let him know who you are and don't hurt him."

"Banyon will not be harmed," Dean lied with a straight face.

After they had settled on the couch in Pierce's living room, Dean realized that he didn't know how much money Pierce would pay him. "How much will you pay me to complete the mission?"

"Answer this first," replied the old man. "Will you be the savior of the Aryan cause?"

"I'm equal to the task. I'll be the savior of the Aryan race. I'll complete your mission."

"Good. When the 'event' is over, the cause will inherit my estate," replied Pierce.

Surveying the house, Dean asked, "How much is it worth?"

"Somewhere in the neighborhood of one hundred and thirty million."

"Dollars?" The amount stunned Dean.

"Plus all the land you saw today."

"All the land?"

"I own five thousand acres."

They spent the entire night going over the plan, which would be involved, and the final outcome. Dean left the following morning, feeling like his destiny was in his own hands. Kroll could not fight him. Dean would control the entire white supremacy movement. It would just take a few more days. It was a glorious time for Dean. All he needed to do was secure the name of the person in the picture. That person held the key to everything.

It was now four days since Dean had spent the night talking to the old man. Pierce's incredible story rattled around in his head constantly. He felt burdened with the weight of the world. Yet he must succeed. He alone was charged with changing the world. Although he knew he was good enough to pull it off, he was less sure about the people around him.

The date was August 6, day two of his clandestine operation. It was nine o'clock in the morning, and he was already suffering setbacks. As he prepared to call Pierce to relay the news that they didn't find Banyon yet, he searched his mind for the right words to soothe his new commander. A lie was clearly in order.

While Dean was overwhelmingly impressed with the old man, Dean asked himself how he could use this information to gain more power. *How do I eliminate everyone in my way? When will I become the Aryan savior?* The need for power was an adrenaline rush even greater than his sexual needs.

He dialed the number, and this time Pierce answered on the first ring.

"Dean, checking in with a progress report."

"Did you get the name?"

"We have secured the products that you requested from his sisters' houses, and all operations were a success."

"Did Banyon give you the name?"

"Banyon's out of town, in Las Vegas, until Tuesday. He suspects nothing, and we'll grab him the night that he returns. We have listening devices in his house and will know when he's home. It's all planned, Herr Pierce." The lies came out smoothly.

The response was instantaneous and resembled the crack of a whip. "Never use 'Herr' again in addressing me. I am Mr. Pierce. This no longer has anything to do with the Germans. It has to do with Aryans. America will be the center of the Aryan empire. Do you understand, Mr. Dean?"

Dean was stunned by the force of the reply but rallied for control. "All the materials are being shipped to you today. You'll have them soon. All arrangements are in place. We'll be able to reach the location within twenty-four hours. The man in the picture will give us the location. I promise you, Mr. Pierce. We will find the box."

"The sisters, you did not harm the sisters, correct?"

"We set up the break-ins just as discussed. As far as they are concerned, it was a prank."

"Good, good, no harm must come to any of them, you understand?"

"No harm will come to the Banyon family."

"Report back to me when there's more information. I've transferred fifty thousand dollars to the account that we opened at my bank. I trust that will cover your expenses for now?"

"Thank you, Mr. Pierce. We will succeed, and the Aryan nation will rise again, thanks to you."

Chapter Nine

At that moment, Colton Banyon was waking up to unfamiliar surroundings. It was dark in the basement room. There was a small window, but since it was belowground, little light filtered in. He had expected to see fluffy curtains, heavy dark furniture, and many bright colors throughout the space. As his eyes adjusted, he realized that the room was furnished almost the same as his own.

He remembered having come to the house last night, meeting the family and twins. They were twins, but only Previne wore the red dot. A married Indian woman often had one placed on her forehead. He was feeling a little uncomfortable. Pramilla had an uncanny ability to keep him off balance—or was it that he was so physically attracted to her that he wanted to believe that she kept him off center? Did she flirt with him, or did he misread only honest concern?

In truth, Banyon didn't know what to make of his current situation. All he knew was that a strange exotic woman had protected him and furnished him with a place to stay for the night. He had uncanny luck. Things had a habit of turning around for him just when he was facing disaster. Pramilla had even offered him a very strange job. The job entailed returning to his boyhood home. He pondered the prospect of returning to the old haunted house. He also wondered why she really wanted to visit his old house.

He was brought back to the present by a knock at the door. Still lying in bed naked, he answered.

"May I come in?" came the throaty voice of Pramilla.

"I'm still in bed," he replied. "Give me ten minutes, okay?"

The door swung open just as Banyon had said "okay." Pramilla stood there smiling, dressed in a man's T-shirt, which hung over skimpy white shorts. She was braless, and her feet were bare.

"Wake up, sleepyhead," she breathed, staring at Banyon's exposed chest. "We have a lot to talk about." She glided over to the bed and effortlessly raised her leg to begin poking the bottom of Banyon's feet. He had to pull his legs up to his chin to prevent her from seeing the change in the contour of the covers. She stood with her leg in the air for another ten seconds and then pivoted, lifting her leg straight up toward the ceiling. She did this while caressing the inside of her thigh with her long slender fingers. Banyon was breathing heavily.

"I just finished my yoga. I'm very limber, don't you think?"

"Yes, yes, you are." It came out as a small croak. She was overtly flirting with him.

"Why don't you get up and shower? The bathroom's right over there." The slender arm was once again raised, with the index finger pointing toward the bathroom. She was giggling.

"I'm naked, you know." He baited her with a suggestive voice.

"So am I, under this T-shirt," she shot back. She starting shaking her body, head thrown back and chest pushed out. Banyon could see the outline of buds growing under the influence of friction and the fluid sway of firm breasts. Then she started walking toward the side of the bed, giggling, hips grinding, her hair swinging from all the motion. Banyon suddenly wondered if she had been a pole dancer at a strip club. She certainly moved like one.

He was near panic now, mind racing at a hundred miles an hour. He was trying to find some way out. Somehow this didn't seem right. Men pursued women, not the other way around. *What about May?* He had to do something to stop this. He tried to think of how to stop her aggressiveness. Instinctively, he threw up the only defense that he knew would work—tickling. Banyon knew that when women are aroused, they become very sensitive and are susceptible to tickling.

As she drew into his trap, Banyon grabbed her wrist with his right hand and drove his left hand under her defense. He made contact with her flank and then began tickling. It took her one second to shriek and twist away from his attack. Five feet away now, breathing heavily, with hands on hips, she glared at him. "Not fair," her sensual lips pouted. "Don't you like my body?"

"Actually, I'm a leg man," hoping that the fish would take the bait. In her sexually aggressive mode, Banyon was sure that she would want to present her legs to him, just as she had the rest of her body.

"Oh," was the cooing reply. She turned around, bent over, and placed both of her hands on the ground, keeping her legs straight.

At that precise second, Banyon bolted for the bathroom, grabbing his pants in the process. Switching on the light, he turned on the shower and wondered if the cold water would have any effect. He could hear her out there, a feline after her prey. Was she making the bed or beating it?

"I'll be out in ten minutes," he said to the door.

"I'll bring your breakfast down here." Her reply seemed cheery to him, not laced with the scorn that he expected.

Banyon decided to dress quickly and get upstairs before she returned. When he opened the bathroom door, he noticed that the bed was made. He crossed the room and grabbed the bedroom doorknob. The door was locked.

Chapter Ten

At the same time, Detective Heinz was just walking into the small kitchenette of the police station in an attempt to replace the coffee he had finished. At first, he didn't see the object lying on the small table to the right. Then he noticed what could only be described as lots of hair, a large amount of human hair. A soft moan came from the hair as he let out a chuckle.

"Loni, are you resting or doing some kind of mystic exercise?" An amused smile underscored his remark.

"I'm dying, don't you have any respect? My Chinese herbal cure will start to work in fifteen minutes. I still have one more hour of allotted sleep before I return to work."

"Hey, if you are not feeling well, I can't hold you to your promise. Take all the time you need—you being a girl and all."

The head popped up. Bloodstained almond eyes, outlined by dark circles, were throwing daggers at him. Tight lips with a pained pout had replaced the usually confident smirk. There was the puffiness in her face that Heinz had seen many times before, even on his own mug.

"So, this is how you look in the morning?" He said it in a pleasant way, not wanting to face a harassment suit for his remark.

"Very funny. Do you kick little children too? You knew I was on the job last night until late or, rather, early this morning."

"Of course you were. After all, you went bowling. Had a few beers, did you? I know you needed to play the part up to the hilt. You probably even got someone to buy you a beer." He was getting into it now—maybe there was a crack in this tough but beautiful facade.

"It was eight beers actually." She was official, even when having a near-death hangover. "I hung around and bowled six games while attempting to collect information. My cover was good."

"Somehow I can't picture you bowling," continued the detective. "I'm sure everyone couldn't wait to talk to you at the alley. You being straitlaced, proper, and interrogating each person as he passed." Sarcasm dripped from his words.

"I was state champion of Hawaii in 1979," she said, again with no ego. "I know how to bowl, and I had three 200+ games last night—that gets you noticed. Bowlers all like to talk to good bowlers."

"Okay, I didn't know that you spent a misguided youth in a bowling alley. I can't imagine any skinhead types talking to you, seeing as how you are Asian."

"That was the easy part," she said as she stood up. "I wore a skirt."

He saw her shoeless feet, then shapely legs; they just seemed to disappear where her hair started. *Where was the skirt?* She brushed her hair aside to reveal a black micromini leather skirt, size 2 or 3. She tilted her head in that now familiar "I got you" way and placed her hands on her hips.

"Oh," was all he could muster. He suddenly pictured her moving down the alley, ball in hand, sliding gracefully, releasing the ball at the proper time—and every man in the place stopping to watch. She certainly had an effect on everyone she met, he thought. Was she trying to send a signal? Or was she simply so determined to succeed that she would do anything to get what she wanted? She was definitely attractive, but he felt that there was no chance to melt that iceberg.

"Well, are you going to ask me about what I've learned, or are you just going to stand there and stare at me with your tongue hanging out?"

It was the terror of a woman speaking like she knew what you were thinking that had kept Heinz a bachelor all these years. "What did you find out?" the whipped puppy dog asked.

"I found out three things that I am confident will lead us to a resolution in this case." He watched her with interest as her small delicate fingers counted off. "First, the Ultimate Tattoo Parlor on Route 20 is the place that Dean meets his snitches. I suspect that it's a hangout for white supremacy types. Second, most of the people in this village do not like Dean. Several—I have their names and addresses—have been shaken down by him and three other guys friendly with Dean. I also have their names and addresses. It is small potatoes, but nonetheless real illegal activities. I don't know if we can get any of them to roll over and testify, but if we can get him for something else, I think they'll jump on the bandwagon. And third, there's a meeting at The Altar of the Creator church this evening at eight o'clock in Aurora. It would be a good idea to do a little stakeout, don't you think?"

"Special Agent Chen, you amaze me," Heinz said and meant it. "How did you find out about the church meeting?"

"I found that out from Marge, whom I met in the ladies' room. Lots of talk in there, you know. Marge was one of Dean's victims. He recently abused her when she was drunk and had rough sex with her. She warned me to watch out for him. She also knew about the meeting. It seems that Michael Dean has been bragging about a major type meeting at the church."

"Loni, that was dangerous. You can't run around with all those bad guys. These thugs are trouble, and you're—"

She cut him off with, "I'm what? Just a girl?"

"Yeah, I deserved that," Heinz admitted as he wondered if she was a feminist. "How'd you find out about the tattoo parlor?" He asked this in an attempt to change the subject.

She just glared at him, face turning red. Her posture suddenly changed, and he noticed that he faced a more subdued person. "I kind of went there."

"Well, who told you about …? Hey, wait a minute, don't tell me you got a tattoo," a stunned Heinz said.

"I needed to do recon. I found out a lot of information there. It was the right thing to do," she said defensively.

"Does it hurt?" a sympathetic Heinz asked.

"Hurts like hell, I can hardly sit down. But I like it."

"Well, the cost of your tattoo had better not show up on your expense account, for … I can't approve what I can't see," Heinz joked.

"I never cheat on my expenses—you just want to look at my ass," she complained a little too strongly.

"Well, now I know where it is, and probably half of Streamwood has already seen it while you were in the tattoo parlor."

"It represents my name in Chinese," she said, pulling up her micromini to reveal black thong panties and a smooth rounded cheek. In the center of the right cheek was a small tattoo—a butterfly.

Heinz spilled his coffee and retreated to the bathroom again. As he left the room, he said, "I'm still not paying for it."

Chapter Eleven

Walter Pierce hung up the phone. His life's work would be done in a few days. It had all started so many years ago with his good friend Wilhelm. Wilhelm Canaris was a brilliant man. He was also Pierce's mentor. In 1941, Canaris approached him with an earth-shattering assignment. He was being sent to America.

As the old man ruminated about the assignment so many decades ago, he was lifted in spirits at the realization that his mission would finally see completion. Although he could not complete the mission in 1942 as planned, he could finish it now. The timing was right. The neo-Nazi, white supremacy, and Aryan causes were taking hold all over the United States, not to mention several other countries. People were tired of losing jobs to foreigners. Airports and government agencies were bilingual. You could even collect unemployment pay without speaking English. Come to America, you don't even have to learn the language; we will even pay you to stay home once you qualify for unemployment benefits.

After 9/11, many began to fear immigrants, avoiding people who were not white. The ineptness of the government agencies—lack of communication, turf issues, and failure to report career-threatening information—was a critical factor. The current administration was chock-full of bureaucrats who said they were working to stem the flow of illegal aliens, while they actually campaigned for amnesty for such illegals. This all would change when his mission was complete. Pierce had believed in his mission for a very long time; he would stop at nothing to complete it and was sure it would be complete soon. This made him happy.

Yes, everything was falling into place, just as Wilhelm and he had planned. Canaris and Pierce would go down in history as the ones who changed everything. It was all going to happen in just a few days.

Pierce sat on his couch thinking. He knew that Dean was lying. Pierce was a master at reading and manipulating people. Dean was a moron. He had suggested that Pierce was a sleeper. Pierce realized that he was somewhat like a sleeper, but he had activated himself.

He was, in fact, an American. He had lived almost all his life on Long Island. He had spent only a little over a decade away from the island. He did want people to remember him. He had already decided to write down his early life. He wanted people to see who he really was back then, before the mission. He sat down at his desk and continued to record his history on a Dictaphone.

"I was born on November 14, 1911. I am almost a hundred years old as I speak. My parents were Emma and Wolfgang Becker. They resided on Speonk-Riverhead Road in Speonk. The house my father built did not have a street address. It was simply RFD #1. My father came to America in 1890 and opened a nursery on land he bought from a local farmer. He was a gentle man and kept mostly to himself. Since he was often lonely, he sent back to Germany for a wife. She never accepted America and hated the many different people that she met here.

"She was quite a bit younger than my father and had a difficult time living in 'the country,' as she called it. My first memories were of walking around the yard, watching my father tending to trees and bushes. The back of the yard had a huge smokestack that burned coal to heat the greenhouses in the winter. Our home was also heated by coal, and Father constructed an underground tunnel that led from the smokestack pump house directly into the basement of the house. There was a hidden door in the basement of the house, behind the furnace. I had often played in the tunnel. Coal could be brought over from the pump house without getting dust and soot all over the house. Father was clever that way.

"In the early years, I had a wonderful life. There were people to take care of me. We had a maid and a butler. When I was twelve, Father bought a sailboat, and we would sail the Great South Bay for hours. High school was easy for me. I played baseball for the Westhampton Beach high school team and was in the chess club. I had many friends; some of them were very wealthy. When I was old enough, we would take the train to New York City to go to the many nightclubs.

"The problem was my parents. They never seemed to get along. One day, I got home early from school and found my mother in the arms of the butler. Actually, they were shamelessly frolicking on the parlor room couch. She didn't even stop when she saw me come in. She just stared at me and said, 'I dare you to tell your father.' It was then that I realized that Mother didn't care about Father at all, and the butler was imported from Germany to be her lover. I wondered about the maid, since she was also from Germany. I didn't have to wonder long.

"Heidi, the maid, was about thirty years old. She was not particularly pretty, but she did have huge breasts. That night, she knocked on my door, naked. I didn't know it at the time, but Mother put her up to it. It was either have sex with me or be sent back to Germany. Heidi was also having sex with the butler, Willy, and didn't want to lose those privileges, not to mention being sent back to Germany. So the choice was easy for her.

"In my senior year, I found out about several secrets that my house held. Father was home and in his bedroom at the bottom of the stairs. My door opened to reveal Heidi, dressed in only a short nightgown. 'How did you get by Father?' I asked. She opened the door to the upstairs closet and pressed a latch in the back. The whole wall opened out, and I saw a small landing and a ladder running up and down. She closed the door and went to the ladder, climbing up toward the attic. I followed her, watching her fine ass sway as she climbed. She pushed on the door, and we were suddenly in the attic. She stretched out and pulled a cord, lighting up the attic. I could see that the trapdoor was well hidden. We entered the large unfinished attic, and she whispered in my ear that there were other doors. I was stunned: I'd lived in this house for all these years, and the maid knew more about my house than I did.

"She walked a few feet and opened another trapdoor and motioned for me to look down. I saw a closet. There was a trapdoor in the closet. She closed the trapdoor and walked over to a third door in the corner. This one had another ladder, and we climbed down.

"We only went down one story. She pushed the wall, and it opened into the front attic. The house had a second attic that ran the length of the front of the house. It was just an open area and was low, as it was the leftover space from the intersection of the roofline and the inside walls of the rooms. The main entrance was in the guest room. I was amazed. But we weren't done yet. We made our way back to the original ladder, and she climbed down to the main floor. There was a small landing there, and she showed me that it led into the back of the pantry. Finally she climbed down to the basement, and we found ourselves in a small room between two of the bricked-up basement rooms. It was bare and had only a light hanging from the ceiling.

"Heidi knelt down and pushed on a section of the brick wall, and it opened. We found ourselves in the furnace room. She told me that Mother showed her all the hidden passages and made her swear not to show them to Father. I knew that Mother designed the plans for the house; Father just paid the money. Now I realized just how devious my mother was. She had designed the house so that she could travel throughout the house without my father ever knowing, probably to dally with the butler.

"All winter long Heidi and I spent the nights on ladders. Her room as well as Willy's was in the basement, so Father never knew what we were doing. I was enjoying my life and had no view of the future. Shortly after Christmas of that year, I received a letter from Yale, informing me that I had been accepted into the prelaw school. Heidi and I romped through the rest of the winter and into the summer.

"On August 29, 1929, I left for college. I told my parents that I would come home every two weeks and meant it at the time. College was the ultimate rush. There were football games, parties, and an incredible number of good-looking women. I was in heaven and soon forgot my promise. My new friends were a who's who of industrialists' children.

"Then disaster struck, beginning on October 24, 1929. The stock market fell. It continued for several days, and soon about 40 percent of the total market was gone. Several of my friends had to leave school, and I was concerned for my own family. By phone, Father told me that we were fine and I should continue at school. I decided to come home for Christmas.

"We were rather subdued during that holiday season. Father really didn't know how bad his business was, as there was never much activity in the winter. He would have to wait until later in the year to know exactly where he stood. Heidi and I made love several times, but something had changed and I didn't know what it was. Mother was now talking about Germany again and how it was going to rise. She was getting newspapers and magazines at a regular rate, and her family's business was growing again. The name of Hitler started to crop up in her discussions. I couldn't wait to get back to school to be with my friends.

"Spring came, and not only was my family a lot poorer, but it seemed that everyone wanted to discuss world politics now. We discussed Communism and the problems in Europe. It didn't interest me much, but there was romantic talk about war. School had turned to drudgery, and I was glad when the semester ended.

"When I came home, I realized that much had changed. Father's business was hanging by a thread, and he spent most of his time wandering around the yard. Mother had become militant and was talking about the stupid American president and how Germany was going to teach everyone a lesson. She wore a kind of uniform—it was all brown—and she started discussing Hitler's plans. From school, I knew that Hitler was a fanatic and had a shady way of campaigning.

"The biggest surprise was Heidi. She'd put on so much weight. I didn't grasp that she was pregnant until she came to my room the first night home and told me that it was mine.

"Things got worse the next day when Mother announced that she was leaving Father and going back to Germany to run her father's company, at least for the next few years. Willy and Heidi were going back too. Father didn't appear to even hear my mother's announcement.

"I followed my father into the yard and tried to talk to him. He was a stubborn person and told me that I should go with my mother to protect her from herself. I asked him to go with us, and he replied that he could never go back to Germany. He had too many enemies there, and besides, he wanted to stay in America. He'd been in the USA for over forty years, and this was now his home. It was my homeland too, but I feared for Mother, and of course, there was Heidi."

At that point, Pierce decided that he was very tired. He shut off the Dictaphone. He would finish his story at his lawyer's office. He would do that soon, as there wasn't much time left for him—the voices in his head told him that.

Chapter Twelve

Banyon didn't know what to make of his situation. Here he was locked in a room, waiting for breakfast from a lovely creature who displayed all the tendencies of a sexually crazed woman. She wanted to hire him, yet it was a job he didn't want. He did not want to go back to the old house. People were chasing him for something or some reason, and he didn't even have a clue as to what it could be. The local police considered him a wacko. He was broke and couldn't even return to his house. Did any of this make sense?

The sound of a knock filled the little room. "Come in, it's open," he said. When the door slowly opened, Banyon considered making a break for it but hesitated. In walked Previne, dressed in a multicolored sari.

"Good morning," she said demurely.

"Where is Pramilla? You didn't have to bring me food, Previne," Banyon said.

"Pramilla had to talk to people in India," the shy woman said, then turned to leave.

"Wait," Banyon said. "It would be impolite for me to eat alone."

She turned, flowed to the chair near the little couch, and sat down with her knees together and hands folded on her lap. She bowed her head slightly. On the tray were fruit, dry toast, orange juice, and tea.

"You're quite different from your sister," he remarked, trying to draw her out.

"We're actually the same." The reply came in the same voice as her sister. For a quick second, Banyon wondered if this was Pramilla, dressed up to be Previne. Could even Keri tell them apart? "We are identical twins, except I'm wilder than my sister."

Banyon looked up at that remark. "Why would you say that, Previne? Pramilla is very outgoing, and you're lovely and quiet."

"First looks are deceiving, don't you think? In India, my sister and I were both dancers. We were always in demand because we were twins. I always earned the most money."

"What kind of dancers?"

"Why exotic, of course." Previne announced it proudly. "It's not quite the same as your strip clubs here, but it was fun." A smile lit her face. Based on the early morning performance by Pramilla, Banyon was now stuck with images of the twins twirling and swaying, sitar music in the background, candles burning, and myriads of mirrors.

She continued to entertain Banyon, who hung on her every word. "But we had to stop. We'd grown too old. No one wanted us to dance anymore. That's when we came to America."

Calculating in his head, Banyon said, "That was two years ago, right?"

"Yes," she said with a shake of the head.

"How old were you when you stopped dancing?"

"We were twenty-four." She spoke again, as though hearing the next question in Banyon's mind. "We started when we were twelve." When shock registered on Banyon's face, she added, "Things are different in India."

"And you are the wild one?"

"Most definitely."

Banyon had read that people grew up at an earlier age in Asian countries, but it was still hard to think of these beautiful women as being old at twenty-four. Quickly he asked, "Pramilla said that your father deals with guns in India. What did she mean?"

"Pramilla is somewhat of a kidder."

"Well, she seems to know a lot about guns." Banyon pressed the issue.

"Our father is a journalist for the largest newspaper in New Delhi. He covers much crime. There is a Mafia in India, much bigger than here. He learned much about guns and taught us to be aware of such things."

Banyon realized that he enjoyed talking to Previne. She was a good conversationalist. Pramilla was a lustful, aggressive woman; Previne was sensitive, understanding, and equally as beautiful. *What a choice.* "If I can ask, who is Pramilla calling?"

"She's the American correspondent for the human interest section of my father's paper," came the proud answer from Previne. "She wants to do a story about ghosts. Your talk of ghosts got her excited—she can hardly control herself."

"You can say that again," Banyon replied. Just then his phone rang. It was a recruiter friend. The recruiter just got off the phone with the owner of a company. He had just bought a general merchandise housewares company and was in the process of firing the president. He had asked for Banyon, by name, to interview for the position. The owner wanted Banyon to fly to New York to interview at the Hilton Hotel in Manhattan on Tuesday of next week. The recruiter felt that this was a hot one and Banyon stood a good chance of getting the position—that is, if he were modest in his salary requirements.

Banyon inquired as to what the opening offer was. The recruiter replied, "Somewhere around three hundred thousand dollars."

"Book it, Danno," was Banyon's reply.

Detective Heinz left the bathroom for the second time this morning only to return to the kitchenette to pour more coffee. He had just filled his cup when Agent Chen came bounding out of the next room. She took a flying leap and slammed into him, wrapping her arms around his neck. She seemed to scramble up Heinz's much larger body and planted a hard kiss on his lips. He spilled his coffee on his pants again. He was confused.

She whispered in his ear while hanging from his neck like a necklace, "He's right behind me, been chasing me around desks for five minutes. Where have you been?"

Officer Dean was leaning on the doorjamb, a leer on his face. He was clearly enjoying seeing Chen hanging there, micromini and all. "I didn't know that this one belonged to you," Dean said in his sleaziest voice.

Chen dropped down, ran behind Heinz, gripped his large bicep in a strong hold, and peered around his body. Heinz felt that she needed protection and rose to the occasion. "What are you doing here?" he demanded. "Why are you chasing my girl?"

"Sorry, Chief, I thought that she was a hooker needing a little love."

"Don't talk stupid talk to me." Heinz was now past being civil. "You apologize to Loni right now." The implication was clear. "*Now,* Dean." This was said with thunder.

"I'm sorry, Loni, I was just kidding," Dean said, realizing that he had bigger fish to fry right now and didn't need to have a hassle with Heinz. But he had decided that someday, when Heinz wasn't around, he and the little slant-eyes chick were going to play Okinawa.

"What're you doing here? Your shift ended hours ago!" Heinz raged.

"I needed to put in some paperwork, so I came back to the station. Remember, I found the stolen van and the plates too. But since I've found you, I'm taking a week off, starting now. I have a big meeting at the church tonight, and then we're going off for a couple days to a retreat. We're going out of town."

Nails dug into his arm, but Heinz had already put two and two together. "You wouldn't be going to waste your money in Las Vegas, would you?"

"Never been and never going," Dean said, shaking his head. "No, we're heading up to Wisconsin and camping out. You can't stop me, I have the time coming."

"I wouldn't think of it, Michael. We'll really miss you, though," Heinz said through gritted teeth. Dean backed out the door as if he couldn't trust anyone in the room.

"I could have taken him," Chen said, examining her nails.

"Sure, that's why you were standing behind me."

"I was playing my part," she said as she looked at him with now clear almond eyes.

"Next time, kiss better. You were so clumsy that you spilled my coffee again." He said this as he headed to the bathroom one more time.

She was standing by the bathroom door, tapping her foot like an impatient wife does when hubby is late. Heinz opened the door, looked out, and went back in.

"You can't stay in there forever," she fussed.

"You can't come in here either."

"I'll hurt you," she all but screamed.

"What're you going to do—pull my hair? That is, if you can reach it." Then he started to laugh. When he opened the door, she was bent over laughing, and the tension had vanished. They returned to his office to talk. After all, there were other people about, and they were acting like they were having a lovers' spat.

Heinz spoke first. "Come on, we have several places to go. We need to go see the tattoo parlor, and we're definitely going to stake out the church. In between, we have to interview a friend of Dean's."

"I thought he only had three friends. We know they'll be at the church."

"Well, in analyzing the report you gave me, I discovered the name of Ula Woods."

"I'm going to change into pants first."

"That would be a good idea."

"Can I bring my guns?" she asked in a serious tone.

As they walked out the door, the fax machine rang. A single piece of paper was printed. It had some notes on it and a picture of a man with a "shit-eating grin."

Chapter Thirteen

Dean entered the storefront door of the Altar of the Creator. The church was located in a small strip mall in Aurora. He was feeling satisfied with himself.

He had driven to downtown Chicago to pay a sexual visit to Patty Rowe, the FBI clerk that accessed the databases in an attempt to locate the print on the picture. Patty was a mousey woman who craved any attention. Dean gave her some attention, but mostly he liked to humiliate her and treat her roughly. On this visit he had gone too far.

From the emergency room at the hospital, Patty called a friend at work and asked her to send a fax. Love had turned to hatred in a heartbeat.

Chapter Fourteen

Driving the police cruiser, Heinz turned to Chen. "Can I ask you a question?" He noticed that she had changed into skintight leotards and also added an oversized police windbreaker, just like he wore. The windbreaker came to midthigh.

"Is it about the case?" she queried.

"No, it's personal."

"Then, no."

"Why are you such a hard-ass?" he asked with slight irritation.

"Let's not bring that up again."

"Cut the crap, you know what I mean. You're very competent, yet you approach everything like a hard-ass. You jump in and don't think about the consequences. Your antics last night have me a little worried. What happens if on one of your adventures, someone decides to rob a bank or even something worse. I'm not so sure that you wouldn't go along, just to get the goods on the bad guys."

"I would never do anything illegal. I'm a cop. Personal sacrifices are part of the job. I accept that. I am not a martyr. I'm a minority woman, cursed with my looks, with no one respecting my brain. My father wanted a boy—he got me. I try to make him proud of me." She was talking so fast and with such force that Heinz felt that he had touched a nerve. He almost missed the turn into the tattoo parlor parking. Chen added one more statement. "Stop talking now, or I will pull out your hair." From then on, they had a switch that could stop any conversation without penalty.

As they entered the front door, a man greeted them. He was about forty with long shaggy hair. Tattoos covered arms that protruded from an Italian undershirt. Heinz guessed correctly that he was the owner.

The eyes of the man twinkled. "Hi, Loni, you looking good, babe. Want another tattoo?"

He then looked at Heinz and sensed that he was a cop. He became wary. "No refunds. She came in here on her own. I did nothing wrong. She wanted the tattoo, I only touched her where she wanted the tattoo, I checked her driver's license, and she is over twenty-one. You can't hassle me, man, I know my rights. You got a warrant? I'm a respectable businessman."

"Have you exhausted your vocabulary of legal clichés? What're you afraid of?"

"Relax, Timmy, we're not here about my tattoo," Agent Chen said with a soothing voice.

"Good," Timmy said. "Because it was righteous work, man—all the guys thought so."

Chen walked over to the tattoo wall and pointed to a particular tattoo. "You get much call for this one?" Her slender finger was pointing to an exact replica of a swastika.

"No, man, I don't get calls for that one; it's just there for show." It was obviously a statement made from fear and paranoia.

"I saw at least two people with that tattoo here last night," Chen remarked. "Are you telling me that those guys have a better place to have their tattoos done?"

"No, man. I'm the best, the best there's ever been."

"Well, how about it, punk?" Heinz was playing the bad guy. "Maybe we should go down to the station house and have a little chat."

"If you promise not to take me there again, I'll talk," he said.

"You've been to the station before?" asked the detective.

"Let's just say that it wasn't a good experience."

"How many have the tattoo?" Chen interrupted. "You want to look up your records?"

"No need," Timmy replied. "I've done a total of five of those tattoos."

"Do you have the names of those men?" Chen asked.

"What do you need the names for? These people play rough."

"What people play rough? You'd better explain, or we're taking you in, got it?" Detective Heinz shifted his posture to look more aggressive.

"Okay, first of all, they weren't all men. One was a woman, and one is a policeman," a suddenly submissive Timmy said.

Both Heinz and Chen spoke at the same time. "What policeman, what woman?"

Timmy looked hard at both cops. "What's this about?"

"We can't tell you; it's official police business," Agent Chen said.

"You're a cop? I don't believe it, especially the way you were prancing around here flirting with the guys and showing off your tattoo last night."

Heinz's fist started to clinch. "Give me the names." There was rage in his voice. "I'm not going to ask twice."

"Okay, okay, keep your shorts on. You've got to protect me, man. Dean will kill me if he finds out."

"I want the rest of the names. Write them on a piece of paper. Then maybe we'll talk about protection."

Quickly Timmy grabbed a piece of paper and began to write.

Finished with his writing, Timmy waved the list of names in the air and said, "I need witness protection."

"Why would you need that?" questioned Chen.

"I know more about this than you think," came the reedy reply.

Loni and Carl were once again riding in the cruiser. They were on their way to the house of Ula Woods. Agent Chen hardly took up half the seat. She was on her laptop and was pounding away furiously. She had not said a word since leaving the tattoo parlor. Instead, she had retreated to the official machine-oriented world where she sometimes lived. Heinz started clearing his throat to get ready to speak, but that was as far as he got.

"I'm sorry that I let you and the department down by being compulsive. I shouldn't have gone to the tattoo parlor by myself," she said while continuing to type.

"The only person you let down has to be yourself."

There were small tears in her eyes. "I have no expectations for myself."

"Loni, I'm trying to be your friend here, not your interim boss."

"How could you possibly understand? You're a man, white, handsome, with a personality and charm, and the head of a police department. I'm a nothing and will always be a nothing and have nothing to look forward to," she whined like a little girl.

"Look, you are an agent with one of the best law enforcement agencies in the country. It's not a mistake that you're working on this case—you are good."

"I'm actually just an analyst for the state. When you called, I was sitting in my boss's office, showing him my legs to get him to give me something to do. While he was talking to you, he decided to use me for this case. I've never worked in the field before. He just wanted to get rid of me. All I know is how to use my body to get what I want. Don't you see I'm hopeless?"

Heinz knew that this was her first case. In the beginning he was just looking for someone to do analysis work. But things had changed, and her outlook in life now bothered him. He also wanted to be near her, although he was not sure why. He'd only known her for a little over twenty-four hours, but it had been the longest and most exciting twenty-four hours of his life.

"What if I told you that I might have an opening in the department after this is over, and I want you to consider working with me in Streamwood?" It was said professionally, but there were undertones of personal need.

She stopped typing and fixed her gaze on Heinz. "You're just trying to make me feel better."

"On the contrary. I need new blood in the department. I need you to help me clean up the department. I know I want to stay here now, so will you come to work with me?"

"Can I bring my guns? Can I dress anyway I want?"

"You can dress like Chuck Norris if you like."

"Who's Chuck Norris?" A blank stare was set on her tear-streaked face.

"He's a good guy—a black belt."

The mood had changed in the car, and Chen was back to business. "Timmy, the tattoo man, gave us some good information, don't you think?"

"He certainly filled us in on Dean's operation, his connections to the church, and now we know who all the white supremacists are in town, not to mention knowing who set the fire last week."

"When we get to the house, I'll play the good guy," Loni said.

"Actually, I think you can play a better bad guy than me."

"Right, Chief." There was a mischievous tone in her voice.

"Don't call me 'Chief.' Call me 'sir,'" Heinz said as he pulled into the driveway of the small house.

Chapter Fifteen

As Pierce sat at his desk, the voices in his head told him that something was wrong. The voices had never been wrong and were there to guide him in the effort to complete his mission. They had again been talking to him on a steady basis for only a few years, but he had learned to trust them. This phase of the plan wasn't supposed to take this long. He picked up the phone to make a call. The call was to Colton Banyon.

Back in Chicagoland, Banyon along with Pramilla and Previne had decided to go out for dinner. His cell phone rang just as he and the twins were about to get into the car.

"Is this Colton Banyon?" a deep voice asked.

"Yes, it is. Can I help you?"

"Your consulting agency was recommended to me. I'm writing a book and need some insights into business philosophy. You do that kind of work, don't you?"

"Well, I'm really a management consultant, but I do know a lot about business philosophy, especially at the retail level." Banyon was now calculating a cost in his head. He usually charged two hundred and fifty dollars per hour to have his brain picked.

"One of my associates will be in Chicago tomorrow morning. Do you think that you could meet with her for, let's say, four hours? We'll pay you five hundred dollars per hour."

"I didn't catch your name." Banyon was frantically looking for a pen and paper. A useless proposition, since he never carried such things unless going on a client call. Previne handed him both.

"My name is Walter Pierce."

"And you said you're writing a book?"

"More of a plan," the voice replied.

"What, specifically, would you be interested in?"

"Well, my associate will only be taking notes, but my interest is in the future of retailing. I want to learn about the changing environment and the continued impact of dollar stores. My associate will bring a check drawn on my bank for two thousand dollars."

"I'm kind of busy at the moment." Banyon was considering the job interview that was coming up in three days. Not to mention the twins and the fact that someone was after him.

"I'm sure that you're very busy, and so am I. I'm calling long-distance, from eastern Long Island. I won't take up any more of your time."

"Did you say eastern Long Island?" Banyon asked with some measure of excitement.

"That's correct, from Westhampton to be exact."

"That's very interesting," Banyon said. "I grew up in Speonk and graduated from Westhampton High School. Wow, talk about coincidences."

"So you'll take the job?" Pierce said, pushing the issue.

"I'll be happy to meet your associate. How about the Marriott on Cumberland? It's by the airport. Does ten o'clock sound right?"

"Splendid," replied Pierce. "By the way, she's doing some research on several people for me. Would you mind looking at a few pictures to help identify some locals from Westhampton? They'd be in their fifties now. A client of mine is trying to identify some old pictures."

"I'll do better than that," Banyon said with enthusiasm. "Since they'd be my contemporaries, I'll bring all my old yearbooks and pictures, and maybe we can match them up."

"That would be wonderful."

"Mr. Pierce, how will I know your associate? What's her name?"

"All you have to do is be there. She'll find you."

Pierce hung up the phone and smiled. Pierce couldn't help admiring his finesse. His plan was now back on track.

Two minutes later, Dean's cell phone rang. He was at the church with Joe Kroll. They were practicing their speeches for the evening festivities. Kroll enjoyed hearing the flow of words in his head. He was looking forward to his oration tonight and didn't want to be disturbed. But when Dean showed him the ID on the phone that told him it was Pierce, he stopped practicing and listened in.

"Michael Dean here."

"I am very disappointed with you, Dean. You have not delivered the name yet."

"I told you that Banyon's in Las Vegas and won't be back until Monday," Dean lied smoothly.

"That's strange, since he's meeting one of your people tomorrow morning at the Marriott."

"But, how, what …?"

"Shut up and listen, you weasel. This is what I want you to do," Pierce said with true anger.

"Yes, sir," Dean replied.

Dean closed the cell phone. His discussion with Kroll lasted for three minutes.

"Judy, I have a job for you to do, baby," Kroll called to his wife.

Part Two
Ula Woods

Chapter Sixteen

From across the street, Agent Chen studied the old three-story with a sagging front porch. There were several columns and a lot of fancy trimming, reminiscent of old Europe. It was quite similar to the house next door, which she had learned belonged to Michael Dean. The difference was that this house was in disrepair. Paint was peeling, boards on the porch were not maintained, and several screens were ripped. There was a driveway next to the house that separated it from Dean's house. Parked in the driveway was a new gold Lexus. The front door to the house was open, and a screen door led into a dark interior.

"Let's go," said Chen.

They walked across the street and over the uncut front lawn, climbing the three stairs onto the porch. Stepping up to the door, Heinz searched for a bell but found none. Instead, he banged on the screen repeatedly. Finally a boy of about twelve appeared at the door, staying half-hidden in the shadows. "What you want?"

"Your mom home?" Heinz asked.

"Nope," he said too quickly.

"Are you home alone?" Heinz continued.

"What you hasslin' me for? I ain't telling you nothin'."

"Do you remember me, Bobby? We met last year when you were involved in the car accident with your bike."

"I don't know nothin', and I ain't saying nothin'," he replied with continued disrespect.

"We just want to say hello to your mother. Is that her car in the driveway?"

"I ain't talkin'—you got a warrant or something?" Bobby said. "And my name ain't Bobby. It's Robert."

Out of the corner of his eye, Detective Heinz saw movement. It was Chen.

Chen walked over to one of the columns that supported the porch and began to climb it like a seasoned gymnast. Reaching the top, she flipped over onto the roof of the porch.

The boy stood watching her with eyes so large that they might pop. He then yelled, "Mom, the cops are breaking in—there's one on the roof."

Heinz groaned inside and was thinking Chen had once again displayed her tendency to act rather than to think. There was movement now in the back of the house, and Heinz could see a woman sprinting up to the door. She skidded to a halt.

"Good to see you, Mrs. Woods," he greeted her.

She, like her son, stood in the shadows. His senses were alerted. "If you ain't got no warrant, you in big trouble. We gonna sue." Ula Woods stood defiant, her hands on her hips.

A meow distracted him. Agent Chen was standing next to him and cradling a small kitten in her arms.

"I saw this kitten in peril on the porch roof," she stated. "I barely had time to climb up and save his life. Is this your cat? She doesn't have a collar, and by the way, no pets are allowed outside unleashed on weekends in Streamwood. Now, to whom shall I make the ticket out?" Her look was stern.

Heinz stood there bewildered. Did she plan this to draw out Mrs. Woods, or was she just being impulsive?

Chen continued, "I also noticed that your car is blocking half of the sidewalk. That's a nonmoving violation, with a seventy-five-dollar fine attached. If you can't pay, we can impound the car until you come up with the money. At the police impound, we can't take responsibility for anything that may happen to it, and it will probably be searched as well. You can expect it to be gone for a week or two."

Mrs. Woods remained silent. Heinz stood back and folded his arms.

The tension was growing. Subtly, Chen slipped in, "We're on to you, Mrs. Woods." Then she continued, "Your car—it is your car, isn't it?—has a good-sized dent in the front fender. I hope that you've reported the accident. It'll just take a minute to check, okay? Oh, if you haven't reported it, well, we'll have to take you down to the station for an 'interview.'" She used her fingers to indicate a quote for emphasis. "Do you need to get your purse with proper ID? Of course, there's—"

Mrs. Woods now appeared in the doorway. "Get away," she admonished.

Loni continued, "We can get a warrant. It would take a few hours. We could wait across the street and—" Of course, there's …"

At that point Mrs. Woods said, "Stop." She pushed the screen door open and said, "Let's get this over with."

Heinz gestured with his hand for Agent Chen to go first, acknowledging her successful implementation of a good plan. Chen, however, did not move.

"Are you inviting us into your house, even though we don't have a warrant?" she asked.

Speaking in a cultured voice, Ula Woods said, "Considering the circumstances, it would hardly serve me to attempt to prevent this inevitable conversation. And, yes, this is how I actually talk. The rest is just for show."

Agent Chen turned off the tape recorder that had suddenly appeared in her hand. Since they were invited, the Woods woman could never deny that she had let them inside her house. "Okay, let's go."

The inside of the house did not resemble the outside. The hall was dark on purpose, but at the end of the short passageway, an open door led to a large room that had hardwood floors and white leather furniture—Italian, thought Heinz. There was a wall-mounted flat high-definition TV, surround sound, a large grand piano, and two abstract paintings that took up half the wall.

Walking to the large sofa, Ula Woods gestured with her arm for them to sit. Smoothing her skirt, she sat reclined in the overstuffed chair, crossing her legs as if to give an interview. Heinz sat; Chen stood. A triangle of sight lines was established. Robert was standing in the doorway. Mrs. Woods said, "Robert, return to your studies, please. Your piano teacher will be here in two hours." The boy said nothing and left.

Heinz noticed bruises all over Mrs. Woods. Her left eye was nearly closed and very puffy. She grimaced whenever she moved.

Mrs. Woods was in her midforties, very slim, almost bony, with short black hair in curls. Heinz asked the first question. "Are your bruises from the car accident?"

"I would offer you coffee or tea," she said as she ignored the question. "But I don't feel up to it."

There was an awkward silence now between them. Outside, a bird was calling to its mate. Chen continued to scan the room. Heinz opened his notebook and pretended to write down some notes. He then looked up.

"We have several questions." Heinz was beginning to set the groundwork.

"About what?"

Agent Chen was not about to wait for his questions. "I want to see the tattoo."

There was a flicker in Mrs. Woods's right eye, but she quickly recovered. "I do not condone tattoos."

"Mrs. Woods, we have this problem." Heinz ignored the response. "We know you have a swastika tattoo. That alone would not be an issue, but the other people with the same tattoo are under investigation. Then there's the problem of your name showing up in six accident reports in the last two years."

"Actually, that's twenty-one. I didn't have a chance to tell you, Carl." While riding in the cruiser, Agent Chen had done a little more analysis and cross-referenced all of Ula's children and uncovered a gold mine. The information had come from Timmy, the tattoo man.

Chen pressed on. "We know that your three children all have different last names. When I cross-referenced this information, I found a lot more incidents. You don't appear to be very protective of your children. I'm recommending to DCFS that your children be taken from you for what can only be interpreted as child neglect."

Chen watched as Mrs. Woods shifted in her seat. Her eyes glowed with a little moisture, and her left hand started to shake.

It was Heinz's turn now. "I believe we have more than enough evidence to get a warrant. We can get one in less than two hours, have it delivered here, and then begin to take your life apart. Will we find anything in this house that could connect you to a crime? There are a lot of nice things in here—you have receipts, I assume? What do you do for a living, Mrs. Woods?"

Movement in the hallway caught the attention of Heinz. Standing in the doorway were her three boys and the older man that looked like a knuckle dragger. The two older boys had broom handles that had been fashioned into lethal weapons. Robert said, "You want us to whap them side the head, Ma?" The knuckle dragger stepped into the room and was three steps from where Chen stood. There was fear in Mrs. Woods's eyes.

In the blink of an eye, Agent Chen assumed a stance, kicked out, caught the knuckle dragger in the crotch, kicked his feet out, and dropped down on top of him, attaching handcuffs with the speed and skill of a rodeo cowboy.

Standing, she looked at the stunned boys. "Next. How about you? You're my size."

Detective Heinz pointed at Mrs. Woods. "Stop them. You're all in enough trouble already. Assaulting an officer will lead to more jail time."

"Boys, please stop. Put down the sticks and go to your rooms. I'll call you when I need you."

"Too late," Chen said. "I'm going to cuff them all. We can't trust them; they might decide to attack again." To the boys, she said, "Up against the wall *now*. Carl, throw me your cuffs. I only have two more sets on me."

Heinz pulled his cuffs and threw them to Chen. He wondered where on her small tight body she hid three sets of cuffs, not to mention the tape recorder.

The only sound was a soft moan from the knuckle dragger.

Mrs. Woods heaved a sign of resignation. “It’s over, and thank God. I’ll tell you the whole story. I no longer care. I just want this craziness to stop. Let me make sure that my brother’s unhurt.” She hobbled over to the knuckle dragger.

The Woods woman spoke softly. “Leroy, we have to give it up. The boys are starting to become ganglike again. There was never supposed to be any violence. I don’t know what’ll happen to us, but we can’t go on anymore. We need to cooperate with the police before it is too late.”

“But what about you?” Leroy asked. “What will happen to you?”

“Look at my face. He beats me regularly, he uses me, I’m totally submissive to him.”

“Who beats you?” Heinz inquired.

“Michael Dean.”

Chapter Seventeen

"My story will take some time to tell," Mrs. Woods said. "Can I at least put my boys on the couch and turn the TV on for them? They'll do as I say."

Chen was shaking her head no, but Heinz was sympathetic. "All right, but the cuffs stay on."

"Each of you please introduce yourselves properly and mind your manners."

The youngest boy stepped forward. "My name is Robert Evans, and I'm thirteen years old." He then went over to the couch and sat down.

"My name is Kevin Toms. I'm fifteen."

"I'm Ruben Jones. I'm sixteen."

"I guess you know that I'm Leroy. Leroy Givens is my name, and I'm Ula's brother." He got up with his hands still cuffed behind his back and waddled over to the couch.

Chen said, "We're now up to twenty-five incidents. I didn't know about the brother but saw the name four times on the reports."

Mrs. Woods shook her head. "There're a few more to talk about."

They had proceeded to the spacious kitchen. Mrs. Woods and Detective Heinz were now seated along the marble center island. The kitchen had all modern appliances and was very clean. Chen continued to stand like a prison guard—eyes searching, posture alert, ready to pounce.

Heinz had his notebook open and a pen in hand. "I hardly know where to start."

Chen said, "You'd better Mirandize her before we talk."

Mrs. Woods gave a short quick laugh and then was serious again. "If you do that, I'll have a right to contact my old friend and lawyer. I'm afraid that by the time you're able to question me, it'll be too late for all of us. I could waive my right to counsel, but what would be the point? We are guilty of many crimes. Can we just talk? It'll save us a lot of time."

Chen asked the first question, "What's your real name?"

"I was born Ula Givens. My married name is Woods. I've been married only once. Someone killed my husband over twenty years ago, near his dental office."

"Tell me about the tattoo," Heinz asked. "It doesn't make sense for a black woman to have a swastika tattoo."

"Michael made me do it." She pulled open her blouse and exposed her left breast. On the underside just below the nipple, there was a three-inch tattoo that completely disfigured her breast. She went on to explain.

"I've known Michael all my life. He thinks he owns me, that I'm his slave. He wanted to brand me so other men, especially black men, wouldn't want to be with me. He said he was afraid that I'd get AIDS from them, and then he couldn't have his brand of sex with me."

Mrs. Woods then started her story. "I'm going to tell you about my life with Michael Dean. You must let me tell everything before you arrest me. Agreed?"

Heinz readily agreed.

Chapter Eighteen

"I was born in this house in 1958. My family and I had a nice life here, but I didn't have many friends. In 1963, the Deans moved in from Wisconsin. I was very happy because they had a child. I couldn't wait to play with him. But Michael's father, Manny, hated everyone and didn't want his boy playing with a black. They turned out to be not ideal neighbors.

"Cora, Michael's mother, only did one thing. She did it often. She screamed. Many nights I could hear her screaming, begging for him to stop. The next day we would see her with bruises and black and blue marks. Michael's father could be brutal and set up parts of the basement to look like a dungeon. For years I heard sounds coming from the basement, and I was becoming more than curious.

"His father was a drinker. Frequently a few friends showed up for drinking parties in the backyard. I spent many hours sitting in trees in the woods watching their parties."

"So was his father a racist?" asked Chen.

"Oh, he was more than that. He was an old Nazi. But no one could prove it."

"So how did a black girl get connected with the son of a racist?" Detective Heinz inquired.

"Well, it was about sex. We were both teenagers by then and had met in the woods behind our houses. One thing led to another, and we had sex one night, with neither of us knowing how to do it. He was gentle until the end. He just finished, zipped up his pants, and said, 'See you tomorrow.'

"We had sex from then on. We even developed a system to communicate. We used a small white cloth. We hung it outside our bedroom windows whenever we wanted to see each other. Although we were in the same school every day, we couldn't talk. No one would understand. Blacks and whites didn't mix in those days."

With pencil poised, Detective Heinz asked the next question, "Was Dean violent then?"

"Mostly on the football field, as I recall."

"When did he show signs of violence?"

"It happened in my senior year. My mother died in March 1977 from cancer. A disaster happened one week before school was finished. I was sleeping in my upstairs bedroom when the door to my room opened, and my father entered. He closed the door and approached the bed. He had been acting very strangely since my mother had died."

"I will never forget his words. 'I've been hearing things about you and your white boyfriend,' he said. 'The Lord has told me to punish you.'

"Then my father started to hit me. The next morning, I got up, and there were several bruises on my face and a big bruise on my belly. It hurt, and I cried before getting dressed for school. Father was not home when I got downstairs.

"When Michael saw the bruises, he went insane and beat up two smaller boys at school. He, of course, got off with a lecture from the football coach. He could do no wrong," she said sarcastically.

"Well, he seemed to care for you then," Loni pointed out.

Ula let out a small laugh. Then she continued.

"Cared about me? He didn't care about me. In fact, he up and left and screwed up my life completely."

"What do you mean?" Detective Heinz questioned.

"It happened on July 4. I'll never forget it. We had gone on a date to celebrate his birthday. After the fireworks, we made love. He had turned eighteen that day. It was one of the best times ever. Michael then got dressed and said that he had to do something. He left me at the bowling alley.

"He showed up an hour and a half later with his friend Gary Baum. Gary tends bar now at the bowling alley. Michael was smiling, and I was sure that tonight would be the most favorite night in my life. We drove over to the grocery store parking lot because he said that he wanted to talk. It was late, maybe 1:00 a.m.

"I remember his exact words. 'I have something to tell you. I'm leaving for boot camp in three hours.'

"I was shocked.

"'I'll write you, and I'll see you when I get back.' He was leaving me without any concern about me.

"'Don't count on it,' I said through the tears.

"'I have to go,' he said. 'I took care of everything for you, you'll see, everything you asked for.' And he was gone."

"What a son of a bitch," Loni bellowed.

"Agent Chen, you have no idea. The real devastation came later when I arrived home only to find several police cruisers in my driveway. They said that my father had committed suicide in our garage."

"Do you think that Dean had anything to do with the apparent suicide?" Detective Heinz asked.

"I didn't think that then; I was too full of despair to even consider it. I had lost my boyfriend and my father in the same night."

"But now do you think that he was involved?" Heinz questioned.

"Yes," replied Mrs. Woods in a grief-stricken voice.

"Okay, you were eighteen, alone, and had Leroy to take care of. What happened next?" Loni asked.

"As it turned out, my father had planned well. He had purchased a large insurance policy on himself. The insurance company didn't want to pay, but the funeral home director knew a shyster lawyer named Seith Paul. Seith got my money somehow and has been my lawyer ever since."

"I noticed that a lawyer named Paul has represented you and your children in several scams. Is this the same guy?" Loni inquired.

"Seith liked the money and has no ethics. He worked out of his gold Cadillac and chased ambulances until he hooked up with us."

Heinz was making notes in his book. "Check out death of Thomas Givens in 1977. Run background on Gary Baum. Check out a lawyer named Seith Paul." He already had Woods, Dean, Leroy, and the three boys on the list.

Ula was crying now, and this prompted a question from Heinz. "So you had enough money to survive—why go into the crime business?"

"It happened because Michael came home."

"And when did that happen?" Heinz continued.

"He came home three days after his mother and father died in the car accident. That was in 1988. He gave me a key ring with his house key on it to watch the house until he could move in. He already considered me his slave."

Suddenly a phone was ringing. Woods said, "That's my cell phone. Should I get it?"

Heinz said, "Fine, but Loni will need to listen in on the conversation."

Mrs. Woods crossed to the pantry door, where her bag was hooked, and extracted her cell phone. "Hello," she said. Agent Chen was standing next to her. She had moved her long hair away from her ear to listen in. She had spread her leotard-clad legs and was leaning forward. Heinz thought that she looked like a mime.

"Yes, Judy, what can I do for you?"

"Judy Kroll," Chen mouthed to Heinz.

"No, Leroy can't drive you. He is tied up at the moment."

Chen's lips mouthed. "Needs a ride."

"Besides, he knows him from a sting we did last year."

Chen's shoulders gave a shrug.

"Call Billy Brown, you have his number—we've used him before. He'll do it."

"Okay, you're set then? Good-bye."

Heinz had already added Brown's name to his list.

"What was that about?" the detective asked.

Woods replied, "That was Judy Kroll. She's having a meeting tomorrow with the guy we did a sting on last year. She wanted to use Leroy to be her driver and act as bodyguard. The meeting's supposed to be about collecting business information, but actually she wants the guy to identify a picture. Strange, don't you think? They're going to pay him money too."

"Where and when?" Heinz was already organizing the stakeout.

"Tomorrow morning at ten o'clock at the Marriott," the Woods woman answered.

Heinz now added Judy Kroll to his list of names. "What is the guy's name?" Heinz asked.

"Colton Banyon," was the reply.

After he had recovered from the unexpected twist, Heinz asked, "How is the Altar of the Creator connected to all of this?"

"I don't know much, I was going to explain. But I do know that this all has to do with some big meeting tonight at the church. I know that they're scheduled to go to Long Island on Sunday. We're supposed to drive them to the airport. Michael's made all the arrangements. We're just the maid and butler, you know."

"Do you know what the meeting is about?"

"Only that several deacons from around the state and some more white supremacy leaders from around the country will be there. Some big announcement, I think."

Heinz had already filled his notebook with potential crimes and suspects and asked Loni if she had a notebook. Loni produced a new one from somewhere on her body and handed the warm notebook to the puzzled detective. Mrs. Woods was giving the boys something to drink and was changing the channels on the high-definition TV. Mrs. Woods came back into the room. She was ready to reveal the next part of her journey through life.

"So here it was 1988, and Michael was coming home. I was thrilled but frightened. What would happen to me? Would we finally settle down, or would some new event keep us apart?

"One night I let myself into his house through the backdoor and found myself in the kitchen. It was spotless with a sprinkling of dust. Walking down the hallway, I found the house was set up identical to my own. The difference was the furniture was very dark and made of heavy wood. Everything was well-worn; it all reeked of tobacco. Upstairs was more of the same. I entered Michael's room. It was set up for a teenage boy, as there were T-shirts and jeans in the closet and very few personal items, with the exception of a picture of Michael playing football, a picture of Michael in a suit, and a picture of Michael that showed him at a camp. There were other boys in the camp picture. Men with guns were in the background, and to my horror, a Nazi flag was flying in the picture. A signature at the bottom read "Frank Collins—Fuehrer." I suddenly remembered that when we were in high school in the late 1970s, the American Nazi party was creating a huge uproar because they wanted to hold a rally in Skokie. Skokie was heavily Jewish, with many concentration camp survivors living there. Frank Collins was the leader of the movement. Michael was one of them, a Nazi.

"I was stunned and decided to leave. In locking the door, I noticed the other key on the key ring. Then I remembered, Michael had told me his parents had a locked room in the basement where Manny and Cora 'played.' I couldn't get down the stairs fast enough. At the bottom of the stairs on the right was a door. I stuck the key in and turned the lock.

"The room was dark and musty. I managed to locate a light switch. The lights were dull. The walls were painted to look like a dungeon, and there were hooks on one wall with various ropes, chains, whips, and other torture devices. I was horrified and yet intrigued. I didn't know at that time that this would be my dungeon too. When Michael returned home, he introduced me to the devices."

"But couldn't you just say no?" asked Chen.

"You don't understand," Ula shot back vehemently. "He threatened me. He had worked on his plan for a long time. He said that he had evidence that I had murdered my father. His friends would swear to it. He was also going to be a policeman in Streamwood. He even threatened to have Leroy arrested on a trumped-up charge. I had to protect Leroy."

"Please continue," Detective Heinz requested.

"It took three more months to totally destroy my will. Michael said I was a slow learner. But I learned to be exactly on time, to anticipate his moods, and to even predict when he wanted sex, rough as it was. It became clear to me that whenever he was challenged or got frustrated, he would want rough sex. Once in a while, though, he would even satisfy me during one of our dungeon visits, and believe it or not, I craved it."

"In other words, he had made you into a slave," Agent Chen pointed out with what appeared to be a measure of sympathy.

"I just wanted a good man, but what I got was a monster."

Chapter Nineteen

"What do you know about the church?" Detective Heinz asked as he tried to move the interview along.

"I first heard about the church when Michael had one of his monthly meetings. I was the entertainment and waitress. I served them, and they groped me. He had just started his meeting."

"'I have good news,' he said. 'A friend of mine has returned to Illinois and has started a church. We're going to be a chapter of the church.' They all started to laugh and acted as if it was a joke. Michael was turning red.

"'Listen, you idiots, this is the best thing to happen to the cause in decades. I worked with Joe Kroll in the army. Kroll is a lawyer now. He's smart and knows how to get things done for the cause. By starting a church, it prevents the government from looking too closely at us. The base church will be in Peoria. What can be wrong with that?

"'What we need to do is to start collecting money to finance our movement. Joe thinks we can get twenty chapters going by the end of next year, and we will also take over a couple of other white supremacy churches, by force if need be.' The boys liked that statement. They were always up for a fight, especially if they ambushed the victim and outnumbered him three or four to one.

"'Mark my words, someday we'll have a huge membership, lots of money, and we'll be the leaders of the Aryan cause. Don't you want to be part of that? Now here is what we are going to do. Teddy, you and Harry are going to Peoria to meet with Joe. He'll give you all the paperwork we need to declare ourselves a church. I'm going to set up an operation that will get us some money so we can recruit other members. One more thing, I want each of you to read this book.'

"'What for?' blurted Harry. 'I haven't read a book since high school.'

"'It's called *The Turner Diaries*, and it's about the violent overthrow of the government. It was written by a former assistant to George Lincoln Rockwell. Rockwell was the first leader of the American Nazi Party. Believe me, the Aryans win. It also tells how to make plans and even make bombs. Joe Kroll thinks that it's a blueprint to achieve our goals, so read it. Is everyone in agreement?'"

Heinz asked Mrs. Woods to stop for a few minutes. He was seeing red before his eyes. Every law officer in America knew about *The Turner Diaries.* Timothy McVeigh, the Oklahoma City bomber, had been an avid reader of the book. He had also been an enthusiastic promoter of the book at gun shows. The Murrah Federal Building bombing had remarkable similarities to the bombing of the FBI building in the book. *The Turner Diaries* was first published in 1978, and the Oklahoma bombing took place in 1995. In between those years, a lot of white supremacists read and believed in the book. Apparently so did Michael Dean. Detective Heinz was now determined to nail Dean and his "church." He was having trouble calming down and decided to call Colt Banyon.

Back in the spacious kitchen, Mrs. Woods was ready to continue.

"Michael's great plan was simple extortion. He figured that it was time to tax those that he felt were inferior. This was most people. He would use his church members to collect the tax, and if there were any problems, he would be called in to arbitrate as the police. The plan was simple. Michael was careful to not be too obvious. He made periodic arrests of blacks and Hispanics, often planting evidence to ensure convictions. The arrested people almost always had previous records. The Streamwood police captain was not a problem. He was an old-time city cop who had passed his prime but was friends with the mayor. He had less than twelve years until retirement. Michael was always ready to take care of anything that came up and was so gung ho that Captain Miles didn't worry about the department. He went fishing.

"By 1992, Michael's operation was netting about six thousand dollars per week. One of my chores was to keep the books. Michael sent most of the money to the Peoria church, although he kept two thousand for himself and a thousand for me each week. By then, he had made me quit the part-time job at the hospital I had taken to survive financially. My job now was to serve the church.

"One day a report came in to the police department that a woman's car was stolen. I don't remember her name. Anyway, Michael knew where to look for the car. He found the car in half a day. The woman was so happy that she offered Michael a reward. He took it, deciding that this was a good way to make more money. He could also utilize Leroy and his gangbanger friend Billy Brown. A systematic plan was introduced that converted Leroy into a car thief. The scheme started to net Michael another thousand a week; I got a hundred dollars, and Leroy got four hundred, which he had to split with Billy. The group also developed contacts in other towns and then traded information on cars to steal.

"The church grew to thirty members, far less than Michael had promised, yet all were making lots of money. Michael purchased the title of deacon of the church. Teddy, Harry, and Gary, his friends, were also big shots for the cause. One of them—I don't know which one—had the title of sergeant of arms, strange for a church. They had all gotten tattoos at Timmy's parlor as a sign of leadership. Michael's was a huge swastika on his back, with the word 'Aryan' below it. He apparently never took his shirt off at the station, so no one knew about it but us.

"The main chapter of the Altar of the Creator was flourishing as well, but Michael wanted his own building. They had always met at Michael's house, and he was paranoid that the feds were taping them. They eventually moved to a storefront in Aurora. That is where they hold their meetings now.

"As bookkeeper, I wrote a check to the church every month from the checking account. It was listed as the Ary-Inn Corporation. Michael and I were the cosigners.

"In 1994, we embarked on a new venture. On the way to stealing a car, Leroy and Billy were rear-ended at a light. They were all right but called Seith Paul from the car phone. Seith instructed them to moan and say that they needed an ambulance. In a few minutes, Michael arrived with Seith right behind him. Michael knew Seith but had never used him in any of his schemes before. This one would make much more money for all of us.

"We staged fake accidents, and Seith would always show up in seconds, passing out his card and attending to the poor, defenseless, hurt victim, who was actually one of us. This worked a good number of times. Our average settlement was nine thousand dollars. But Michael was worried that some insurance company would put two and two together. So the final plan called for new and different people to get into accidents. I was told to obtain a foster-parent certification and to bring in young boys who would cooperate because they had been involved in juvenile crime.

"I've really tried to keep them out of trouble; I've been a good foster parent. They're getting a good education and can be controlled."

"But once a criminal, always a criminal," Chen quipped.

"That's the whole story. I don't care what you do to me. The last beating that he gave me has cleared my mind. I can't do this anymore. Michael's ruined my life, not to mention Leroy's, several people he's killed, and those poor boys' in the other room. Seith is as bad as the rest of them and should be punished too."

Heinz said he needed to ask a couple of questions, but first he asked Chen to call the state police to come and transport all the suspects to the station. He also made a note to call Seith Paul and have him show up at the station at seven.

"So the Banyon accident last year was a setup?"

"His was one of the easiest scams. We made a lot of money off of his insurance company."

"When did you get the tattoo?" he asked while reading from his notes.

"That was four years ago. I made the mistake of sitting on my porch and talking to a black man, who was actually someone that I met at the grocery store. He carried my groceries home, and we had tea on the porch. Michael drove by in his cruiser and saw us. That night he beat me bad and told me that he didn't want me to give him AIDS from a nigger. Later, he dragged me over to Timmy's place and had him do the tattoo. Of course, his friends were there. Michael believed that any man seeing the tattoo would run. I never tried to find out."

"You said that you kept the books for the operation—do you still keep them?"

"Yes, they're on my computer. I use a computer program to record them. The ledger has all the transactions since 1999. Before then, I used a handwritten ledger. It's in my desk."

Heinz said, "Loni will need to take the computer and the ledger." Chen took off like a shot.

"How many accidents have you recorded?"

"Before 1999 we didn't really keep track. Since then, I have recorded forty-eight. I don't know where they get the additional extortion money. I think Gary keeps that list."

"And about how much money have you taken in since 1999?"

"A little over three million dollars."

"Do you know the other members of the church?"

"Since they moved to Aurora, I don't see any of them. I think Michael likes it that way, as it keeps me from knowing who's watching me."

Heinz next asked, "Do you mind if we take a short break? I need to confer with Agent Chen. I should cuff you to the door," he added.

"Don't worry, I want to get this over with; we won't run." Then she turned and went to check on the boys.

Part Three
Connections

Chapter Twenty

As soon as Ula Woods left the room, Heinz pulled Chen close. "This is getting too big for just us. We have too many leads and so little time. We can't trust anyone in the Streamwood department. Got any ideas?"

Chen suggested that because of the interstate members and the plans to go to New York, they might call in the FBI to do the surveillance on the church. "The FBI is the best at that. It would free up a lot of our time. I know who to call and could set it up. We have about three hours before the meeting starts. Time is short, but the FBI has a long list of issues with the church; they will be there. I hate to let others in on our gold mine here. But I think it's the right thing to do. What do you think?"

"I think this case is bigger than we can imagine," Heinz commented.

Agent Chen had just returned from the cruiser, where she'd spoken to Agent Greg Gamble of the Chicago office of the FBI. Her head of long black hair virtually hid her face, but Heinz could detect the smile of success and accomplishment there.

Gamble had quickly understood the situation and agreed to have four agents at the church by 7:30 p.m. They would be armed with special mikes and cameras. All the people that entered the building would be photographed, and a sound recording of the meeting would be made. The information would subsequently be brought to the Streamwood Police Department, where a task force would be set up. The immediate mobilization of a large number of white supremacists caught the attention of the FBI.

The questions went on until the state police showed up with three cars and a van. They would have to investigate every crime, every report, and every connection since 1988. Not to mention the possible homicides. *Wait until the insurance companies find out about this. They will all be looking to get their money back.*

Heinz walked outside and dialed his cell phone, connecting to Banyon's cell phone.

"Mr. Banyon, it is Detective Heinz. How're you doing? Listen, can you stop by the station at say 7:00 p.m.? I need to talk to you about something. Your name has surfaced again, and you may know more about this than you think."

"What do you think I've done now?" Banyon angrily retorted.

"No, we don't suspect you of anything. We need your help."

"Can I bring Pramilla?" Banyon asked.

"Yes, you can bring Mrs. Patel."

"We will be there at 7:00 p.m."

Everyone was now Mirandized and loaded into the van. The computer and ledgers were entrusted to a cruiser. The state police, having obtained a warrant, were checking all over the house for more evidence and clues. Heinz considered getting a warrant for Dean's house, too, but decided they didn't want to tip off Dean until they could digest all the evidence.

Dean would be concerned about Mrs. Woods not being home, so Heinz had her call his answering machine to say that they all had gone to look at a summer house in Indiana and would be back on Monday night.

Heinz would get someone from the station house to watch the Dean residence until everyone had been arrested.

It was about six o'clock in the evening. Heinz and Chen were standing on the porch. Everyone had gone to the station. They had to be there by 7:00 p.m. As they walked to the car, he could see that Agent Chen had something on her mind. She had been restless and fidgety all afternoon.

"What's on your mind, Agent Chen?"

"Well, we have about forty-five minutes before we need to be at the station. Do you live near here?"

"Actually, I live only about a mile from here. Why?"

"I'd like to see your place," she said with a mischievous smile.

Detective Heinz got in the car, turned on the lights and siren, and peeled rubber.

Chapter Twenty-One

Back in Westhampton, Walter Pierce was seated at his antique desk. The front gate buzzer rang. He got up and walked slowly to the front intercom. He carried his trusty Luger.

"Who is it?" he croaked into the intercom.

"I've got a package for a Walter Pierce," a deliveryman said.

"Please, walk up the drive."

He opened the door and hid the gun. The deliveryman was clearly in a hurry as he jogged to the door carrying a two-foot-square package in brown paper. Pierce signed for the package and closed the door. He watched through the small window until the man passed outside the compound. He then closed the gate and walked to his desk, hugging the package.

Once in his office, he ceremoniously cut the box top and started to take out the contents. After he had laid out all the bounty, he closely examined each one. He knew what each medal represented.

To Walter Pierce, these medals were his reward for all these years of service. The fact that no one would ever know he had them was of no consequence to him. There was no one left alive that had any idea about who he was and what he had been charged with. He sat there and awarded each medal to himself, citing the reason that he should receive each. He then pinned each one on his suit coat and stood at attention for several minutes. A rush of accomplishment ran through him.

He could have gone to many stores and even had someone get him medals on the Internet, but Pierce didn't want any old medals; he wanted the Banyon family medals. It had been an obsession since he first heard of the medals from the voices. They were almost his constant companions now. They were filled with joy. It seemed that the nearer Pierce got to completing his plan, the more joyous they became. Now the medals were his, the voices were singing, and his plan was progressing splendidly. But he had more work to do.

He picked up the phone to call his old acquaintance Professor Raymond Davies. Davies was much younger than Pierce, being only forty-three. To

Pierce, he was always "the kid." Davies was a professor of archeology at Stony Brook University. Davies answered the phone on the first ring.

"How are you today, my friend?" a congenial Pierce asked.

"I'm just fine. Bet you're calling about Monday?"

"You'll be there Monday night, I trust?" Pierce was apprehensive, as his associate was not always reliable. Davies sometimes got lost in his work, and time had no meaning.

"I wouldn't miss it for the world," Davies replied with sincere interest.

"Good, and don't forget to bring your assistant. This will be the biggest archeological find of the century—I guarantee it. We'll need you to verify the translation of the tablet. I have kept this tablet secret for over sixty years. It must be exposed to the public."

"Will you have media there?" Davies inquired.

"Everyone who needs to be there will be there," Pierce coyly replied.

"I'll see you at 8:00 p.m. then."

Chapter Twenty-Two

Heinz and Chen had arrived at the station house at exactly 6:45 p.m. As they entered the station, they walked into complete chaos. People were everywhere. The "Woods gang" was sequestered in the back cells. Seith Paul was handcuffed and confined to the interview room. The open area had at least three times as many people seated as usual. Several sat three to a desk. Agent Greg Gamble, a mountain of a man with a slight Southern drawl, had settled in Heinz's office, and the two Streamwood police officers on duty were seated in the lobby. They had been asked to turn in their guns and to wait for Heinz to return. He asked them to wait one minute while he straightened out the situation. He walked into his office and asked Gamble why he had taken his men's guns.

"I didn't know whom to trust. Sorry. If you are vouching for them, we'll give back their guns."

Heinz returned to the men and told them to go to Dean's and Ula Woods's houses and stake them out. Both men gathered their guns and left. Heinz returned to his office. He sat down at his desk to confer with Gamble.

"Agent Gamble, I know that you're heading up the FBI part of this investigation. However, remember, this is my station house, and I'm in charge of it. I care about what happens in my department and anything that's connected to Streamwood. I need to know about everything you're working on so I can see how it fits into my case."

"Captain Heinz, there's enough here for everyone to take credit. We may be able to shut down the most organized white supremacy group in the country. That is all I care about."

"Okay, we've got that cleared up. By the way, I'm not a captain, just babysitting until they hire a full-time captain."

"Don't worry, pal, when this bust is over, we're all going to get promotions—this is big."

Suddenly Agent Chen burst into the office. She tossed Heinz the fax that had come in earlier. "A clerk at the FBI bureau in Chicago sent this in. She was seeing Michael Dean until he got too rough with her. She said he gave her the picture two years ago. This is the photo that started it all. Colton Banyon's fingerprint showed up a year ago as a match to the print on the picture."

"A year ago?" Gamble questioned.

"We took his prints when he was hauled in because of a sting that the Woods gang had set up. Apparently he had not been fingerprinted since before we had a database," Heinz offered.

Gamble asked a question. "The picture was taken in 1970. What do you think it all means?" For once, Agent Chen could not come up with an answer.

"I don't know," admitted Heinz. "But Banyon is due here any minute. Maybe he can shed some light on this."

At five minutes after the hour, Colt Banyon came strolling into the station with both Patel women, one on each arm. As they walked up to the service window, everyone stopped to stare. Heinz jumped up and headed out to greet him, a broad smile decorating his rugged face.

"Colt, thanks for coming in. Good to see you, Mrs. Patel. This must be your sister?"

"You may address me as Ms. Patel." It was Previne speaking.

"And you can call me Carl. This is Agent Loni Chen from the state police and Agent Greg Gamble from the FBI." The girls, in unison, looked Loni up and down, turned back to Carl, and then turned up their noses.

"Let's go into the interview room, shall we?" Heinz pointed the way. After they were seated, Heinz brought out the picture and placed it in front of Banyon. He asked if Banyon recognized the picture.

"Where did you get this?" Banyon responded.

"It was sent to us by the FBI's Chicago field office, which got it from a Michael Dean. Does that name ring a bell?"

"Is he the same Michael Dean from this station?" The question was filled with contempt.

"You should be happy that you don't know him better—he's a white supremacist."

A light of recognition went on in Banyon's head. "This has to do with my break-in, doesn't it?"

Pramilla said, "And my attack."

"We think so. But the picture came in over two years ago, yet your break-in was only two days ago."

"I've absolutely no idea why it took so long to find me. The only time I've been fingerprinted was when I was drafted. I was included in the first draft group in 1967. I was also fingerprinted when you pulled me in last year. Maybe there's a connection?"

"Yeah, I'm sorry about that. We're still investigating, but it appears that your accident was planned."

"I told you so," Banyon said. Although he was not a vindictive person, Colt felt the thrill of vindication now.

"Okay, a year ago you were fingerprinted. That would have activated the database. Can someone check to see if anyone had a flag on Mr. Banyon's prints match?" Agent Chen was already opening the door to the interview room and heading out to investigate.

Heinz turned to Banyon. "While we're waiting, what can you tell us about the picture?"

"That's easy. It's a shot of Lorenzo. He has this 'shit eating' grin that you could never forget. He's a good friend of mine, has been since the sixth grade."

"What's his last name?" Heinz had a pencil and paper in his hand.

"It's actually Lawrence Bell, but everyone called him Lorenzo, the Latin lover. I don't think he's Italian or anything, but he was hot-blooded." He then added, "Lorenzo's kind of a nickname; you won't find it on any documents, yearbook, or anything."

"And where can we find Mr. Bell?" Gamble interrupted.

"He lives in Silicon Valley in California. He had a very successful Internet business and sold out a couple of years ago. He's a man of leisure now. He couldn't be part of this; I've known him forever, and he's no white supremacist. I'll call him if you'd like."

"Well, it appears that someone is looking for him. Got any ideas?"

"No, not a clue," Banyon said, scratching his head.

"Do you remember when and why this photo was taken?"

"Yes, I do. I took the picture. It was during our senior year of college. Lorenzo and I had a great relationship since he was good at science and I was good at history, art, and all the humanities. Sometimes we would help each other on projects. We both took geology in our second semester senior year and had to do a paper on some local geology. We agreed to partner and decided to do the paper on the formation of eastern Long Island.

"Most people don't know this, but Long Island was formed by several glaciers and not by a single glacier. Long Island was the terminal moraine, or where the glacier ended and drained. The glacier stopped and receded and came back and receded at least three times. We wanted to prove the hills in the middle of the island were a different glacier than the north shore. At that time, 1970, the more-than-one-glacier theory had not been proven.

"This picture was taken at the second highest hill on eastern Long Island. A gun club owned the land, and Lorenzo and I dug a big hole. You can see it in the background. We counted the striations in the sand. We also did this on the cliffs on the north end of the island a few miles away and compared them. They were clearly different. We got an A."

"What is that metal pole in the background? There is something written on it. It looks like a marker. It says 19-42." Heinz announced.

"During World War II, the land was used by the army and air force as part of a huge military training base. Pieces of metal are scattered everywhere in those woods. The marker was already there, so we dug our hole by it. The landscape is very monotonous on that part of the island."

"Could you find that spot if you needed to?"

He nodded. "I grew up in that area. I remember the view from the spot. You could see a long way from there. I'm sure I could draw a map to the location, but—"

Heinz interrupted, "Have you ever found markers like that in other parts of the woods?"

"Well, no, now that you mention it. Do you think this could have something to do with my break-in?"

Agent Chen had just returned to the room and pushed a piece of paper across the table to Heinz. It had a name on it. Michael Dean had put a flag on Banyon's prints. He'd done it a year ago.

Chen announced, "There are too many coincidences to ignore."

"And this could be another one," Heinz interjected. "We suspect that Dean and several others are landing at MacArthur Airport on Sunday. That's in eastern Long Island, isn't it?"

"That's funny," Banyon said. "We're going there too."

"Why are you going to Long Island?" Chen inquired.

"I don't know that it is any of your business," replied Banyon.

"Just answer the question." Agent Chen was clearly irritated.

The twins gave Agent Chen a show of sharp teeth that said, "Back off, bitch."

This was not lost on Banyon. "Actually, I have a job interview on Tuesday. Monday we are going to have a look at my old house. You remember, I told you about that."

"Is your old house near the site of this picture?" Detective Heinz asked.

"A couple of miles away," Banyon answered.

"Why are you going to your old house?" Chen continued to probe.

The twins were staring at her with a look that could freeze water into an ice cube in ten seconds.

"Actually, Pramilla is a journalist and wants to do a human interest story for a newspaper in India."

Switching topics now, Heinz asked, "I understand you have a meeting tomorrow morning at the Marriott?"

"How'd you find out? I just got the call this morning." Banyon was indignant; he hated it when everyone knew about his business.

"Well, that's another coincidence," Heinz remarked. "The person that you will be meeting with is the wife of Joe Kroll. Her name is Judy Kroll. She's posing as an assistant to someone, but we don't know who or why."

"How do you know that?" Banyon could not believe that they had this information. Maybe there was a bug on him.

"The usual driver is part of a gang that we're investigating, and the topic came up during our interrogations. So, what did they tell you to bring?"

"They asked for a report on the future of retailing, nothing that would require a ruse. Wait, Pierce said to bring my pictures, as he was trying to identify some people from Westhampton. They could be trying to identify Lorenzo, I'm sure of it now. As I already mentioned, only his friends called him Lorenzo." He continued, "Pierce brought up Westhampton just when it seemed that I wasn't going to accept the job. Whoever Judy Kroll is, she will undoubtedly have a copy of the picture tomorrow. She may want me to identify Lorenzo or the place in the background. I'm betting it's the location they're after. Whoever's managing this operation is sharp. He didn't want to ask me directly because I might not have taken the picture and maybe I wasn't even there when it was taken. The only person who was directly involved is Lorenzo. We know they've had the picture for at least two years, but I only become active on the project in the last year, since my prints were identified. This is a mystery."

"You didn't by chance get a first name from the man that called you? Even if it's a false name, it would be something."

Taking out his cell phone, Banyon replied, "He gave his name as Walter Pierce. His number's also available on my phone."

Agent Gamble promised to check out Pierce and the phone number.

"Colt, let's discuss this meeting tomorrow," Heinz said. "I don't want you to go there by yourself. Agent Chen will accompany you. She'll pretend to be your assistant. I'll also be in the lobby somewhere, and I want you to wear a wire. Agent Chen will fit it on you before you go in."

"We're going with Colt," Previne announced.

"No, you are not. These people have a bad track record of violence."

Agent Chen countered with logic. "I'll have my guns. You'll just disrupt things and be in the way."

"How do we know that you can protect Colt? You're so—if you excuse the expression—small," Pramilla remarked. Sarcasm dripped from her voice.

"I can vouch for the fact that she can handle almost anything. She can protect Colt, me, and the whole hotel, if necessary."

The twins turned to look at each other; they sometimes communicated without using words. But, Previne suddenly commented, "Oh, Detective Heinz and Agent Chen have a relationship."

"What do you think is buried in the ground?" Gamble asked Banyon.

"Captain Kidd buried a treasure somewhere on eastern Long Island. And to this day it hasn't been located. There were other pirates, of course, and they often buried treasure. It could be buried treasure that we're looking for."

"You're telling me that this whole case is about buried treasure?" Gamble stated in disbelief.

"I don't know what to think, except what else could it be? That area is called Speonk, and it's located just below the fork of Long Island at one of the highest land points. The area is all scrub pine for miles and miles. It would be easy to lose track of something buried in the ground."

"Speonk is a funny name," Previne commented.

"It means 'high land' in the local Indian dialect," replied Banyon.

Banyon now turned to the FBI agent. "Agent Gamble, do you think Lorenzo is in any trouble?"

"I'm not clear about that. Maybe we should contact him," he replied. "We may want to have the local FBI put a watch on him."

"Hand me my phone. I'll call him right now," Banyon requested. He hit the speed dial, and the phone was ringing.

"Hello, Larry speaking," a voiced answered.

"Bell, what's happening?"

"Well, today I decided to take up golf. I went out and bought some clubs and shoes. It was fun. I didn't buy any golf balls, though—too expensive." Larry was legendary for his frugality.

"How are you going to play golf without golf balls?" Banyon was a 10 handicap and had been one for many years.

"That's what I have friends for. I'll borrow from them, at least until I can find balls in the woods."

"Well, I'm glad that you'll be giving up skiing for golf. You should act your age," Banyon chided his friend.

"Who said I'm giving up skiing? I just booked a trip to New Zealand for a month. I leave tonight at midnight."

"That's great, but let me tell you why I called. I'm at the Streamwood police station with the FBI and have to ask if anything strange or unusual has happened to you in the last couple of days."

"Define 'unusual'—this is California."

"Like strange phone calls or a break-in."

"No, nothing like that. Say, what's this all about?"

"Remember way back in college when we did the geology project on the glacier on Long Island?"

"Yeah." There was hesitancy in his voice.

"Well, one of the pictures I took of you has turned up in a big-time police investigation. In the picture, you're standing by one of the holes we dug, and you had the 'grin.' In the background, there's a marker of some kind, and we think that it may have something to do with what's going on here."

"Colt, I'm getting old. Sometimes I can't remember what I had for breakfast. I don't recall anything other than our digging the holes and getting an A on the report."

After hanging up the phone, he explained that Larry Bell was probably not the target and that he had no idea what was going on.

One of the agents from the outer office came in with details on Walter Pierce. He gave the data to Agent Gamble and left. Gamble began to read out loud.

"He doesn't have a record of any kind. There are several lawsuits over business deals, but nothing that says that he is any kind of a bad guy." Gamble continued, "There is no record of his birth. He just appeared in the 1940s. He went on to work for a bank in 1942 as a teller. Nothing is recorded up until then, but that's not unusual for that time period. In 1946, he and several friends purchased a large tract of land in Speonk and formed a—"

"Gun club," Banyon cut in.

"That's correct. He then sold off some pieces of the land on the northern and southern ends while starting a real estate business. In 1960, he bought a restaurant, the Wheel & Tack."

Banyon cut in again, "I know that restaurant—it was on Tanners Neck Road in Westhampton. I worked there."

"Another coincidence," observed Chen.

Gamble continued, "In 1966, after acquiring a local construction company, he incorporated into a stock company. Then a marina, the Great South Boat Bay Company, was added to the portfolio. Finally in 1975, he bought a fastener company, Ajax Fasteners, located in New York City."

"What does a fastener company make?" It was Previne.

"Nails, screws, anything that fastens things together. It's big volume, if you can keep your price down," explained the businessman Banyon.

Gamble was still reading out loud. "It appears that the Walter Pierce Company, LLC, made a lot of money from buying land on Dune Road and building houses on the land. He's very wealthy, with over one hundred and thirty million dollars in assets. He resides on Tanners Neck Lane in Westhampton," Gamble concluded.

"I'll bet it's on the land where the Wheel & Tack used to be. A friend from school told me that the restaurant was torn down several years ago," Banyon pointed out. Then he added, "Another coincidence."

Agent Gamble was wondering what all this had to do with the white supremacist movement and the meeting at the church.

"I think I need to interview Mr. Pierce and see how he fits into all of this."

"Can you have some agents in New York also check the location that's in the picture?" Banyon asked. "That is, if I give you directions."

"Can you remember how to get there?" Heinz inquired.

"I'll write down the directions and draw a map. I'm sure the area hasn't changed much over the years. I mean, the hill couldn't disappear, could it?" Banyon took out a piece of paper and began to write. "Take the Speonk-Riverhead Road north until you pass the fourth fire lane …"

Gamble asked, "What's a fire lane?"

"Well, the forest on eastern Long Island is mostly scrub pine because the ground is sandy. The ground doesn't retain water and can get very dry in the summer. All of the woods on that part of the island are a big tinderbox. The police are always chasing people out of the woods, but there are many hiding places. Mistakes happen, and fires get started. The great fire of 1980 was started by a lightning bolt and burned over a thousand acres before it was put out. The fire departments use the fire lanes as a firebreak and as a way to reach the remote areas. It's like a big grid, and each section is a big square. I've no idea when these roads were built, but they've been there ever since I can remember. They may have been built when the area was part of the military base."

Banyon went back to writing. "At the fifth fire lane, turn right and go down the road. Then cross two more fire lanes. Turn left on the third lane and go north for about a half mile. You'll see the crest of the hill. Park the car and head into the woods on your right. Stay on the crest of the hill. When you can see the fork of Long Island directly in front of you, you have reached the spot. If the marker's still there, you should see it." He then added a hand-drawn map.

"Will there be an X to mark the spot?" Gamble asked sarcastically.

"I don't know. Maybe you should look for a notch on a tree or a skull and crossbones too," replied a joking Banyon. "If your men can't find anything, I'll be out there on Monday, and then I'll find it for you."

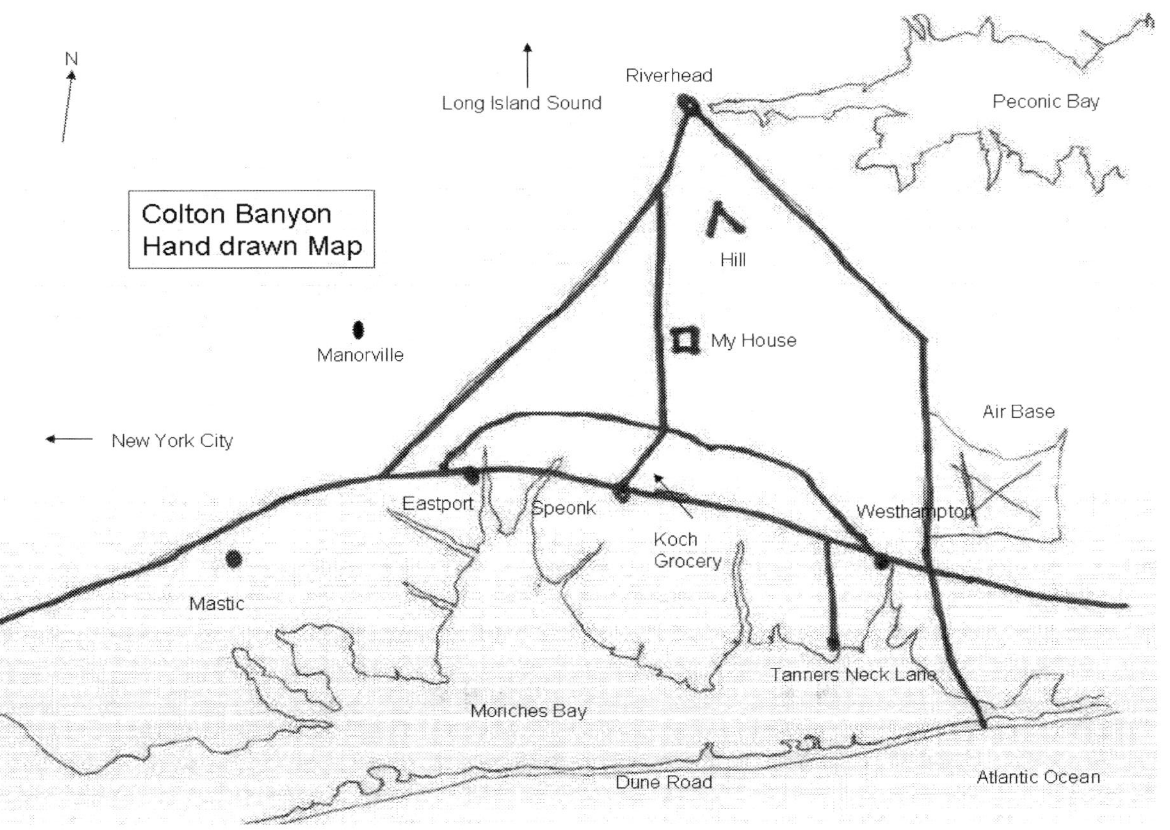

N
Long Island Sound
Riverhead
Peconic Bay
Colton Banyon
Hand drawn Map
Hill
My House
Manorville
Air Base
New York City
Eastport
Speonk
Koch
Grocery
Westhampton
Mastic
Tanners Neck Lane
Moriches Bay
Dune Road
Atlantic Ocean

Chapter Twenty-Three

Back in Westhampton, Walter Pierce was hosting a rare party. His restaurant catered the affair. Stella was his date. All seven presidents of his company's divisions were there, including the president of a newly bought manufacturing company. He had brought them together to tell them that he was going to divest himself of all his divisions. They would each have a chance to buy their division via an initial stock offering that was arranged to take place within the next week. He would personally lend each of his managers the money. Soon he would have little use for the money.

The president of the new company was perplexed. He followed the old man out to the patio, where there was no one to hear. "You just bought my company, and now you want to divest it? I don't get it."

Walter replied, "You don't have to worry about it—you are fired. You made a lot of money on the sale of your company, so be happy."

"You can't do that; I have a contract," the irate manager said. The president had been a difficult negotiator during the buyout. He had run the company into the ground with micromanagement and poor decision-making, usually based on his ego. This caused the company to be put on the market by the conglomerate that owned it. Of course, Eddy Dufeey blamed everyone else. His Elvis-like haircut was also annoying.

"On the contrary, I can buy you out of the contract, and I just did. Here's your check. Now, please leave."

The former president was furious. He began to call Pierce names. In anticipation of the outburst, Walter produced a recorder. "You, my friend, will never work in this industry again. This will be to the benefit of humanity. Now get the hell out before I call the cops and they toss you in jail." Finally the man left, still in a huff.

Pierce was enjoying himself immensely. He had bought a new suit, which he decorated with his medals. No one asked him about the medals, and he didn't care. What did these people know of medals?

All his other presidents were inside celebrating while Walter stood at the patio wall. He was taking in the view of Moriches Bay. Only a couple more days and everything would be set right, he thought.

He planned everything. He even knew what the tablet said. To be certain, Himmler had put a translation in the box, but it was Canaris who actually had the translation done by one of his people. His people also verified that the tablet was original and authentic. Over two years, he fed Professor Davies a few characters at a time, so he had already translated the tablet without knowing it. There'd been so many concerns; now there were none. The verification of the translation of the tablet and the original copy were in his wall safe. Later tonight, he would give Stella a ticket for a cruise. All was going splendidly.

Pierce believed that it was the right time to implement his plan. In fact, he was told to start it.

The voices came to him two years ago as he was reading an article about some sniper killings in Europe. The voices were in his home and spoke in the familiar riddles. "Follow the path." The killings were blamed on the neo-Nazi movement. Pierce was horrified to learn that the Nazis still had a following in Europe and decided to research the subject. For months, he had a driver take him to the library in Riverhead. He spent hours at a time catching up on the movement. What he found was very disturbing.

While the neo-Nazi movement was small, the white supremacy movement was growing. It included the KKK and many splinter military movements, Nazis, skinheads, bikers, and many more. They all had one thing in common—the belief that whites were superior. The word "Aryan" appeared in all of their literature. There were literally hundreds of these groups in the United States alone, not to mention Europe. There were pockets of strength in Africa, Asia, and even Australia. Their members numbered in the millions, if you believed the literature. The library had adequate facilities, and he was able to hire a librarian to do further research. All he had to do was read the materials and give her direction.

The movement was not only large but was growing. The use of migrant workers and a high level of immigration were forcing many people in some developed countries out of middle-paying and into low-paying jobs, particularly in Europe and America. The result was a growing hatred for all people not indigenous. Blacks, Hispanics, and Asians were becoming targets for the supremacy groups. It was going to continue to get worse. Pierce could see that.

Chapter Twenty-Four

A party of sorts was also going on in Aurora. The four FBI agents were hard at work, identifying people entering the church and setting up sound equipment. Agent Krist, a twenty-year veteran of crime fighting, was in charge of the Aurora stakeout. He was using his computer to compare faces with the FBI database. "Something big is going down here," he noted to the other agent in the truck that was parked in the lot behind the church. They had arrived at 7:30 p.m. and had set up several listening devices that were aimed at the storefront and allowed them to hear every word said inside the building. Video cameras were set up next and finally high-powered cameras with long lenses to record everything. Two additional agents sat in a car in the front. They could hear everything through their earphones.

"There's a who's who of supremacy punks here. Are we taping now?" Krist asked the other agent.

"Yes, I'm getting everything on tape. Those creeps are mostly talking about how successful they are and how many times they got laid this week, typical punk stuff so far. Wait! I think the meeting is coming to order now—Joe Kroll is addressing the troops."

Inside the church, Michael Dean watched Joe Kroll as he stood tall on the front podium. Dean scanned the crowd of over one hundred people that showed up for the meeting. It was by invitation only.

Kroll now spoke. "My friends and associates, I've gathered you here tonight to celebrate. 'Celebrate what?' you ask. Celebrate the awakening of the Aryan nation. That's correct, the Aryan nation. I, and I alone, know things that will change everything for our cause. By the middle of next week, I'll be leading you into the first year of Aryanna. Aryanna will be our own nation. It will be seeded with over five thousand acres of land, and we'll expand from there. Before you leave today, you will have to sign a confidentiality agreement and a document that swears your allegiance to me, your new leader."

Michael Dean sat in the back. He gritted his teeth to control his rage.

Dean hated that Kroll was on the podium. He had done all the work, and Kroll took the credit. The plan outlined by the old man was Dean's plan. He should be the leader—Pierce had told him that he was the "savior." Dean smirked to himself as he considered the additional plan that he had put into motion to achieve his goal. He had implemented his plan ten minutes before the meeting. He'd set up Joe Kroll. He recalled the conversation with satisfaction.

"Joe, I just got off the phone with Walter Pierce. There's been a slight change of plans."

"Son of a bitch, did you screw up again?"

"No, Joe. Pierce said that he only has one hundred million to donate to the cause. He didn't want to be misunderstood by the delegates. You know how they might react if the numbers didn't add up."

"What the hell happened to the rest of the money?"

"He didn't say."

Kroll was carefully observing the crowd, letting his opening comments sink in. Next he was going to tell them about the money. *That would get their attention.*

The old man had told Dean that one hundred million of his estate would go to the cause; the other thirty million was to stay with the old man or didn't exist. There were some nonbelievers out there. He might have to remove them. He hoped Teddy was taking notes on the skeptics as he had been instructed.

"We're already strong. There are twelve branches to the church. Aryanna will be a religious country, run by the Altar of the Creator. In addition to the land that I've mentioned, we'll have one hundred million dollars in assets. That is my commitment to you, my gift of loyalty, and my sacrifice to the cause. Can any of you challenge that gift? I've studied the American legal system. We can declare our land to be independent of the United States when we're ready. This will be a new beginning, a whole new life for all of you. You'll have money, status, and everything you want. Especially you'll have the freedom to believe as I know each of you truly believe. We believe in the Aryan cause. Accept this gift. Stand with me." The applause was deafening, and everyone was on their feet.

But Joe Kroll was just warming up.

"When everything is revealed, millions of people will come forward. Our depressed brothers will see the evidence that will guarantee that the Aryan cause will multiply. The Aryan cause will become the cause of all great white people. They'll come in droves, bringing their skills, knowledge, and desire to Aryanna."

Joe Kroll knew he could not divulge the actual place that was to be Aryanna, nor could he reveal that he did not really have the tablet yet. No one knew the details about Pierce except Dean, and Dean was too paranoid to share the information. But Kroll had a plan for getting all the information and getting rid of Dean. It would happen when he got his hands on the estate. However, he knew he had to tell the congregation something about the colossal discovery in order to win them over. He needed to follow the outline of the old man's plan as passed on by Dean. He'd been on the podium for an hour, ranting and raving about all his plans and good fortune. Maybe he might have to stretch the truth a little, but after the tablet was properly documented, he would be forgiven.

"Now let me tell you why the good white people of America will rise against their oppressors and the inferior scum that are taking over our rightful world. It all started in the 1930s. A group of German scientists were helping a country to modernize when they found something, something that would forever change the world.

"They found an original tablet with the history of the Aryan race. It's true. It's all written on the tablet, and I have the tablet. The German scientists found the historical tablet in some ruins of a fortified town in northern India.

"You see, my friends, the Aryan race began a thousand years before the birth of Christ. The Aryans were the first people to build a fort. They settled in the northern part of the Indian peninsula and had to fight to protect their race. They often sent out groups to settle other lands, and they had a network that went all the way into present-day Europe. They were very clever and were the true people to invent gunpowder, which they gave to the hated Chinese to appease them. They invented printing. They called it Sanskrit. They recorded their history on a single tablet. It is this tablet that the Germans found.

"The good people of the Aryan race prospered for many centuries and had vast holdings of land and slaves. They had large farms and many animals that they sold to the 'others' to support their nation. Their women were beautiful and good child bearers, and the men were tall, handsome, and blond.

"Their laws were righteous—marriage only within the nation. They were the masters of their time. They were the perfect society.

"But there was much to fear from the 'others.' There were many savages at that time. The 'others' were stupid and lazy, but they wanted everything that the Aryans had. This caused the downfall of the nation—they were sabotaged. The main settlement was wiped out by a plague that black Indians brought from the south. Many of the outposts survived and had to go underground. I am a direct descendant of the original Aryan race, just as many of you are.

"Yes, my friends, this is the true history of the Aryan race. It tells of the great achievements and success they had and the benefits of protecting the race, just as we will do. This is our bible, our message from God, and our new constitution. It will give all Aryan peoples the strength to come forward and unite under Aryanna."

Everyone was on their feet again. Some stomped their feet; the church rocked.

A buzz filled the air throughout the church. Kroll had one more task before he opened the floor for questions.

"Thank you, everyone. Please settle down. There is much work to do. Our good fortune will not go unnoticed by our enemies. We must prepare to defend the people we love and ourselves. Gary Baum has a plan, along with the charter for each one of your chapters. From this moment on, you and all your members are all under the protection of the Altar of the Creator. Each of you will meet with Gary and provide him with a list of all your members and the resources that you can bring to Aryanna. We need to inventory our assets so that we can develop a battle plan to eliminate our enemies, one at a time.

"Finally all Aryan people must have a tattoo of a swastika on the back or neck. Women are expected to have a tattoo on the breast or in the crotch area. This will enable us to identify friend from foe."

With that, Kroll slipped off his tie and ripped off his shirt. He turned around to expose his fully tattooed back.

The applause, once again, was thunderous.

Joe Kroll was sweating and felt completely spent. Yet he also felt the sweet thrill of victory. He had inspired his audience for two hours. He laid out his plans and asked for commitments. He now opened the floor for questions.

"When can we see the tablet?" was the first question.

"I have it in my possession. We will announce the finding of the tablet and the location of Aryanna on national TV on Monday night. So watch your sets." He grinned.

"Where has it been all these years, and why is it in your possession now?"

Kroll made a mental note to get rid of the man who asked the question. "The tablet has been hidden and protected by one of us. The time to reveal it is now."

"What will we do after we sign up new members?" was the question posed by a second man.

"First, consolidate our holdings. Then we'll build a huge church on Aryanna. The church will be the center of our government until we can declare our independence. It's all in the plans."

The questions continued until well after 3:00 a.m.

Chapter Twenty-Five

Detective Heinz and Agent Chen now left the Banyon interview and went to talk to Seith Paul. He was seated on a chair in the other interview room. He was fuming. "I have my rights. You can't hold me. I need a lawyer. No one's read me my Miranda rights."

Detective Heinz let him rant. "So far you're only a material witness. Are you demanding that we book you for some crimes?"

"You either book me or let me go," an angry Paul shot back.

"You can have it your way, but before we book you, I should tell you that we have the entire Woods gang in the cells down the hall. They've produced evidence that says you are part of a big conspiracy. From initial analysis, I think that you're looking at a very long jail time."

Paul quieted down. He shifted in his chair.

"I want a DA in here," he demanded.

"Why would you want that, Mr. Paul?" Chen asked. She slid a paper and pen over to Paul.

"I want to make a deal. I'll need protection. I want the witness protection program and a new car, and I want to be moved to Florida. I want food too," he demanded.

"Write everything down that you want to say—don't leave out anything, as we have a lot of evidence already. I'll call the DA and get you a piece of pizza," Heinz offered.

"Can I have ribs?"

Agent Gamble was watching from the room next to the interview room. When Heinz came in, he said, "This whole thing is busting wide open. I bet you can get the Woods woman to roll over on Paul."

"Yeah, you're right, but I can't help thinking that Ula Woods is more of a victim here than a mobster. This guy Paul, though, is sleazy and would sell out anyone to save his own skin. I would not trust him to do the right thing. I'll bet he blames Dean and the Woods woman for everything and says he couldn't say anything because he's their lawyer and was constrained by lawyer-client privilege. Everything else will be just a coincidence."

Gamble glanced through the one-way mirror and said, "Look at him—he's regaining his confidence. He just pushed his card over to Agent Chen. I can just imagine what he's telling her. Let's listen in." With that, he pushed a button on the wall.

Paul was speaking to Agent Chen. "That's right. I think you have a case. They're treating you like a second-class citizen; I know because I'm a minority like you. Look, they leave you in here to watch me while they make all the decisions. You won't even get credit for the collar of the gang. I can help you. Just tell me what they have on me. I'll make sure you get a big settlement."

Gamble was starting to get nervous.

"Just wait," Heinz said. "I've learned to trust Chen. And besides, would you have Paul as your lawyer?"

When Paul looked down to write some more, Chen put up one finger for the men behind the mirror to see and then pounced.

Suddenly she produced a recorder. "Well, Mr. Paul, we're now adding charges of attempted bribery and a second count of attempted conspiracy to your jacket. I don't think these charges will have any impact on the Woods case; they're separate. I'd say that you're going to be in court for a long time and in jail even longer. Hope you don't have any enemies in the state pen." She ordered him to rip up that garbage that he was writing and start over with the truth. "I'm a very vindictive woman and might come across the table and cut off your balls with my ancient ball-cutting knife. I'll just say that you attacked me. Who would believe you?" She started up the recorder once again.

Paul was suddenly sweating. He threw the pen down. "I have it all on tape—names, dates, and people involved. Is that worth something?"

The interview with Seith Paul had proven to be another gold mine. The records found in his car and office filled in several blanks the Woods's records had left unclear. Detective Heinz did not make a plea bargain deal with Paul, other than to ignore the potential charges that he'd picked up in the station. Meanwhile, the FBI agents were interviewing the Woods gang.

Agent Gamble left for New York to visit with Walter Pierce. He also assembled half a dozen New York agents to visit the place that Banyon outlined with a map. There was little more to do until the voice tapes from Kroll's meeting came in. They were not expected for several hours. Heinz directed his attention to Agent Chen.

"Want to get something to eat? You've been going all day without a break."

She looked at him with true admiration. He seemed to trust her judgment and actually did want to be around her. "I want to hear your siren again."

Chapter Twenty-Six

Colt was once again lying in bed in the Patel basement. He had showered and shaved. He was so perplexed by these twins. They seemed to move in unison, and yet they were worlds apart in personality. One was an intelligent, graceful companion, and the other an unsuppressed adventurer. Colt admired both. *The spell they cast over me is overwhelming*, he thought. *I'm powerless to defend myself around them.*

He was also troubled by the fact that he might be cheating on his girlfriend. While Colt rarely felt guilty about anything in his life, he wondered if age had affected his ability to feel guilty. On the other hand, he was very aroused now and actually felt kind of proud that he still could have these feelings.

The door opened. Despite the darkness, he could see that she had on a nightdress. He pretended to be asleep.

She walked over to the bed and stood before him.

"Hi," he said.

"No talking," was the reply. "Just lie there and be quiet." Her voice was hoarse with lust. "Don't move; I want to enjoy you. Just let it happen. Colt, let me take my time."

"I'm all yours, Pramilla."

"I'm the wild one," was the reply.

Oh my God, thought Colt. This is Previne. I'm in trouble now. What am I going to do? "Previne, what's your husband going to think?"

"We've been telling you a lie; I'm sorry. Keri, June, and May are my brother and sisters."

"You mean that you're all one family? I don't know if I'm pleased or more upset. Why play these games with me?"

"Sometimes I'm Previne, and sometimes I'm Pramilla. It depends on the circumstance. We've used this deception to fool people in India, and we kept it up here in America.

"Why did you wait so long to tell me this?"

"When Pramilla first met you, she was very attracted to you. I did not want to interfere. But I've grown attracted to you as well. We have decided to drop our charade. Do you hate me now?"

"I don't know what to think. So neither of you is married; is that at least correct?"

"Neither of us is married—that is correct."

"And are you Previne, or are you Pramilla?"

"I'm really Previne; I won the coin flip."

"What coin flip?" asked Colt.

"To see which one of us would go first. Pramilla lost but will be along shortly."

That night Colt was able to cross off number 3 on the list of things he wanted to do before he left this earth. The feeling of guilt had melted away.

Chapter Twenty-Seven

Chen lit a cigarette. She and Heinz were standing on the patio of his apartment. Heinz had a big stogie that he had saved for a celebration. For the first time in his life, he felt that he knew where he was headed and who would be going there with him. He had to admit that sometimes she was a little scary, with the hidden-items trick and the lightning speed with which she did everything. His main problem was trying to keep her slowed down enough for the rest of the world to catch up.

"Have you considered my offer?" he asked her through a cloud of smoke.

"Which one was that?"

"I want you to come here and work with me—that offer."

There was an unexpected pause. "I don't know. I'm not very good at my job, and I'm not very experienced, and you know people only want me around because I'm pretty and …"

Heinz knew enough about the Chinese culture to know that she was begging him to ask her to work with him. The Chinese, especially their women, had a habit of acting modest to a fault when under pressure. While inwardly confident, they often would point out their faults, rather than say they wanted something, especially something personal. So he rephrased.

"Too late. I've already asked your boss to cut you free to work in Streamwood. He said he was proud to let you go." Heinz had not actually called the man yet, but he would.

"That son of a bitch couldn't wait to get rid of me. I'll take you up on your offer, at least until something better comes along."

"Keep talking like that, and I'll pull your hair."

So it was settled: she would come to work in Streamwood and become his partner, friend, and maybe more.

Chapter Twenty-Eight

Michael Dean arrived home at almost 4:00 a.m. He immediately noticed that the Woods house was dark. He got himself his tenth beer of the night and sat down in the living room. His insatiable greed had started him on a course of confrontation with Joe Kroll. It was time to implement the next stage.

Dean speed-dialed his phone to call Teddy and was waiting for the phone to ring when he noticed his message light was blinking. *I'll get that later*, he thought.

"Teddy, it's Mike."

"What's up? It's late, you know." Teddy was slurring his words.

"I thought everything went great tonight, didn't you? I've got one question for you, though. Remember when we had our private meeting with Joe? I told him there was one hundred and thirty million in the kitty. During the speech tonight, he said there was only a hundred million."

"Yeah, man, you did. Kind of funny, don't you think?" Teddy was more alert now.

"Kroll's insane, you know. He's consumed with being the 'king' of Aryanna." Dean now had Teddy's full attention.

"He had the other leaders virtually sign over their club memberships and incomes. The Altar of the Creator is now one of the largest private churches in the country. He must want the thirty million for himself," a vengeful Teddy said.

"Meet me tomorrow around noon, and let's make some plans for dealing with Mr. Kroll."

"I'll see you at your house—you bring the beer."

Checking his messages, Dean was enraged to find out that Ula had left town, especially when he was tense and needed her to release his frustration.

Chapter Twenty-Nine

Early the next morning, FBI Agent Greg Gamble and two additional New York agents were on their way to Westhampton, specifically to Tanners Neck Lane. The two New York agents picked Gamble up at MacArthur Airport late on Saturday night and drove out to Riverhead, where they stayed in the local Holiday Inn along with six other agents. At breakfast, he briefed the half-dozen field agents on their mission. Gamble spent more than a half hour explaining the assignment to the six agents. Several men on the digging detail thought this was all great fun.

On his lap in the car was a map of the area, as well as directions to the Pierce home. The map depicted just how small the island was. In some places it was only eight miles from the north to the south shore. A narrow slip of land ran along the south coast. Only a mile or so separated it from the mainland. He knew the sandbar was a couple of hundred yards wide, running from Brooklyn almost to the end of Long Island. It was referred to as Jones Beach near the city Fire Island in the middle, and Dune Road from Mastic on out to Southampton. A total of over one hundred miles of great sandy beaches lined the route. Land prices were astronomical. At one time it had been a continuous island, but weather and man interfered to make openings into the huge bays for boats.

Gamble studied the map as Agent Booth filled Gamble in on the geography. "Is the area what you expected?"

"Actually," said Gamble, "it's not at all as I expected."

Agent Booth chuckled. "Wait a few more minutes, and you will see what the Hamptons are all about. The interior of the island is pretty bland, but the ocean area is something else. Let me give you a few facts. The Gulf Stream comes very close to the shore along this part of Long Island, giving it a moderate climate. Not too hot in the summer and warmer in the winter than in the city. They don't get much snow here. When it does snow, it doesn't stay long. While it doesn't get very cold, it does get pretty raw and windy. Beaches and water are everywhere, and that attracts celebrities, wealthy New Yorkers, and people who want to get away from the concrete jungle for a few days. Many locals rent their houses out for the summer—for big money, I might add. On weekends some houses have twenty or more people staying there. In the summer, the population here can quadruple; yet in the fall and winter, these are sleepy little towns. On places like Dune Road, a plot of land could go for a million dollars or more. Maybe we'll have time to go down to the beach. Many of the houses are one-of-a-kind designs, and some are built on stilts to protect them from bad weather. The whole island was formed by a glacier."

Gamble interrupted him. "I know about the glacier thing. How far to the Pierce house? I'm getting sick of hearing how cool the Hamptons are. After all, I live in the flat, dry, cold Midwest."

Chapter Thirty

The alarm had awakened Banyon. He opened his eyes and realized he was sandwiched between two darker-skinned women. Both were facing him with one of their arms draped over his chest. They were also stirring. Warm brown eyes were looking at him from both sides. "Good morning, ladies," he greeted them.

"I don't want to get up yet," said Previne.

"I don't either, but I have to meet Agent Chen at the police station in less than an hour."

"We're going with you," Pramilla said.

"Well, at least one of you is because someone needs to drive me. Now one of you will have to move, or I'll have to use my secret weapon."

"I love when you talk dirty," Previne said.

"He means that he will tickle you, the vicious bastard," Pramilla laughed.

With that, they all bounced out of bed. The twins started to stretch, and Colt forgot to go to the shower. They were so graceful and athletic.

"Why don't you join us?" Previne said through pouty lips.

"I'm afraid that I'd only get stiffer and be late for my meeting," he joked.

Both girls stopped. They were twin bookends, naked and beautiful. They started toward him.

"Oh no," he said. "I couldn't, really, I couldn't."

He ran into the bathroom and locked the door.

Chapter Thirty-One

The agents reached the end of Tanners Neck Lane, and Gamble marveled at the view. The bay in front of him was wide and sparkling blue. Several sailboats with their colorful sails ran along the far side of the bay. The air was rich with the smell of the sea—a perfect place to live. They walked up to the compound and pressed the bell. After a short wait, a tinny voice inquired, "Who is it?"

"Mr. Pierce, please."

"Who are you?"

"I'm Agent Greg Gamble of the FBI. May we speak with you?" Gamble was attempting to sound nonthreatening.

"Very well. Please walk up and leave your car where it is."

As they strolled up the long driveway, they noticed the front door open. An old man stood in the shade of the small porch. He was dressed in a white shirt and tie, but no jacket. "My name is Walter Pierce. Please come in."

They entered the house and were directed to the back patio. The agents assumed seats under the big umbrella. The sun was so bright that Gamble kept on his sunglasses, and no one seemed to mind. The old man did not offer them anything.

"Mr. Pierce, you sure have a nice house here. Do you live by yourself?"

"Well, my boy, I have a housekeeper, but she's away on a cruise, so for this week I am on my own. I would offer you coffee, but I don't know how to make it."

"That's okay. We'll try to not take up too much of your time, Mr. Pierce."

"You may call me Walter."

"Walter, how long have you lived in the area?"

"I was born in this part of the country, and I have lived here all my life. I built this house several years ago."

"The only information that we have been able to gather about you starts in 1942. We would like to fill in some blanks about your background."

"Why are you here?"

"Your name came up in a routine investigation. We need to fill in a lot of blanks. Can you help us?"

"Actually, I have nothing to hide," replied Pierce. "If you will allow me a minute to collect some papers, I can fill you in. One of your men can go with me if you like." Gamble nodded, and Agent Booth followed Pierce into the house.

His credentials were complete. He had his original U.S. passport and papers that had been signed in 1936 in France that legally changed his name to Walter Pierce. Thanks to Wilhelm Canaris, he had actual bona fides. He gathered the information and returned to the patio.

"I left the USA for a period of time when I was a teenager and spent time in Europe. While there, I had my name legally changed. When the war in Europe interrupted my stay, I moved to England and eventually returned to the USA in 1941."

He handed the passports over to Gamble, along with the papers that legally changed his name. Canaris was really clever and had forged the stamps of France and England as well as the USA on the passports, with the dates that Walter gave the agents.

"At the time, it seemed appropriate to change my name," Pierce added as Gamble accepted the documents. Pierce watched Gamble study the papers.

Pierce realized the FBI had connected him with Banyon. He needed to stall their investigation for just a little while. He thought telling the truth was the best route to that.

"Do you know a Colton Banyon?" The question did not catch Pierce off balance.

"I know of him; I've never met the man," Pierce replied coolly.

"Can you explain that?"

"He was born in the area," he replied. "We're a small community here, especially in the winter. His family had dinner in my restaurants, and I believe that Mr. Banyon used to work at the restaurant I owned right here on this very spot."

"All right, fair enough," Gamble noted. "But can you tell us why you're having people meet with Mr. Banyon this morning in Chicago?"

"Of course. There are two reasons for the meeting. One is to get a copy of Banyon's view on the future of retailing, and the other is to see if he can identify a picture of someone I believe he knows."

"And why are these important?" Gamble asked.

"On Tuesday Mr. Banyon is interviewing for a position in one of my companies, although he doesn't know it yet. I wanted to get his viewpoint before the interview, so I would be able to ask pertinent questions. The recruiter I hired to find a new president for my company presented me with several candidates. Banyon was one of them."

"Actually, I do know that he's planning to be in Manhattan for an interview on Tuesday." Clearly, Gamble was fishing.

"At the Hilton," Pierce filled in.

"That doesn't explain why you want him to look at the picture."

"That is even less complex. I found that picture maybe six years ago when I was cleaning out some materials from my old restaurant. I found several pictures, and as amusement I've returned them all to my former employees. They all sent me letters and current pictures of their families. It gives me great pleasure to discover how my old employees are doing. This one picture could not be identified. No one named Lorenzo was in any yearbooks or local school materials. I can show you the materials if you want."

"How is it that you came to hire Joe Kroll?"

"Who?"

"Joe Kroll, the man you hired to find Colton Banyon."

"Never heard of him."

"Then whom did you hire?"

"I hope that I'm not in trouble. There was a fingerprint on the picture. I didn't know it was Banyon's. I thought it was Lorenzo's. I placed many ads in magazines to see if someone could identify the print. You know, mercenary magazines—they all promise their readers to find people. Anyway, Michael Dean—that's his name—Michael Dean answered the ad and told me that he could find the person whose fingerprint was on the picture. Since I didn't hear from him, I figured he'd just taken my money. Then he suddenly called after a year and said he knew to whom the print belonged. It belonged to Colton Banyon. It's been another year since then. Dean did not make contact with Banyon, so I contacted Banyon myself and set up the meeting. You know, kill two birds with one stone. Have I done something wrong?"

"How well do you know Michael Dean?"

"Just by talking to him on the phone—is this about him?"

"All right, just one more question. Do you know where the picture was taken?"

"Yes, as a matter of fact, I do. It was taken on my land near the high point."

Gamble reserved the most important question for the end of the interview. "Do you know why that marker is in the background of the picture?"

"No, not really. Maybe it's the marker for Captain Kidd's treasure."

Chapter Thirty-Two

Teddy parked in the Dean driveway at 10:00 a.m. and entered the house through the back door. Dean was seated at the small table in the kitchen and didn't even look up.

"Michael, we have to talk," Teddy started. "I've been thinking about what you said last night, and I think that we're being set up. We can't trust Kroll."

"You're telling me? Remember, I was in the military with him. I'll bet that he has some plan to get rid of all of us. It'll probably happen in the woods. We need to make certain we have some guns when we get to Long Island."

"How are we going to do that? If we have guns, Joe will see them."

"Teddy, you forget that I lived in New Jersey for a while before I left the army. I made a few friends there—I'm going to call them."

Chapter Thirty-Three

Officer Lopez was one of the two policemen sent to watch Dean's house. He was just having coffee around 10:00 a.m. when he noticed Teddy's car entering the driveway. He immediately contacted Detective Heinz, who was on the stakeout at the Marriott.

"Chief, this is Officer Lopez. We're at the stakeout at the Dean house, and there appears to be someone home. A visitor just arrived."

"Dean's in his house?"

"He must have slipped in late last night, sir."

"When did you leave last night?"

"Sir, we were here until 3:00 a.m., and no one came by. We returned around 8:00 a.m. I thought you told us that Dean was away in Wisconsin."

"I told you to stake out the house until relieved. Maybe that wasn't clear enough."

Lopez paused. "Do you have any instructions? He's one of us."

"Lopez, listen to me carefully and do what I tell you. If you have any questions, you should ask them right away, not when it is convenient. Got it?"

"Yes, sir."

"Michael Dean's been implicated in several crimes and is now considered very dangerous. I need to know his movements and what he's up to. Can one of you get close enough to hear what he's saying? Make sure you identify the visitor."

"I think we'll call the station and get a mike out here. The FBI must have someone there to man it. The station's only five minutes away."

"Do it, and don't call me back. I'm undercover right now. Use your judgment, and I'll call you when I'm done."

"Okay, Chief."

Lopez hung up the phone before Heinz could tell him to not call him "Chief."

Chapter Thirty-Four

Banyon and Chen were going to drive to the rendezvous to meet Judy Kroll. The twins dropped Colt at the station door. After parking, they went inside to check out Agent Chen's outfit. She was dressed in a severe business suit in pink with a not-too-short skirt. Her hair was all rolled up into a bun, and she wore glasses. The twins approved but did comment to Banyon that pink was not Chen's color. They watched with great concern as Chen attached a mike to Banyon's chest, ready to take over if she showed any attempt to fondle their toy. When the procedure was complete, they were all smiles and decided to go out for breakfast. Heinz was already headed for the hotel. Chen was driving, and Colt couldn't help but notice her shapely legs as she hiked up her skirt to allow for better leg movement.

"Loni, you look very nice today."

"I'm seeing someone," she replied tersely.

"I know that; you and Carl make a great couple. Maybe when this is over, we can be friends."

"Why would you want to be friends with me?" She seemed stunned by the remark.

"You can never have enough friends. My gut tells me that you're a very honorable person and clearly intelligent. Why wouldn't I want to be friends with you? Don't worry, I'm not after your body, and besides, you are too young for me. I just thought you might like to have a friend who didn't have any demands on you other than to know you. I do have experience with Chinese women, you know."

"I'm not Chinese. I'm a second-generation American, born in Hawaii of Chinese parents," she said proudly.

"Forgive me for this, Loni. I'm trying to be your friend, but you have a huge chip on your shoulder. I used to have one. Finally I decided that it was better to treat people at face value and accept what happens. If someone betrays me, I see it as their loss, not mine."

"It's different for you. You're older and have done many things. I haven't accomplished anything."

"Why would you say that? You are very bright, attractive, clearly in good shape, and you are an agent with the state police. I think that these are wonderful accomplishments."

"Do you flirt with all women?"

"Actually, I like to make people feel comfortable around me. If flirting does that, I'm happy to oblige. Like I said, I have no expectations. My life has been full for a long time, ever since I realized that the only one to control my life should be me. I've spent a lifetime trying to understand motivations in people, and my instincts are very good. You would be a good friend if you could get past the lumber on your shoulder."

"Do you always make so much sense?"

"Only to my friends."

She said nothing for a long time, then blurted out, "I have this problem of always jumping into a task to beat everyone else. It's inbred." She was opening up a bit now.

"You're a compulsive person. I'm one myself," Colt said. "We have to learn to channel our compulsions to achieve longer-term goals. Being compulsive probably has to do with your background. Want to talk about it?"

"Are you going to psychoanalyze me?"

"Maybe that's why you are so reckless—to prove that you're as good as a man."

They reached the hotel. On the way in, Agent Chen put out her small arm to halt Colt just outside the building.

"Okay, I'm going to be your friend. But let me warn you, I'm very high maintenance," she said with a smile.

Colt replied, "What real woman isn't?"

Chapter Thirty-Five

Pierce's doorbell rang for the second time in less than an hour. The voice at the gate told Walter his car had arrived. The driver was instructed to drive up to the house. Pierce was on his way. He was going to his lawyer's office. He had enjoyed the FBI agents who left his house ten minutes ago. They were so polite and correct. *It must take a special person to do that work.* The voices had warned Pierce that the FBI was on the way. The FBI took the letters that he had written to his former employees and believed Pierce's story about Dean. Pierce thought that it was too easy to stay one step ahead of everyone.

Walter Pierce was in his lawyer's office. Trent Rogers had been Pierce's personal lawyer for over forty years.

"Walter, you look tired. Are you getting enough sleep?"

"Too much sex—you know how it goes." Pierce was being cagey.

"You're changing everything—wills, giving things away, and being more generous than you have ever been. Either you've suddenly found religion, or some bug has found you."

"Trent, I'm not dead yet, just taking some precautions. I have a few surprises for you too."

"Okay, we're set up in the conference room, just as you requested. Just you, me, and the tape recorder. Shall we reconvene there?"

They walked down the hall to the conference room. It was comfortable and well-appointed. Laid out on the table were all the papers that Rogers had prepared for Pierce to sign. He did this without reading the details. What would be the point? Rogers had been his close associate for many years and would not attempt to fool Pierce. There was honor at stake.

Finished with the legal papers, Pierce prepared himself, taking out some notes and papers from his briefcase and lining up all his medals in front of him. He handed the surprised Rogers a recorded tape. "I recorded my life up to 1930 last night. Please make sure that it is included." Rogers nodded yes.

Pierce then indicated for Rogers to start the recording.

PART FOUR
Walter Pierce

Chapter Thirty-Six

"My name is Walter Pierce, longtime resident of Westhampton, New York, and this is my story.

"For more than sixty years, I have been living a lie. Walter Pierce is an assumed name that was given to me by the Abwehr in 1936. I am and have been a spy for a former German government. I am, however, an American citizen. My real name is Wolfgang Becker II.

"Mother and I arrived in Berlin in the early fall of 1930. Leaves were still on the trees, and the weather was warm. I could understand why Mother missed the city. Everything was very clean, and people were dressed in suits and dresses. The music was dark. There was an undercurrent of excitement and intrigue buzzing about the coffee and teahouses. Political posters were tacked on every tree.

"We settled in my grandfather's home, an estate really. I met Grandfather Franz for the first time. He was a gracious man, who was seventy-something years old with muttonchops on his face, a monocle in his eye, and a watch on a chain in his pocket. He walked and talked like royalty and truly believed that his will was stronger than anyone's. He always was fully dressed in a uniform, and his left side always seemed to be closer to the ground from all the medals that he wore there.

"Grandfather was a true Prussian general. He was a neighbor of the great Otto von Bismarck, the first chancellor of United Germany. Grandfather was educated in the ways of the military. He saw his first action in the siege of Paris during the Franco-Prussian War in 1871. He was a distant relative of William II, who became emperor of United Germany in 1888. As a result, he became a leading general in the very active German military machine. After World War I, he retired; and in 1920, he bought a small company that made pistols and other guns. The gun was only marginally usable, so Grandfather decided to go into the ammunitions business.

"Grandmother had died soon after my mother was born from a disorder that could not be treated. We never knew what it was. Since Grandfather was almost always away at war, a nanny—who fanatically believed in discipline and tradition—was placed in charge of raising Mother. Grandfather had wanted Mother to eventually run his company, and now she was going to have her chance.

"My first six months in Germany were spent with Grandfather. He was a man of honor and someone to be respected. He told me tales of war, political intrigue, and the power of a good leader. He drummed into me the reasons for sacrifice and protecting those weaker than me. He explained the personal satisfaction that he received from each medal on his chest. I had originally wanted to return to America but realized that the time spent with Grandfather would be short and could not be refused.

"Some days we would walk out by the pond on his estate, and he would tell me all about the good things in Germany. He told me that Germany had the best scientists, the finest art and culture, and the German compulsion to organize everything. He also described the paranoiac nature of the current politics and told me about Communism and how it was affecting Germany. He feared a hysterical backlash and a move to ultraconservatism; while this was good for his business, it was not an honorable way to make money.

"Eventually we came to talk about my father. The Becker and the Franz families were friends for many years, going back to feudal days. My father, Wolfgang, had served in the military under Grandfather. He'd been a captain but lost his nerve on the battlefield. It had happened before to soldiers, and usually the soldiers were court-martialed and shot. But Grandfather interceded, and Wolfgang was sent home in disgrace. His family wanted nothing to do with him. They did the logical thing and sent him to America with some money and forgot about him. Grandfather was the only one who corresponded with him, as he understood his shame. When Mother had grown and started to display radical behavior, Grandfather was unsure of what to do. Father, who wrote that he was in need of a wife, solved his problem. Grandfather ordered Mother to go to America to see if it truly were the land of opportunity. Such were the ways of Prussians and the reason that I was there."

Pierce continued his story. "Mother was happy in Germany. She was the life of every party and was always off to lectures and demonstrations. She told me that it was good for business. She suggested that I should go with her to represent the family and do deals with the men that she was not able to reach. At that time, Germany was still a man's world. My grandfather warned me not to go, as most of what was discussed at the parties was poison. Nevertheless, I attended some of the parties.

"It was at one of these parties that I met the husband of one of my mother's friends. His name was Wilhelm Canaris. Canaris changed my life. He became my mentor and set me on the path that has brought me here today.

"The first thing I noticed about Wilhelm was that he had as many medals as Grandfather. He noticed me looking at the medals. 'I know your grandfather; he and I have traveled in the same circles,' Wilhelm told me. I was surprised that he knew Grandfather and that he knew my name. As time went by, I came to understand that he seemed to be well-informed about everything that was going on in Germany. He was in his midforties then and already an admiral. We took up a discussion about his career, and he told me that he'd been a fairly successful captain on submarines during World War I. Actually, he had been a hero of the war, but Wilhelm was always modest and never wanted to be the center of attention.

"I enjoyed talking to him, as he had many life experiences. He asked me many questions about America. He read a good deal, he told me. He did not really mix with many of the fanatics that Mother clung to and preferred to stand in a corner and observe. He seemed to learn from just watching, and I was drawn to him like he was the Pied Piper.

"After a few hours, he said that he would like to talk to me further and gave me his card. 'Come by the office on Monday, Wolf,' he said. From then on, he called me Wolf, and I called him Admiral.

"For the first time since coming to Germany, I was interested in something besides my family. Bright and early on Monday, I went to downtown Berlin, to the admiral's office. It was in some nondescript brick building, and there were guards at the door. The admiral had left a pass for me, and I found myself walking through halls that echoed with my steps. I entered an office and was greeted by Greta. Greta was the secretary that all executives dream about. She was in her midtwenties, slim, with a pretty face, and wore a dress that accented her figure. Her deep-throated voice was cheery. I was so captivated that I missed the inside door opening and the admiral standing there. He cleared his throat, and I was jerked from my fantasy. He waved me in. I wondered how he knew that I was there, but that was the admiral.

"His office was typical German. There was nothing out of place. A huge safe was in the corner. Before sitting down at his desk, he motioned me to a chair. He was a short somewhat frail man. I was about six foot one and 180 pounds at the time and would have appeared to be a giant next to him. We exchanged pleasantries about the party, and I noticed for the first time that he had the most intense eyes that I'd ever seen. They took in everything.

"'How would you like a job?' he asked.

"I had never worked in my life and wasn't sure how to answer. 'Doing what?'

"'You would be a personal assistant to me,' he replied. 'I have need of an English translator and someone who could advise me of American things. Also, I need someone who is willing to travel with me throughout the Mediterranean region and write down observations of what we see. You would travel with me. We have extensive influence in that part of the world, and you would learn much from the travel.'

"'How much would it pay?'

"'You will get the grade pay of a lieutenant; that's not much pay. But then, there are few expenses on the job and lots of perks.'

"I knew that I did not really need the money. Grandfather had arranged a generous monthly allowance for me. I asked him how soon I could start.

"'Greta has the papers and will be taking you to lunch to explain your duties. Please report to this building tomorrow.'

"After signing all of the papers, I had lunch with the intriguing Greta and was home by midafternoon. Mother stopped me in the hallway and announced that she wanted me to take a more active role in the business. She said I was a just a playboy and would never amount to anything. When I told her that I was now working for Admiral Canaris, she became very quiet. Then a broad smile replaced her frown. I asked her why she was smiling, and she said Canaris had just joined her favorite political party, the Social Democrats.

"I knew little of German politics, but I did know that Social Democrat was another name for the Nazi Party. What I did not know at the time was that Grandfather and the admiral were close friends, and both wanted me away from the politics that my mother adored. They had cooked up my position to keep an eye on me.

"My secretary was an older woman that took no guff from anybody like me. Her name was Hilda, and she ordered me around and told me what had to be done from the time I entered my office until I left. Most of the time, I translated English documents to German.

"After a couple of months, I got a message to go to the admiral's office. He greeted me warmly and inquired about my work. I was sure that Hilda was reporting to him regularly, but I proceeded to tell him how interesting my work was and how it helped Germany. Satisfied with my answer, he said, 'How would you like to take a little trip to Italy?'

"'Of course, if you require me.' My heart was racing with excitement!

"'Good, meet me here tomorrow. Plan to be gone about a month.'

"'Why are we going there?'

"'The Italian trip has three objectives. First, to check out a dictator named Mussolini, who is becoming somewhat powerful in the Mediterranean. Second, we will take a warm weather holiday in Sicily, and, third, to talk.'

"Mussolini was a seemingly friendly person, who ran his country with an iron fist. He made some forays into other countries with mixed results. The admiral desired to know if the Italians were interested in an alliance. Germany would provide arms and expertise, and Italy would provide soldiers. After a week, we were off to the south of Italy. The impressive mountains overlooked ancient coves where the water was a deep blue. The small towns along the coast were picture-perfect. The admiral had a large sailboat waiting, and in less than a day, he and I were on the water. We sailed all over the Mediterranean for three weeks; we never shaved, and we dressed in shorts.

"During this time, the admiral and I talked extensively. He explained that Germany was moving toward a military state and Hitler would eventually be the ruler. He said he was very concerned about the true objectives of the Nazi party. He further explained that he was a patriot first, and if his country were to go to war, he would fight, but he had grave reservations about the probable German leadership.

"The admiral said that bullets were the visible part of the war, but the knowledge that one had about the enemy was the way to win a war. I never forgot that.

"In the fall, I was once again summoned to the admiral's office and told that we would be leaving immediately for Morocco. I'd never been to North Africa and was unprepared for the desert. It was so hot and dry that I felt the indigenous people living there must have had no other alternative to survive.

"We met with a Spanish general named Franco. He headed an insurrection and was the dictator of the small colony of Spain. He had bigger plans—the control of Spain. Our job was to learn of his abilities and to offer him aid. Both Italy and Germany aimed to dispose of the current Spanish Republic. The meeting went well. The admiral told me that when the day of the revolution came, we would be there to see how the new German weapons performed during battle. It was, so to speak, a test of our military superiority.

"From 1931 through 1934, we traveled all over the European continent, visiting with leaders and opposition forces, depending on whether they were an ally or an enemy. Hitler had taken complete control of the German government and declared himself the Fuehrer of Germany. The German war machine was in full swing. Grandfather's company had plenty of business, and Mother was very active in the Nazi party. The pace in Germany was electric. People went back to work, and many government projects were being implemented. The admiral and I had time to go sailing during all of our visits, and he continued to tell me that there were big concerns on his mind. As always, I listened.

"On New Year's Day in the year 1935, Canaris was named head of the Abwehr. He was now head of the entire military intelligence network for

Germany. He was the head 'spy.' In his new duties, the admiral was also in charge of counterespionage and inherited agents in many places. The work was so interesting that I asked him to admit me to the spy school he had just opened. He agreed, and off I went for almost a year. It truly hardened me and made me see up close the horrors of things a spy could do.

"While I was in spy school, Hitler got a new law passed. It was called the Nuremberg laws, and they deprived Jews of citizenship. It did not take much imagination to understand what was really going on in Germany.

"The Olympics were held in Berlin in 1936, and the admiral sent me a ticket for several of the competitions. He said he needed to talk to me. I noticed at once that he had changed. He seemed to be listening to someone over his shoulder, but I dismissed it as paranoia. During the events there was much noise, and he whispered into my ear. He said he was very upset by the new policies of the Fuehrer and wondered if I might be interested in learning more. The admiral was my mentor and had always given me good advice and counsel. I, of course, said yes.

"A month later I graduated from the Abwehr spy school and was reassigned to the admiral. We left almost immediately for Spain and the civil war. Franco was happy to see the admiral, and it was clear they were friends. We spent our time following the front and watching the German equipment chew up the Republican forces. During this time, I learned that many Americans were fighting on the side of the Republicans. One group was called the Lincoln Brigade and had many notable American members. The admiral asked me if I could infiltrate the group and gather some of their plans. He gave me a new passport in the name of Walter Pierce and told me that it was a perfect cover.

"I had learned that a simple plan was the best plan and walked into the camp as if I had just come off the lines. What I heard was very upsetting. The Americans hated Fascists, and Germany was a Fascist country. To a man, they thought there would be war in Europe, and the United States would be drawn into the conflict. They would come with guns blazing.

"Back from my first great spy adventure, I reported what I had learned to the admiral. He seemed to already be aware of the information. The admiral said that it was just a test; he already knew everything that I had gathered.

"On the next sail trip, he wanted to talk seriously.

"'Wolf, you need to understand that Hitler and his cronies will destroy Germany. The main objective for Germany should be to gain territories that have resources like oil. But I have to tell you that the Fuehrer is consumed with developing a master race and building an empire. If things do not change, I feel that some of us will have to take steps to eliminate him. I know what I say is treason, but I will fight for my country and try to counterbalance the Nazi programs. I need to know that you are on the side of an honorable Germany.'

"'I have many mixed emotions, Admiral. I'm both German and American and do believe in honor. Germany is strong and mighty, so we will win the concessions that we seek.'

"'Wolf, that is only a subplot; Hitler wants to exterminate all Jews. Next it will be blacks, Catholics, and any group that he decides is not fit to live in the new Germany. It can never stop; can't you see that? Wolf, I have set up an organization to fight the Nazi regime. Will you be part of it with me?' I did not have an answer.

"We returned to Germany to find that Grandfather was gravely ill. Mother had no time for him, as she was collecting orders and going to meetings and parties. She had taken up with a Gestapo major, and he goose-stepped around the house as if it was his. Grandfather died in January 1937, and my life was very empty. Then his lawyer contacted me and informed me that I had inherited all of his money. He said in the will that he had earned it honorably, and it should be mine. The sum was almost eight hundred thousand dollars and was on deposit in a Swiss bank. Mother didn't really care, as she got the company and the house. Her new friend immediately told me that I had to move out, as there were party meetings to be held at the estate and I was not a party member.

"Two days later, after I found a new apartment, I walked into the admiral's office and told his secretary, Greta, that I wanted to see him.

"'He's been waiting for you,' she said airily. She showed me in.

"'Admiral, I want to be part of the organization that we discussed.'

"'Your grandfather would be proud,' was all he said. 'Meet me for dinner tonight at my villa. Be there at eight o'clock.'

"That night, when I rang the doorbell, Greta answered. Inside I found Hans Oster, the number two man in the Abwehr and two other people, one of them a priest. The admiral explained that he had set up two sides in his organization. One side did legitimate counterespionage work, and the other side worked against the atrocities of the Nazis. The people in the room were the leaders of the second group. I now was part of a treasonous organization."

Suddenly Rogers reached over and turned off the recorder. "Walter, you never told me any of this, why?"

"I saw no need as it was all in the past. I didn't even meet you until the early sixties. We all have things to hide."

"As your lawyer, I'm telling you that you could be accused as being a war criminal."

"Trent, there is much more to come. So let me get it out, will you?"

After a brief pause, Pierce continued. "The admiral and I left for Spain in mid-1938. The Nazis were planning to use Spain for a base to attack the British at Gibraltar. We had the dual task of talking Franco into letting Germany use his country for a base and talking him out of it, but that was the admiral. In the end, the admiral convinced his friend to be neutral. Franco did manage to keep Spain out of the conflict and all of World War II.

"Next we traveled to Czechoslovakia to help refuges flee from the German invasion of 1938. The admiral had people and resources everywhere, and we managed to save numerous lives. During this trip he told me he was not sleeping well and felt possessed. He told me that he had been hearing strange singsong voices in his head. They told him things and alerted him of current events. Each morning he would know how to handle any situation that developed.

"We visited Poland in 1939. Hitler had already invaded and had wiped out the weak military defenses. While we were there, news came of an attempted assassination plot on Hitler. The admiral said it was good that we were out of the country when it had taken place.

"In Poland, I had my first taste of battle. We were traveling in a small convoy of five staff cars. Some partisans were hidden in the woods. They raked the cars with machine-gun fire. Since the admiral and I were in the third car, we had time to draw our guns and fire. I never heard such intense firepower. There must have been twenty machine guns shooting at the same time. Suddenly I was hit in the shoulder. I collapsed on top of the admiral. Both of us went down on the floor of the staff car as the shooting continued. I woke up in a hospital. A nurse informed me that an admiral had brought me there.

"Although I was still in Poland, this was a hospital run by Germans. It took me three months to recover. When I returned to Berlin, all that the admiral said was that I had earned a medal."

After a few moments of silent reminiscence, Pierce continued his story. "By the summer of 1941, Germany was winning on most fronts and had carved out a huge part of the world. It was then that we first came across the 'ultimate solution.' It happened on another trip to Poland to inspect our counterespionage network. We both were taken to a concentration camp to interrogate some prisoners. I won't tell you what I saw, because it was beyond comprehension. That night we attended a party at the commandant's house. About thirty high-ranking officials from the camp attended the party. There were women from the camps there, and they were all nude. There was more than one woman per man, and we found out that the commandant had promised them food—if they took care of the men. These women were non-Jews from conquered countries, and their only reason for being alive was to service the men. The admiral's prediction had come true. After Jews, who would be next?

"Our desire to work for the Nazi regime ended that night. We were now working exclusively to stop the war and to eliminate Hitler. There were two more attempts on Hitler's life, and the admiral had actually arranged meetings with officials of the Allied forces to try to stop the inevitable crushing of Germany. All failed."

CHAPTER THIRTY-SEVEN

PIERCE WALKED AROUND the office to stretch his legs. Rogers put a glass of tea in front of him. He took a small sip, and then he turned to Rogers. "Now the adventure starts," he announced.

Then he continued to recount his adventure in Berlin. "One day I was summoned to the admiral's office. Arriving there, I met Gestapo guards at the door. Had they discovered our plots? I was escorted inside. There was Heinrich Himmler, head of the Nazi intelligence group, the Gestapo, along with the admiral. They were having coffee. The two men waved me in.

"'I understand that you were born in America,' Himmler said. 'I'm also told that you speak and read English and have a father there.'

"'Yes, that is correct,' I replied as I stood at attention. Himmler never told me to be at ease.

"'Good. Then you will be going home soon,' he stated.

"Himmler explained my role as a supportive one. I was to translate, provide food and shelter, and make contacts as assigned in America. Two seasoned agents were to accompany me on a very secret mission. They would be transporting a case that was to be put into the hands of some people in America. We could not fail—the future of all Aryans was at stake.

"'I am prepared to serve my Fuehrer,' I said immediately.

"'Good. Canaris will give you the details of your mission. You will leave in three months.'

"'Heil, Hitler,' I saluted before leaving the office.

"I promptly went to the bathroom and threw up."

After again pausing to stretch his legs, Pierce continued. "Later that afternoon, Greta delivered a handwritten message to meet the admiral at his boat on the river. I was to be on the watch for a tail, as Himmler was known to trust no one. The message said to burn the paper when done. I was truly a spy now, a spy in a foreign country.

"I never knew if I was being followed, but I took no chances. I used the evasive techniques that I was taught in spy school. I arrived at the dock and climbed aboard the Canaris boat. The admiral was already there. We quickly cast off and headed out to the middle of the river.

"'I have three things to tell you, Wolf,' the efficient admiral said.

"'I have many questions.'

"He ignored my reply. 'I am afraid that the Gestapo is on to me or at least has some suspicions. Two of my agents have been caught in Poland. You realize that the Gestapo can get you to say anything if captured.'

"'Oh, my God, what are you going to do?'

"'I'm serving my country. What happens to me is not significant; there are many of us working against the Nazi regime. I will be all right.'

"Somehow I didn't believe him. 'But—' I was cut short.

"'The family news is even worse. Her Gestapo major has confiscated your mother's business. He has decided that it is too important for the war effort to be entrusted to a private citizen. I believe that he was disappointed that you inherited your grandfather's money. Her house is also in his hands, and I feel that it is only a matter of time before she will be arrested.'

"'How can that be?' I was incredulous. 'She has been a Nazi supporter from the beginning.'

"'That matters little when they want your possessions,' the admiral said.

"'I must go see her. Maybe we can get her out of Germany.'

"'Wolf, listen to me carefully, I will help her, but only after you reach America. If I act too early, the Gestapo will recognize the plot and recall you. What is at stake here is far more important than the few of us.'

"'Admiral, I'm scared.'

"'And well you should be! Remember your training and believe in God, my son. I will protect you as much as I can; I promised your grandfather that I would look out for you.'

"'I'm so confused I don't know what to do,' I said with panic in my voice.

"'You will do your duty, Wolf. You have no choice.'

"'But what is my duty, Admiral?'

"He went on to explain. 'Listen carefully. Do not write anything down. The two agents that are going with you will be referred to as Bernard Hall and Andrew Adams. Their real names will not matter. Hall is a thug and a killer. He will be in charge of security for the box. Adams is a communications expert. There will be other spies dropped off with you. I have made arrangements with the Americans to have them apprehended. You need to know where they keep the box at all times. Hall will have the names of the people that he will be contacting in America. We need those names. He probably will not have them written down, so you need to be patient. The names are the leaders of the Nazi party in America.'

"'What does the box contain?' I asked.

"'The box contains the verified history of the original Aryan race.'

"'I don't understand.'

"'A few years ago, we accidentally stumbled onto the origin of the ancient Aryan race in India. A tablet with the history of the race was found. The people that found it did not fully understand what they had found. I was given the assignment to translate the writings, and eventually we discovered the truth about the Aryans. The translation that I passed to Himmler is not correct. I made some changes. I told Himmler that the tablet would be valuable to use in America, where the war effort against Germany is rising. I told him that if we could use the American press and our leaders in America, we could get much exposure. The American Aryans would rise up and stop or at least hinder the war efforts. Germans are the single largest ethnic group in America. This would be of great advantage to us. Your assignment is to make sure that happens.'

"'Admiral, that could change the course of the war,' I declared.

"'I truly hope so. I expect that it will shorten the war by years.' There was no mistaking the zeal that the admiral displayed in telling me this. Had he lost his mind?

"In the late spring, I left for America on a secret mission that I truly did not understand. The admiral wanted me to make sure that the tablet got to the proper destination. At the same time, communications with Germany were to be disrupted while he ensured the capture of the spies being sent to America with me.

"At the docks in France, I met my companions for the first time. Both Hall and Adams were just as the admiral had described. The other six spies did not reveal their names. For security purposes, we were known to each other as #1 through #9. My number was 6.

"One hour before departure, I heard my number, 6, called. The captain told me that I had a visitor.

"As I left the U-boat, I saw Greta on the docks. She looked beautiful. She was anxious to see me. As I drew near, all eyes were on her as she put her arms around me and gave me a wonderful kiss. I never even felt the packet that she slid into the inside pocket of my coat.

"She breathed into my ear that the admiral wanted me to have the packet, but warned me that I was not to look at it until I was in America. She promised that it would explain everything. As she let go of me, she began to cry. Before disappearing into the night, she thanked the captain for letting her see me off.

Rogers again turned off the recorder. "Wait, are you saying that you became a spy for the Nazi regime? We can't let this get out. You will most certainly be arrested."

"They will not find me," Pierce coolly replied.

Pierce pressed the button on the recorder. "The trip across the Atlantic was uneventful. Clearly the other spies had not spent much time on the water, as evidenced by their near-terminal seasickness. We nine spies spent our time practicing our English and talking about sports and other American things. Not all of the spies had been to America before. We were each given a thousand American dollars. It seemed like more money than we ever should have, yet we knew that we would be in America for an extended period of time. What would I tell Father about Mother's situation? I spent a lot of time thinking. I was truly looking forward to returning to my house and walking in the woods, just as when I was a child. I wondered about how large the trees had grown. My companions would be introduced as friends from school in Germany.

"Finally on June 13, 1942, we sighted land, and the operation commenced."

Pierce drew a long breath, and then he continued. "At midnight we surfaced, and a collapsible rubber boat was put over the side at a place called Amagansett. Numbers 1 through 3 climbed into the boat with explosives and clothing. They rowed off into the darkness.

"They had the bad luck of running into a young coast guard seaman named John C. Cullen, stationed on the beach. It was dark that night, and a fog was rolling in. The coast guard had a rescue station in Amagansett. Cullen was patrolling the beach. Each patrol guard was responsible for three running miles of surf. Cullen didn't have a gun.

"He stumbled onto the three spies as they were unloading their boat. They told him that they were fishermen and that the heavy box was full of clams. The Germans thought that the best way to get rid of Cullen was to bribe him. They offered him three hundred dollars to look the other way. This confirmed his suspicions that these men were not fishermen. He took the money and walked off.

"Once out of sight, he ran to the station to report to his supervisor that the Germans were invading. It took several hours to gather a response, as other guardsmen had to be called onto duty. By the time eight coast guard members returned to the beach, the men were gone. But the Germans had done a poor job of burying their explosives. The cache was uncovered in less than an hour.

"What was significant that night was not that they were the first three German spies on U.S. soil, but rather that the landing changed how the

American government responded to the crisis. By midmorning on this small part of the beach, the following government agencies had assembled: the coast guard, an army detail, the FBI, naval intelligence, and members from the Eastern Sea Frontier group. There had been no sharing of information. All were working the case separately.

"Finally some bureaucrats decided that the FBI should head up the investigation. From then on, for all possible spy landings, the FBI would take the lead.

"Meanwhile, FBI undercover agents were placed in an East Hampton restaurant where the owners were suspected of having ties with German nationals. An agent was placed as a clerk at the local fish market and another agent at a gas station in Montauk. The three German spies were arrested within two days. On June 27, J. Edger Hoover, director of the FBI, announced that an additional three agents had been captured in Jacksonville, Florida."

Rogers quickly remarked. "Yes, I remember that. We were all very scared that Germany was invading"

"But you didn't know that the FBI knew of the spies, did you?"

Returning to his personal story, Pierce continued, "The next day in the early morning, we went over the side in a dense fog. We paddled toward the beach, and I saw the opening for the bay. Since I had grown up here, I told the others to paddle through the opening. It was so foggy that no one could have seen us even if there had been someone on the lookout. I told them to keep paddling, and we eventually crossed the bay to land at the end of a dirt road known as Tanners Neck Lane.

"Rather than bury the boat, I had them deflate it in the reeds along the bay. We started to walk toward Father's house, which was some six miles distant. I was happy to be on land again, especially American soil. The night was still. Hall was having trouble carrying the tin-lined box, but he would accept no help. I was looking forward to sleeping in my old room and harvesting some fresh vegetables from Father's garden. My spirits were high.

"Everything was going well until we reached the corner of Speonk-Riverhead Road. There in front of us was a wire fence that ran as far as the eye could see down the road. A large sign said *Government Property, No Trespassing.* Hall asked me in German, 'Vas ist dis?' I told him to speak English. We set off like the fence meant nothing. I didn't know what else to do.

"As we walked down the road, I became more and more wary. *What was going on?* About half a mile down the road, large elms leaned over the road. I knew that my house was still there. As we drew up to the house, I could see that it was inside the fence. There were no lights. The place was very eerie. 'Let's go,' I said as I climbed over the fence.

"Tire tracks ran along the perimeter, meaning that patrols would be along soon. We sought cover by sprinting to the old pump house. The place must not have been used in many years. The electricity was off. We used our flashlights to look around. I tried the old hand pump to the well. After some work, I was able to get water to come out. We all drank our fill. We were also hungry. I wanted to explore the house to discover what had happened to my father, but I did not want Hall and Adams to know its secrets.

"Suddenly we heard the roar of an engine. Peeking out the door, I spied a jeep with two army sentries driving past the fence. It was 5:00 a.m. Eventually we learned to pace our activities by observing the sentries that came by every hour. It was just starting to turn light now, and I noticed the fruit trees that Father had planted. I told the others to stay put while I ran to the different trees. I picked apples, peaches, cherries, pears, and black walnuts for dessert. After our feast, we settled down for some sleep before deciding what to do.

"We had slept about two hours when we were awakened by the roar of airplane engines. It sounded as if there were hundreds of them. I jumped up and looked out the window of the pump house. Four fighters circled the area. Suddenly they went into a dive and came roaring over the pump house, missing the tall stack by only a few feet. To my horror, they started strafing my house with machine-gun fire. I wanted to cry. The one place that had made me happy was getting shot up. Before I could react, I saw more planes with bombs under the wings.

"Then I saw that the target was not the house, but the smokestack near the pump house. Bombs rained down on the smokestack. I yelled for Hall and Adams to take cover, knowing that it was already too late. The bomb concussion alone would kill us all. The released bombs dropped down with a distinctive whistle. The smokestack was beginning to crumble. We waited for the explosion that would end our lives. After twenty minutes, all was quiet. Four bombs were sticking out of the ground at an acute angle. One had hit the stack and knocked it down. Fortunately, it had fallen away from the pump house. One bomb had buried itself in the ground up to the tail fin, as if there were a hollow area under it—like a cave or tunnel. I wondered if it had hit the tunnel to the house or whether there was another tunnel. All three of us stood in fascination, wondering when the bombs would explode.

"It was Adams who first noticed that a trickle of sand was leaking out of one of the bombs. We went outside to take a closer look and discovered that the bombs were duds, filled with sand. It suddenly occurred to me that this fenced-in area was a training base. My father's dream house was being used as a practice area to learn how to kill Germans.

"By ten o'clock we realized that the training was over for the day. Hall said that our first order was to secure the box. I suggested that we bury it in the woods for now and that way we would not have to carry it around. Hall and Adams vetoed that idea and set the box behind the well pump in a corner.

"I wanted to visit my old house to see if I could find out anything about what had happened to my father. We went to the backdoor, and finding it unlocked, we entered. The house was much as I remembered it, except for being empty. All the rooms were bare of furniture, and many of the windows were cracked and broken. Several shell casings lay scattered in the rooms. There were holes through the walls where the planes had strafed the house. Adams and Hall wanted to go back to the pump house to sleep. I told them that I would be along after I spent some more time in the house—and specifically in my old room.

"I decided to read the packet that Greta had given me months ago on the dock in France. In the packet were several things: my original passport in my real name, another thousand dollars, a note from the admiral, a war medal, and a translation of the tablet. The note from the admiral was in his handwriting.

Dear Wolf,
I'm writing you this note to tell you that am very happy to have known you. I only hope that we can meet again. The mission that I have sent you on is more important than you think. The translation that is included in the packet is the actual translation from the tablet; it is genuine. Have an expert in America verify translation.
You must complete the mission and have the tablet revealed to the public by American Nazis. No man has ever had a more important task. I know that you will succeed.
Always Your Friend,
Wilhelm
P.S: I have also enclosed a medal—a medal for an honorable man.

"As I read the translation, I began to understand the admiral's plan. The admiral had indeed developed a strategy that would shake the world and probably destroy the Nazi reign. I then knew that I must implement the plan.

"It was eerie in the old house. A warm breeze filtered through the holes in the walls and windows. It made a continuous whistling sound, and suddenly I felt that there was someone looking over my shoulder. It was then that I first heard the voices. They said, 'Listen to the admiral. He has helped us, and now it is your turn.' The voices were exactly as the admiral had described them. I wondered why they were haunting me. Was there more than one? Were they men or women or both? I also wondered if they had left the admiral and attached themselves to me. Was I going crazy? Were they somehow connected to the tablet? 'Who are you?' I screamed, but the voices never replied. I finally reasoned that there was some sort of divine intervention, something supernatural, something unexplainable guiding me. I was sure that it had to do with my mission.

"I suddenly felt I had to make plans to succeed in my mission. We needed a place to stay and find good cover until the tablet could be revealed. 'Use the tunnel,' a voice suggested.

"I decided to see if the old tunnel was still passable between the pump house and my house. In the basement, I found the secret latch. The door opened easily. I turned on my flashlight. The passage had not changed since the last time I had walked it. I thought one of the bombs had penetrated it, but there was no evidence of a cave-in. As I reached the pump house, I took a chance on Adams and Hall being asleep. The trapdoor opened quietly, and I realized that they were not there. *Where had they gone?*

"I immediately went to the box and attempted to find a way to open it. As I studied the latches, it occurred to me that Hall would have added extra security. I decided to leave it alone. 'Disable the radio; no longer make it able,' a voice directed me. I remembered that the admiral told me to disrupt communications. After opening the back, I took out a tube and banged it on the floor. Satisfied, I set it back. Next I rummaged through Hall's pack, hoping to find the name of the person who expected the box. I could find nothing. Feeling dejected, I climbed back through the door and returned to the house.

"A voice using a riddle told me to take the hidden ladder up to the second floor. I had just replaced the wall in the closet when I heard a noise on the steps. The stairs creaked as I had remembered. I rounded the corner to find Hall coming up the steps.

"'We were wondering when you would come back down,' he said.

"'I guess that I was lost in thought,' I replied. 'Let's pick some fruit and have dinner.'"

Once more Pierce paused to remember the events of that long-ago night. Then he continued, "That night, Adams said that we needed to check in with the submarine. He took out the wireless and turned it on. It didn't work. He took off the back and found a damaged tube.

"'The wireless is useless,' he said. 'Without this tube it will not work, and I do not have a spare.'

"We all started to curse in German. Hall was slamming his fist into the wall.

"'Well, at least we have a backup plan,' Hall finally said to my horror.

"I inquired as to the details.

"'The first team that we put ashore is our backup. When we make contact, we will use their radio.' He was more confident now.

"'How are we to make contact?' I had not been briefed on this. Clearly there were parts of this mission that I was not privy to.

"'There's a German grocer in town. The first team will contact him, and he will point them to us. One of us needs to go grocery shopping.'

"'I'll go,' I said. 'I speak English better than you do and know my way around.' It would afford me the opportunity to discover the whereabouts of my father.

Chapter Thirty-Eight

Pierce again took up telling his story. "It was about a mile and a half to Hoch Meats. When I entered the store, an older man behind the counter met me. He was huge and stood over six foot four. He probably weighed more than two hundred and fifty pounds. 'How are you, Wolfgang?' he asked. 'I have been expecting you.'

"'Good to see you, Mr. Hoch.'

"'So, you are finally back.' It was a play to find out where I stood.

"'That's correct; I have been over on the continent for several years.'

"'And how is my friend the admiral?' He was staring at me. 'He told me to call you Wolf to verify that I work for him. It is his pet name for you, no?'

"I didn't know whether this was the Nazi Hoch or the German Hoch talking. 'I'm on a mission.'

"'I know. Come in the back so we can talk.'

"In the back room we settled at a small table. 'The other group will not be coming, you know.' Hoch had taken the first step.

"'Why is that?' I asked.

"'Because I called the FBI and told them where to find the idiots. I have worked for Canaris before, in submarines.'

"I couldn't see someone this huge fitting in a submarine and was skeptical. 'You were stationed in a sub?'

"He laughed. 'Not exactly. I worked as a procurer. Met the admiral during the First World War and have worked for him since. He is a true hero. I despise the Nazis, and I'm an American now. My son Frank and I will do whatever you ask.'

"'First, tell me about what has happened to my father. We went to the old house, and it is now under control of the military.'

"'I'm sorry to tell you that your father is dead. When the government confiscated the land in 1936, I heard that he hung himself in a closet. I thought you knew. We sent a message to your mother, but she never replied. He had returned to Catholicism when you left, and the church got what was left of his estate. I'm so sorry, Wolf.'

"I was truly shaken by this, but the hatred for my mother now overshadowed my grief. 'Thank you, I appreciate your concern.'

"'Wolf, what can you tell us about your mission?'

"'Not very much, I'm afraid. I was told to destroy the communications, which I did. I'm to ensure that the box we carry gets into American Nazi hands. That's all there is. By the way, Wolf is no longer; I'm Walter Pierce now. The two agents with me are Bernard Hall, who is security, and Andrew Adams, for communications. Neither of them was entrusted with the name we need to complete the mission. The Admiral told me that Hall would have the name, but he was wrong. The name is the secret leader of the organization in the United States. I don't know what to do.'

"'Well, your mission may be over. Have you seen the news lately?'

"'No, we've been at sea and only landed last night.'

"'The Allies have invaded North Africa.'

"'When did this happen?'

"'They hit the beaches over a week ago. They are moving rapidly inland. Your mission may be cancelled.'

"'No, I doubt it. The mission is really big and still needs to be completed.'

"'Just tell us what you require,' Mr. Hoch replied."

Again Pierce moved about the room before continuing his story. "I returned to the pump house and told Adams and Hall that the first team had not reported in yet. I had collected a sack full of groceries, and we ate well that evening, although we could not risk heating the food. I told the other men that we would have to lay low for a few days while communications were reestablished.

"After a week we were getting tired of hiding. Finally Adams suggested that we should rent a room and obtain transportation.

"The next morning I walked into Riverhead, the largest town in eastern Long Island, and bought a car for cash. Next I searched the newspaper ads for a house to rent. It was just north of town. It was a big house with a driveway leading to a garage in back and far enough from neighbors that we would not be under constant view. I drove back to the old house and realized that I could not park the car along the road, as someone might see it. I decided to pull it over near the house and jack it up as if we had a flat. I could always explain that I had run over to the house to see if anyone was there to help me. The plan worked fine, and in a few minutes, the three of us were in the car heading north.

"Hall, always concerned about security, said that we needed to hide the box somewhere besides the rental. I knew just the spot and pulled over by one of the fire lanes. We once again jacked up the wheel, climbed over the fence, and set off down the lane. We made a left turn that brought us to the top of a hill, where we could see for miles.

"'This is the place,' I announced.

"Hall said, 'This is fine, but we need to mark the spot with something.' We agreed to come back with some sort of a marker the next day.

"We moved into our furnished house. Hall found a metal pole and some paint in the garage. He wrote on the pole '19-42.' It was, of course, the year that we buried the box. We returned to the fire lane and put up the marker. Precisely thirty steps south, we had buried the box.

"We spent the summer waiting for some sort of communications. Each week I went to the Hoch grocery store. I bought all the different newspapers to keep track of the war. It was in late June when I read that the other six spies had been apprehended. We knew we were in trouble and had no choice but to wait for some communications from Germany. We learned one more thing—Germany was getting pounded.

"One day Mr. Hoch told me that he had a message. Adams was with me and quickly read the message. It had come by regular post from Germany. It was coded, of course, but still passed through without any censorship.

"The message said that a submarine would be one mile off the coast of the lighthouse on Fire Island on September 25 at 4:00 a.m. We were to obtain a boat to meet the submarine. The submarine would bring us a new wireless radio and new instructions.

"As head of security and the strongest of the three of us, Hall decided that he should be the one to steal a boat to meet the submarine. I knew that I was better on the water, but Hall was clearly more macho and was looking forward to the adventure. The voices told me, 'Let him go; there will be a big blow.' The morning before had been windy and raw. I knew that the ocean would be rough, but Hall insisted that we go. We left at midnight and drove through Remsenburg. We parked at the dock. The wind was tremendous, and it was raining. I warned Hall not to go, that it was too rough, but he leaped off the dock and into a twenty-five-foot wooden boat with a small cabin. He told us that he would be warm and dry in the cabin. He jump-started the boat, checked the gas, and cast off. We watched him disappear in the dark.

"At 5:02 a.m. the second largest hurricane to ever hit Long Island crossed over the shoreline on Dune Road. The Great Long Island Express of 1938 had been the worst to ever hit the island. It killed 390 people. This storm was the second worst. The nor'easter, as they call it, was the strongest kind of storm. It was preceded by a twenty-five-foot wall of water churning along at about seventy miles per hour.

"Adams and I were standing on the dock when we heard a tremendous roar like a train and noticed that all the water was being drained from the bay. 'Tidal wave,' I screamed at Adams, and we ran to the car. We leaped in, and I gunned the engine, leaving rubber on the slick road. We raced down the straight road, hoping to reach high ground before the wave hit. I could see the wave in the rearview mirror—huge, all engulfing, roaring down on us.

"The road ended abruptly. We had to choose right or left. I went left, and thirty seconds later, we were hit by the wave. It had dissipated down to a ten-foot height. Yet it rolled us over like a toy. We were just passing a field, and we rolled inside the wave for about one hundred yards or more before slamming into the back of a motel. Adams was in the back of the car, and I was sprawled across the front seat. The windows held, and we were on our side, underwater. Getting my bearings, I realized that our little submarine was not going to stay sealed for long—we had to get out. Adams had a huge gash on his head but otherwise seemed all right.

"'Andrew, we need to get out of here. The windows will soon break, and we will drown.'

"'How are we going to get out? I'm not that good of a swimmer, you know.'

"'I'm going to kick out the front window, let water come in, and then we'll swim out. Once we get to the surface, we'll find something to climb onto or something that floats. Are you ready?'

"I kicked the front window, and it collapsed inside. Water came rushing in, and soon the cabin of the car was full. I made sure that Adams was behind me before swimming out and rising to the surface. Water surrounded me. I was happy to see that the top of the motel was above the waves. I swam to it and climbed on the roof, helping Adams get his footing.

"We sat on the roof for two days before we were rescued. The electricity stayed out on the whole end of the island for another eight days. The army had to come in to help save people. Forty people died that night, including Bernard Hall. We never got the radio.

"Adams and I were on our own now. We went through Hall's things in the hopes of finding something more to help us. All we found of value was a Luger. Adams and I spent hours debating the mission and what we would do.

"Our orders were to wait until contacted, so that's what we continued to do. Fall came, and we started to run short of money. I went to Mr. Hoch. He advised me to get a job. Hoch's mood had also darkened.

"In November 1942, I took a job working at the North Fork Union Bank as a teller. Adams had no marketable skills, as he had been in the army since he was sixteen, but he sometimes hired out on some of the fishing boats in the area. We tried to stay away from the German community, as we believed that many of them were now spies for the Americans. It was a lonely life.

"One day I was on my usual run to the Hoch grocery store. Upon entering the store, I could tell that something was wrong. Frank Hoch was now behind the counter. He was perhaps sixteen. 'Where's your father?' I asked.

"'He's in the hospital,' the boy replied. 'He had a heart attack yesterday. I'm here alone. Mother is by his side.'

"'I'm sorry. Is there anything I can do? Do you wish for me to help in the store until he gets back?'

"'Mr. Pierce, I don't think that he is coming back.' The boy had tears in his eyes. 'He did want you to get this message, though. He had his attack right after he read it.' Frank handed me the paper.

"In seconds I was crying too. The Gestapo had tried to arrest the admiral for attempting to assassinate Hitler and for treason. Somehow the admiral was able to persuade them that he was not part of a plot and was, in fact, in Italy at the time. But the note said that he was under surveillance, and we all knew what that meant. The message continued with a warning that Adams and I were being recalled and would be told to bring the box. A submarine would meet us off of the lighthouse again on February 1.

"'Do not mention this to Andrew. We cannot go back, you know.'"

Chapter Thirty-Nine

After pausing to wipe his teary eyes, Pierce continued his story once more. "In the middle of March 1943, Mr. Hoch died. Adams and I drove to the funeral in Remsenburg. There were perhaps two hundred people there, most of German extraction. Several people were on the periphery taking pictures. I was certain that they were FBI. I nudged Adams that we should leave. A man who hailed me by name stopped me.

"'Good afternoon, Mr. Pierce.'

"'Who are you?'

"'I am Agent Paul Williams of the OSS,' he replied.

"'What can I do for you?' I looked him straight in the eye as we were trained to act.

"'You are how old?'

"'Thirty-two.'

"'Do you have a draft card, please? Someone your age should be in the army.'

"I was nervous now. Adams, who was ten years older, turned to the man and said, 'This man is a war veteran. Walter, show him your recent scar.'

"I opened my shirt to show him the big scar. 'It happened in North Africa.' I had become an adroit liar by this time.

"'I'm sorry to have bothered you.' He held out his hand for me to shake and passed me a piece of paper.

"I told Adams that I needed to say good-bye to Frank and told him to go to the car. I then read the note.

> *You are in grave danger. Trust no one. Meet me at the all-night diner in Riverhead Circle at 1:00 a.m.*
> *A Friend*

"I was truly terrified now. How did Adams know about my scar? 'Trust no one,' the message said. What of Frank? I knew that the OSS was the Office of Strategic Security, and they were very similar to the Abwehr. Why were they contacting me?

"In the car I decided to find out how Adams knew about my scar. As usual, the simplest plan was the best. 'How did you know I had a scar?'

"'I thought you might catch that,' Adams said.

"I was now getting tense. 'That is not an answer.'

"'Bernard and I were given extensive background about you. Some in high places felt that you might have mixed loyalties to the mission.'

"That night I slipped out and went to the diner as instructed. Upon entering, I saw Paul Williams seated in the corner, and I walked over to the booth. I looked around to see if anyone was paying any attention to me, but I could not see anyone suspicious. 'Mr. Williams,' I said.

"'Nice of you to come, Wolf.' This gave me a shudder.

"'Why did you call me Wolf? My name is Walter.'

"'I have been sent by Bill Donovan. Do you know who he is?'

"'The name means nothing to me.'

"'He is the head of the OSS and has been in contact with Wilhelm Canaris. You do know who he is, don't you?'

"'Why are you interested in me?'

"'I have a message from the admiral. Donovan and Canaris have met before and are going to be meeting again shortly. They are trying to end the war clandestinely, you know.'

"'Just give me the message that you are sure should go to me. Maybe then I can figure out what this is about.'

"'That's fair. The message is this: The Nazis have sent a Gestapo assassin. She has managed to reach America and is looking for you. It seems that she wants the box, whatever that is, and has orders to eliminate you and the other agents with you. Apparently you missed the rendezvous that was included in your instructions. Yes, we have known about the three of you for some time. Hall has gone missing, hasn't he?'

"'Why would you deliver a message to a foreign agent? I just don't get it.'

"'We know about your mission and would like to capture the Nazi leadership in America. While the OSS is not supposed to be working on U.S. soil, Bill feels that this is very important and can end the Nazi movement in America. We will catch them all in one place. Don't worry, your box will be safe and locked in a secure facility, never to be seen again.'

"I suddenly realized that the admiral was at work here, that he was somewhere behind the scenes. This would be a typical diversion while getting me information. 'If I had such a box, it would already be secure. Do you have a name or a description of the Gestapo agent?'

"'We don't know her name, but she is of average height and slim build. Her eyes are green, and she had red hair when she was last seen. One more thing, she has a one-inch round mole on her leg, in the middle of her thigh. That is all we know. But she is very dangerous and has already killed several Germans in New York City while seeking information. She interrogates with a knife and then kills her informants. As you can imagine, we want her off the streets.'

"'What do I do if I meet her and survive?'

"'Here's my card. It has a telephone number on it. If you see her, call me. We will take care of her. Any questions?'

"He put out his hand for me to shake. 'I never thought that I would be doing business with a German spy,' he said.

"'I'm an American,' I replied while standing proudly."

Pierce finished his tea and then continued. "Everything was changing for me. My partner was a question, my grocer was a question, and the OSS was a question. The admiral was somewhere behind the scenes, but I knew his influence was limited, and I started to carry the Luger.

"A month passed. I went to work at the bank, and Adams went to the docks. We were just treading water, and my mission was not moving ahead. News on the war front was bad for the Germans. Everybody knew that Italy would be invaded soon.

"One day a man came into the bank. He said he wanted money to be transferred from an account in England. He explained that he was buying a house in America and needed the money for a down payment. I had no idea money could be transferred without going to the specific bank where the money was on deposit. The bank manager greeted the man and handled the transaction. Later I asked the manager to show me how it was done. He was happy to show me the telex machine and explained the operation. I was amazed. Now I knew I could access the money my grandfather had left me if I needed it. This was good news indeed.

"Spring was in full bloom when the trouble started. The FBI had done a sweep of the docks and arrested several people who did not have papers. Adams was one of them. I did not find out about it until I arrived home that night to discover FBI people swarming over my rented home.

"'Who are you?' the FBI agent demanded.

"'I live here.'

"'Do you have identification?'

"'I have a driver's license and my passport. They are inside.'

"I retrieved the documents and handed them to the agent. He said nothing and instead wrote down all my information in a small notebook.

"'Do you know an Andrew Adams?'

"'Of course. He's my roommate and has been for years. Has something happened to him?'

"'He didn't have papers on the dock when we did a sweep looking for illegals, especially Germans. He's German, correct?'

"'I thought he came from Wisconsin and had been on Long Island for many years, since he came back from the Lincoln Brigade.'

"'So he's a veteran?' The FBI agent seemed perplexed by my comment.

"'Yes, he fought against the Germans in Spain. I know where his passport is hidden. I can get it for you.'

"I went into his room and knew that I had to dump the gun while fetching Adams's passport. This was going to be tricky, as there were police all over the place and the agent was following me. I went to Adams's room and picked up the carpet on the floor to gather his passport. I also noticed some cash and a matchbook cover. I would look at this later.

"'Here,' I told the agent. 'Can I go with you to bring Andrew home?'

"'Only if you don't mind sitting around while we check out his passport.'

"'I'll follow you in my car, okay?'

"He agreed.

"We left in a multicar caravan. Along the route, I slid the gun under the front seat of the car. When we arrived at the local FBI headquarters in Riverhead, I was told to wait in the outside room. It was an hour before Adams appeared. Back in the car, I asked him what had happened. He said that the FBI, without warning, showed up on the docks and arrested anyone who didn't have papers.

"'Did you see anything unusual on the docks?'

"'I don't know. There was this woman there that I have seen before. She was buying some fish when the FBI came. She disappeared, but she had been on the docks for several days, you know, hustling. She gave me a matchbook cover.'

"'What did she look like?'

"'Slim, long brown hair. She had green eyes.'

"I checked to see if the gun was still under the seat. It was.

"The next day I was at Frank's store when I heard on the radio that there had been a knifing at the docks. I called Adams immediately. The phone rang with no answer. Had the killer zeroed in on him? I made one more call."

Chapter Forty

Pierce went to the bathroom and then continued. "On the way home, the voices came into my head. 'The road ahead has trouble on it; change your plan a bit.' I had to act fast to protect my mission, so I stopped at the fire lane. It was directly on the way and ran down the path to the marker. At first I planned to dig up the box and take it, but a freshly dug hole would be obvious. Besides, I didn't have a shovel. I was panicky. Then I realized once again that a simple plan was always the better plan. I grabbed the marker, pulled it from the ground, and slid it back into the ground thirty paces due east of the original site. The sandy ground was soft. With the use of a stick of wood as a hammer, I drove it back into the sand. I threw the stick as far as I could and kicked dirt into the old marker hole. Then I covered it with some pine needles and leaves. The box was still in the same place, but now that the marker was moved, it would be nearly impossible to find the box.

"Back in my car, I was dirty, sweaty, and already ten minutes behind schedule. I floored it.

"Turning off my lights, I coasted into the driveway of our rental and had the door open with my finger on the button that turned on the overhead light. The lights were on in the house. Yet there didn't seem to be anyone around. Suddenly there was movement on my left. I dropped down outside the car door and reached under the seat for the Luger. Before I could find it, a hand grabbed my shoulder and spun me around. All I saw was the barrel of a gun.

"'Where have you been?' Paul Williams asked. 'I got your call and headed right out to your house. There hasn't been any movement since I got here. Are you sure that it was the green-eyed assassin? And that she was after Adams?'

"'He told me he had seen a woman hanging around the docks. She fit the description, except she had brown hair. I think she picked up Andrew's trail on the docks.'

"'You may be right. Let's go see what's going on.'

"Stealthily we moved to the window in the front. Williams peered inside. 'No movement here.' We tried the door, and it was unlocked. The hair on my neck was standing up. We entered the house as quietly as possible and worked our way to Andrew's room.

"There was blood on the bed and no Adams. Could this be our girl? Would she have taken him to bed to find out what she wanted? Where was the body?

"As Paul checked out the other rooms of the house, I had an urge to pull back the carpet. Sure enough, there was the matchbook cover that I had seen earlier, along with the money and passport. I scooped up the cover without Williams seeing me do it.

"'Paul, you have to trust me. I think I know where they are. I think she has taken Andrew to look for the box.'

"We were quickly in my car, speeding toward the fire lane. Williams was beside me, checking and reloading his gun. How would I get my gun from under the seat?

"'Do you think she will kill Andrew?'

"'So far her informants have had a short life after she talks to them. We have given her the name of the Black Widow.'

"'Paul, what happens if we find her?'

"'Let me worry about that, as I'm authorized to do whatever it takes to finish this.'

"'I still don't understand why you are willing to help me.'

"'My orders are to find and to eliminate the Black Widow. I'm not to interfere with your mission. Just watch and observe and report back when things heat up. I told you, we want all the Nazis. War makes strange bedfellows, Wolf.'

"'My name is Walter, please.'

"'Okay, Walter. Now you can tell me about the matchbook cover in your pocket. I saw you pick it up. I am a trained agent, you know.'

"I reached into my pocket and gave it to him. 'I don't know what that is about. I saw it under the carpet a couple of days ago and was going to look at it to try to figure it out. It's unlike Andrew to keep anything like it. It's not a secret, as far as I can tell. He said the woman gave it to him.'

"Williams turned over the cover to study it. As we reached the fire lane, there was another car parked by the side of the road. No one was in it. I shut down my car. 'We walk from here.'

"He slipped the cover into his pocket. With his gun drawn, he jumped out of the car. I pretended to have to tie my shoe and grabbed the Luger. Paul was writing down the license plate. We were then off to the hunt.

"It was a full moon that night, so we could see quite clearly. Of course, the Black Widow could see us too. I could tell that Williams was concerned about entering a dark wood with me at night.

"'The box is buried in the woods,' I said. 'I know the way.'

"We were very quiet as we walked down the fire lane. I couldn't imagine failing my mission after all that I had been through. I was not going to let that happen. After all, I was a trained agent too. I would survive.

"As we got close to the clearing, I whispered to Williams that we would need to go in through the woods. He said to walk slowly and not to make noise. He did not understand that I was a trained spy. The shadows were maddening. It was hard to tell what was in front of me. I started to shuffle my feet in the sand so that I would not step on leaves or twigs. This seemed to work, but progress was slow. I now knew what it felt like to be in the middle of a war—searching for the enemy, trying to be quiet, and watching everything. I was scared.

"Eventually we saw the clearing and a mound of dirt. We waited in the bushes for some time. Finally Williams crawled out and peered into the hole. He stood up, shouldered his gun, and then waved me over. I was very concerned now.

"Adams was lying in the bottom of the hole. His throat had been cut. Williams was cursing and kicking the ground. I just fell to my knees and cried. Adams didn't deserve this—she was after the box and me. I knew that the box was still safe but also knew that the Black Widow was not yet finished.

"'We are in trouble now,' Williams said. 'Now that she has the box, all she has to do is to kill you. I'll never find her alone; I'm going to need help.'

"'No help,' I said. 'She will be looking for me real soon, probably at my home right now. She doesn't have the box; I moved it.'

"'Moved it to where?' Williams asked.

"'To a secure position.'

"'You're not going to tell me?'

"'The fewer people know about this, the better. If she gets me, then the box is gone forever.'

"We decided to bury Adams in the hole. I said a few words in German over the stark grave and resolved to kill the Black Widow in revenge.

"Reaching the car, we found that one of our tires was slashed. We changed the tire and drove back to my house. 'Do you think she is at my house?'

"'No, I don't think so,' answered Williams. 'If she was setting anything up at your house, she would have cut the distributor wires. She just wanted to stall us long enough to get away.'

"'So what do you make of the matchbook cover?'

"'It has a skull and crossbones on it. That is all—no message, phone number, or anything. I'm going to take it to the lab to see if there is a hidden message or some prints on it.'

"'Paul, maybe you should stay around this evening.'"

Chapter Forty-One

Once more Pierce stretched his legs. Then he continued, "The night was uneventful just as Williams predicted. The real action started a week later, at the bank. I had just transferred ten thousand dollars to my account from the Swiss account. My mood was improving. Suddenly I realized there was someone at my teller window. I looked up and into a pair of the greenest eyes I had ever seen. The woman was indeed handsome and rugged looking, like a farmer's wife would be. Her hair was blond.

"'Could you change a twenty for me? I need some singles and fives, please.' Her voice was light, with only a slight British accent.

"'Do you have an account here?' I asked her automatically.

"'I just want some change. Be a good guy, please.'

"'Do you have identification?' I asked. 'We don't want any counterfeit twenties.'

"She opened her purse and produced a social security card with the name of Sally Hand on it. The address was located in Oyster Bay, about fifty miles west of Riverhead.

"'You are a ways from home.'

"'I need change for the train,' she said, 'to go home.'

"I made change and handed her the money without a word. She turned and left. I palmed the twenty, changed it for one of my own, and wrapped it in my handkerchief. I wanted to give it to Paul Williams.

"At lunchtime I decided to walk up the street to the diner. As I entered, there was Sally Hand, sitting in a booth crying. As I walked by, I tipped my hat and kept going. Five minutes later, she slid into my booth.

"'I'm so distraught; I need your help.' She was crying real tears.

"'What's wrong?'

"'I missed my train. The next one's late, and there's no one to pick me up.'

"'That's nothing to cry about,' I said. 'You will just get home a little late.'

"'You don't understand—my husband has left me here, in Riverhead, and he's not coming back.'

"'I'm sure that it isn't that bad.'

"'Yes, it is. He's gone and never coming back. He has a new girlfriend and wants to lose me. I don't know what to do.'

"'I'm sorry,' I said. 'I just can't help you.'

"'Oh, please, could I just stay at your place until I think things through?'

"I was finally getting the picture. She wanted to try to seduce me and pump me for information before cutting my throat. But Ms. Hand didn't know that I was onto her. Maybe I could get a message to Williams and have him capture or kill her, just as she did to poor Andrew.

"'You can stay at my house until I get home from work.' I gave her my address even if she didn't need it.

"'Oh, you are so kind, I need a little time to freshen up and will be there when you get home. Thank you. You know my name, but what's yours?'

"'My name is Walter Pierce,' I said. 'My roommate, Andrew Adams, may be home though. Just tell him that you are a friend of mine.' I watched her eyes for a sign but could detect none. She was good, but I was going to make sure that she never killed again.

"'I like the name Walter,' she said seductively.

"When work ended, I decided to leave my newly transferred money in the bank. I also called Williams, but he was out. I knew that I would have to handle this myself. I made a plan.

"I pulled into the driveway and parked my car. As I came near the front door, I decided to look in the window. There she was on the couch with only her slip on. Her hair had been combed, and she looked every bit the seductress.

"My plan was simple. As I opened the door, she bounced off the couch and came across the room toward me. As she got close, I balled my fist and cracked her across the mouth. She went down like a leaf.

"I felt better now. My hand should have hurt, but I didn't feel it. She didn't look so tough now. Sally Hand, the killer, knocked out by a sucker punch. *I should kill her right now.*

"She lay at my feet in a heap. The slip had ridden up, revealing a nearly translucent thigh with a mole. For the first time, I realized that Sally was beautiful. She looked to be under thirty years old and didn't appear to be very muscular.

"I picked her up—she wasn't very heavy—and took her to the bed. I went into Adams's room and got several belts, returning to tie each arm and leg to a corner post on the bed. There she was, looking like a sleeping teenager, lying on her back with just a slip covering her body. I needed to question her. The spy school had taught me many techniques, most of them violent. If I needed to use the proven techniques, they were available to me. But first I wanted to collect information.

"I left the room and went looking for her purse. I found it behind the hamper in the bathroom. It was well hidden. I emptied the contents on the floor and sifted through the usual woman paraphernalia. Her wallet contained fifteen dollars. The purse seemed heavier than it should, so I shook it. There was something in the lining. I opened the purse and noticed that there was a flapped-over secret compartment.

"The compartment was hidden, but the heaviness of three knives could not be concealed. They were professional killers' knives, all very sharp and well-balanced. I guessed that she could throw these knives as well as stab with them. I knew that I had found my killer. The lovely Sally Hand was nothing but another misguided Nazi. I now felt that I was justified in doing away with her. The only considerations were where to stash her body and would I get my questions answered. I took the knives with me.

"Back in my bedroom, she was still unconscious on the bed. I knew about spies. There is always a backup plan. I needed to search her. It sounded silly, but I knew the rules—search first. I started with her feet; something could be taped there. Her feet were small and quite pretty. I ran my hands up her legs and felt the smoothness of her thighs. She had a mole the size of a dime on her right leg; it didn't detract from her silky leg. The slip moved up, and I suddenly realized that Sally was indeed a redhead by birth. The fire red hair was sparse and neatly trimmed. She had narrow hips, which accentuated her hip bones. I felt a stirring that I had not recognized in a long time.

"The belly was flat and smooth; her belly button hid nothing. I pushed up the slip; a pair of medium-size perky breasts were revealed, with nipples large and brown. I looked for a tattoo on her flank, but there was none there. While most Nazis had a number and SS markings on their left flank, I didn't think that there would be many women with the markings. I turned her on her side to inspect her back. To my surprise, there were whip-mark scars crisscrossing her upper back. I continued up the arms and found them to be small and delicate. There was a surprise there too.

"Tattooed on the underside of her forearm were several numbers. Makeup had been used to try to cover them up. I'd seen these same numbers in the same place on people's arms in Poland in 1939 in a concentration camp. Had she been in a camp? Was this all a ruse to fool me?

"I checked her hair last, and sure enough, I found a razor blade taped to the nape of her neck. It had tape on one end for a grip and could be a deadly weapon in the hands of an expert. Sally, no doubt, was an expert.

"I was done with my inspection. I used the slip to test the razor. It was sharp all right, and the entire slip had been sliced open from top to bottom and been peeled back like petals of a flower. I don't remember doing it, but I was starting to feel a primal lust that could only come from being in close proximity to a naked beautiful woman. I was looking at her—taking in the seductive pose of her body, thinking that Adams was probably having sex when he was kidnapped, wondering what it would feel like to have sex again. I was starting to lose control. When humans are in a hopeless situation, they often turn to sex. I was on the edge. My member was throbbing in my pants.

"'Well, are you going to fuck me or beat off, you sorry excuse for a man?' Sally Hand asked in a husky voice that told me that she had been awake for more than a few seconds.

"'I have a few questions for you.'

"'Your kind all think that a woman is just someone to be used and abused. Come on, get it over with. Or are you a pansy?'

"'I told you that I have a few questions for you.' I was twirling the knives and making it look like I knew how to use them. It got her attention.

"'Yeah, I know your questions. Which hole would you like it in first? Come on, asshole, I can take it. There is no need for knives. I've been raped before, many times.'

"Her language was both disturbing and erotic. I wasn't sure which of my emotions was winning the battle. Was this a ploy?

"'Bet you never even touched a girl before.' She was playing me now, but I didn't care. I reached out and slapped her breast. It felt good.

"'That's it, that's it, do it again. I know you want to. I need it.'

"I was watching her as her green eyes filled with something. I was sure that it was lust. Her nipples had turned hard, and her hips were grinding in a circular motion. *She likes this,* I thought. *Or was she trying to get me to untie her so she could attack me?* I rolled her on her side and slapped her small ass. She yelped and begged for more.

"'Pull my hair,' she said. 'Pull it like a rag doll.'

"I was standing close to the bed and ran my hand down her body; it was on fire and wet between her legs. *My God, if this is an act, she is good.*

"I was feeling very sexually charged. Would it be wrong to have sex with a tied-down woman? I'm going to kill her anyway. Maybe a little release for both of us would be good. I was starting to think crazy. Vivid pictures were crowding my brain.

"'Twist my nipples; use both hands … do it hard.' Sally was talking dirty, and it was turning us both on. *Was this wrong?* I couldn't think past obeying her commands.

"Her hips were rotating. Her strong legs were clenching and unclenching, trying to draw up but held in place by the belts.

"'Walter, do something—don't just stand there. Can't you see I'm ready? Fuck me, Walter.'

"The anticipation was a big part of the game for her; but Sally wanted it now. I, however, wasn't ready to give her what she wanted.

"'What's wrong with you—can't you see that I'm more than ready? Give it to me, you bastard, I can't wait any longer, you son of a bitch.'

"'First question: Why did you kill Andrew?'

"'Fuck me first.'

"'Answer my question.'

"She was resigned now, but I could tell that she didn't want to go there. 'Andrew killed my family and husband. He deserved to die. It happened back in 1938. He raped me viciously, and then he passed me around from Nazi to Nazi, just because I was a redhead. I wound up in a concentration camp when they were done with me. I got beat up a lot. You've seen the whip marks. I wanted this mission to find Andrew and kill him.'

"Holy shit, I might have been at the same camp. But she was still a killer.

"'What do you know about a matchbook cover with a skull and crossbones on it?' I asked my second question.

"'That has the code for the local phone number of the head of the Nazi movement on Long Island on it. I was supposed to deliver it to you or Andrew, and if you refused to complete your mission, I'm supposed to kill you. When I saw Henrich—that's his real name—on the docks a couple of days ago, I gave him the matchbook.'

"'I've known Andrew for over two years. He was not a violent person.'

"'Get serious, he's left a trail. There have been three rape killings on eastern Long Island over the last two years. All of the woman were sodomized after they were dead—a Henrich specialty. Go to the library; check it out.'

"'Don't worry, I will check it out. What is the name of the local Nazi leader? What's the code on the matchbook cover?'

"'I don't know that; they don't trust me either. I was told to give you the cover and you would figure it out. All I know is that it leads to the phone number.'

"'How is it that you became a killer for the Nazis?'

"'I was a knife thrower at the Warsaw circus; I'm good with knives. When I was in the camp, the Nazis thought that I was always very cooperative with their little games. I can swallow knives. I had a special arrangement with a major at the camp and cooked up the killer image. I took care of a few people for them in Poland, and suddenly they sent me here on this mission. I speak

English, as you can see. I was educated in England. I wanted this mission to avenge my family. The Nazis knew, they *knew*, that I would find Henrich.'

"'What were you doing on the docks?'

"'When they sent me here, they told me that the fishing docks were a backup communications drop. I recognized Henrich. I also needed money. How do you think that I got the twenty? It was an easy matter to find out where he lived.'

"'And then you cut him while in the bedroom?'

"'I didn't cut him there. The blood was already there. When I questioned him, he told me that it was from another woman. I suspect that you will be reading about her any day.'

"'I found Andrew's body in some woods. You cut his throat. How did you get there?'

"'So, that was your tire that I cut—I thought that it was the police's. You're right, I did kill him. I told him that I wanted the box. He said that he would get it for me if I didn't kill him. Silly boy. There was no box in the hole that he dug.'

"'You said that your mission was to pass me the cover or to kill me and take the box—take it where?'

"'There's a man waiting every day at noon on the steps of the Forty-second Street Library in Manhattan. He wears a red hat. I'm to deliver a note from the local Nazi leader that says that you have delivered the box. Or I'm to give him the box; you would be dead, of course.'

"'And what do you get?'

"'I get my freedom—I can just walk away.'

"'But I haven't broken the code yet. What are you supposed to do while I'm figuring it out?'

"'That's the fun part. I'm supposed to seduce you, so how about it? At least undo my legs.'"

Pierce continued his story. "The next morning, I called in sick. I wasn't really sick; in fact, I was feeling very satisfied, but I had work to do. I drove to the Speonk station and caught the 8:00 a.m. train to New York City. I got to the library at ten o'clock and spent the next hour and a half reading the local papers. Sally was right—the big news was about a young female high school student who was missing. There were also stories over the last two years about other women who had gone missing and turned up dead. How could I have been so wrong about Adams? We all were very cautious around each other. But his activities were far worse than I could possibly comprehend. We had been through a lot since we had landed in America; it just didn't seem that he was capable of such viciousness. Still, he was a Nazi.

"At twenty to twelve, I went outside and parked on the steps, lighting a cigar. I had a good view. I watched as a scruffy young man in a red hat leaned against the wall directly below me. I didn't look at him; I was looking for others. There were two. They clearly were not from America. Hair too long, clothes too shabby, and bad shoes. They were European, probably from Germany. So Sally was right about this too. I began to feel sorry about chaining her to a pole in my basement, but I left water and food and even a bucket to pee in. It was better than the camps she had been in. I was changing my attitude about her. She was very attractive to me, and her mouth was stimulating. She was also great at sex. She was smart and could carry on a conversation. Not many women I had met could do that.

"I decided to call Paul Williams in his New York office and fill him in. I also wanted the matchbox cover. I was dialing his number when it hit me. I had deduced that the skull and crossbones on the matchbox meant poison but couldn't crack the code beyond that. It suddenly popped into my head. It was the phone number of the head of the local Nazi party. He, therefore, was 'the one.' The rotary dial on the phone had letters on it. If I dialed p-o-i-s-o-n-1, I would reach the Nazi.

"A woman answered the phone. I asked for Paul Williams. 'He's no longer here,' she said. 'How did you get this number?'

"'Paul gave it to me to call in case of an emergency. Give me his new number?'

"'I'm afraid that is impossible. Let me transfer you to Mr. Helms.'

"Soon I heard, 'Helms here, what can I do for you? What did you say your name was?'

"I hung up. I was on my own. I decided to go home.

"Sally was still in the basement and was actually happy to see me. She had made the best of her position and didn't seem the least bit nervous in seeing me. 'Well, dear, how was your day?' She was actually being cheerful. 'I've just been hanging around waiting for you.'

"'I figured out the code, checked on the murders, and found out that there are three men waiting for you at the library.' I didn't tell her about Williams. 'Sally, we have to talk.'

"'Why don't you unchain me and talk while we are having sex?'

"I did unchain her and told her to go take a bath. I would talk to her after she was cleaned up. I just kept underestimating this woman.

"Several hours later I finally came up for air. Sally's body had a language that made men unable to speak; everything about her screamed lust. Her body was something to be used and abused. She loved every second of it. The problem was that when she was turned on, which seemed to be all the time, you could not carry on any type of a conversation. She smothered you with sex. Her thrusts were like a knife, tearing all normal needs from your body. She was an aphrodisiac. As a result, it was very late when we finally could talk. She didn't want to, but I held back and got out of bed.

"'I'm not done with you—there are still two parts of you that I haven't explored,' she said.

"'I told you that we have to talk,' I said. 'Sally, there is real trouble out there. The Nazis never give up, you know. There are three watching for you, a local Nazi leader looking for me, and who knows how many are still hidden? Almost everyone I know has already been killed. They haven't gotten me yet only because I have the box hidden. They will kill you when you have finished your mission and deliver the box or a letter to the man in New York.'

"'The mission is over for me. I accomplished my goal. I don't give a shit about your box. Don't worry, I can take care of myself. I just need to make a little money on the docks, and I'll be out of your hair.'

"'Look, I've been thinking, I am tired of all this shit. Germany is going to lose the war. We just have to be alive when this is over, and the whole Nazi thing will be gone. No one knows who we are. We can just blend in and live a real life. We only have to make it to the end of the war.'

"'Walter, don't include me in any of your plans. I'm too restless, too angry, too full of revenge. I want to kill people. Someday I will be killed too. It doesn't matter when. Until then, I want to live life to the fullest.'

"'I have a plan,' I said. 'I have some money. We could go abroad and hide until this is over. I have enough money to last a very long time. We could be safe and comfortable and live life just as you want.'

"'Walter, I told you, I'd never let a man try to take care of me again. Too many men have brutalized me and left me for dead. The thought of killing them is all that has kept me going. I will not take a handout.'

"'Okay, I'll pay you a hundred dollars a week to be my bodyguard. You can earn your own money and still hide with me.'

"'Do you pay me for sex too?'

"'If you want.' I truly did not know how to answer that question.

"'I'll charge you five dollars per trick. I don't want you to go broke. Is that okay?'

"'Do I have to pay cash every time, or can I get a little credit?'

"'I'll extend credit up to fifty dollars a week,' she said, laughing.

"'But one more thing,' I said. 'We need to eliminate the guys in New York and the local Nazi leader. We need to leave no trace, or they'll find us. Do you agree?'"

Chapter Forty-Two

It was time now for Pierce to recount his contact with the Poison One. "'Hello,' a deep voice boomed into the phone. The voice had just a whiff of an accent, enough to tell me that I had found my man.

"'I'm looking for the Poison One.'

"'And who are you?' came the reply.

"'I'm the deliveryman,' I said. I could hear a restaurant or deli in the background. The sounds were European.

"'Fine, I'll give you an address …'

"'No, I don't trust you. Here's how we will meet and transfer the box.'

"I told him to meet us at the western tip of Dune Road. It was unpaved, and he would have to walk to the end. We could see anyone coming. Sally was hidden in the high dunes and flat on her belly, looking through a pair of recently purchased binoculars. I was offshore in a stolen fifteen-foot boat.

"We set our plan in motion the day before, when we went to dig up the box. We took it to the bank. I resigned my position, much to the chagrin of the manager since there weren't many men available to work in a bank at that time. I told him that I wanted to rent the largest space in the vault for my box. It was three feet wide by three feet high. I paid him three years' rent in advance. I withdrew twenty thousand dollars from Switzerland and was off.

"First we went on a little shopping spree to gather our tools for the assassination and then paid Frank Hock a visit, giving him half the money. He was overwhelmed. He vowed devotion for life. I simply asked him to keep an eye open and to run an ad in the *New York Times* on Wednesdays if he needed me for anything. I didn't want to tell him where we were going.

"The first part of our plan seemed to be working as we both spied a man making his way toward us over the dunes. I had told Sally that once she knew I had spotted the man, she was to slide over to watch the ocean side. I was sure that Mr. Poison One would not be alone and would try to eliminate me.

"I pulled the boat to within twenty feet of shore and hailed the man.

"'Over here, my friend.'

"'Why are you in a boat?'

"'Let's just say that I feel safer here,' I said. 'Now be a good boy and wade out to the boat to get your prize.'

"'I may kill you for this.'

"'That has occurred to me.'

"He took off his shoes and socks and while doing so revealed a gun in his waistband. Not too clever, I thought, typical Nazi. He then entered the water with his hand on the gun. He reached the boat when the water was waist-high.

"'Let me see the box,' he ordered.

"'I'm sorry to tell you that it was destroyed in the hurricane.'

"'Too much is riding on this, you know. Stop fooling around and give it to me, or I'll add another notch on my gun.'

"'How many men did you bring with you?'

"'I have two, and they have their guns trained on you, my friend. One sign from me, and you're dead. Do you understand?'

"'Do it,' I said. Sally had already given me the all-clear signal.

"He raised both hands and yelled, 'Now.' Nothing happened. A flicker of fear passed through his eyes, and he reached for the gun. Too late! I had the Luger in his face.

"'Drop the gun in the water,' I said. 'I guess your men got lost. Give me your wallet.' His name was Robert Hunt. He lived in Mastic.

"'I need to make sure that you are the Poison One.'

"'How dare you question me?' There was the arrogance I expected.

"'Remember, I have the gun. I need to be satisfied that you are the Poison One before I do anything.'

"'Okay, what do you want to know?'

"'Who sends you instructions?'

"'Why, they come from Himmler, just like yours.'

"'Okay, you are correct. How do you get information?'

"'There are three men in New York that have a radio. They deliver messages directly to me. My organization follows my orders.' He said this with the force of a fanatic.

"'This is also correct, but could be guessed.' I was now getting ready for my big move.

"'Where do they live?' As I said this, I pulled up a suitcase in the boat—I knew that his greed would take over.

"'They live in an apartment in Astoria—it is part of Queens, Thirty-fourth Street and Astoria Boulevard, under the name of Heller. Now give me the suitcase.'

"'Just one more question,' I said, toying with him. 'How many people are in your organization? I need the exact number of members, not just those who are active.'

"'My records are complete and in my desk, I assure you. There are thirty-three, all German men. Now give me the box.'

"'Ja, Herr Hunt. But let me tell you something. Everyone who has come into contact with this box has died. Do you want to take that risk?'

"'For the glory of the Third Reich, for the glory of all Nazis, I and I alone will lead the Aryan race to its rightful place. We will snuff out the Jews, cleanse the population, and control the world, Heil Hitler.'

"'Okay, if you say so.' We had drifted out from shore, just as I had planned. He was up to his chest in the sea now. I grabbed the suitcase, which had two hundred pounds of bricks in it, and moved it to the railing. As he reached for the handle, I looped a handcuff over his wrist and attached it to the suitcase.

"'Herr Hunt, the case is very valuable. Here's the key. Oops, I dropped it into the water. Oh, by the way, it's also very heavy.' With that I pushed the case over the rail, and Hunt and the case disappeared below the surface. I knew that I had just killed a man, but he had it coming. Over the last three years, the Long Island Nazi group had been responsible for four terrorist attacks on different utilities and had killed more than ten innocent people on Long Island alone. I had learned all of this at the library. My first face-to-face kill was a pleasure. This man was not a good German fighting a war—he was an ugly brute, who was in it for the fun and excitement and, most of all, the glory. He loved to kill. The only question for me was which side was I on: American, German, or Nazi? Had I become one of them?

"Stop," shouted Rogers. "You killed someone? Walter, this is bad very bad. I can't let you record a confession."

"He needed to die," Pierce spat back.

Pierce returned to his story. "I started up the boat and ran into the shore. Sally was there and climbed into the craft.

"'Did you remember to take your knives?'

"'I got both of them.'

"'Are you all right?'

"'Nothing a little trip to a warmer climate won't heal,' said Sally. 'Did you get the information?'

"I flashed the wallet. 'Got the address of our friends in Queens and the location of the list of Nazi members in the Long Island chapter. Let's go hunting.' We drove the boat back to the dock and jumped into the car.

"Hunt's house in Mastic was nondescript. There didn't appear to be anyone home. We put on the rubber gloves that we had bought and went around to the back. The backdoor was open. We went in and found no wife or children. I wasn't surprised.

"The list of the members was in a ledger in his desk. Along with it we found fake passports and several blueprints of the electric company and other utilities. I guessed that he was an engineer. The number that I had called was a restaurant where he and his members hung out. I made sure that the number was in plain view on the desk. Astoria was next on our list.

"The city offered us an advantage in that there were other cars and people on the streets. The Astoria section of Queens was mostly German, but we would pass. We watched the address of the spies for over three hours. They eventually came out, intent on their daily library visit.

"As soon as they were out of sight, Hand and I gathered our stuff and headed into the building. Hand picked the lock, and we were soon in their apartment. 'The three nothings,' I called them. Their names would mean nothing to anyone, but their apartment was a warehouse of information. We found maps, documents, and, finally, a radio. They had quite an operation, all neat and tidy. We put down the bag of materials that we had collected at Hunt's house and made sure that we had our gloves on. I wrote the phone number of the restaurant on a matchbook cover. I had found it at Hunt's house. I wanted to make sure of the connection between them and Hunt. Mission accomplished, we then sat down to wait.

"About four in the afternoon, one of the 'nothings' returned. As he entered the door, Sally cut his throat, ear to ear. She was expert at this, smiling as she did it. The other two 'nothings' were a half hour behind. We had moved the first 'nothing' to the middle of the room, and they saw him immediately. It was too late to run, as I had them covered with the Luger. They were little men, real tough when they had you outnumbered, but proved to be cowards when at a disadvantage.

"'Take out your guns and knives, or she will cut you both, just like your friend.' We had ski hats on and had cut holes for our eyes and mouths. We looked like the devil himself to them, and they did as asked.

"I ordered them to drop to their knees.

"Sally tied both of them up in minutes. We secured them to the radiator. Our job was almost done. I wrote out instructions, including where to find Hunt and his friends. Now it was time to go.

"We called Paul Williams's old number from New Jersey. 'Hello, this is Helms, what can I do for you?'

"'Listen carefully. The Nazi espionage ring in New York has been broken. Go to Thirty-fourth Street and Astoria Boulevard in Queens. Enter the Heller apartment. There you will find two spies who are alive and tied up, one dead, and everything you will need to completely close down the ring. You must hurry, as the men are resourceful.'

"'Who is this?' he asked.

"'An American.'"

Pierce was now ready to relate what happened after they broke up the Nazi ring. "The cottage that we rented in the Bahamas was right on the water. The salty smell of the ocean reminded me of home. The constant drive of the waves was very soothing. After two weeks, I was starting to calm down and enjoy the beach.

"We sold the car in Philadelphia and boarded a train for Miami. In Miami we secured a boat that would take us to the Caribbean. We settled on Paradise Island in a small two-bedroom cottage. The trip had been well planned, and our steps were covered. No one knew where we were. This was truly paradise. Sally could not handle the sun very well, being a true redhead, but managed to be out on the beach much of the day—naked, of course. She had gained a little weight, and her figure had really filled out. Her hair was flaming red now, and freckles were popping out everywhere. She attracted attention from all the men. I was jealous.

"I spent my time reading and lazing on the beach. It occurred to me that I wanted to finish getting my college degree. Finally I enrolled in Nassau University. I was surprised to find other men like myself there. Most were draft dodgers, but some were veterans from England.

"We spent our free time drinking exotic drinks and smoking Cuban cigars. Life was good. I didn't even hear from the voices now.

"I read the *Times* every day and was pleased to read about how the FBI had cracked a major Nazi ring on Long Island. A total of forty men were arrested. Several plans were uncovered. Irreparable damage had been done to the Nazi organization in the United States. The FBI announced that it was all part of a continuing investigation. No mention of an anonymous tip or of several dead men. It didn't bother me; I knew who planned and did the work. The murder of Hunt didn't really bother me, either. I thought about it once in a while. I knew that it was cruel, but I couldn't feel the least bit of sympathy for him. I felt that I deserved a medal for my efforts, but no one knew who I was.

"The *New York Times* arrives in the Bahamas three days after the initial printing in America. It was a fine spring Saturday on the beach, or was it Sunday? The days just rolled on without much change. Anyway, the first message from Frank said, 'Wolf, call home.'

"'Frank, how are you?'

"'Wolf, it's good to hear from you. I did as instructed. There's bad news from Germany.'

"'What?' It was all I could muster.

"'The admiral has been arrested and sent to a concentration camp, as were Oster and the priest. Greta has gone missing, and your mother has been declared insane. I'm so sorry—is there anything that I can do for you?'

"'Were there any new instructions from Germany?'

"'I think they believe you were taken in the big roundup of the Nazi organization in the fall. Did you hear about that?'

"'I read about it in the paper. Thanks, Frank, we will talk again.'

"There were worries again in my life. The last few months were easy and fun. Now reality was once again setting in. The Abwehr connection was gone. My mentor and friends were in prison, and I worried about Greta. I hoped that she wasn't in some camp like Sally had been. What about my mother? What were they doing to her? They took her business and her house and now declared her insane. If she had stayed in America, none of this would have happened. Sally noticed the change in me. She tried to cheer me up with sex. Sex cannot replace fear in one's heart.

"In June 1944, I read of the Allied invasion of Europe. The detailed account went on for pages, and it appeared that the Allies were going to win the war. I wondered how much of the news was real. Was it all propaganda? I had learned about propaganda in Germany and recognized it as a powerful tool. My friends at Nassau College were all excited and upbeat. Some talked of going home and getting into the war; I stayed quiet. I had done my part, even if no one knew it. I kept reading the *Times* to follow the advance of the Allies.

"I was consumed by the war. I spent all my time listening to the radio, reading papers, and talking to people about the progress. Someplace along the way, I forgot that I was in paradise, and my employee became restless. She was high-maintenance, and I wasn't even paying her ten dollars a week for her favors. Nor did I notice that she had become plump. One day when I returned from school, she was gone. A short note lay on the table.

Dear Walter,
We always knew that it couldn't last. I didn't love you like you needed. My life has been over for some time, but I enjoyed the vacation with you. I'm going back to Europe. I'm going to fight the Nazi terror. My family and my honor require me to do it. We did good things over here. I will do good things over there. You were a good partner, and I will always have a little piece of you with me. I must now go alone.
Love,
Sally

"I can't say I was devastated. I always felt she would go; I just didn't know when. But now that I didn't have anyone to look after me, I spun out of control. There was only one month of school left. I was drunk on graduation day and missed the ceremony. Rum was my passion. I put it in everything, including my coffee. I went to the local Bahamian bars and got into fights over the local women and eventually discovered that I could forget my troubles for weeks at a time. I hit bottom. Everyone continued to leave me. Was it a curse?

"One day I was lying on the beach and heard lots of people cheering and shouting. I was too preoccupied to find out what had happened. After awhile, all was quiet. It was the fall of Germany, and I had missed it. About four months later, as I sat at the bar in a joint, I heard cheering and shouting again; however, I was too interested in the bottle of rum next to me. It was late that night before anyone told me that Japan had surrendered. We were fighting Japan? What had happened to Germany? My buddy wanted another swig. Then he blurted out that Germany had surrendered in the spring, Hitler was dead, and Germany was now divided. Divided? What did he mean? He took another swig, and then he elaborated. The United States, France, and England each got a piece of Germany, and Russia got a big piece. Berlin itself was divided.

"I stopped drinking that night. I missed everything. What happened to the admiral? And what happened to my mother? Greta? Could I go there to find them? I had to know. It was time to become human again. I spent the next week at the American consulate. I was seeking information. I found out that I could fly to England since the Bahamas were a protectorate of England. I could take a boat to France. Germany was devastated—there were no guarantees, but I could get there; that was something."

Chapter Forty-Three

Heaving a sigh of relief, Pierce continued his story. "I arrived in Germany in October 1945. There was a chill in the foul air. The stench of death, defeat, despair, and famine was more pervasive than the cold front. Military police were everywhere. Every German appeared to be on the verge of starvation. Vacant looks told of true defeat. Germany was gone. I brought cash but found out that Germans were prohibited from having American currency. Most business was done by barter. Cigarettes became the new money. Whole cities were gone, and nothing but rubble remained. So many people displaced or killed! Germany would never come back. The Nazis were gone forever, and so were many good Germans.

"I had both a driver and a bodyguard. I was warned that there were still some renegade groups of people who refused to surrender and were dangerous. The consulate would not let me enter the country without protection, even though I told them that my mother was in Berlin. Of course, I could not tell them that she shared my real name. Perhaps they felt that anyone who wanted to go to Germany had to have a good reason.

"The driver turned onto the autobahn, one of Hitler's projects. Suddenly we came to a roadblock. At the roadblock, the Russian guards would not let us pass, telling my driver that the frontier was closed. Frontier? This was the heart of Germany. Berlin was just down the road. My driver ask how we could get into Berlin, They just laughed and told us that we could not pass through. We must return the way we had come.

"Eventually we found that we could fly into Berlin, although we would have to wait two weeks before a flight was available. It was the longest two weeks of my life. Our accommodations were fair. We could not escape the horror of the war. No matter where I went, I saw death and destruction, even in the countryside. Burned-out and bullet-ridden tanks, airplanes, guns, and trucks littered the landscape. Mercifully, our plane would leave in the morning.

"Berlin was not as bad as I had heard. Some sections had escaped total devastation. My mother's house was located in one of these sections. When we reached the front of the house, we found many American jeeps in the driveway. It was now a command post. I walked up the drive and was stopped by an MP. I requested a visit with the commander and was ushered into my grandfather's library. There sat a colonel who said his name was Hayes.

"'What can I do for you, Mr. Pierce?' He picked up my name from the passport.

"'I'm looking for the owner of this house.'

"'I'm afraid that he is dead, and the house is now property of the U.S. government,' Hayes retorted.

"'No, the owner before the Nazis took it.'

"'That would be Emma Franz, of the munitions Franz empire, wouldn't it? Why do you need to find her?' He had grown very suspicious now.

"'Yes, that's right; she is my aunt.'

"'Are you German?'

"'I'm an American, born and raised on Long Island.'

"'No shit! What part of Long Island?'

"'Westhampton, to be exact.'

"'No kidding? I grew up in East Moriches, on the north shore.'

"'Colonel Hayes, East Moriches is on the south shore.'

"'Okay, just checking if you were really from there. We get a lot of desperate people coming in here. So, Emma Franz is your aunt?'

"'That's right. Can you tell me where to find her?'

"'It's not good news—she is in an asylum. The war has taken its toll. I'll give you the address.'

"The asylum was worse than I expected. It was an old hospital that had been used as a jail during the war. There were bars on the windows and a big fence around the compound. It was a prison without guards. The administrator told me that I could find my mother in the garden, even though it was rather cool that day.

"I recognized her right away. She was seated properly on a barren bench. She did not appear to notice the weather. Actually she didn't notice anything, according to the administrator. She was off somewhere—nobody knew where.

"'Hello, Mother,' I said. There was no reaction. I was suddenly overwhelmed and started to cry. I sat with her for hours. She never moved. That night I contacted the consulate and asked about taking her to America. They told me that it could be done in about eight to ten months. They gave me the name of a doctor.

"I visited my mother for four weeks straight. The doctor was happy to have a paying customer, but he was not able to help Mother. He said that she would be catatonic until she died. I really didn't know what to do. I didn't care about the money it would cost to take care of her in America; it was just that I wasn't sure that I could stand seeing her this way. I was feeling very dark sitting on the bench with Mother, when I heard a familiar voice.

"'Hello, Wolf.' It was the admiral's wife, Winnie. 'I heard that you were in town. I come to see your mother once a month. We were good friends before the war. I think it has been bad for all of us.'

"'I don't know what to say,' I stammered.

"'Nothing needs to be said—we take care of our own. I will watch over your mother until neither of us needs watching; I have nothing more to give. She did care for you—she just couldn't say it. She got caught up in the moment.'

"'I'm sorry about your husband. He was my friend and mentor. I respected him more than any other man that I have known.'

"'Here,' she said, handing me a crumpled letter. 'He wanted you to read this. It came from his prison before he died.'

Dear Wolf,
I'm sure that you are well. I trained you to be. Your mission now is to protect the tablet. Don't let it out until the right time. I trust your judgment and can only tell you that I enjoyed our relationship. My time and work is over. I hope that I made a difference. I'm sure that you will tell me all about it when we see each other in another life.
Yours Truly,
Wilhelm Canaris

"I went back to the Canaris home and found that it was now a small apartment in central Berlin. Their two children had grown up since I had seen them but were frozen in time in a picture on the small mantle.

"Both died during an air raid in 1944. Winnie told me they had been her great joy. Now her only reason for living was to help people she knew, Mother included. I asked what I could do. She did not reply. I told her that I was considering taking Mother back to America. She told me that Mother hated America and would prefer to stay here. I understood. I then asked if she needed any money, and she started to cry. She told me that she had nothing and would soon be on the street. I had forgotten how proud some people were. She was destitute but would not ask for help, even from an old friend.

"So we made a deal, a business transaction. Germans always respected a good deal. I would pay her to watch Mother and to send me notes of any progress. She could continue to help all her friends. I felt good and knew that Mother would be with friends. In addition to money, I had sympathy.

"I visited Winnie several more times and helped her to move to an actual house that had tenants. It would be her house from now on, since I bought it for two thousand American dollars.

"One night I asked her about Greta. She told me that Greta was in Siberia. She had been captured by the Russians and exiled to the tundra. I felt sorry. She did not deserve her fate.

"It was now late winter in Germany. I spent over three months in locating people, visiting with them, and trying to understand the reasons for what had happened. I tried to find out whether anyone remembered my mission. I found no one. I stayed away from rum. I turned to beer, sausages, and bratwurst, and my waistline showed it. I was becoming a typical German businessman—balding, out of shape, and making deals everywhere.

"One day I was having a little breakfast of three eggs, sausage, apple pancakes, and coffee when I decided to read the *Times*, something that I had not done in months. I was paying more attention to my food than the paper, but the ad was unmistakable: 'Wolf, Urgent.'

"'Frank, how are you?'

"'Thank God you called. Another two weeks, and it would be too late.'

"'Too late? For what?'

"'Your house, Walter. Your house is up for sale.'

"'What? How could that be?'

"'It was in the paper, Walter. The military is giving up more than half the base. There are five thousand acres going up for auction on March 30. You can buy back your old house.'

"'Frank, this is great news. I'll head home immediately.'"

Chapter Forty-Four

Pierce took a moment before continuing, getting his thoughts in order to continue his story on the other side of the Atlantic. "The trip back to America gave me time to think. America was really my home, whereas Germany had been a cause for me to be compulsive about. I could regain my boyhood home. I would be happy then. My only concern was that I might not have enough money left. I spent my inheritance like a madman for over two years. I hoped it had not ruined my one chance to be happy. When I arrived in New York, my first call was to my banker in Switzerland. He told me that I had only spent the interest on my money, and not even that—I was a millionaire.

"The real estate sale—or should I say 'auction'—took place in the courthouse in Riverhead. There were many people there. All wanted a piece of the land. I wanted it all.

"The auctioneer said that we could bid on any part as long as we bid in five-acre lots. He noted that the fire lanes that traverse the area were property of the county and made rights-of-way for the land in the forests. As a result, he said, any parcel was accessible by road. There were large topographical maps of the area on the wall. People could use a grease pencil to mark areas that they wanted. The going rate was fifteen dollars an acre. If more than one person wanted a parcel, then it would be auctioned off to the highest bidder. It all seemed to be quite fair. However, I was not interested in fair, just in getting my house.

"The actual auction would start in a half hour. I had circled the entire map and sat down to wait, feeling confident and relaxed. It was then that I heard a small commotion and turned to see what was going on. In the middle of the room, there stood a soldier with a young woman. He had on full military dress, and I could not help but notice the medals on his chest. I did not know what they stood for. I asked Frank, who was seated next to me, who the man was.

"'That's Stan Banyon. He's a true war hero,' he said. 'He comes from Eastport. He's still recovering from injuries he suffered in Burma during the war. He lived in the jungle for two years with Merrill's Marauders—most did not make it back. That's his fiancée; she's from the city someplace. Guess that they want some land to start a family.'

"'Maybe I'll let him have a little piece of my land,' I chuckled. Actually I was extremely jealous. Everyone paid attention to Banyon, and you could see that they all felt that he was a hero—his medals proved it. I was a hero too—only no one fussed over me, and I had no medals. He also had a woman, and I did not.

"The gavel sounded to begin the auction. There were over twenty overlapping circles on the map, so I knew it would take a long time. First awarded was the land that was not in dispute. I was awarded the first 2,650 acres for the going rate of fifteen dollars an acre. For fewer than forty thousand dollars, I instantly became the largest landowner in Speonk and maybe in the entire county. Actually, I bought the land under the name of the South Fork Gun Club. It was a name that Frank and I cooked up.

"The first real competition was with a man named Karmmerer, who owned a real estate business. The one hundred acres he wanted were smack-dab in the middle of the entire plot, and it was one of the highest places in the area. At thirty dollars an acre, he gave up. The next fifty acres went for twenty-five dollars an acre, and so it went. I did let a couple of people buy land on the very fringes of the south and north, but the rest would belong to me.

"Finally we were down to the most western portions. The sections along Speonk-Riverhead Road were prime property. So far I had 5,500 acres, at a cost of less than one hundred thousand dollars. I decided to let the people south of my house win the auction; it would be good to have neighbors. All three got their land for fifteen dollars and fifty cents per acre. Everyone was surprised and pleased. I thought it would be good press and happy neighbors for me too. Now came the big one—the land I really wanted. But something was wrong: the auctioneer was talking to Banyon and not pounding his gavel. I stood up and bid a hundred dollars per acre and was ignored. What was going on?

"Soon the auctioneer came to the podium and made an announcement. A ten-acre parcel was awarded to Stan Banyon. I stood up again and screamed, 'There was no auction! I was robbed; that land is mine.' Everyone looked at me like I was an ogre, Scrooge, or maybe a fanatic land-grabbing outsider.

"The auctioneer explained that as part of his discharge, Stanley Banyon was guaranteed by law to have first rights on any government land up for auction after the war. It was part of the GI bill, and it ruined my miserable life. Any attempt by me to get the land would be perceived as criminal.

"Frank and I paid our money, but it wasn't as happy an occasion as I had hoped. It was then that I started a different life and developed plots that survive today.

"I was staying with Frank in the small apartment over his store. I hadn't heard from the voices for many years, and I thought that they were gone. Frank's mother had died while I was in Germany, so he now lived alone. I sometimes felt sorry for him. He was only in his mid-twenties and had no woman. The long hours at the store and taking care of me left him little time to find a woman. He was perhaps more lonely than myself, if that was possible.

"I was hard on him. I rediscovered my old friend rum, and we were having a swell time. I wallowed in my misery, fevered with the contempt that I felt over the failure to purchase my house.

"One night we decided to go out to dinner at our favorite restaurant, Lenny's. We had gone there often, and we became friendly with the owner. The place was wall-to-wall people in the summer. We were privileged to have a table reserved for us. We were seated at our table, admiring the many women in the place, when Lenny came by and sat down with us. A bottle of rum decorated our table. Lenny poured himself a drink.

"'You know, Walter, I'm going to sell this place.'

"'Why?' I inquired. 'This place is a gold mine.'

"'Yeah, in the summer, but in the winter we don't get much business from the locals, and I haven't had a Saturday night off in over twenty years. I have a good manager, but I want to see Florida before I die—I'm over sixty, you know.'

"It made me think about my life. It was the opposite of Lenny's. I was always on the move. I had been to so many places that I had no roots. My mind was on other things—and then I saw Banyon. I could not mistake the black wavy hair and the pencil mustache. It was Banyon, coming out of the kitchen, dressed in a chef's hat and carrying a boiled lobster the size of Texas.

"'What's he doing here?' I slurred.

"Lenny looked up. 'Oh, Stan works here on weekends. He was a cook during the war, works fast and cheap. He's trying to make extra money so he can get married and move into his house.'

"My brain was swimming. I saw blood before my eyes, and I recognized the signs of a new compulsion taking root. I wanted to make things as difficult on Banyon as I could.

"'I'll buy your restaurant,' I offered. My main purpose in rashly agreeing to buy the restaurant was to fire Banyon. I had not intended to, but I had now become a restaurateur.

"As it turned out, Frank and I became partners. He supplied the meat and all the food with the exception of the fresh fish. Banyon took care of getting the fish, and we all made money. When I sobered up, I realized that the investment was more important than punishing Banyon, who turned out to be a good chef. Besides, I could keep an eye on him, and he was also good to drink with. He drank a shot and then a beer, a lot of them. It wasn't that I had gotten over my envy of his getting my house. On the contrary, I thought that I could get him to sell me the house someday.

"For three years I drank, chased women, and paid little attention to my land and business. Everything kind of ran by itself. In the evenings I would go to my restaurant and sit at the best table, greeting people and offering a drink from my rum bottle. My money continued to grow. Every week I went to the bank where I had worked during the war and deposited the currency. I kept paying on the vault space that held the tablet. I just couldn't think of anything to do with it.

"In February 1950, I got a call from Winnie Canaris. She said that Mother had passed away. I decided to go to Germany to attend the funeral.

"Germany had changed in just those few short years. It was again bustling with activity. People were not starving, and many of the cities were in the process of being rebuilt. There was something else that sent a shiver down my back. Everywhere I went, there were posters and newspapers talking about the Iron Curtain and the ultraconservative right-wing hawks that opposed Communism. I knew who the Communists were and was pretty sure that the hawks had another name, the White Supremacy Party. Could it all happen again? Who was the greater threat?

"Mother's funeral brought out only a few people. Most of the people she had known were already dead. I needed to protect my new identity, so Winnie took the lead. At the burial site, I noticed several men on the perimeter. It was like Frank's father's funeral all over again. They were undercover police or secret police or KGB or CIA or God knows who. I decided that I needed to return to America on the next flight.

"The Nazi Hunters were actually several groups of people that were looking for the many Nazis that had escaped capture and were still at large. They reasoned that some Nazis would probably come to Mother's funeral. All they got was me.

"I was 'detained' as I entered my hotel and taken to a location that was foreign to me. They were hard people, and I was treated roughly during the trip. I kept telling them that I was an American, but they just kept cuffing me to keep me quiet. Soon I was seated in a metal chair with a bright light in my eyes. Then it started.

"'What is your name?' The question came from a distance.

"'Walter Pierce, I'm an American. What do you want with me?'

"'What is your real name?'

"'Walter Pierce,' I replied. The first punch was in the stomach. It knocked the wind out of me.

"'What is your name? Why were you at the funeral of a known Nazi?'

"I knew how this would progress and decided that I would take a chance before I had no teeth or unbroken bones in my body. I was sure that the admiral would have destroyed my records and no one would be able to prove anything. The only problem was that these men were fanatics and would believe what they wanted to believe.

"'My born name was Wolfgang Becker II—Emma was my mother.'

"'Ah, now we are getting someplace,' Ira Gold, the interrogator, said. 'So, you are a Nazi, eh?'

"'I am not and never have been a Nazi. I'm an American. I was born in New York and lived there until I was nineteen.'

"'And then you came here to help the Fuehrer.'

"'No, my mother came back to care for my grandfather and to run the family business in 1930. I stayed a little while and then left. I was never in the army. I never fought for Hitler.'

"'I find that hard to believe, considering your connections. Did you know Admiral Canaris?'

"This was a dangerous question and so early in the interrogation; I was scared now. 'Of course, he was a friend of my grandfather, and Winnie was a close friend of my mother. Why are you questioning me? I have done nothing.'

"'How did you get the name Walter Pierce?'

"'In 1936, in France I changed my name legally. I knew the war was coming and didn't want a German name. It interfered with my activities.'

"'So, you were a playboy, shirked your family responsibilities, and even changed your name to stay out of the war? How did you escape being drafted by the Germans?'

"'I told you. I'm an American.'

"'We will check on that. Tell me where you were between 1930 and 1945.'

"'I told you, I was a playboy, traveled all over—check my passport.'

"'I'm particularly interested in the years 1932 through 1936.'

"'Well, I went to Italy and then to Spain, to help in the Lincoln Brigade. It was very sexy and romantic. I have nothing to hide. Check it out.'

"'Okay, that is all for today. You will be our guest while we check your background.'

"I was interrogated for four months, during which time I had to recount every step I made. I was kept in a cell in a large house outside of Munich. It was very lonely. Even the voices would have been a welcome guest, but they weren't heard from. There were several other German men there, and I avoided all of them like the plague. I didn't want any of them to recognize me and sell me out. The fanatic Nazis were good at stabbing each other in the back when they themselves were threatened.

"I was able to keep in touch with Frank, but I was sure that my mail and phone calls were censored. I believed that my story would hold up and I would be released soon.

"Gold started another session with a rehash of old news. 'You are familiar with Winnie Canaris?'

"'I told you that she was a friend of my mother. Of course, I knew her.'

"'Are you aware that she was interrogated just after the war ended?'

"'I assumed that she was, but I had no contact with her until 1946.'

"Ignoring my answer, Gold continued. 'As part of her statements, she mentioned that her husband traveled to visit Mussolini and Franco in the years between 1932 and 1936. She said that he was traveling with a young man named Wolfgang Becker. That was you, was it not?'

"'Yes.'

"'Well, Mr. Pierce, I'm afraid that you are going to need a lawyer. We are going to prosecute you for war crimes. Take him away.'

"The trial was long and drawn out. My lawyer told me they had no real evidence that I was a Nazi and I would be set free. I told him that I was, in fact, not a Nazi. He didn't believe me either.

"I was interned for the duration of the trial, which lasted over four years. The prosecution kept asking for delays, as they would capture another Nazi and they waited to interrogate the man before moving forward. They were sure they would find someone who could prove that I was a Nazi. They didn't know that everyone who knew of my position and mission was dead.

"Finally in March 1954, they declared a mistrial and let me go. It was called a mistrial because they wanted to arrest me again when they had more evidence. I didn't care by then. I left Germany as soon as possible, vowing to never return.

"I walked from the train station in Speonk to Frank's grocery store. He was surprised to see me. Immediately he invited me to stay with him until I found a place. He noted that I looked different. I had lost over twenty pounds, and my hair was all white, even though I was only forty-three years old. I felt tired and worn. I wondered about the fact that my real name and my assumed name could now be connected. It was all a matter of record in Germany. All someone would have to do was read the transcript of my trial. Would this mean that the remaining Nazis would be after me? Who was still alive that knew of my mission?

"Things had changed in Frank's apartment. The drapes had been updated, something a man didn't do. There were some pictures of Frank and a dark-haired woman at the beach. It was clear to me why he liked her, but it was not clear why she liked him. I went to my room and found new sheets and a new bedspread. I was both ecstatic and worried. Our little group didn't need another member. Had he told her anything about me? Was she a plant by some organization? God knows there were enough people after me. *Was I being totally paranoid?* I decided to talk to Frank to feel him out.

"'Frank, it seems that things have changed.'

"'Yeah, I got myself a girl now,' he replied. He was over ten years younger than I was and now in his prime to land a woman. The question for me was 'Is she the right one?'

"'Where did you meet her?'

"'Actually, she came in for a job interview at Lenny's. I hired her, and next thing I knew, we were a couple. It's been very lonely without you around.'

"'What do you know about her?' I asked with greater interest.

"'Walter, don't worry. Ann is local, a part of the Raynor family. She went to Eastport High School. The family has been in the area since the middle of the 1700s. They were some of the first settlers of this part of Long Island.'

"I was feeling better, so I inquired about the restaurant. Frank said, 'I made her the manager of the restaurant. The guy that was there quit two years ago, and I needed someone. Also, Stan Banyon quit two months ago. He went to work in his father's grocery store in Eastport.'

"Suddenly the whole Banyon thing came rushing back—the loss of my house, the respect that Banyon attracted, my need to somehow overshadow him. *Did I really hate him?* My compulsion was back with a vengeance. I started plotting almost immediately to get what I wanted, but first I needed a car and a place to live.

"The next morning I felt refreshed and ready to face my new world. I didn't have many creature needs, as my bank account was bulging. My needs were psychological—on the level of acceptance and how I viewed myself. My ego was growing. I borrowed Frank's car and drove to the bank. I intended to withdraw some money to buy a car.

"The bank manager greeted me at the door. He was the one who hired me more than a dozen years earlier. We chatted for a while. I learned the bank was on hard times. It was a family-owned bank. The family didn't get along, and when their grandfather died, everything landed in court. The bank was up for sale. If they didn't find a buyer soon, it would close due to the lack of cash flow. Things looked bleak.

"While I was in the bank, the voices in my head came back. I was completely dumbfounded. Why did they return now? I did not hear them during all the years I was stuck in Germany. They kept saying, 'Buy it, we fit.'

The evidence was strong, and the voices convinced me. Their effect on me was very powerful—*why now, why in the bank?* I wondered if the tablet stored in the bank controlled the voices.

"While at the Cadillac dealership, I realized that owning a bank would be good for my investments. I had all this money in Switzerland. I had more than five thousand acres of land that could be sold; with the buyers needing financing and the cash flow from my restaurant, not to mention Frank's cash flow, we would survive. Eastern Long Island was growing, and I could not think of a good reason not to own it. So, I headed back to the bank in my new Cadillac and made arrangements to buy it. The manager would stay on, with a small piece of the business. Not bad for my first day back in America!

"Nineteen fifty-four was turning out to be a good year. For the first time in my life, I felt wanted, useful, and happy. I found a small house right on the Moriches Bay in Remsenburg. A sailboat was added to my growing list of possessions. Frank married Ann, and they lived above their store. They were frequent visitors to my house, but that Thanksgiving I received a call.

"'Walter, it's Frank.'

"'Good to hear from you, Frank. So what time should I get to your house for Thanksgiving?'

"'Well, that's the problem. Ann and I are going to spend Thanksgiving with her family. You understand.'

"'Of course,' I responded. 'Have good time,' I lied.

"I was alone again and didn't like that feeling. I decided to go to Riverhead and eat at a German restaurant there. I made the mistake of taking Speonk-Riverhead Road. I avoided that route since returning to America. I usually went the longer way past the air force base. As I sped up the road, I approached my old house. I slowed down. Several cars were in the circular driveway, and many kids were playing football on the front lawn. More than two dozen people hung around the porch, and they all seemed to be happy. They waved as I went by. My face became red, and my anger grew. Why should these people be so happy when I was heading up the lonely road all by myself?

"All that evening, I obsessed over my loneliness and Banyon's success in life. I had everything—money, position, and possessions—but didn't have anyone, especially tonight. The waiter understood and kept the rum flowing well into the night. They threw me out at midnight. I was very drunk. All that I could think about was my house. I wanted my house. It was my connection to the past, my heritage, and was even surrounded by my land. The only reason that Stan Banyon owned my house was because he had some medals. In my drunken stupor, I decided I needed to steal those medals. The medals belonged to me. I deserved them, and once I had them, the house would be mine again.

"I hatched the plan in my head as I was attempting to drive back home. It was simple really; I was incapable of anything complicated at the time. I would sneak into the house and steal the medals. I entered the last fire lane and parked my car in the woods behind the Banyon house. I headed to the back door, and I noticed the old pump house and diverted my route. Using a flashlight, I found the trapdoor in the pump house. The tunnel was just as it had been in 1942. As I entered the basement, I realized that I was not only sober but also very excited.

"This was a true adventure, with a clear measure of danger. After all, Banyon could probably still shoot a gun. For the first time in a long time, my body felt alive. My senses were tuned to any noise, my hearing alert. My mind also cleared. I would not steal the medals tonight but instead would do some reconnaissance. I would put to use the skills I had been taught many years ago in spy school.

"It only took me a few minutes to ascertain that the Banyons had not discovered the hidden room or the ladders inside the walls. They were probably too busy repairing the many bullet holes and replacing the broken windows to realize that the walls didn't match. I was elated. Some secrets of my house remained only for my use.

"I moved very slowly. I checked each rung of the ladder as I climbed to the second floor. Finally I reached the attic and paused, not sure of what to do next. I sat there for over an hour before I went to the trapdoor in the closet and pulled it up. The closet door was open, allowing me to see into the room. Two little boys were sleeping in twin beds. I climbed down to the front attic and realized that I couldn't see anything and had no idea where the parents were. It was going to be more difficult than I imagined, but I was up to the task.

"Coming out of the pantry wall, I found a huge supply of food in the pantry. How many people lived in the house? I went to the door and opened it very slowly. It creaked, and I heard someone say, 'What was that?' I retreated quickly, back through the wall and down to the basement. It was time to leave. As I was opened the secret door to the tunnel, an eerily single male voice whispered into my ear, 'Please come back; I have so much to show you.'

Rogers once again interjected, "So now we are adding home invasion, trespassing, and a whole bunch of crimes. Walter, I had no idea. This can never get out to the public, you know."

Pierce replied, "Stop whining. There is more to come."

Pierce continued. "Once safe in my car, I recounted my little adventure. The voice from the house was different, yet somehow seemed familiar. Was this voice connected to the tablet too? It didn't speak in a riddle. I knew one thing—I wanted to find out more. Next time I would be prepared.

"I spent weeks thinking about what happened. What were the legal ramifications if I got caught? I could go to jail. I could not let that happen. Yet I was drawn to the old house. Something there satisfied what I yearned for. I began plotting; there was so much to learn.

"That winter was unusually severe. On Long Island, that meant snow, snow that stayed. As a result, my plans were delayed. This wasn't war, just a little skirmish, and I had other things to do.

"As usual Frank was my sounding board.

"'Frank, I decided to start a real estate business,' I told him.

"'Good idea,' he replied. 'You could use it to sell some of our land and finance the whole enterprise through your bank. You could make three markups on each land sale.'

"But I paid a price. I had to be near the office in Riverhead most of the time, and when I wasn't, I was showing clients property or buying up farmers' lands. There was also the restaurant to look after and the bank work of signing documents. In addition, I was moving my money from Switzerland, a little at a time. The pace was hectic. I didn't have time to obsess. I would drive by the Banyon house every few months to try to figure out when they were home and how many people were living there. I had a plan, but neither the time nor the chance to implement it.

"The opportunity came on Memorial Day, 1956. At noon I was heading down Sunrise Highway in Eastport. All of a sudden, a foot-patrol policeman stopped my car.

"'Pull over to the side of the road,' he said. "'The Memorial Day Parade is marching through. Cars are not allowed on the street until the parade passes.'

"The policeman did me a big favor, but neither of us knew it at the time. Since I didn't want to take the long way around, I decided to pull down a side street to watch the parade. There might be some prospective buyers in the crowd.

"The parade was like many others that I'd seen, except for one thing. Stan Banyon was walking with the American Legion group. There he was, carrying a large American flag, and people were cheering for him and his friends. I suddenly noticed that his wife and several children were at the parade. This was my chance.

"I ran to my Cadillac and bolted down the road. It took me twenty minutes to reach the Banyon house. I figured they would be at the parade for at least another hour, which would allow me time. I cruised past the house, and as anticipated, it was deserted.

"I entered the house from the tunnel. I promised myself to be out by one o'clock. I wore gloves, and I carried a bag filled with tools. First I checked the downstairs. There were eight chairs around the dining table. Two big couches were in the living room. The parlor that my mother loved was walled up and made into a bedroom. No doubt, it was Stan Banyon's bedroom. I had no access to the room and decided to move on. Upstairs there were four bedrooms, the one with the trapdoor in the closet and three others that faced the front of the house. They were adjacent to the attic. I walked through each room. The second room had grandparents' clothes in the closet. The third had things that belonged to a single man, an uncle perhaps. The final room was decorated all in pink.

"I located the medals in a drawer in the master bedroom. I wanted to take them, but that would bring down the law, and my ultimate plan would be discovered. After completing a full reconnaissance, I left. No voice spoke to me on that trip.

"When I told Frank about my adventure, he was very angry.

"'Walter, I know you are obsessed with your old house, but you could get into real trouble by going there. You can buy any house you want. Why do you covet this old house?'

"'Somehow, it is part of my future,' I replied. 'I cannot help myself.'

"It wasn't until the winter of 1957 that I was able to start my plan to win my house back. It was a cool and windy night in December. There were many trees in the yard, mostly fruit trees. When the wind blew, they made rustling noises. Branches snapped; leaves whistled. Night was eerie in the old house, and I was going to make it scarier. I was dressed in black and covered my face. No one would recognize me. I put on kids' sneakers.

"I waited until I heard the two boys in their room. Then I came out of the hall closet. I put my foot on the top step and pushed down. It creaked, just as it had when I lived there. A little voice asked, 'Who's there?' I shot back into the closet.

"I could hear panic calls of 'Mom,' and then feet coming up the stairs. That was all for the night. I went home, believing I was on the right course and would have them out of my house by spring. Only once did I hear a voice in my head. "Watch out for the little one." I assumed the voice meant the boy, but why?

"After awhile I became a regular visitor to the Banyon house. Sometimes I would open a door and leave it open. I also tilted pictures and moved things on counters. Sometimes I listened to their talk and found they were tougher than I suspected. They said the magnetic pole caused disturbances or wind coming through the old house caused the pictures to tilt. But I could tell that they all were a little spooked. It was time to step up my plan.

"One night I let myself down the trapdoor in the boys' bedroom. They were deep sleepers. The youngest one was Colton Banyon. I walked over to his bed and saw that he was facing the wall. I sat down on the bed and stayed there for a few minutes. I could smell his fear. The boy was awake now, but afraid to move. When he began to tense up, I knew he would turn over and face his ghost, so I got up slowly and leaped to the closet. I didn't know it then but found out later that in my haste to climb up the hole, I accidentally hit the ceiling with my sneaker and left a shoe print.

"The boy was screaming that someone was in the room. Feet pounded up the steps, and I could hear harsh words from Stan Banyon.

"In a drunken voice, he said, 'Quit your crying before I give you something to cry about.'

"'But, I'm telling you there was someone on my bed. Maybe he's under the bed,' the boy cried.

"'So what do you want me to do, look under it?' Stan Banyon slurred.

"'Yes, please,' cried the boy. Banyon grabbed the kid and threw him on the floor so he could look under the bed. Then he left.

"Suddenly I felt ashamed. I was causing trouble for a child. I wanted Stan Banyon out, but instead, all I was doing was creating a phobia for a child. The voice talked to me that night. 'Do not harm the boy; you will need him,' the voice said.

"I did not go back to the house for over two years. I'm not sure if it was the terror of being caught or that I was afraid of the fear I was instilling in my prey. I was also worried that the voice in my head would come out again. It was both soothing and demanding. It told me things and gave me advice. It treated me like a child but always made me think. This voice was very different from the voices of my mission. I realized that single voice was connected to the old house. Or was I going crazy? In any case, I wasn't sure I wanted to continue. Stan Banyon's drinking had confused me. I admired him for what he had done during the war. We were alike in that—we had many horrors to keep buried in our brains. I also continued to drink too much. The difference was that I had no children to abuse.

"My next trip back was to satisfy my curiosity more than anything else. I wanted to see how the family was coping and if there was anything new. I heard the cries of a baby. Was it a boy or girl? I found the room with the baby and ascertained that there was a new girl in the house. There were some other changes. Everyone looked bigger and older.

"On my first trip to the house, I drilled several holes in the walls that allowed me to see into the upstairs bedrooms. I was discreet and hid the holes well. I reasoned that if the Banyons found the holes, they would just think that they were left over from the time the house was used for target practice. There was one thing that I did not consider—wallpaper. The young girl's room was wallpapered, and the hole had been covered over since my last visit. I almost burst out laughing. The boys were in their room, and the quiet one was tinkering with a radio. He had it all apart on the floor, studying the parts. The younger boy was drawing pictures at a desk. They were very intense about their work. I studied them for a while and wondered if all boys were so quiet.

"The voice was very loud that night. 'Take a good look; understand what you see.' Then it said, 'Work for the future; you will be needed.' That night was the first time that I saw the voice. He was sometimes in color, sometimes white, always smoky, and never stationary. He pulled me to the ladder—'Understand what you see.'

"I made my way down and through the pantry. It was quiet, except for the TV blaring in the background. I chanced a peek around the corner. The wife was on a couch, reading a book. Stan Banyon was glued to the TV. Next to his chair was a table with six empty bottles of beer.

"I spent several hours going from room to room that night, learning about the family and their habits. I also decided to get out my drill again.

"Nineteen sixty also bought earth-shattering news. I was perusing the local newspaper when a small article jumped out at me. It was a blurb from a news service and said a war veteran named George Lincoln Rockwell had formed a new political party—the American Nazi Party. Rockwell vowed to attend civil rights meetings and demonstrations to spread his hatred of blacks and Jews. They were back. After only fifteen years, the Nazi movement was again making news.

"By 1961, I was regular visitor to the Banyon house. I tried not to scare them too much. The Banyons had another baby, another girl, and the house was really crowded. There were seven Banyons, an uncle, and, at times, some grandparents. I did not know how they were able to feed all those people, but they did. Stan was getting worse. His drinking was changing his personality. The younger boy, Colton, was always in trouble because he did not understand about drunks. The rest of the kids tried to be quiet and get along with their father, but Colton was independent and often took the brunt of his father's condition.

"The problem was made more complicated in the sixties by the imminent war in a far-off place called Vietnam. One night, I heard them arguing.

"Stan opened the argument. 'I fought in the big war, and both of you will fight in this war.' I wanted them to stay out of it.

"The older boy, Jim, replied, 'Dad, I signed into the navy. I leave for boot camp in two months.'

"'The navy is not the army. You belong in the rangers like me.'

"'They have special schools. I'll learn a trade. What is wrong with that?' Jim tried to reason.

"'What about you, Colton?' Stan asked.

"'I'm going to college.'

"Stan Banyon had lost in both cases and turned further to his cold, foamy friend."

"Visiting the house was not the same with the boys gone. Banyon's mother had moved in with them. I realized that she was too much like my own mother. She was very opinionated and straitlaced and kept everyone else on edge. I tried scaring her, but she totally ignored me. No wonder Banyon was so tough. I decided to visit only on holidays when everyone was there. The voices were quiet too. That was 1966."

Rogers cut in, "I know that you purchased several other companies after 1966. You must have been too busy to visit the house?"

"I was not only busy with my companies, but I was continuously reminded that Nazis still existed."

"What do you mean?"

"Another wire service article caught my eye. George Lincoln Rockwell, head of the American Nazi Party, had been assassinated by one of his own men. Since he was a war veteran, he was scheduled for burial in the national cemetery at Culpeper. However, his followers refused to remove their swastika armbands and had been denied entrance into the cemetery. No one knew where his body was buried, just like Hitler.

"My only passion became reading everything I could find about living Nazis. There were many articles. I soon realized that there were modern Nazis, but they had changed their names. In fact, they had many names."

"What names?" Rogers asked. "This makes no sense."

"Trent, there are too many to discuss, but they all have one goal—white supremacy. It was the same goal that the Nazis had preached. Then things got worse."

Rogers jumped in. "Something happened, what?"

"It happened in early 1986. I received a devastating phone call. It was from Ann Hoch."

"'Frank died. It is blamed on heart attack,' she said.

"'I don't know what to say, Ann. Frank was always my best friend.'

"'He loved you too, Walter. Nothing will be the same for either of us.'

"I became a recluse. My restaurants sent me meals. My only companions were Stella, my housekeeper, and sometimes the presidents of my various companies. Of course you were there many times, Trent. I wasn't sure that I wanted to continue. But something kept pushing me to keep studying the new white supremacists.

"In the summer of 1986, another newspaper article caught my eye. A white supremacist named Richard Scutari was sentenced to sixty years in prison for racketeering, conspiracy, and obstruction of interstate commerce. The charges stemmed from his part in an organization known as the Order. They attempted to establish a separate white state by forming an army, committing assassinations of alleged enemies—including government officials—establishing a war chest, acquiring money through armed robberies, and recruiting new members. The Order was implicated in such activities as a Brink's armored-car robbery and the assassination of Denver radio shock jock David Berg, both in 1984. The leader, Bob Mathews, died in a shoot-out with the FBI in December 1984. They were back."

CHAPTER FORTY-FIVE

FINALLY PIERCE BEGAN the final episode of his story. "Banyon sold the house in 1987, and I bought it through a shell company. I thought this would change my life. But when I got a limo to drive me out to visit it, my mood only worsened. The house was empty and looked its age, just like me. I realized that I was very old and broken-down; I would never be active again. My life was over. I wanted to leave this world. There was no reason to continue. The voice was very loud on this trip.

"He kept chanting, 'Your time is near; a plan will appear.'

Rogers noted. "I set up the shell company for you. I thought that you were hiding money somewhere."

"No, it was to buy the house. Only Frank Hoch knew the real reason for the company."

"Later that year, I went to Banyon's funeral. He had a military burial in a military cemetery with a twenty-one-gun salute. I was jealous. I would not get such treatment. Yet I was a great success in life, and he was a failure. He left a big family to remember him. I would leave no one.

Pierce looked very tired, but continued. "It was at that funeral that I decided that I needed to have some purpose to my life, some accomplishment, and leave some sort of legacy, but what?

"My plan, as always, was simple. I knew history often repeated itself, and this was the case now. The supremacy movement would become a political force again and start a new version of the Reich. My plan was to follow through on the promise I made so many years ago. I would bring out the Aryan tablet for the entire world to see. The voices agreed. There seemed to be joy in their sounds. They were like angels to me—guiding me, pushing me, and assuring me that I could do it. I finally understood that the voices were some kind of guardians of the tablet. Who they were and how they were attached was still a mystery. The single voice that I heard when in my old house was part of the many voices connected to the tablet, but that voice was sending me separate messages. Why? It was also clear to me that the voices would never leave until I did their bidding.

"First, though, I would need help. I needed the full translation of the tablet to be authenticated. That was when I hatched my plan to find an archeologist. I had my driver take me to Stony Brook University, less than an hour away, to attend a lecture. There I found Raymond Davies. I recall the conversation.

"'I am collecting ancient art and am in need of help to categorize and authenticate the art,' I said.

"'How much will you pay?' he replied.

"'I will give you a grant to help him with your expenses. I will also send you an assistant.' Over a period of two years, I fed him small pieces of the characters on the tablet, and he filled in the blanks, one by one.

"Now I was ready to implement the next part of my plan. The voices told me I had to be careful. I could not just announce that I had the original history of the Aryan race. It had to be found, recovered from a hidden place. I thought hard about how to do that. I also wanted to understand the extent of the movement in America, and I wanted to be rewarded for all my more-than-fifty years of effort.

"I needed to find the strongest and most fanatical group to do my bidding. The mercenary magazines would be my vehicle. They are thinly disguised advertisements for fighters for hire, and I guessed that many of the subscribers would be supremacists. The angle was that I needed to find someone in a picture. The voices led me to a picture in the old house. What was remarkable about the picture was that it had the original marker that Hall, Adams, and I had put in the ground in 1942. It also had a fingerprint. The voices told me that it was Colton Banyon's. I knew that once I found the right group, the members would find Banyon and assume that the picture held the key to the location of the tablet.

"Michael Dean was my answer. My decision to hire Dean was lucky from the start. I had him steal Stan Banyon's medals to prove to him that I was a fanatic. I, of course, knew where Banyon lived. I had confederates living right next door for the last year. And before that, there had been others to keep an eye on him. Banyon was pivotal to my plan.

"I failed to realize that Colton Banyon did not have his prints on file. I spent two years waiting for Banyon to be found by Dean. Suddenly his prints appeared a year ago. I spent the last year developing and nurturing my plan. I decided to implement it immediately. The next and final phase will be completed on Monday.

"This is my complete story. I have been a spy and a murderer. I have deceived people, been a voyeur ghost, destroyed some people, and now have a chance to set everything straight. I will not fail."

With that, Pierce collapsed.

Rogers rushed to his side and realized that Pierce was exhausted. He had been talking for more than three hours. The old man waved him away and eventually was able to sit up straight. He looked at his old friend and saw the amazement in his eyes.

"Walter, is this all true?"

"Every word."

"My God, can I get the rights to your book?"

"You cannot let this out until I'm gone, Trent. You are my lawyer, client privileges and all."

"Walter, I've changed my mind; your story needs to be told. I'll donate all earnings to a charity of your choice. It's just too incredible not to be told."

"You will have to write the last chapter, Trent, as I will not be around to write it."

Part Five
The Tablet

Chapter Forty-Six

As they entered the hotel, Agent Chen was thinking that she was having more fun than she'd ever had. Finally she had a chance to show what she could do. She had actually taken a lover, had a new job prospect, and made a friend. She was determined and would try extra hard to make sure this adventure came out positive for everyone. Then she could start her new life. She was somewhat concerned about the friendship thing—she wasn't sure that she knew how to be a friend, but she would try very hard to please Colton.

Heinz sat on a couch in the corner of the lobby. He was pretending to read a paper. A woman was nervously waiting near the check-in, dressed in a too-short dress of green with a belt that hiked up her hemline.

Banyon walked over to her. "I think you may be waiting for me."

"Well, hi," she cooed. "I expected a professor type, not someone so handsome."

"Let me introduce you to Loni Chen, my assistant." The woman looked at Chen and pretended that she wasn't there.

"My name is Judy Kroll, and I have something for your eyes only, Colt." She pulled out a check and waved it in the air, brushing her lips as she let him look at it.

"Perhaps we should sit on those couches over there," Banyon said.

Judy Kroll's hips were the main attraction as she crossed the room. Banyon thought that Mrs. Kroll was attractive and, more importantly, was someone who had more experience with sex than reports. When she sat down, enough of her thigh was exposed to interest Banyon. Banyon sat across from her. Chen sat at the other end of the couch. Opening his bag, Banyon pulled out the report he had printed, along with a business card and a legal pad to write on. It was a ritual that allowed him time to evaluate the posture, mannerisms, and attitude of his adversary.

"Would you mind giving my assistant the check before we start, just so we don't forget?" Banyon was dripping with charm.

"I'm not used to paying up front," Judy Kroll replied, flicking her long lashes as she spoke. Reluctantly she extended her arm with the check toward Chen. Chen recrossed her legs, then took the check with the tips of her long fingernails. Her smile to Banyon required little interpretation.

Chapter Forty-Seven

Meanwhile, the FBI agents, sent to the high point on Pierce's land, were busy digging. "Got something here," one yelled out.

Agent Booth rushed over to find that he had uncovered a skull and bones. Had they discovered Captain Kidd's treasure? Pirates sometimes killed and buried the men that carried the treasure. This prevented them from divulging where the treasure was buried. Volunteering to help with burying treasure was a risky business. Upon closer inspection, Agent Booth realized that some clothing and shoe soles were with the bones and would be identifiable. This was an unsolved death. Work immediately slowed as they began to collect evidence.

Agent Booth whipped out his cell phone to call Agent Gamble at the motel in Riverhead.

"Gamble, this is Booth."

"What have you got for me?"

"We found a body, but no treasure."

"A body? Was it near the marker?"

"It was thirty steps due south of the marker."

"Huh? I think that Pierce has some explaining to do. Keep working."

No sooner had Gamble hung up the phone than it rang again.

"Gamble here."

"This is Agent Krist."

"Where've you been? I've been waiting for your call."

"I needed some sleep and some time to analyze the tapes from last night. I was also told you were not available until eleven o'clock."

"So, are you going to keep me in suspense?"

"In a nutshell, Pierce has promised Dean something like a hundred million dollars, over five thousand acres of land, and an ancient translation of the Aryan history. Dean intends to start a new nation on the land that Pierce has promised him. The new nation will be called Aryanna. Many splinter groups will join them under the Altar of the Creator banner. This is big. We know that they've required a list of all members from the splinter groups. The lists are being kept in the church."

"Christ!" muttered Gamble. "Thanks for the update. You had better put some surveillance on the church. Have them stop anyone from taking any papers out. Also, get a warrant to search the church for subversive materials. Don't go in yet. Wait for me to tell you when to hit it."

As Gamble sat and pondered his new knowledge, he realized that Pierce had told him several lies. He grabbed his gun and, with two escorts, headed back to Tanners Neck Lane.

Chapter Forty-Eight

Joe Kroll was feeling good. He had dispatched his wife to get the location of the marker. He knew she would not fail. He told her to use her sex to get the location. After all, no man would pass up her sweet ass. His intention was to immediately head off to the spot and secure the tablet. He instructed Judy to call Pierce and tell him she knew the location, but not give it to him. This would enable the group to get there first. Although Kroll wanted the money and land, what he really craved was the tablet, and he wanted it before anybody else could claim it. He rented a private plane to fly him and four others to Westhampton Airfield, only a few miles from the Pierce land. He also rented a van. He then assembled Gary, Teddy, and Harry and called Michael. He instructed them to bring guns.

Michael Dean could not believe that Kroll decided to bring guns. Dean, thinking that only he and Teddy would have guns, had made arrangements with an Italian friend that he met during his stay at Fort Dix, New Jersey. Anthony was to deliver two guns to Michael on Monday afternoon on the island. Now he had to change plans; he needed backup. Dean opened his cell phone.

Anthony wanted fifty large to cover Dean's back. Anthony would supply two shooters with submachine guns to take care of Dean's needs. In the end, Dean agreed, and they discussed the specific plan.

Chapter Forty-Nine

Seith Paul was resourceful, determined, and connected. He obtained a cell phone while in the lockup. Another Streamwood policeman had snuck it in to Paul. The policeman was under investigation, and Paul promised that he could get him off.

Billy Brown knew that most people saw him as a street-smart black gangbanger. But he wanted out of the current game with Dean and thought that this job might accomplish that. He was watching from outside the Marriott Hotel. The large front windows afforded a clear view of the lobby. As ordered, he had driven Judy Kroll to the meeting. He recognized Detective Heinz and hoped that he would not have to use his gun. He didn't see any other cops, but they could be hidden. *What was Kroll up to?* Seith Paul had just called him, and Billy had promised to update Paul if anything were new.

Paul knew something big was going on. He had been involved in crackdowns and cleanups before. He used a cell phone like a weapon and spoke to several gang members and a crooked cop that he knew. It took him two hours to find out about the surveillance on Dean's house, the FBI tapes from the church, and the mission of Heinz and Agent Chen. He learned about the planned flight to New York and the guns. *What the hell is going on here?*

Chapter Fifty

In the middle of the stakeout, Heinz's phone rang again. A little irritated, he answered it.

"Patrolman Lopez here."

"Lopez, I'm on a stakeout—I can't talk now."

"It's important, sir," he said. "Dean is flying out today. He's taking a private plane, and he mentioned something about guns. We picked this up from their conversation; it has all been recorded like you wanted."

"Today?"

"Yes, they want to get to this meeting place before it's scheduled and dig up something. I don't know what."

"Okay, this is all part of my stakeout. Good work. Stay with them. Tail them to wherever they are going and get information on the plane and where it's headed."

Heinz dialed Gamble's phone. He appeared to be an executive making business calls on his cell.

"Gamble, Heinz here. I just learned that Kroll, Dean, and some others are flying out in a private plane to Long Island. I expect to get their flight plans soon and will pass them on. I think they will have guns on board."

"Thank you for the update. By the way, we found a body at the marker site. It seems that this whole business is about an ancient tablet concerning the Aryan race. Pierce supposedly has it, and the Altar of the Creator wants it. At least we can nab them for interstate transportation of guns. We'll pick them up at the airport. One more thing—Pierce has disappeared."

"Pierce has disappeared?"

"Yeah, we missed him by a couple of hours. I'm going to round up all of these sleazebags now, raid the church, and figure this out later."

"Wait," said Heinz. "Maybe we should let this play out a little longer so we can get to the bottom of it. What do you think?"

"It is risky. I'll give it some thought and call you back."

Chapter Fifty-One

As Banyon was finishing his presentation on the future of retailing in the lobby of the Marriott, he noticed that Judy Kroll was yawning. "So, in conclusion, I feel that the landscape will continue to change. Dollar stores will continue to grow, and there will be more consolidation in the mass market."

As he recapped his presentation, Judy came alive. "Colt, that is so fascinating. I do so love strong men who make bold, hard thrusts into a subject."

As Colt handed the presentation to her, she grabbed his hand and stroked the back. Agent Chen was inching close to the edge of the couch, ready to pounce like a panther. Suddenly Judy got up and seated herself right next to Banyon, so close that her thighs were touching his. She leaned closer, and her ample breasts brushed his arm. Banyon mouthed to Chen for her to stay put. He knew that Judy would try to get the location of the marker.

"Sweetie, why don't we lose little brown eyes here? We can go up to my room to discuss the rest of my questions."

"I'm comfortable here for now." He had a little twinkle in his eyes.

"I could make you more relaxed. I could give you a Japanese massage while we talk."

"I'm okay, really. What else do you need to know?"

She took out a picture from her bra and showed it to Banyon. "Do you know who this is? Where was it taken?" Her hand was on the inside of his thigh.

"Sure, that's my buddy Lorenzo. He was helping me dig the hole that you see in the picture."

"I love when you talk dirty. Do you know the exact location?"

Banyon was starting to feel a tingling inside. Judy was good. Even though he knew that she was after the location and sex was the catalyst, she was good. "I can write down the exact location, if you wish. But how did you get this picture, and why do you need the location?"

"My employer found this picture and wants to identify the person in it.

He also thinks that it's on his land. He wants to put it in his archives. He's very rich."

"Well, I took the picture, but I wonder how your employer was able to get it." Banyon was digging for information.

Judy Kroll seductively said, "Write down the directions, and I'll tell you."

"I can do that," Banyon agreed. He then wrote the exact directions that he had given the FBI the day before and even drew another map. Judy now had her hand on Colt's privates and was attempting to massage them. When he finished the map, he handed the paper to Judy.

"So, how did he get it?"

"You will have to ask my employer. I don't know."

"And how do I contact your employer?" Banyon asked.

"I'll give him your number."

"I don't think that's good enough."

"It's the best that I can do," she replied. "Come on, I'm so hot now."

Chen suddenly said, "Take your hands off of him." She became unglued and unprofessional. "Colt is not interested in you. I'm his friend; I know."

"Look, slant eyes, this is between Colt and me."

Chen was off the couch and standing over Judy. "You take that back. There is no need to call me childish names."

"I'll call you anything I want, Chink." She then pushed Chen, causing her to fall over the table. She sprang back so fast that Judy didn't have time to prepare.

The fight was on. Chen pulled Judy up by her hair and looked her straight in the eyes. "You have nothing over me," she said.

The two women were suddenly wrestling on the large coffee table. The sight was surreal. Two good-looking women were rolling around on a low table, pulling hair, each doing their best to humiliate the other. Chen kept slapping Judy across the face. Judy reached out with her free hand and grabbed the front of Chen's blouse, ripping it open, bra and all. Agent Chen went to cover up her breasts with her hands. This afforded Judy the chance to throw her off.

Agent Chen rolled over and sprang to her feet. She then roundhoused Judy and knocked her to the floor, leaving her dazed and spread-eagled for all to see.

"Now who is superior?" Chen asked as she walked toward the ladies' room.

Judy lay on the floor—clothes ripped and legs askew.

Banyon got up to help her to her feet. "Are you okay?"

Judy said nothing but quickly got to her feet. She adjusted her dress as she walked out the door.

Chen managed to pin her clothes together in the ladies' room. She said nothing to Detective Heinz as she left the building. She turned to Banyon and ordered him to drive. There was a frost in the air. Banyon shot a side glance at Chen. She had done a good job with a couple of pins. But you could see that her legs had some bruises, and her beautiful hair was less than perfect. He felt proud of her for trying to defend him but also needed to tell her that it wasn't necessary.

"Are you all right?"

"I was trying to protect you, my friend. Now I'm in trouble," she muttered.

"You should worry more about Carl than me. You need to talk to him to make him understand what happened."

"It sure seemed like you were letting her get to you," she cried out.

"Look, I knew what I was doing. I didn't want her to be suspicious. By the way, that was a nice punch you threw." He smiled at her while saying it.

"I didn't think you noticed." She smiled back at him.

"I would notice," he replied. "Are we still friends?"

"Always," she replied and kissed him on the cheek.

"She couldn't hurt a flea," Judy told Billy. "God, I'm so hot." She was seated next to Billy Brown in the front seat of the car. They had left the hotel, and Brown had pulled into the parking lot of the nearby Transworld Center to allow Judy a chance to rearrange her clothing.

"So, what was that fight about?" Billy asked.

"Wait, I have to make a call to someone. Give me your phone," Judy demanded. She dialed Pierce and reported that she had the map.

"What is this about?" Billy asked.

Her response was not understandable as she was busy opening his clothes. He looked over and saw her purse and opened it. The map was clearly visible. Billy knew how to get Judy to spill the beans.

Brown was on the phone to Paul. "Seith, you ain't gonna believe this. These freaks are after some sort of Aryan history thing. It proves that the Aryan race is better than everyone else. Some guy is giving them something like a hundred million dollars and a lot of land on Long Island. They think that a whole bunch of supremacy freaks will join them and start a new nation. Judy told me. This is scary, man."

"So, that's what this is all about. The feds are on the case too. The only problem is that if the feds get the tablet, it will surely be in the news and would accomplish the same thing as if Kroll got it. Blacks will be chased back to Africa or worse. I knew that these assholes were trouble. How did you find that out?"

"Let's just say that Judy Kroll can't keep a secret when she is hot."

Chapter Fifty-Two

Agent Chen was standing in Detective Heinz's closed-door office with her head down. She felt ashamed. She hadn't changed yet and looked like a refugee from a foreign country. Heinz was yelling at her. "Just tell me why. Why would you pick a fight with Judy Kroll? You knew that we needed evidence. How stupid can you possibly be? What if she had some shooters nearby, huh? Well, say something."

"I … I …," was all she could say; she was crying.

"You continue to be a loose cannon, always trying to bull through everything. You could have gotten all of us killed. What do you have to say to that?"

"Carl, please, let me explain." Real tears flowed down her face.

Banyon, who was listening in the other room, decided to intervene. He threw the office door open.

Heinz loaded up. "What the hell are you doing in here? Get out."

"Why are you screaming at her? It was my fault," he said.

"What the hell do you mean?" Heinz demanded.

"Judy was feeling me up and looking for a mike. I was afraid she was about ten seconds from finding one. None of us thought she would be so bold with me. I was feeling violated. Stop yelling at Loni; I asked her to help me. She didn't even start it—Judy pushed her. You saw it. All Loni was trying to do was to prevent Judy from finding the wire, Carl. She's a hero. I didn't know what to do. She's one resourceful woman. She even sacrificed her dignity to help me—she did nothing wrong."

"Is that right, Loni?" Heinz's voice softened a little.

Banyon knew that Chen would not stand up for herself, as it was part of her upbringing. Damn Chinese heritage. They are too humble sometimes. He stepped over to Chen and hugged her. "When we're done with this mess, I owe you a dinner, okay? You can bring anyone you want, even this pigheaded chauvinist."

Banyon continued to hug her and felt a tiny peck on his cheek. He knew that she realized that he had saved her.

"Well, uh, you know, maybe I didn't have all the facts. You're right, Colt. If the roles were reversed, I would have reacted differently. Thanks for giving me all the facts. You know this is hard work and—"

"Carl, tell her that you're sorry already, and then she can stop hiding behind me."

"Yeah, well, Loni, I am sorry. Do you forgive me?"

"Wait," said Banyon, "don't answer yet." He closed the blinds. Someone pinched his butt as he walked out the door.

Chapter Fifty-Three

Only a few feet away, Seith Paul was hard at work on his illegal phone. He believed that he found a way out of jail. He also knew the right buttons to press to get his way. He realized the impact of the tablet, but his goals were, as always, very selfish and financially oriented. He would depend on the publicity to get him off. If he got his hands on that Aryan tablet, he could get a lot of money from the freaks and then snitch on them to the police. The cops would have to let him go. He would be a hero, another Martin Luther King. People would invite him on their TV shows. He would get endorsements and maybe even a movie.

"Billy, I've been thinking. If the Aryan tablet gets into the hands of the cops, we're in just as much trouble as if it were in Kroll's hands. They would have to let it go public. The Aryans would still be able to use it to send us back to Africa. The answer is to steal it ourselves."

"Yeah, man, I know that. But how we gonna do it?"

"From what I can gather, the meeting for the exchange will take place tomorrow night."

"Yeah, that's true, man. But some of those guys are going out today to jump the claim and get the tablet. Wait, I've got the number for the old geezer who has the tablet. The number is in my cell phone—his name is Walter Pierce."

"Good, give it to me. I'll call him and warn him that they are getting in early. Hopefully Pierce will get the tablet and keep it under wraps until the meeting, right?"

"But what does that do for us? I mean, will he even believe you? Remember, he's a Nazi."

"I'll think of something."

"But they'll find out that someone called and tipped off Pierce."

"Yeah, but by then it will be too late."

"What the hell are you thinking?"

"I'm thinking that it is about a sixteen-hour drive to the spot on the map. If we get together about a dozen of the boys with guns, you could get there in time to steal the thing before the meeting."

"But how we gonna get the thing if you tell Pierce to hide it?"

"Let me worry about that—I'm a lawyer, remember."

It took Paul two hours to decide what to do. He then called Pierce.

"Hello," Pierce said into the phone.

"Walter Pierce, please," Paul opened.

"Who is this?"

"My name is Bob Wilkosz. I'm a reporter with the *Sunsetter News*."

"What do you want, Mr. Wilkosz?"

"Some informed sources told us that you plan to announce a discovery tomorrow. It has something to do with an Aryan historical find. I want to confirm the story and see if you'll allow me to come and take some pictures. Our readers love this kind of stuff."

"Sir, even if your paper, which I call trash, was reputable, I have no comment."

"Well, sir, as I understand it, several white supremacist types are flying out to see you this afternoon. They have directions to a secret location. It seems that they are going to dig up some artifact that you have knowledge of. Am I getting close?"

"Mr. Wilkosz, I'm over ninety years old. What would I be doing with an old artifact? I can barely see, and I don't read Aryan. Ha-ha! Good day to you."

Paul hung up his phone. He thought Pierce was an arrogant son of a bitch. He sounded German to him. *Bet he is the head Nazi.* At least he now knows trouble is on the way. I'm sure that he will hide the tablet. Paul had bought some time. He needed to check in on Brown but waited until the late afternoon. He had other calls to make.

"Billy, are you on the road yet?"

"Yeah, man, I got twelve guys in two vans. We'll be in Westhampton by noon tomorrow. I'll call you when we get there."

"I spoke to Pierce, told him that the 'boys' are heading his way. I bet the package isn't even at the spot. This guy isn't stupid. There is more to this plan. I'll work on it. Man, this is big—lots of money involved. Don't worry; you'll get your share. Call when you get there."

Brown hung up the phone. He knew Paul was only thinking about the fame and money. Paul didn't give a shit about anything or anyone else. If this thing were to get into the papers, every white dude will think that they have a right to push blacks around. *Well, he has news—the boys and me are gonna get that Aryan thing and destroy it.* He didn't want that stuff lying around.

Chapter Fifty-Four

Banyon was waiting in the police station lobby for the Patel girls to pick him up and take him to the airport. *Things are looking up.* He earned two grand today and was vindicated on the accident that happened a year ago—and no one was chasing him. He made some new friends, both male and female. To top it off, he landed a job interview on Tuesday and now was going traveling with two delicious ladies.

Suddenly Chen appeared. She had changed into black stretch pants and a white T-shirt. Her hair was brushed and lay long and flat against her back. She had applied some makeup and lipstick. She looked stunning.

"Hi," she said to Banyon in a soft voice.

"Hi, yourself."

"Colt, I want to thank you for saving my career and maybe my personal life as well."

"That's what friends are for."

"No one has ever done anything like that for me before. Why did you do it?"

"I wanted to show you that friends could be your best asset. You need to learn to let people help you. Besides, it was my fault."

"How can you say that?"

"When we decided to become friends, I didn't tell you the rules. Friends do not judge friends. They wait to be asked before they help, and they help when asked, regardless of the circumstances. Do you understand?"

"It sounds different when you say it that way. I just wanted to protect you from her."

"Loni, please stop protecting me unless I ask for your protection, okay? You do not need to do anything to keep me as a friend. I'm your friend, period."

"Colt, how can I ever repay you? I have so little to give you. I have been raised to always repay my debts. I have to give you something."

"Give me a smile; trust me, it's worth it to me."

"There must be something—"

Banyon cut her off.

"Look, I love flirting with you and being your friend. You are a most unusual woman. It's a long life; let's just see where it goes. Okay, now give me a big hug and wiggle while you are hugging. Then let's go have a cigarette."

"That sounds too much like foreplay," Loni remarked.

"I know," he replied.

As the Patel girls pulled into the parking lot, they saw Agent Chen and Banyon smoking a cigarette out in front of the station house. As was their usual style, they just looked at each other to communicate.

"Trouble" flashed between them. Banyon walked over to the car and got in the back.

"Did you bring my bag?"

"Why do you need a change of underwear?" The frosty reply came from Previne.

"Why would I need a change of underwear?" he repeated in an equally frosty tone.

"I noticed that your girlfriend changed her clothes."

"Look, you two, stop being jealous. Loni saved my bacon today. Her clothes got ripped; that's why she changed. I never touched her."

Pramilla interceded. "Previne, leave him alone. We are heading out for a great adventure. Let's have fun, okay?"

"Okay, you are right. Colt, I'm so excited. So your son Mitchell will pick us up?"

"Yeah, he told me he would."

"I can't wait. Is he like you?" Pramilla asked.

"I don't even know how to answer that. You girls measure things in a different way."

"Has he ever been to your old house?" It was Previne asking.

"Sure, he was a teenager when the house was sold. He stayed there many times with me."

"So, he has seen the ghost too?"

"He says that he has. By the way, I have to tell you that I'm not comfortable with our breaking into the house at night."

"Don't be silly, Colt. We aren't going to break into the house; I have a key," said Pramilla.

"How on earth did you get a key?" asked a puzzled Banyon.

"We have a key because we own it," Previne continued.

"What?"

"That's right," said Pramilla. "From the stories that you told us, we are sure that the house is truly haunted. Is Mitchell as sexy as you are?"

"Wait, you are changing the subject. How did you get a key?"

Previne answered, "I told you. We own the house. We bought it yesterday. A shell company owned the house, and the owner was willing to sell. We made him a good offer. This is very exciting."

"Why would you buy my old house?" asked a confused Banyon.

"That is simple, silly one," Previne replied. "Once we connect with the ghost, the house will be famous, and I will own it."

"That seems a little too convenient," a skeptical Banyon noted.

"Do you want me to get in the back with you to celebrate?" She started to climb over the front seat and landed on his lap. Banyon could not help but wonder what they were hiding.

Alarms were going off inside Banyon's head. How could they have bought the house so quickly? How did they find the owner? Who financed the purchase? *And every time I try to find answers, they gang up on me with sex.*

Chapter Fifty-Five

Heinz walked into the lockup to check on Dean's friends. Ula Woods and the boys were still sitting in custody. He wasn't sure how many charges were going to be levied against the gang, but they would be off the streets for a long time. The assistant DA on the case told him that there would be a year's worth of trials. Also, there would be issues involving charging them separately or jointly on some counts. Then, of course, there would be the usual plea bargaining and trading for information on other members and on and on. The DA, who was twenty-six, felt that he would be well into his thirties before it was over. Dean and the other cops involved also created different scenarios. Streamwood was going to be a busy station for a long time.

As Heinz passed the cell where Paul was being held, he heard Paul talking to someone. He peeked around the corner and saw Paul sitting with his legs crossed. He was leaning against the wall and acting like he was in his office. He was talking on a cell phone. Just then Paul looked up and saw Heinz standing there.

Shit. "B., gotta go, I think I just lost my phone privileges. You know what to do, bye."

Heinz stuck out his hand. "Give me the phone, Seith. You know you aren't supposed to have a phone in here."

"Sorry," was all Paul said as he handed him the phone.

Some time later, Heinz stopped by Chen's desk. He could smell the sweetness of her shampoo. "Hey, good-looking, have you recovered enough from your ordeal to find out who Paul's been talking to on this cell phone?" He handed her the phone.

"Carl, you snuck up on me."

"I want to tell you that everything's all right with me, but unfortunately there are too many people around right now."

"Anywhere, anytime, Chief."

"Right now I need to find out how Seith managed to get a cell phone into the lockup and who he was calling. Can you get the job done?"

"In a heartbeat. I will also find out who the phone is registered to and do a background check on them. I'll meet you in your office in about an hour."

The phone was ringing as Heinz reached his desk. It was Lopez.

"We followed Dean to the Schaumburg Airport, where he and four others took off in a private plane to Long Island—destination is Westhampton Airport. We met up with two FBI guys here as well. They were tailing two other gang members. Dean, Kroll, and three friends are on the plane. I have the flight plan and plane ID. They also rented a van in Westhampton. What do you want me to do now?"

"Good work, Lopez. Return to the station for a new assignment. Can you put one of the FBI agents on the phone?"

"Yes, sir."

"Hello, Agent Krist here," came a voice from the phone.

"Krist, this is Detective Heinz. Did you get any further instructions from Gamble?"

"We're to be ready to investigate the church, probably tomorrow. I'm about to call Agent Gamble now. He's in the area where the plane is headed."

"Good. I'm coming out there. One of those men is a cop from my department. I want first crack at him, okay?"

"I'll tell him, but he won't like it. This is FBI jurisdiction."

"Just tell him I'll speak to him in person when I get there."

About an hour later, Chen entered Heinz's office along with Agent Krist. She handed him a sheet of paper. It listed all the calls made by Paul, the actual owner of the confiscated phone, and the list of the phone numbers that were called. There were six calls to Billy Brown, three calls to the station house switchboard, one to a bank offshore, and one more call to Walter Pierce's cell phone.

"What the hell is going on here? Everyone is talking to Walter Pierce," Heinz commented.

Chen suggested that he call Billy Brown. Heinz dialed the number, and Brown answered on the first ring.

"Billy, this is Detective Heinz. We have put a statewide APB on you. It would be best if you came in voluntarily to discuss your role with the Woods gang."

"Nice try, Heinz," Brown replied. "For your information, I'm already out of Chicago and not coming back. You do what you want with Seith—he deserves it." There was a sharp click.

"We'll probably never find Brown," Heinz said. "My hunch is that he cleaned out some bank accounts. Maybe even some of Paul's and is heading to someplace warm. What do you think?"

"I agree," said Krist. "But I'm really confused about this call to Pierce. How does Paul know him? And how did he get the number?"

Before Heinz could answer, the phone rang again.

"Gamble here. Pierce may be in trouble. The Kroll gang will be here in about an hour, and they mean to contact Pierce. I don't know what Pierce's game is yet, but I don't want him hurt."

Heinz suggested calling his cell phone to tell him that the boys would be early. "I have his number right here."

"Hmm, good idea. Give it to me."

Gamble was angry with Pierce but decided to not let him know it. He dialed the number and spoke. "Walter Pierce, please."

"Who's calling?"

"This is Special Agent Gamble from the FBI. We met this morning. Do you remember?"

"Of course, Agent Gamble. But, tell me, how did you get my … never mind—you are the FBI, after all."

"Right. Have you recently spoken to a Seith Paul?" Gamble was trying to set Pierce off guard.

"I don't know any Seith Paul. The only call I received was from a reporter with some rag. He wanted an interview. Of course, I declined."

"I see," said Gamble, somewhat confused. "Mr. Pierce, where are you? We went back to your house to find you gone."

"I have urgent business around town. Don't bother to stake out my house. I won't be home tonight."

"Mr. Pierce, we believe you are in danger."

"If you are referring to Michael Dean, I already know that he's heading my way. Don't be concerned. Dean can't find me; that is, he can't until I want him to. I am adequately protected, my boy."

"Mr. Pierce, we found a body in the ground on your land. What do you know about it?"

"A body, you say?" said a surprised Pierce.

"Yes, that is correct. It had been in the ground for some time."

"Agent Gamble, I own a lot of land, and I haven't killed anyone on my land. I'm just a businessman. Where did you find the body?"

"It was found near the marker in your picture, sir. Care to explain that?"

"No, I can't. We can discuss this on Wednesday if you like; I'm free then."

"Sir, I strongly urge you to turn yourself in today. We have an APB alert out on you, and if we find you, you will be arrested."

"I am sorry, my young friend, but your questions will have to wait." With that, he hung up the phone.

Chapter Fifty-Six

Mitchell Banyon waved to his father and the girls at the luggage area. He was a strapping young college graduate with a slightly receding hairline. The girls were fascinated. Previne was analyzing the younger Banyon as they stood waiting for their luggage. "He doesn't really look like you, but he has your savoir faire. He's a little taller than you and twenty pounds lighter, but he's your son all right. He talks like you too."

"Mitch, can I talk to you for a second?" Banyon asked.

"Sure, Colt," he replied.

"It's Dad to you, Mitchell."

They moved outside so they could talk without the girls listening. "Mitchell, you'll need to watch yourself with these two. They're all flirt and more, if you know what I mean."

"Good job, Dad. These girls are my age. How do you do it?"

"I don't think I did anything. They are very aggressive, and I don't think they have been honest with me. Don't make a fool of yourself, okay?"

"Yeah, like you never did."

"We are not talking about me here—we are talking about you."

Mitch saw the girls coming through the doors with the luggage. "Let me help you with that," he offered. "Which twin are you?"

"I'm Previne, and she is Pramilla, and we do so love the Banyon family."

When they got to the car, Mitch suggested that his father do the driving. He threw Colt the keys and climbed into the back, a little too eagerly to suit Colt. The two girls slipped into the backseat too.

Chapter Fifty-Seven

While other groups were working on plans to find the tablet, Robert Spita of the New York State Crime Commission was already on the scene. Through a phone tap on some local mobsters, he determined that a possible crime was in the offing. His plan had been laid out in Manhattan some eight hours ago. The commission had determined from phone calls that some Chicago thug had called the local boss to get two shooters for a hit. It was to take place on eastern Long Island. A call had instructed the shooters to go to a location in the woods off Speonk-Riverhead Road and wait for a whistle. The shooters were to take everyone out except for some guy named Michael.

Crime commission agents were now hidden in bushes below the peak of Pierce's marker. Crouched behind a tree, Captain Robert Spita was eyeballing the shooters.

"What're they doing?" inquired his brother Richard.

"They're just sitting against some trees and eating doughnuts," replied Robert. "Bruce, what do you see?"

Bruce Conn was their good friend as well as a sharpshooter. Conn had a keen eye and lightning reflexes. The three friends had been on the task force almost ten years and had been through all sorts of adventures together. They often pawned themselves off as local businessmen, going to shows, having dinners with accounts, and even golfing a little now and then. Most people did not realize that they were undercover cops. They were relentless in their pursuit of Mafia thugs and had spent many nights on stakeouts. From experience, they knew how to hide in plain sight.

Six members of the force blanketed the woods, surrounding the shooters. They were waiting to see who would show up. They could arrest the shooters for carrying submachine guns, but the shooters would be back on the street before the task force could get coffee. The success of the present venture would rest on timing and fast moves. All the men were on edge. Due to the nature of their business, they neither sought help from nor notified any other government agency, including the FBI, about their plans. They were on their own.

Kroll was talking to the other Aryans on the plane. "Right after we land, Teddy, you get the van, and we'll get the luggage. It will be after six o'clock here, and I don't know exactly how far it is to the site. I don't want to be there in the dark, so we need to move fast." He asked Dean if he had the directions.

"Got them right here, Joe," Dean assured him.

"When we get to the site, follow Michael; he's been in the vicinity with Pierce. You could get lost in those woods and really screw things up. Once we get to the site, we'll need to dig. We have to buy some shovels."

"Won't Pierce be pissed if we dig up the box? He's promised us a lot of money and valuable land. We don't want to screw that up, do we?" Teddy asked the question without expecting an answer.

"I want the tablet," Kroll said a little too fiercely. He then changed tactics as everyone looked at him with confusion. "That's the beauty of my plan," said Kroll. "We're going to bury the box again, but not where Pierce thinks it is. That way we can get him to sign all the papers, and we'll have leverage. Keep in mind that he's a fanatic and wants nothing more than to complete his mission."

At the same time, the FBI was mobilizing in the lot behind FBI headquarters in Riverhead. Gamble was in control of nineteen agents, all outfitted with bulletproof vests, flak jackets with "FBI" on them, and baseball hats. They had at their disposal a high-elevation helicopter with look-down infrared radar, headset communications, detailed maps of the area, pictures of the known church members, complete plans for location of cross fire sites, and even a coffee container for the boys. They were in readiness, down to the last detail.

Agent Chen and Detective Heinz made their plans while driving from MacArthur Airport. They decided to piggyback with the FBI. Their only goal was to arrest Dean since Dean needed to be interrogated in Streamwood.

Back in the woods, there was a noise. Robert whispered into his mike, "What's that?"

"It's a cell phone ringing in the woods," Richard answered.

"The fat one's talking on the phone," Robert overheard Conn saying. Conn was located in a tree, about a hundred feet away from the shooters. "Oops, he just hung up. They're on the move."

"Everyone, stay put. Let's see where they're going. Rich, you take point. Don't let them out of your sight."

The warm late summer air was wet with humidity; the shadows were lengthening. The task force crept stealthily through the woods, all on the lookout for enemies behind every bush. The shooters weren't hard for Spita to follow. The fat one could only waddle. So it took them twenty minutes to reach a new location. Then Captain Spita dispersed his men. Conn climbed up another tree, affording a view of the surrounding area. With his face black and dark clothes, he blended into the foliage.

Joe Kroll was seated in the front passenger seat of the van. "Let's go. We want to get there before dark. I want to hold the tablet while I still can see it in real light. Wait, Gary, turn around; you idiots forgot the shovels."

Gamble was in the lead Ford Blazer. "What do you think? Are they doubling back to lose any tails?"

"I think you're giving these guys too much credit," said the driver. "They don't strike me as being that bright. They just forgot to buy something. They aren't prepared the way we are."

It was ten minutes after seven when Conn observed a car coming up the fire lane. "They are moving fast—they must be our guys. I'll get some pictures."

Captain Spita ordered his brother to shadow them into the location.

Conn reported that there were five of them. "They are all carrying shovels and guns. It looks like a hit all right, but for whom?

"Stay put; let's see what happens."

The FBI was three minutes behind Kroll's men and closing in fast. Gamble called in the helicopter to get a position on everyone. The helicopter would be there in six minutes. Meanwhile, he deployed his men. All twenty men entered the woods on their predetermined course.

Michael Dean announced that they were at the location on the map. He pointed to the marker.

"Christ, there's already a hole here. Its thirty paces south of the marker. The box is gone," wailed Teddy. They all stood there in shock. No one knew what to do. They had been double-crossed.

Michael was angry. Within minutes, he should have had it all. He knew that the shooters waited in the shadows, fingers on their triggers. He didn't know that the task force people were on the balls of their feet, all ready to pounce.

Dean whipped out his phone and called Pierce. "Pierce, you double-crossed me, you bastard," he hollered into the phone.

"Ah, Michael, how wonderful to hear your voice," Pierce replied.

"Where is the box?"

"Calm down, my boy; it is in a safe place. I thought you would go directly to the location. You don't follow directions very well. I told you to be there at 8:00 p.m. tomorrow. It will be revealed then, not before. And don't try to find me; you can't."

Gamble's headphone erupted almost at the same time. "This is chopper 1. I'm getting many body signatures—at least thirteen near the site."

Gamble knew they would be outgunned. The FBI routinely employed a three- or four-to-one ratio to ensure success. "Everybody, stop and take cover."

"What are we going to do now?" asked Teddy.

"I'm going to go get drunk," said Kroll. There was a rage in him so great that he wanted to hunt, but he knew that could jeopardize everything. "Throw your shovels into the woods, where you can find them tomorrow night if we need them."

"Kroll's group is coming out; everyone else is staying put," the chopper pilot noted.

Gamble had figured correctly. "They thought that the box was in the hole, but it's not. Pierce is controlling everything. We're done here for tonight. We need to come up with a better plan for tomorrow. Okay, everybody, it's over for tonight. I need four volunteers to follow these two groups of unknown guys out of the woods and to find out who they are. Call out."

Kroll told his men to leave the woods. He wasn't paying any attention to their surroundings; otherwise, he might have noticed that there were too many shadows around. Instead, he was lathered in a rage. Kroll wanted the box. Dean wanted the box and wanted Kroll dead. Gary, Teddy, and Harry were enraged because they knew that Kroll and Dean would be unbearable for the next twenty-four hours.

Gamble had two men follow the shooters, who were, in turn, being followed by the crime commission group. Two more of Gamble's men tagged along behind the crime commission group. The rest of the FBI group was instructed to follow the Kroll group, even though there was a transmitter and a receiver on the Kroll van. Eventually they all reached their cars, and the

FBI put transmitters on all the vehicles. The spotters got license plates and called in the numbers.

The FBI was the first to recognize the situation. A trace on the commission's vans identified it as law enforcement. At 7:30 p.m. Gamble studied the report that was printing out on his in-room printer at the Holiday Inn. He decided he needed to talk to someone. He called his office in New York, and they referred him to the police commissioner of New York City. The commissioner admitted there were several undercover operations going on, and only one group had enough authority to do a stakeout without submitting a report—the organized crime group. He also supplied Gamble with a phone number.

Robert Spita was sitting in his room, also at the Holiday Inn, with all five members of his stakeout crew. He was chewing on his cigar and muddling over the possibilities. *What the hell is going on here? We follow the shooters into the woods, and five skinhead types show up with shovels. The shooters hide in the woods, and then about twenty other guys show up, and everything stops. The skinheads throw their shovels in the woods and leave. The shooters leave another way and come to the same hotel that we are in. Was it a hit gone bad? And if so, why are the shooters still staying here instead of going back to the city for a little pasta?*

The phone on his hip started to buzz, and he grabbed it, expecting to be talking to the office about the license plates.

"Yeah, what have you got?"

"Is this Captain Spita of the Crime Commission of New York?"

"Who the hell is this, and how did you get my number?" he said by way of answer. The rest of the crew grabbed their guns and took up positions around the room. Conn peeked out the window but saw nothing. This group had been ambushed before, so no one was willing to take any chances.

"This is Special Agent Greg Gamble of the FBI. I need to talk to you."

"About what?" Real concern crept into the captain's voice.

"About today in the woods just south of here, that's what. We were there too and need to know what you were doing there. This is a very important government investigation."

"I don't know what you mean."

"Don't stonewall me. We're staying at the same motel here in Riverhead. We found you before you found us, okay?"

Suddenly very concerned, Spita walked to the window. "Where are you now?"

"Right next door," replied Gamble. "Meet me in the hallway."

Spita snapped his phone shut. He hand-signaled his men to cover him. Then he opened the door and slipped into the hallway. Gamble was standing there with phone in hand.

"We have some talking to do," Gamble said. "I don't know why you are here, but maybe we can work together."

"I generally don't trust the bureau."

"All right, then, I'll buy."

"Let's go," said Spita. "Let me get the boys—you can buy for them too."

"Why am I not surprised?" said Gamble with a smile on his face.

Chapter Fifty-Eight

The Patel girls wanted to stay in the old house overnight. Banyon suspected that there was more to their desire than was mentioned. To appease them, he agreed to stay late into the night at the house. He wondered what they all would do there since the house was empty. They had stopped at the hardware store for some flashlights and a lantern. They also stopped at Wal-Mart to get some blankets and pillows to sit on and a scrabble game to have something to do. They would camp inside the house and wait for the ghosts. Banyon hoped that no one would start telling ghost stories.

They were seated in one of the bedrooms upstairs, with the windows open for a breeze. A lantern lit the room. It was just after dusk, around 8:30 p.m. Colt had to admit that it was cozy there, and the girls were even more alluring in the shadowed light. Mitch was completely engrossed in the situation and was enjoying himself immensely.

Then suddenly there was a noise.

Previne grabbed Mitch's hand, and they took off down the hall. Pramilla rushed to Colt's side and slammed herself against him. She said, "Are you scared?"

"I'm too smart not to be scared. That noise sounded like a door slamming. It might be intruders," he said.

"You do not believe?" asked Pramilla.

"Remember, I lived here. I'd rather believe that there are intruders."

"Well, I can't wait to see the ghost."

"Come on then. No sense waiting here, let's explore," a reluctant Colt replied. He grabbed a flashlight and took her hand in his as they left the room.

Pierce was irresistibly drawn to the house that night. He had come to deliver the translations from his safe and wanted one more night to visit his past. He had Rogers drive him to the back entrance. From there he walked through the familiar woods to the backdoor. He used his key to enter the house. He went to the basement and opened the hidden door in the furnace room.

The box was where he left it on Saturday. It was important that the box be located where Pierce put it, or his plan would not work. After the bank closed, he and Rogers went there to meet the manager, who opened the vault. The box had been in the same vault for more than a half century. Then they drove it to the old house and hid it. It was all part of the plan for tomorrow, and everything was going according to schedule. Pierce heard noises in the house. He had to take a peek but needed to be careful. One slip, and all would be lost.

After some time, he made his way to the front attic and peeked through the dusty holes. There was no one in the room. Only a lantern and some blankets. *Where are they?* He let out a moan and used the flashlight to send a stream of white energy through the hole and into the hallway—just as he had done so many years ago.

"In here," someone yelled.

Four people entered the room and began to look all around. Pierce was delighted. The women were beautiful, and there was Colton Banyon with them. There was also someone who could only be Banyon's son. Pierce settled in to wait. He knew that Rogers would stay put. He had told him that he would be gone an hour.

After about twenty minutes of looking, listening, and calling out to the ghost, everyone seemed to give up.

"He's here; I know it, I feel it," said one of the girls.

"How do you know that it's a he?" asked Banyon.

She just stood there with her mouth wide open. Before she could answer, Pramilla said, "We should stay quiet, Previne. Maybe the ghost doesn't want us to be too noisy. I have an idea—let's play scrabble. That's quiet, and maybe he'll appear again."

Pierce watched as she opened the box and set up the board. Banyon seemed to be amused.

Previne went first. They all made a word, and then it was Pramilla's turn again. She put down "devoor." Colt challenged immediately, before he even thought. "Oops," he said. "Hey, we don't have a dictionary."

Previne said, "Well, I do have my PDA. It has a spell-checker. It's good enough, isn't it?"

They finished the first game and were about to start another when they heard a noise. The hunt was on again. As the people left the room, Pierce slipped out the attic and down the ladder. The single voice told him that everything was right. Pierce was in a good mood as he left the old house.

Now in the bar at the Holiday Inn, Agent Gamble and Robert Spita were getting to know each other. "So, are you going to tell me why you were in the woods?" asked the captain.

"I think that you should go first. I'm FBI, remember?"

"I know that the FBI is famous for stonewalling other law enforcement agencies," came the quick retort. "You are on my turf, you know."

"The USA is my turf, my friend. I'm not here to stonewall you. I'm chasing a bunch of white supremacists that have killed, conspired, threatened, and even carried guns across state lines. They are not nice people."

Spita asked Gamble why he hadn't arrested them in the woods.

"Well, there is something else going on that I can't tell you about yet. Tell me why you were there."

"We work on Mafia crimes. Someone from your group called the local boss and asked for two shooters. We were following them. It looked like a hit was going down; then it stopped."

"Yeah, well, they didn't find what they were looking for in the woods, so they will be going back tomorrow night."

"At least I now know why they had shovels. So who are my guys supposed to hit?"

"That, my friend, is a good question—I don't know."

"My boys and I will be there tomorrow."

"Tell you what, you be responsible for the shooters. I don't want them. I'm after a larger goal. Just stay out of the way, okay?"

"What time does it go down?" asked Spita.

"Eight o'clock in the same woods."

"Okay, pal. Let's have another."

Teddy wanted to be drinking, but Kroll had forbidden it. "So, what time is this going down?"

"I told you, eight o'clock in the same woods," Joe Kroll exploded in rage. He had all that he could do to control himself. It was rage from being outfoxed by Pierce. He knew that he should be very excited about tomorrow—the most glorious day in history. But all he wanted to do was rip out someone's heart.

Chen and Heinz had checked into their hotel. It wasn't easy to find one in the Hamptons in summer. Most hotels were booked as much as a year in advance, but they found a place in Quogue. They could have stayed at the Holiday Inn in Riverhead, where all law enforcement agencies were guaranteed a room, but it was not very romantic. The courthouse was less than a mile away, so it was very popular with the guns and cuffs clientele. As they had hardly slept in three days, they were completely exhausted. Dropping their bags in the room, they headed to the bed.

"You want sex?" Chen asked.

"Too tired," Heinz replied.

"Good."

"I've got to call Gamble and tell him that we're here before we sleep."

Heinz dialed Gamble's cell. "Greg? Hi, this is Carl Heinz. Sounds like you are in a bar?"

"Yeah," said Gamble, with a slight slur. "What you want?"

"Loni and I are here on Long Island. We want in on the show tomorrow. We want Dean—he is one of mine, you know. I hope you don't object."

"Well, this is getting to be just one big happy party, isn't it?"

"What do you mean?"

Gamble explained about the New York State Crime Commission and the deal that he had just made. Then he ordered Heinz to stay out of the way. "After this is done, you can take Dean back, but we may want him for questioning too. Do you agree?"

Chapter Fifty-Nine

Raymond Davies was at his desk in his small house near the Stony Brook University campus. He was preparing his speech for the following night. This was going to be the greatest archeological find of the century, and he would be the lucky one to announce it. He knew that he would become famous as the man to authenticate the true history of the Aryan race. And Walter Pierce was even paying him for something that he would have done just for the glory.

"What time did you say we need to get going?" asked the small voice. The young woman often stayed at his house and seemed to be very interested in his work.

"I told you, sweetie, we are expected at the old house," replied Raymond Davies. "So start getting ready around six." When he told her about the translation of the symbols that Pierce had given him, she insisted that he bring her to the ceremony. What Davies couldn't figure out was why Pierce was having him make the announcement at the old house. What did it matter? Why not do it at a museum or city hall? Pierce had promised that at least one major TV network would be present and Davies would have the spotlight. He did say that Davies would need to be flexible in his presentation. What did that mean?

He marveled at his good luck, which also included his assistant. She just walked into his office on campus two years ago and asked for a job. She had proven to be brilliant, funny, and a good companion. The deep brown eyes always got their way with him. Yeah, he was crazy about this twenty-six-year-old beauty named Myra, Myra Patel.

Chapter Sixty

Walter Pierce was the first of the many competitors to be up and around. "What a glorious day today is! If this is my last day on earth, just give me the strength to complete my mission."

He was on the cell phone to confirm his car rental. He was talking to a limo agency. "Mr. Pierce, are you sure about where you want this guy picked up and delivered?"

"Ron, you have been my limo service for how many years now, twenty? How many times have I given you bad directions?"

"Well, never, I think."

"Okay, then, just have your driver do as I have told you; I'm paying double. It has to be exactly at eight fifteen sharp."

"Okay, you're the boss, and we do aim to please. See you tonight."

Greg Gamble's first call was to the FBI main office in Chicago. He needed to check in with the special agent in charge. He had to be careful about what he said, or the special agent in charge would secure a company plane and show up to take over and steal all the credit. The FBI was nothing if not bureaucratic and seeded with many career-minded employees. His boss was a first-string player.

"Agent Gamble checking in," he said to Special Agent in Charge Dodge.

"Gamble, good of you to check in. You are spending well outside your budget, you realize. Are you looking for buried treasure? Ha-ha!"

"Sir, I know that we are over budget, but we have an explosive situation here. It should all get resolved tonight."

"Good, good, I'll be out there on agency business. Perhaps I'll stop by to see how things turn out."

"That's too bad, sir."

"Why do you say that?"

"Well, sir, the bigger and more important part of the operation is going to take place in Chicago, tonight at five after seven. I was hoping that you could help Agent Krist."

"Bigger part, you say? What is it?"

"We're going to hit the church and several of the perpetrators' homes. There should be some real important finds there. Krist has all the warrants and just needs someone senior to lead him. My guess is that he will leak something to the press. Oh well, he will have to deal with them."

"Gamble, you are right, Krist needs someone to lead him. I'll cancel my trip. I won't let you down. Carry on." The phone went dead.

Colton Banyon awoke with a start. He remembered leaving the old house around midnight. The hotel room was small but well furnished. The Patel sisters had actually left him alone to get a good sleep. He had been dreaming, and his dreams were always major productions. He usually remembered them and then analyzed them to discover the root cause. He felt that dreams were an expression of thoughts clustered in his mind. He knew that his brain worked just fine when he slept, and he had many times assigned a task to his brain before sleeping. Often when he woke up, he would have the solution or direction that he needed. This dream he did not want to remember. He was a dog chasing his own tail. All the other dogs were watching, along with a dogcatcher. The problem was that he had caught his tail, and when he bit it, the tail had turned into the dogcatcher's hand. Things had gone downhill from there. The phone was ringing. "Hello?"

"Dad, this is Mitch. I've got bad news; I have to go back to Jersey this morning. The office called, and they need me right now."

"Bummer," said Colt.

"Good luck. I had a blast. No one will believe me about those two women."

"Mitch, don't kiss and tell. Thanks for your help. I'll call you soon. Bye."

Walter Pierce was making a few more phone calls from his lawyer's office. "I'd like to talk to the producer, please," the crackling voice said.

"Who should I say is calling?" the receptionist asked.

"Tell him that it is Walter Pierce, dear." There was a slight delay as the phone was transferred.

"Walter, how good to hear from you."

"Will you be joining us tonight?"

"We will be there at 8:45 p.m. sharp, just as you asked."

"Splendid. You will bring that young woman too, I assume?"

"Well, Walter, she is our best reporter," replied the producer of the CCN news network.

Chapter Sixty-One

Agent Chen and Detective Heinz entered the room of Agent Gamble at the Holiday Inn. Over twenty agents were sitting around the suite, watching TV and cleaning their guns. Chen had dressed in white shorts and a red tank top, planning to go to the pool and hang out as soon as things were set. Every eye in the room was on her as she glided across the room and sat down at the table.

"Everybody, this is Detective Carl Heinz from the Streamwood Police Department. Michael Dean is one of his officers. Heinz is going to be responsible for escorting Dean back to Chicago." No one said a word. "And this is Agent Loni Chen from the Illinois State Police Department. She is assisting Carl."

Almost in unison, all the men said, "Hi, Loni."

"Let's get to the plan," Heinz suggested.

"My boys and I are going to stay on the shooters," Captain Spita said. "We go where they go. If they shoot, they go down. Any questions?"

"No," said Gamble. He then continued, "Carl, you and Loni stay with Dean and only Dean. We have everyone else covered."

Heinz hadn't pointed out that there were twenty FBI agents and only four unknowns to cover. There would also be Pierce and probably one or two more people—a three-to-one ratio.

Gamble pressed on. "Otherwise, guys, the same setup as last night. The helicopter is due in at exactly eight o'clock. Make sure to have your night-vision goggles, as it will probably turn dark while we're there. Bruce, are you still going to be up in a tree?"

"Yeah, just in case."

Gamble slapped his hands on his knees. "Okay, any questions?" No one had any since they were all experienced operatives.

"Good," said Chen. "I can lie by the pool for a couple of hours. See you boys later."

The room suddenly cleared, with everyone deciding to get some air by the pool. Heinz was getting pissed off now.

Michael Dean was walking along the beach in Westhampton. His mind was working overtime as he decided on the future of the Aryan race. He needed to show the world that he had nothing to fear from anyone. *What title should I hold? Supreme Commander? How about President and Divine Spiritual Leader? No, it is too long. Maybe shorten it to Divine Leader. "God" might seem pretentious.*

He knew he would have to seize control of the membership with force. Some of his closest friends were untrustworthy. He noticed that Teddy regarded him with contempt. They would soon be dealt with. Then there was the question of that stupid Ula Woods. After all, he would need to be free to help the many lost females that would need comfort and guidance during his reign.

He considered several options for a dress code in his empire. Women, of course, had to wear dresses at all times. Government personnel would be provided with dashing uniforms complete with boots and hats. The colors were still clogging his mind, although black was his favorite. Yes, once he had the tablet, he would start a new thousand-year reign.

At noon the Patel girls had finally awakened. Banyon took them to a local restaurant for fruit and juices to start their day. They then begged him to take them to a secluded beach. Using a rented car, he drove them to the western end of Dune Road. They walked along the dunes and found a place where there was a good sandy beach and no one else around. The place brought back memories for Banyon. He remembered in high school, the best times were at all-night beach parties, with huge bonfires, beer, and, of course, girls. He'd been to dozens of parties in these dunes.

Banyon found a dune that was cut away like a small fifteen-foot-high canyon. The trio was only visible from the water, and that's how the girls wanted it. As soon as they got to the spot, the twins stripped down to nothing and plopped down on towels.

Banyon climbed up the dune and sat near the top. He told them he could spot anyone who might walk down the beach and could warn the girls to cover up. Besides, he needed a respite from them. The surf and the wind blocked out the chatter from the twins.

Banyon was lying in the sand at the top edge of the large dune, overlooking the vast ocean. The breeze brushed his face, and the healing sun did its magic on his body. The pounding of the waves was soothing and clarified his thinking.

He was always the stable force in his family. He was the one giving advice and pushing people in the right direction. For the last couple of days, he put everything on hold and had become someone with whom he was not comfortable. He knew that he needed to refocus and to set new objectives.

His first priority was to gain employment, and the upcoming interview was critical to his future. He needed to distance himself from the Patels. He decided to tell them that it was over. He began to consider the entire weekend as some type of middle-aged rebellion, although the journey had not been all that bad. He was vindicated on the accident from the previous year. No one was chasing him anymore. *So, why was he so upset?*

His instincts told him that the Patels were not who they appeared to be. The whole trip to Long Island was a set up. And every time he attempted to learn more, they smothered him with lust. He did not know what or who was involved, but he hoped it did not have anything to do with the white supremacists and especially with Michael Dean. He knew the FBI was looking for a guy named Walter Pierce, and the land around Banyon's old house was owned by Pierce. They all seemed to be connected, especially when a key for the old house suddenly appeared. *Why was he involved?*

"I hope that he can't hear us," Previne said with a giggle.

"Sister, you worry too much. Colt is wondering why he is here. Can't you see that he is lost in thought? Otherwise, his eyes would be on us," observed Pramilla.

"He has been great fun. Do you think that he suspects anything?"

"Yes, I believe that he is starting to put it together, but it will all be over in a few hours. We have nothing to fear."

"When should we tell him that we have already begun to move out of the condo?"

"Are you going soft on me, Previne?"

"No, of course not, I just think that he is a decent man and deserves the truth."

"Well, he will get the truth. Tonight will be soon enough. We will tell him about our move. I wonder if he will miss our little sexual encounters? If we had more time, we could have fulfilled his every fantasy, don't you think?" Pramilla smiled as she thought about it.

"I think that I will miss them too," responded her twin.

"It will be good to see our sister again," said Pramilla, changing the subject.

"Yes, we haven't seen her in over two years, but her work was necessary, just like ours."

"Have you called Grandfather, Previne?"

"Yes, he is failing but said he will hold on for us to return before he stops the curse and dies. I also told him that Wolf would be coming with us. He and Grandfather have discussed more curses, you know."

"But they are both so old. Will there be time to implement?"

"I believe these curses will run long into the future." Previne was very quiet now. She suddenly sighed. "I already miss him. He has done so much for all of us, and now we will help him complete his lifelong vendetta."

"Grandfather has placed many curses. Will they stop when he dies?"

"Pramilla, a curse must run its course. Grandfather taught us that."

"Pity," Pramilla sighed. "I do miss India and will be happy to be back as soon as this is over."

The twins became lost in thought. Their two-year journey was almost over. They would leave on a nonstop to India that very night. All that was left was the finale. That would come this evening. It started when Walter Pierce made contact with their grandfather Abu, once known as the Great Abu. The curse that Abu put on the tablet used ghosts to talk to anyone in possession of the tablet. From 1936 until now, anyone who controlled the artifact heard singsong riddled voices. The voices forced honor onto the owners. Pierce had discovered an additional voice and wanted to free all the voices.

Research pointed him to northern India, and he found Abu Patel over two years ago. Abu agreed to help Pierce complete his mission. The Patel clan was sent to help. But the only way to complete the mission was to reveal the tablet, to publicly display the Aryan history. Pierce needed Colton Banyon to locate the hidden place where the tablet was located in the old house. He himself could not do it, as he was not a respectable citizen. Banyon was and would know where to look.

Pramilla rolled over on her side and addressed her sister. "Walter's plan has sure worked well, don't you think?"

"Or maybe there is a higher force at work," commented Previne.

Chapter Sixty-Two

FBI Special Agent in Charge Dodge was cleaning up his desk before going out into the field. His idea of cleaning up his desk was simple. Any written requests for money or equipment that were left in his in-box went unread. He simply stamped them "denied" and sent them back to the sender. If it were important, it would resurface. As a result, Gamble's request for helicopter support that evening was denied. As FBI special agent in charge, he kept his desk always clean. He went into his private bathroom to shower and shave in order to present his best face to the TV cameras.

Gamble and his men were already on station. Captain Spita and his crew were also there. Conn, as usual, was up a tree. Everyone wore Kevlar vests, and about half the men had shotguns. The rest had pistols, tear gas, masks, and stun guns. Gamble hoped to record the discussions as evidence, so mikes had been placed around the clearing, and two men minded the equipment from a van on the Speonk-Riverhead Road. The men in the van also monitored the bug and tracking device on the Kroll van. The FBI pulled their vans off the road and camouflaged the vehicles with branches. A car manned with two agents prepared to follow Kroll to the spot.

The shooters worked their way to the site from another fire lane. They also wanted their car hidden from view. Richard Spita had stealthily followed the shooters and now took up his place in the woods with the others.

Agent Chen and Detective Heinz took a separate car to the site. Their plan was to grab Dean as soon as the action started and hustle him away from the FBI and crime commission, to avoid the eventual bureaucratic nightmare that was sure to follow.

Meanwhile, back at the motel, there was trouble brewing.

"But you can't go," said Previne.

"Watch me," answered Colt. He had come to a decision while sitting on the dunes. He decided that he did not need another night in the old house.

He would head to the city to prepare for tomorrow's meeting—that would be his priority.

"Colt, you promised," said Previne. "We are paying you, remember?"

"Money isn't everything," Colt replied as he closed his suitcase. Pramilla was nowhere to be found. When they returned to the motel, Banyon announced that he was through with the whole ghost thing. The girls were in a panic. Pramilla immediately left to make a phone call.

"Colt, sweetie, you're just tense. Let me give you a massage. It will make you feel better." She undid her dress strap and let it drop to the floor. She had nothing on under it.

"Previne, sex isn't everything, either. You girls use sex like a weapon. I'm going to close my eyes and walk out the door. If I don't look at you, I can escape your spell. I'm leaving."

"Don't be a fool, Colt." Her voice suddenly had a sinister edge to it.

"Showing your real colors, are you?"

"Tonight is too important. You must be at the house tonight." It was a demand.

"There is something going on here. I don't believe that our meeting was by chance."

"No? How could Pramilla and I set up our meeting? Remember, you met Pramilla in a parking lot, with a detective. It was fate, Colt."

"Yeah, I have this feeling that you are one step ahead of me, all the time—almost like you know what's going to happen before it does. Do you know what will happen tonight?"

"Colt, be reasonable. We need you. We want to be around you, and I think that I love you."

"Previne, you are trying too hard. What are you hiding?"

At that moment, Colt's cell phone rang. "Colton Banyon," he answered as the LCD gave a number that he only vaguely recognized.

"Mr. Banyon, this is Dan Broadwater. You have an appointment with me in Manhattan tomorrow."

"Yes, sir. If you are confirming my appointment, I will be there."

"Actually, something has come up." This set off a sudden alarm in Colt's head.

"Has something happened?"

"No, not really. I was just wondering if you mind driving out to eastern Long Island to visit with me. I'm being detained with other business and won't be able to make our meeting on time. I do want to interview you but need your assistance. We could reschedule, if you desire, but I want to close the position soon."

"Just tell me when and where, and I will be there. As it happens, I am on eastern Long Island as we speak."

"Splendid," said the voice. "Trent Rogers, my lawyer, is located on Main Street in Westhampton. Let's meet at nine thirty tomorrow morning at my lawyer's office."

"Dan, I grew up in Westhampton. I know where his office is. I'll be there on time. Thanks for the call."

"Good-bye, my boy."

Pramilla returned to the room to find Colt and Previne squared off as if in a fight. Previne was, of course, naked, and Banyon had his eyes closed.

"What's going on?" asked Pramilla as she tried to slip her cell phone into her small purse. Banyon had been peeking. In one swift move, he grabbed her arm and took the phone.

After pushing a few buttons, he said, "Funny, I just got a phone call from this last number in your phone. What was the name of the person to whom you were talking, Pramilla?"

"Oh, Colt, it's not what you think," a frustrated Pramilla said. "You have a right to be mad, but don't blow this whole operation because of our ineptness." She then dropped to the floor and started to cry.

"Okay, just tell me what is going on, please. What operation? It sounds like a James Bond movie."

"We can't," both girls said in unison.

"Then I'm out of here," Banyon said.

Previne leaped at him and knocked him on the bed; Pramilla jumped on the bed, and both sat on him.

"Now you are going to listen," Previne said. "There is something going on. You are right about that. It has to do with why the white supremacists are after you. We did meet by accident, although we would have arranged a meeting anyway. Pramilla, I, and our sister are all working on behalf of the Indian government."

"Another sister?"

"We do need your help—you're kind of the bait, I guess."

"The bait? What are you talking about? And get off me. I don't want to hurt you."

"Do I have to?" asked Previne.

"Yes," said Pramilla, "get off him now. Let me explain."

"Yes, you have a lot of explaining to do."

"The artifact we seek belongs to the Indian government. It was stolen from us in the 1930s. Walter Pierce has the piece and is willing to give it back to India—that is, if we help him to get you to the old house tonight. It's as simple as that."

"Yeah, but why does he want me at the house? This sounds like there is danger involved. What if the white supremacists show up?"

"Colt, you have nothing to worry about. We are all trained in protection, and there will be newspeople there—nothing is going to happen."

"Newspeople? I don't get it. So the interview tomorrow is just a hoax too?" a disappointed Colt asked.

"No, Colt, it is real. Walter does have a position for you, and we know that you are qualified. We just need to get you to the old house by 8:00 p.m., and we are going to be late if we don't get going now. So, are you going to be a wimp or a hero?"

After some consideration, Banyon said, "I can't believe that I'm saying this, but let's get going. I need the job. After tonight, though, I think that we are finished, do you get me?"

"Well," said Previne, "we are going back to India. Keri is moving us out of the house right now. You will not see us again, unless of course, you come to India. You are invited anytime." She had a smile on her face when she said it.

Chapter Sixty-Three

Billy Brown and his band of tired men were still on the road and headed to the site. He sensed trouble. Paul had alluded to the possibility that the police were onto Kroll. But it did not matter to Brown. He was on a mission to stop the tablet from being released to the public. None of his companions knew what was really going down. They thought that they were stealing a valuable artifact. Each man had been promised ten grand for helping. They each knew that the assignment was dangerous, based on previous experiences with Michael Dean.

They pulled into another fire lane and rolled out of the van. Had they gone down the road just a little farther, they would have found the shooters' car and been more on guard. Instead, they walked back to the main road and followed a deer path to the fire lane by the site. They all crouched together to get final instructions from Brown.

"Okay, now listen up," said Brown. "At exactly 8:10 p.m., we are going to storm the bastards. Everyone needs to start running on my signal—this is important. We want to overwhelm them before they know what hit them. Some of them will probably have guns, so shoot to kill. Any questions?"

As the Altar of the Creator management team pulled into the fire lane, their two FBI trackers reported in and went to their assigned sites. Joe Kroll was dressed in a black suit and white shirt without a collar. As head of the church, he felt that he needed to look the part. His holiness had a .45 in his waistband. Dean and the others were dressed in jeans and T-shirts. They also carried guns. Dean was beyond rage because Kroll had told him to go to a store and buy a camera to take Kroll's picture when he was handed the tablet. Kroll told Dean that he could be the official photographer of Aryanna.

Dean walked into the woods following the unmarked trail that they had passed the night before. They reached the site at 7:45 p.m. and milled around, with nothing to do but wait.

The battle lines were set. Kroll's group was in the bull's-eye. The shooters were out of sight but very near the clearing. The FBI, the crime commission,

Heinz, and Loni surrounded the dig site. Finally Billy Brown and his men were heading toward the site from the fire lane.

Rogers dropped Pierce off at the front door of the old house. Pierce knew that no one would be there. He stood in the center of the old living room.

Meanwhile, Raymond Davies and Myra pulled up in the driveway. They proceeded around the circle and then turned onto the straight driveway that ran alongside the house. When they got out of the car, Myra said she had to get a bag out of the trunk. Davies stood waiting as she rummaged around the trunk.

Myra opened the trunk and then proceeded to bend over into the large opening. Her legs were straight, and she bent from the waist, going down and down until she appeared to be almost bent in half. Her sexy ass was waving in the air and had been doing so for a good five minutes. Davies wondered what she could possibly be doing in the trunk. "Come on, Myra, we are going to be late. Walter is always on time."

The FBI and others were all watching Kroll and his men. Gamble called the van to inquire as to the whereabouts of the helicopter, only to find out that it was grounded due to lack of authorization. *How could this happen?* Suddenly a phone was ringing somewhere in the quiet woods. Almost everyone in the woods reached for his cell phone.

Dean's phone rang at five minutes to eight. He was filled with rage. He expected Pierce to be waiting for him at the spot. He never considered that it would be the other way around.

"This had better be good," Dean yelled into the phone.

"Michael, this is Walter."

"Goddamn it, Pierce. You are supposed to be here."

"Not quite, Michael. I told you to be at the spot at eight. I never said that I would be there."

"What are you trying to pull?"

"Actually, Michael, I asked you to come alone, and you are not alone. So who is deceiving whom?"

"Are we playing games now, Pierce?"

"On the contrary, my friend, this has been the plan all along. Now listen carefully if you want to establish your place in the sun. I am nearby, but I want you to come here alone, do you understand?"

"Yes," replied a now-interested Dean. He looked around at the other men and saw that they were all watching him suspiciously.

"Good, now listen carefully. I have buried a box nearby. It's a fake, of course. I want you to go to the marker and walk thirty steps to the west, then thirty steps to the south. Have your men start to dig there. And when they become frenzied in their digging, I want you to leave and run to the road. There will be a limo waiting for you there. The limo will bring you to me. Do you understand?"

"Yes," was the excited reply.

"Now, get going. You need to be here by 8:30 p.m., exactly."

Dean closed the phone and walked to the marker and stood by it. Everyone was staring at him. Harry asked what was going on. "I have the directions to the box; I know where it's buried. You need to follow me," said Dean, drawing it out and appearing lost in thought. He knew that these men would begin salivating as he theatrically gave the directions. "Get the shovels, boys."

There was a mad scramble to find the shovels. Everyone gathered around the perimeter of the site, poking and probing. The black shadows in the woods went unnoticed. Dean waited until the shovels were all located.

"We take thirty steps due west." They all moved together, with shovels raised like muskets.

"Now we take thirty steps due south," Dean said. They turned in unison and marched thirty paces. "We dig here, boys."

Everyone started to dig at once. There was sand flying and dust everywhere. The agents all crept closer as they realized that the game was finally starting. Dean waited for the exact second that everyone was waiting for, the sound of a shovel hitting something hard. He then took off running. Joe Kroll noticed, and he set off after Dean. The others were lost in their discovery and were now attempting to roll the box out of the hole.

Dean spotted the limo and jumped into the car. He was closing the door when a large hand caught it, and Kroll entered the car. "Going somewhere?" asked Kroll.

"I'm just following instructions from Pierce. The limo will take me to the real site. This site was a setup to shed anyone else with me so that I would come alone. He doesn't like crowds. Pierce told me that the buried box was a fake."

"Okay, Mike, not that I believe a word that you say, but I'm going with you." Kroll showed Dean his gun for emphasis.

The driver took off, without mentioning that a van had pulled out of the woods and was following them.

One of the two radiomen in the van immediately contacted Agent Gamble. "Two of the group have left the woods and entered a limo. Should we follow?"

"Goddamn, yes, follow them. I'm sending backup."

Heinz had been searching for Dean when the call came in over the headphones. He realized that Dean was gone. He said to Gamble, "Loni and I will go. Our car is near, and you can send additional backup as soon as you round up these freaks, okay?"

"Copy," was all that Gamble could say.

Raymond Davies and Myra Patel entered the old house through the front door; which was wide open. Because of the full moon, it was light enough to observe someone standing in the middle of the room. He was just closing a cell phone.

"Walter, you picked a good night for it."

"Yes, but I'm afraid that we have an unwelcome visitor," he said, glancing at Myra. She gave a short nod of her head.

"Walter, this is my assistant, Myra Patel."

"Pleasure to meet you, Myra." Pierce extended his hand. "I've heard good things about you."

"Thank you."

Pierce now turned to Davies. "You know the plan, correct?"

"Yes, I know the plan, but I still don't know why you do not want to be part of the ceremony."

"Let's just say that I do not photograph well, and leave it at that. I need to be in the background. The police will surely want to talk to me, and I must be gone."

"Walter, are you all right? You look as white as a sheet."

"I'm fine, Raymond."

Just then the Patel twins entered the door, all but dragging Colt after them.

"Hello, sister," Pramilla said with a radiant smile.

"Pramilla, Previne, how wonderful to see you again." Myra rushed toward the door and embraced them both.

"Myra, this is Colton Banyon," said Pramilla. He just stared at all three sisters. It was impossible to tell them apart.

"I'm sorry, I don't mean to stare, but all three of you look alike. I mean really alike. The resemblance is uncanny."

Myra laughed. "We hear that often."

"Colt, this is Raymond Davies. He is professor of archeology at Stony Brook University."

Davies just stood there with his mouth open. Banyon turned to Pierce. "You must be the mastermind, Walter Pierce."

"I am Walter Pierce. It's very good to finally meet you in person."

Pierce shifted his gaze as a man entered the door. "Well, this is a cozy little group," Dean said as he walked into the room like he owned it. He had already eyeballed the three women. He could use them in his kingdom. Seeing that Davies was a professor type, he ignored him. He nodded at Banyon, who now was terrified that his prediction had come true.

"Let's get this show on the road, Walter. My boys will see that I'm gone and will be after me soon. Do you have the tablet here?"

"I doubt that they will ever get here," Pierce commented.

Joe Kroll was actually standing on the porch outside the front door. He positioned himself so that he could hear every word said inside, but no one could see him. Heinz and Chen ditched their car just off the long driveway. They now crouched about twenty feet from Kroll in some dense bushes.

At exactly 7:05 p.m., Special Agent in Charge Dodge yelled into his headphone, "Give them hell, boys." Several carloads of FBI agents rushed the church office in Aurora. Seven other groups were on the move to Dean's house, Teddy's house, and five additional places. They had warrants backed up with lots of guns.

Judy Kroll was in the church office when she heard the door crash open and several of the supporters scream. She immediately looked through the hidden peephole that her husband had installed to watch the congregation and saw the FBI pouring into the church. She picked up her phone and hit the speed dial for Joe, but the agents were already in the office and took away her phone.

Teddy wrestled the heavy box from the hole. The men worked up a sweat digging in the sand. As soon as they shoveled out the hole, it would fill up. They dug more frantically. Eventually they dug enough to grab the handle of the box and heave it out. All three men were breathing heavily and gasping for breath. Teddy cut the old leather straps with a knife and threw open the box.

Suddenly Gamble heard a sound in his earpiece, "Oops."

"Repeat." Gamble made an instant reply.

Conn's voice was muffled. "Many hostiles inbound, maybe a dozen. They are running and will reach your location in ten seconds."

Billy Brown was the first to come upon the site. He saw Teddy staring into the open box. Brown took aim on the run. He squeezed off a two-shot burst, and two red holes appeared on Teddy's shirt as he fell over. Harry started to pull out his gun. Gary was lying on the ground, breathing hard, but was able to roll over and pull out his own gun. More of Brown's gang raced out of the forest and into the clearing. They had caught the men completely by surprise. Just as several were taking aim to kill the remaining two diggers, the staccato sound of a submachine gun filled the air.

Billy Brown was the first to die. Three other black gunmen went down in quick succession. Harry and Gary were shooting back now. Bullets were flying everywhere, and the most bullets were coming from the two shooters sent by the Mafia. They had seen the blacks enter the site and did not hesitate to open fire. They stood next to each other, firing from the hip and spreading lethal lead everywhere.

Gamble yelled into a bullhorn, "FBI—drop your weapons and put your hands up."

For a brief second, the shooting stopped. Then everyone started firing into the woods at the unseen FBI.

"Open fire," Gamble ordered.

On command, Conn dropped the fat shooter and was just about to shoot the other one when he threw down his gun. He ran into the woods. Conn said, "The little one is on the run, heading northwest." He dropped from the tree and took pursuit, along with the five crime commission members. They caught the shooter after a half-mile chase.

Gamble was taking stock. There were still five blacks and two white supremacists shooting back. Gamble's forces were seriously depleted. Of the original twenty-eight people, six went after the shooter, and four went after Kroll and Dean. That left him with fourteen against seven. *Not good odds.* Gamble put out an urgent call for more backup. As a result, the two watchers in the van had to abandon their position at the old house and speed back to the old site.

The firing continued for some time. Gamble felt like he was in a war. Men were firing into the dark woods, and other men were returning fire into the open site. Shotgun blasts echoed throughout the forest. Some of the men screamed when they were hit. It was becoming a massacre. Soon the bad guys would run out of bullets. Two more blacks went down. Three-to-one odds were much better. He picked up the bullhorn.

"You are completely surrounded. We have you outnumbered five to one. Drop your guns and put up your hands."

Gary was the first to throw down his gun. Seeing this, the others followed suit. The FBI swarmed out of the woods. In seconds, the men were cuffed. Gamble strolled out of the woods and stopped by the box. Seeing nothing there but rocks, he was puzzled.

Chapter Sixty-Four

Dean was sizing up everyone in the room. Walter Pierce probably had his Luger. The rest of the people were helpless and no threat to him. He knew the professor was there to verify the tablet. One of these women served as his assistant. What Colton Banyon was doing there caused him some concern.

"So, let's get to the tablet. I don't see it here, Walter."

"To retrieve the tablet, we must go to the basement," said Pierce. "We do have to hurry, as the media will be here in less than ten minutes. Michael, I assume that you want press coverage, don't you?"

A little surprised, Dean noted, "The sooner that we get this announced, the better." He then produced an evil smile.

Pierce extended his arm to direct them. Pramilla led the way to the basement door. Myra reached into the bag that she had retrieved from the car trunk and handed each person a flashlight.

"It's dark down there," she said.

Heinz and Chen saw Kroll disappear into the dark house. "I'm going after Kroll," said Agent Chen.

"Then I'm going with you," said Heinz.

"No," replied Chen. "You will make too much noise; I can be very quiet. We'll keep in touch by earphones. You coordinate the backup when they get here." Suddenly she disappeared.

Pierce was about to push on a wall in the basement when he heard something. Joe Kroll had stepped too heavily on a stair, causing a loud crack.

"Ah, I see that our uninvited guest is now making an entrance," observed Pierce.

Kroll came off the steps in a leap and leveled his gun at Michael Dean. "So, you thought that you could have your ceremony without me, did you?" said Kroll.

"Joe, you were supposed to be out of sight. What are you doing, you idiot?"

Dean saw Kroll flinch when he called him an idiot. It was all the time that he needed. Dean struck Kroll's hand like a bolt of lightning, sending the gun flying into the darkness of the basement. He quickly trained his own gun on the little group.

"I'm in charge here, Joe. You told me to be the photographer, didn't you? I'm going to take some pictures with the camera that you made me buy. So, why don't you all pose over there in the corner? Get away from the wall, Pierce." He ushered them all over into the corner in a bunch, the girls in front and the men in back. Pierce, the tallest, was in the middle.

"No pictures," thundered Pierce.

"Too late," said Dean as he hit the flash.

As soon as Colt's eyes adjusted, he noticed that Pierce was missing. He vanished into thin air. "Where is Walter?"

"I don't know," answered Myra. "I felt a rush of air, and he was gone."

"I felt it too," said Previne.

"So did I," said Davies.

"What the hell? People don't just vanish. This is one more trick by Pierce," said Kroll. "And you, Dean, you are a moron. Pierce hasn't signed over his assets yet. Now what are we going to do?"

"I don't know about you, but I'm going to get the box," answered Dean. He went to the wall and began to push. As soon as his back was turned, Kroll rushed at him. Dean, sensing the attack, spun and fired. The bullet passed through Kroll's arm and imbedded itself in the wall. Dean was now taking aim on Kroll, now lying on the floor.

"So, you thought I was stupid, did you? I know you. You just want to take everything for yourself. You wanted to make me the photographer. Well, I'm sick of that; I want it all now. I think that the box is behind this wall. That is why Pierce was about to push on it. I no longer need you, Joe. This is my good-bye."

"You got this all wrong, Mike. This is some type of a setup. Don't you get it?"

Loni Chen had stealthily entered the basement. She was dressed in black and was all but invisible. She was about ten feet from Dean in the shadows. Colt saw Chen. He wasn't sure if anyone else saw her.

"You know, maybe you are right, Joe. I think Pierce planned all this and is nearby. Maybe I can get him to show himself." Dean raised the gun and pointed it directly at Colt. He remembered that Pierce had said that no harm was to come to Banyon. "You have until the count of three," said Dean.

"Loni, help," Colt said. No one else knew what he was talking about.

Agent Chen pounced like a cat. One chop and the gun was gone, bouncing across the floor. She then followed with a vicious kick to Dean's crotch. Dean was prepared. Because of his love of himself, he always wore a cup whenever any physical action loomed. As a result, Chen's kick only knocked him off balance. He bounced off the wall and squared off to face his attacker.

When he saw that it was Loni Chen, he laughed. He was more than a foot taller and about 110 pounds heavier. "Well, well, Loni, no one here to protect you now, so let's play Okinawa." He took a huge swing at her head and missed. She was suddenly by his side, chopping him in the left breast area, breaking one of his ribs. He kicked out with his foot, leaving his rear exposed. Chen was faster. She slammed the tip of her toe up his ass, hitting the bottom of his tailbone. Dean was totally paralyzed. He slumped to the ground. Chen was on him in a flash and had his hands cuffed behind his back before he could move a muscle.

"I'd rather play with dolls than do anything with you, you scum," she taunted. She then turned to Kroll, who was sitting on the ground. She pushed him down on his back and somehow rolled him over before he could protest. She frisked him.

"Can't you see that I'm hurt?" wailed Kroll.

"It's only a flesh wound," answered Chen. She produced a white handkerchief and bound the wound while Kroll was still lying on his stomach.

"Look," said Kroll. His flashlight lay in the dust on the floor. The light shining on the wall clearly showed where a door that opened out had moved the dust. The three Patel sisters ran to the wall and used their fingernails to search for a latch. Previne yelled out that she had found something, and all lights turned to the spot. There was a small hole in the wall and a metal button. She pressed the button, and a sound was heard, followed by a whish. A panel opened. They rushed to pull it open all the way. Pramilla went in first. She saw nothing but a ladder leading up into the house.

"There is nothing in here but a ladder that leads up," she said disappointedly.

"I'll bet that it leads to the box," said Davies. "Walter is always dramatic."

Kroll remained flat on his stomach with Chen above him as she worked on binding the wound. Kroll turned to see into the opening, and his hand touched something—Dean's gun. He grabbed it and spun around quickly, throwing Chen. Before she could recover, he was on his feet, pointing the gun at the stunned policewoman.

"If I had more time, I would frisk you, little one," he said.

Dean pleaded, "Joe, get me out of here."

"Not this time. I'm tired of cleaning up after you. The cops will take good care of you." He picked up his flashlight and waved everyone away from the door. He could hear men running in the house above him. It would be only a matter of time until they located the basement door. He had to move now.

He entered the opening and saw Pramilla halfway up the ladder. "Just keep going, sweetie, and, yes, I am looking up your dress." He grabbed the handle on the inside of the door to slam it shut. There was an inside latch that he pulled closed. He then turned back to Pramilla. "Keep climbing. I'm right behind your behind."

Heinz reached the basement door and leaped down the steps. He found the little group huddled around the wall, trying to open the door.

Chen was almost desperate. "Kroll took Pramilla in there and locked the door. We can't get in. It would take explosives to get in there."

"I'm just happy that you are safe," a relieved Heinz said.

The backup agents had arrived and were beginning to enter the now-crowded basement.

"Colt, you lived here. Where does the ladder lead?"

"I never knew there was a ladder." said Colt. "No one in my family ever found this hidden room. Believe me, I would remember. It could lead to anywhere in the house."

"Everyone spread out in pairs," Heinz said into his radio. "Kroll is loose in the house. He is in a hidden wall with a ladder. He could be anywhere. Set up stations on each floor. If you hear a sound, yell out. He has a female hostage. I'll check the basement."

Colt turned to Previne, "Why are you smiling?" he asked.

"Pramilla can take care of herself. Kroll doesn't know what he's in for. We have nothing to fear."

Meanwhile, the local police and several television stations had intercepted Agent Gamble's call for backup. The race was on. Three helicopters and several vans sped to the scene in the woods, hoping to film some action. Two arrived at the scene just as Gamble had dispatched three carloads of agents to provide backup for Heinz and Chen. The vans never stopped. They rushed off after the agents, who followed procedure and had the strobe lights and sirens going as they pulled out to head for the old house.

The CCN van had pulled up to the house. The anchorwoman was fixing her hair in a mirror. Linda Choi rarely passed a mirror without looking into it. Not that she was vain; she just wanted to always look her best in public. Suddenly she heard a news flash on one of the many monitors in the van. The news flash showed the Chicago special agent in charge of the FBI leading a raid on a white supremacy church in Chicago. The agent was announcing that he had broken a major crime ring headquartered in the church and that so far over thirty alleged criminals were in custody.

She was just opening the door to set up for the interview when another news flash blinked onto the screen. Agent Greg Gamble was being interviewed. He reported that a black gang overran his men while on a stakeout. The FBI was performing surveillance on a group of white supremacists when the blacks came in shooting. There was a major shootout. It happened just up the road from her present location. An undetermined number of gang members were involved. In total, nine people were killed. No FBI injuries reported. When asked why the FBI was taken by surprise, Gamble gave a terse reply that his eye in the sky, the helicopter, had not been authorized.

Davies was perplexed. He knew that Pierce had a plan for everything. "So, where is the box and tablet, and where did Pierce go?"

Colt bit his lip, then announced, "I think I know where the box is and where Pierce went."

"Where?" several people said at once.

"I think it is behind this wall." He pointed to a place on the far wall. He then stepped over to the wall and pushed. As a latch released, a doorway opened. Banyon pointed his light into the darkness to reveal a tunnel. "This tunnel leads to the pump house. I've been inside it before, when I was younger." Colt hesitated for a minute, then announced, "I'm going in. I think he wants it this way."

"I'm going with you," said Chen. "I'm small, and it might get tight in there." Colt was thankful that his friend was going into the darkness with him.

They entered, shining their flashlights into the dusty tunnel. It was made of brick in a semicircular fashion. After about thirty feet, the tunnel turned to the left. The two friends inched their way to the corner.

"Loni, thanks for saving my life. He would have shot me, you know," Colt said.

"You asked for my help. I could not deny you; you are my friend."

They reached the corner and followed it around to a longer section of the tunnel. Suddenly Colt stopped. About twenty feet down the tunnel, Colt saw an apparition. Its hand beckoned to them to follow. Colt was surprisingly calm.

"Where are you taking us?" Colt inquired in a shaky voice.

"Who are you talking to?" asked Loni as she appeared to shiver.

"Don't you see the ghost? It's right in front of you."

She moved a little closer to him and grabbed his hand.

"Is this why I am here? Is this my part of the plan? Are you using me because you know that I knew about this tunnel? Is that it?" Colt suddenly realized that Loni could not see nor hear the ghost. She was definitely spooked and now nestled into his armpit.

"Yessssss …" The wind-whistled sound came back. The ghost continued to beckon them forward. Colt saw him clearly even though he was transparent and looked like something produced by cigar smoke.

"Why can't you see him?" Colt asked his friend.

"Because she is a nonbeliever." It was a feminine reply. It was Previne. She was right behind them. "People who see ghosts are predisposed to believing in them." Previne had followed them down the tunnel.

"Is that opinion or fact?" asked Colt as they followed the gliding spirit.

"I've studied spirits all my life. It's personal knowledge. I've seen this before. Loni, don't worry. He's not here to harm us. He's here as part of a curse."

"Previne, what are you talking about? What curse?" Banyon was confused. "And why am I a part of this curse?"

"My grandfather Abu put a curse on the tablet many years ago in India. The tablet must return to him before he dies, or these ghost spirits will never be free. They have guided all that have been in possession of the tablet, to protect it for all these years." She explained how her grandfather, many years ago, found the tablet only to have it stolen by the Germans.

"How can this ghost here in America become part of your curse? And it still doesn't explain why I'm involved."

"Colt, Wolfgang Becker didn't hang himself in your closet in 1936; he just simply disappeared. That was all a rumor. Did you ever check? I did."

"Well, no, there seemed to be no reason to do that. The ghost was there in the house when my parents moved here in 1946."

Previne nodded. "I will explain. To be part of this curse, Becker had to be in close proximity to the tablet when he died. This means that he didn't die until the tablet was nearby. His death would have been premature, an accident or something. His corpse would not have had a proper burial. And finally, he had to be an honorable man."

"You make it sound like a formula," said Loni.

"It is," replied Previne. "It is how Grandfather set up the curse. That is why there are many voices. They all died under the same circumstances."

"Okay, but how does Walter Pierce fit into all this?" asked Colt.

The reply came from the ghost. "Myyy sonnnn …"

Previne continued. "Walter has heard voices since he became the guardian of the tablet. After many visits to the house, he realized that one of the voices was actually his father. He wants you to find the tablet. We will take it to Grandfather, and he can then release the curse. All the ghost spirits will then be free, wherever they are, including Walter's father. That is why you are here."

"But why me?" Banyon asked one more time.

"Walter could not present the tablet himself—too many questions about his past. You were the logical choice and knew about the tunnel. You are going to be a hero."

They continued to talk as the ghost flowed several feet ahead of them. The apparition summoned them with its smokelike arms as if to hurry them toward a climax. They had completed the walk all the way to the pump house when the ghost suddenly stopped, then turned toward the wall and pointed with a near-solid bonelike finger. Banyon moved forward. Examining the surface with his flashlight, he found the same type of lever that was on the wall in the basement.

The wall opened inwardly, and they all entered a room that was the size of a standard living room. Banyon could see additional rooms off to the right. It was fully furnished in turn-of-the-century furniture. The left corner of the room was completely caved in, as if a bomb had broken through the ceiling. There was a huge pile of rubble. The box was set near the debris.

"Oh, my God," cried Loni. There was a skeleton of a hand near the box. "Look, the arm extends back into the pile of dirt. Whoever this was, he was buried alive."

Colt inspected the bones. "It looks like this happened sometime ago. It must be Becker." Colt was suddenly struck with information. It was a voice in his head. "I lived here for six years. I had no place to go. I died in 1942. Walter was just a few feet above me." Colt turned to ask the ghost a question, but it was gone.

"Where did the ghost go?" Loni asked.

"The ghost has left," Previne noted. "He's completed his task to bring Colt to the box with the tablet in it. He has further work to do tonight."

"I think we should get the box and get the hell out of here. This place gives me the creeps," said Loni.

Colt grabbed the heavy box and headed back the way they came. Loni spoke into her mike. "We have the box and more."

Banyon, Previne, and Agent Chen came out of the tunnel to find that Davies, Myra, Heinz, and several FBI agents were standing there, waiting for them.

"Let's open the box. Everyone, quickly shine your lights here," said Davies. He undid the straps and opened the box. Inside they found the tablet, just as Pierce had described, and two envelopes. Davies took out the tablet and was studying it under the flashlight. Meanwhile, Colt grabbed the two envelopes. He opened one.

"It's in German," he said, frustrated.

"Give it to me," said Myra. "I can read German. I studied it at Stony Brook."

"It is a recap of the tablet, signed by Himmler," she said. "It says that the history of the Aryan race is spectacular. The Aryans invented many things, including gunpowder, printing, and military defense. It says that the Aryan race was a perfect race. The men were strong, and the women beautiful, with the children so smart that some of their best military leaders were under twenty years of age. These people were the first to build a fort to protect themselves against invaders that desired the secrets of their civilization. They sent out many emissaries to foreign lands to help them grow and develop trade with the Aryan nation. The final part says that they are under siege in their fort because the world was in famine and barbarians wanted the Aryan stock of food. It ends there."

"Read the other one," said Previne.

"Canaris signed this one. It says that the history was indeed spectacular. It says that the Aryans were extremely warlike, and every male child was required to serve in the military from the age of ten. They sent many raids into other lands to steal new technology so that they could continue to build their armies. They built a fort to use as a place to mass their armament. By law, they were not allowed to marry outside the race. Consequently, there was much inbreeding—fathers marrying the daughters, brothers who married sisters. As a result, there were many leaders that were not competent. The children who ran the military were taught to be vicious and responsible only to the government. In the end, they became so demented that they began to fight among themselves. Everyone wanted to become the 'supreme leader.' Assassinations became a common occurrence. The race died away, as no one could deal with the constant treachery. A few people left and went to a faraway land. The writer was one of the people who stayed.

"Canaris added that the tablet was found in a place that was probably a bar or brothel. He wanted the tablet to be presented to the media in America so the final truth about the Aryan race would be revealed and Hitler would be eliminated. It's dated August 4, 1942."

"Wow," said Banyon. "If this gets out, it will destroy all myths about Aryans. They will be laughed at, and no one will want to admit that they are one of the chosen ones. Ray, is that what the tablet really says?"

"Yes," the breathless reply came from Davies. "It says one more thing—they were darker skinned."

Banyon was stunned. "Oh, my God," he said. "Do you mean black?"

"Well, it could mean anything—Chinese, Indian, Arabian, or maybe even black. But blacks were not known to live outside of Africa at that time. One thing is sure—they weren't German."

"What does all this mean?" asked Chen.

"It means that the Aryan movement as we know it will no longer exist," said Banyon.

Myra commented, "One thing is sure—we have a date with destiny. Pierce asked the media to be here at 8:45 p.m. That was three minutes ago. Let's go tell them what we found."

Outside on the front lawn, Linda Choi had the driver, who was also the soundman, set up a mike and small podium on the top of the steps of the old house. She watched as the other anchors and newspeople started to get ready to tape footage; none were ready like she was. She was disappointed that the other newsgroups showed up, but she had an edge. She knew what time the show was to start.

At exactly 8:49 p.m., she told the driver to start the live feed. She stood confidently in front of the camera in the light of the bright floodlights that made her hair shine and her eyes twinkle.

"This is Linda Choi reporting live from an old house in Speonk, a small hamlet on eastern Long Island. We have been told that in a few minutes, a leading professor of archeology at Stony Brook University, a Raymond Davies, will be appearing at the microphone. From what we can ascertain, he will be announcing that he has in his possession an authentic written history of the Aryan race. The preservation of the Aryan race was the basis for the Third Reich. Its principles are still followed today by many fanatic white supremacists. Until today, it was thought that the Aryan race had not left any written history of its civilization."

She noticed the soundman pointing to the steps behind her. "We are ready for the interview. But first, Professor Davies will make a statement."

Raymond Davies approached the microphone. With him were Colt, Myra, and Previne. He noticed a very petite black-haired woman standing at the bottom of the stairs. Several other people milled around news vans. He recognized the woman as being one of the best that CCN had to offer. He was ready to speak.

Meanwhile, Heinz and Chen dragged Dean out of the basement and through the backdoor. The FBI swarmed all over the old house but could not find Kroll as he was behind a secret wall. Kroll was holding his gun on Pramilla while they stood on the first-floor landing behind the pantry wall. Pramilla was unafraid. The FBI was within feet of Kroll's position. He didn't know what to do next. Kroll failed to notice the shadowy ghostlike figure standing behind him. His cell phone rang. He thought that he had turned it off. He quickly grabbed it and whispered into the phone, "Who is this?"

"Why, Joe, it's Walter."

"Where are you?"

"I'm nearby. It's time, my friend. The media is waiting, and Davies has the tablet. All you need to do is open the door in front of you and use your hostage to walk out the front door. They are on the porch, waiting for your entrance."

"The friggin' FBI are all over the place; I can't just walk out there, you idiot."

"Joe, don't come apart on me now, just when all of our dreams can be fulfilled. Are you not the supreme Aryan? Can't you hear the crowds cheering you wildly? You must do this for your people, and I will help. There is no one between you and the front door. Go now."

"My name is Raymond Davies, professor of archeology at Stony Brook University. I have in my hands an incredible artifact. It contains the history of the extinct Aryan race. I've had the pleasure of translating the inscriptions and can now reveal the secrets of a race that, up until now, has remained a mystery. This is the only known written history of the Aryan race."

Choi was delighted. This might be the biggest story that she had ever covered.

"I would like to present Colton Banyon. Mr. Banyon is responsible for finding the artifact. I'd also like to introduce Previne Patel and Myra Patel. They …"

Choi noticed that a man and woman had entered the group. Joe Kroll suddenly appeared, pushing Pramilla out the front door of the house. The gun in her back could not be seen by the small group of reporters now pooling at the bottom of the steps.

"Go on, Professor, finish your introductions," said Kroll.

"Our new members are Pramilla Patel and—"

"Joe Kroll. I'm the head of the Aryan movement," Kroll announced as he leaned toward the mike.

"We only just finished the translation, and I assure you that the tablet contains explosive information about the Aryan race. One last comment, then we will open the floor for questions. Joe Kroll is here to accept the tablet. He worked with the owner of this old house to find Colton Banyon and bring him here to help uncover the artifact." He acquiesced to Joe Kroll.

"Thank you, my friend. I accept this tablet as the true history of the Aryan race. As the Supreme Leader of The Altar of the Creator church, I pledge to follow the inspirations written so long ago by the great Aryan race. Hitler could not live up to the standards that my race has set, but I will. I'm announcing today that my church has absorbed several other churches, and our membership is now in excess of one million members. I call on all Aryan people to follow my leadership. We are establishing a safe place for our members. The place is to be called Aryanna, and it will be located on the many thousands of acres of land that surround this old house."

Linda Choi stood at the foot of the steps watching and listening. Joe Kroll babbled about how great everything was going to be and how he was going to run his regime. She also noted that many FBI agents were pouring out of the old house and standing behind Kroll.

"I'm open for questions," Kroll said.

Quickly Choi raised her hand. "Mr. Kroll, there was a big shootout a few miles from here. Several people were killed. Is this event connected to the shootout?"

Choi watched as Kroll turned and saw all the agents behind him. Several of them smiled and nodded. She pushed her mike forward as he spoke.

"We were originally led to a secluded place to search for the tablet. Obviously it was a trap set by the inept American government to prevent me from accepting this historic artifact. The government was afraid that the good white people of this country would overthrow them and bring a hundred-year prosperous regime to power."

Choi raised her hand again.

Kroll acknowledged her again.

"A recent news flash on CCN showed a major crackdown in Chicago. The FBI raided a church and several homes. The FBI has arrested more than thirty people and has warrants for several others. The church was named Altar of the Creator. Do you have any comments about that?"

"What, my church? I've received no information on this." Kroll's voice trembled. "Clearly this is some kind of government sting to prevent me from representing the Aryan people. The tablet proves the strength of our race. We will overcome this insidious attempt by the weak-minded and corrupt government. My church has a long history of helping white people in need. We stand by our record."

"One more question," Choi said. "Can you tell us what the translation of the tablet actually says?"

"No, I cannot, but Professor Davies can. Professor, if you please."

Davies muscled his way to the mike. "Certainly, Joe. The tablet is actually written in the most ancient form of Sanskrit. It appears that the Aryans had no written language. I have a copy of the first translation in German, made by people employed by Admiral Canaris, a German officer and one of Hitler's inner circle for most of the war. In short, the Aryans were a hostile, corrupt, and sexually deviant society. They stole most of their riches and employed children to run their armies. Their real downfall, however, was the concept that they were so superior that they did not allow their children to marry outside their society. In the end, the word 'Aryan' became known as a joke. One more thing: they might not have been white."

"What? No, you are a lying son of a bitch. You are sabotaging my dream. This can't be," screamed Kroll. He filled the airwaves with expletives that later had to be censored from the recordings. "This is some kind of a goddam trick. Pierce told me that everything was set."

Choi continued to watch the podium as Colt suddenly reached out and grabbed Kroll's wrist. He twisted it. Since this was also the arm that had been shot, Kroll screamed in pain, enabling Banyon to yank the gun from him. Several FBI agents stepped forward to grab Kroll, throwing him to the ground and cuffing him. He continued to scream in pain and anger. His last coherent words were, "I'll get you, Pierce."

Linda Choi was pleased. She might receive a Pulitzer for this story.

While the FBI was collecting Kroll, Choi saw Pramilla turn to Colt and said, "You were very brave." There was admiration in her eyes. She grabbed him and gave him a big hug.

"Pramilla, you know that it was really nothing; I was just tired of listening to Kroll's baloney," replied Colt.

"No, you are a legitimate hero," she insisted.

"I saw the gun magazine in your hand. How did you get the gun magazine, anyway?"

"I have my ways," Pramilla flirted. She then added, "It was Walter's father; he was with me in the pantry. Kroll couldn't see him. He took the magazine and also told Walter to call Kroll after he turned on the phone. Quiet now and listen."

Previne stepped to the microphone. "My name is Previne Patel. I am a diplomat with the Indian government and have a diplomatic passport. I claim this tablet for the Indian government. The hated Nazis stole the tablet from a village in northern India many years ago. We want it back. We plan to display the artifact in a new museum in New Delhi. We will leave for the airport immediately." She stepped back from the mike and hugged Davies, then Colt. The other sisters followed suit with the confused men. With that, Previne, Pramilla, and Myra marched off the steps and entered the limo that had originally delivered Kroll and Dean to the old house. They sped off to the airport with the tablet in a diplomatic bag.

Davies returned to the microphone just as the other news reporters finally took up stations at the bottom of the steps. Only Banyon and Davies were left on the steps.

"Well, I guess that there is nothing more to add to this story. If there are any more questions, I will attempt to answer them."

Linda Choi heard a faint sound coming from the house. Then suddenly the old house burst into flames. It was as if the entire structure lit up at once. The explosion shot flames from the windows, and fire spewed out the front door. Banyon and Davies were blown off the steps. Banyon found himself lying on top of Linda Choi, right between her shapely legs.

Choi quickly reached for her dropped microphone. "Are you still getting this?" she asked the photographer. She then pushed Colt off her tiny body.

"Are you all right?" Colt asked.

"This is the best time of my life," she responded as she winked at him.

Everyone had to retreat to the lawn, where they watched the old house burn to the ground. The other newspeople were frantically trying to catch up with all the news, while Linda Choi had already interviewed Davies on a live feed. She smiled into the camera. "This is Linda Choi reporting live from Speonk for CCN."

Epilogue

The next morning, Banyon was awakened from a deep sleep by the ringing of the phone in his motel room. "Your car is here," said the clerk. He'd almost forgotten about the job interview because so much had happened. Many reporters and other people had mobbed him last night, wanting to interview him. Finally Agent Chen came to his rescue and drove him to the motel. It seemed strange to be alone. Banyon had fallen asleep thinking about the Patel clan.

He climbed into the limo and noticed that it was the same driver that had been on duty last night.

"You had a busy night yesterday. Do you always work so many hours?"

"Not usually, but Mr. Pierce was always very good to me," the driver reflected.

"You said 'was.' Do you know something that I don't?"

"Only that Mr. Pierce bought this car for me and said that it was his parting gift if I took care of the transportation last night. My old boss wasn't too happy when I resigned this morning." He handed Banyon his card. "Call me anytime you're in the area."

The limo dropped Banyon at the law offices of Kurt Rogers. Rogers greeted him in the lobby. "Well, I see that you made it through last night," said Rogers as a preamble to their conversation.

"Are you a part of this?" asked Banyon. "I recognize your voice. I talked to you yesterday—it was Dan Broadwater then, wasn't it?

"I've been Walter's lawyer for a long time. His plan was brilliant, wasn't it?"

"Yeah, if you want to be a pawn," Banyon said, referring to himself.

"Let's get down to business, shall we? I have several things for you to sign." The attorney passed the first document over to Banyon. It said that Banyon was now the owner of a fifty-million-dollar business located just outside of New York City. "You also get ten million for working capital."

"I thought that I was here for a job interview," a stunned Banyon replied.

"Well, the interview is over, Colt. Walter wanted you to own this company. He bought it to give to you."

Banyon was nearly speechless. "But why? He hardly knew me."

"Because he used you for a pawn and because he has kept tabs on you since you were a little boy. Any other reasons are confidential," replied Rogers.

"What reasons?"

"I'm afraid that I can't tell you that, but the next document for you to sign is a complete autobiography of Walter. The answers are there for you to read."

"This just keeps getting stranger and stranger," said Banyon.

"Finally we have the last will and testament of Walter Pierce. You can read it if you like, but I can tell you what it says," said Rogers.

"I'm in his will? So he is dead?"

"Let's just say that Walter Pierce has ceased to exist. Your sisters and brother are all in his will. He said that you were the only family he had left."

"But," said Banyon, "I never met him until last night. What's going on here?"

"It's all in the documents I gave you," replied Rogers.

"What does the will say?" asked Banyon.

"In short, the rest of Walter's money goes to charity, approximately one hundred million dollars. The presidents, including you, now own all seven of his companies, Colt. His house on Tanners Neck Lane and several million dollars go to his housekeeper of many years. Finally all his land, which consists of over five thousand acres in Speonk, is to be divided between your sisters and brother, provided that they can agree on which parts to take."

Banyon laughed. "You don't know my sisters—they'll all be at each other's throats for the best pieces."

"Colt, you will serve as the arbitrator. If they don't agree, you can keep it all. There is one last thing." Rogers pulled a small box from his drawer and handed it to Colt. "Walter wanted me to return these to you." Inside the box were all of Stan Banyon's medals.

That evening on the plane ride home, Banyon read the document about Walter Pierce. He was in shock but now understood what had really happened.

He had gone from the law offices to the company that he now owned. He met with the current president and told him that he would stay on. He spent over four hours discussing the operation, and when he left, he made a decision to add three people to the payroll, his three sons. He also decided to open a Chicago office for himself.

Colt entered his home and had just made himself a drink when his phone rang.

"Hello," he said.

"Hi, it's your favorite sister," Jesse cooed.

The next night Colt's doorbell rang. He answered the door to discover Loni standing outside.

"Well, aren't you going to invite me in? I did save your life, remember?" she said with a smile.

"Just this once," replied Colt, smiling.

Loni was dressed in a short gray business suit with her hair tied in a ponytail. She strolled into his house.

"Come and sit down by me, okay?" she asked. Colt did as requested. "I have a lot to tell you," she said as she fluttered her eyes at him.

"First, on a personal note: I'm leaving the state police and coming to work here with the Streamwood Police Department. I'm very thankful for all that you have done for me. You really helped me learn how to deal with men." She stood up and said, "So give me a big hug and wiggle as you do it, Colt."

"I think that I'll keep you as a friend," said a laughing Colt. "By the way, I now own a company. Maybe you and Carl can help me with my business."

"Great." Chen sat back down after the hug.

"Now for the official stuff," she said. "First, the Woods gang will bother you no more. They are all going away for a long time. Seith Paul and Michael Dean have been indicted for murder and conspiracy. They will never see the light of day again. Joe Kroll and the Altar of the Creator have hundreds of charges against them. We found detailed records on all their activities in the church. The men that attacked the white supremacists in the woods were actually part of the Woods gang, under orders from Seith Paul, so they're gone too. Greg Gamble has been promoted to special agent in charge of the Chicago bureau of the FBI. Carl and I have received a personal reward from an anonymous donor that will allow us to live comfortably and a note that suggested that we set up our own detective agency."

"No kidding, I wonder who did that?" Colt remarked as he studied his nails.

"The mayor of Streamwood has ruled that he will allow us to set up the agency, as he also received a donation that is intended to upgrade our station and is tied into Carl's staying on as chief. You wouldn't know anything about that, would you, Colt?"

"I think I know who did it. It will cost you a hug to find out," he replied, laughing.

"Finally," she said, ignoring his request, "we come to Walter Pierce. There are some strange findings there."

"'Strange' would be the right word," said Banyon.

"He has completely disappeared. It's very strange."

"I don't think he's dead. He has disappeared before," Banyon said as he remembered the history of Pierce that he had recently read.

"Wait, there's more. Remember the body we saw in the tunnel?"

"How could I forget?"

"Well, the body has been identified. It was Wolfgang Becker."

"Yes, I know, he was Walter Pierce's father," said Colt.

Loni was shocked. "How did you know that?"

"The ghost told me in the tunnel. You couldn't hear him."

"So where do you think Pierce has gone?"

"Maybe we should use our new detective agency to find him," Colt replied.

Author's Notes

This book is completely a work of fiction. Any resemblance to anyone living or dead is pure coincidence. None of the characters are real, but are a figment of my imagination. It has not been my intention to depict any race, culture, or group in a bad light. It is a simple story.

I must point out that the places and geographical references are all real. The old house mentioned in the book does exist. I know because I grew up there, ghosts and all. I have modified the structure to meet my needs.

Historical people such as Canaris and others were real, and I tried to depict them as they really existed. Historical events like the formation of the glaciers and the German submarine that landed on Long Island were all actual events that I tried to relay to the reader as they were recorded by history. The Great Atlantic Storm actually happened in 1943, not 1942 as in the book.

Finally the book references many white supremacy groups. They are all fictional. Also, as far as this writer knows, there has never been a history of the Aryan race found.

Author's Acknowledgments

This book has been a lifelong desire. I want to thank my family for encouraging me to start and complete the book. They made me work on it when I would rather be doing something else. I would also like to thank my friend Kathy Mayeda for letting me use her as the model for one of the characters and also for her tireless efforts in editing this book.

My sister, Julie Megenedy, was an aid in helping me to remember many Long Island places and events. She gave me much encouragement with her little e-mails that said "give me more."

All three of my sons added support and data that shortcut much of my work, so hats off to you Jeff, Kristopher, and Jon Kubicki.

I'd also like to thank my lifelong friend Larry (Lorenzo) Barber, whose "shit-eating grin" allowed me to bring the characters together.